THE POKER CLUB

ED GORMAN

CEMETERY DANCE PUBLICATIONS

Baltimore

❖ 1999 ❖

FICTION
Gorman,
E,

Dust Jacket Artwork & Design: Gail Cross
Typesetting and Design: Alexander DeLarge
Printed in the United States of America

Cemetery Dance Publications
P.O. Box 943
Abingdon, MD 21009
http://www.cemeterydance.com

First Edition

10 9 8 7 6 5 4 3 2 1

♠

For Evan Hunter and Richard Matheson,
who have taught me so much,
and so thoroughly entertained me while doing it.

♠

WE ARE looking at three men sitting around a poker table. My name is Aaron Tyler and I'm the man in the middle, the slender one with the slightly receding hairline and the sort of sad smile on my face. My wife Jan always says that I never look sadder than when I smile. My mother used to say the same thing to me. The guys in boot camp kidded me about that, too. After college, I enlisted in the Marines. There were no wars to fight. But having grown up in the shadow of a fierce older brother, I guess I had some things I needed to prove to myself and my parents. And after three years as a gyrene, I felt I'd proved them.

The black gentleman is Curtis Reeves. Curtis and I both work at the same law office and are about the same age, early forties. You can see that Curtis makes very animated faces when he's checking out his hand. Right now, for instance, he seems to be whispering to his cards with a certain amount of unmistakable glee.

The more dour gentleman to Curtis' right is Dr. Bill Doyle, MD. In his college days, Bill damned near made All Big 10 his junior year. He's stayed in good shape and he's still got all the old fire. Too much fire, sometimes. There's a bully side to him that you occasionally see, and it's never fun to watch.

You'll notice that there's one chair empty. This is where Neil Solomon usually sits. Neil is an attorney. He's been a good friend for just about twenty-five years, ever since an upperclassman beat the shit out of us at a kegger our freshman year.

You'll meet Neil in a few minutes.

For now, I just want to show you what we look like right before our lives change abruptly and forever.

Because that's what's going to happen.

Four pretty average middle-class guys are about to leave their comfortable old lives behind.

Forty-eight minutes from now.

Forty-eight minutes....

PART
ONE

1

I CAN'T remember now who had the first poker game. But somehow over the past five years it became a ritual that we never missed.

We took turns having the game once a week. Beer and bawdy jokes and straight poker. No wild card games. We hate them.

This was summer, and vacation time, and with Jan and the girls gone, I offered to have the game at my place. With nobody there to supervise, the beer could be laced with a little bourbon, and the jokes could be even bawdier. With the wife and the girls in the house, I'm always at least a little intimidated.

The trouble is, of course, as much fun as I have playing cards, I really start missing Jan and the kids after a few days. Some nights I go in and lie on the girls' beds, with the clean scent of their hair still on their pillows. And then I think of how much I love them. And then I feel a tenderness so overwhelming it almost scares me. Then the fun I have at the poker games doesn't seem like so much fun at all.

CURTIS AND BILL came together, bearing gifts, which in this case meant the kind of sexy magazines our wives did not want in the house in case the kids might stumble across them. At least that's what they say. I think they sense, and correctly, that the magazines might give their spouses bad ideas about taking the secretary out for a few after-dinner drinks, or stopping by a singles' bar some night.

We got the chips and cards set up at the table, we got the first beers open (Bill chasing a shot of bourbon with his beer), and we started passing the dirty magazines around with tenth grade glee. The magazines compensated, I suppose, for the balding head, the bloating belly, the stooping shoulders. Deep in the heart of every hundred-year-old man is a horny fourteen-year-old boy.

All this took place, by the way, in the attic. The four of us got to know each other when we moved into what city planners called a "transitional neighborhood." There were some grand old houses that needed a lot of work.

The city designated a ten square block area as one it wanted to restore to shiny new luster. Jan and I chose a crumbling Victorian. You wouldn't recognize it today. And that includes the attic, which I've turned into a very nice den.

"Pisses me off," Bill Doyle said. "He's always late."

And that was true.

Neil Solomon *was* always late. Never by that much but always late nonetheless.

"Just relax," I said. "Drink a beer."

"Yeah," Curtis said. "Or choke your chicken."

"Or," I said. "Squeeze your blackheads."

"Right," Curtis said, his handsome black face grinning. "Or pick your nose the way you usually do when you think we're not looking."

"You assholes," Bill said. And then started laughing. "You are really a pack of idiots, you know that?"

"Look who's talking," Curtis smiled. "The heavyweight boxing champion of Manor Street."

As a doctor, Bill is a gentle, charming and extremely competent man, the bully side completely hidden. He once saw my daughter through a really frightening spell of rheumatic fever.

"You have to admit," Bill said. "I've been doing a lot better."

"Yes, he has," Curtis said. "He hasn't punched out a nun for at least two weeks."

Bill could be a crazy sonofabitch, but at least he had the ability to laugh at himself. He was laughing now.

"You jerk-off," he said to Curtis.

Curtis gaped down at one of the dirty magazines open on the poker table and said, "You know, jerking off doesn't sound half-bad right now."

"Hey," I said, snapping my fingers. "I know why Neil's late."

"Yeah, so do I," Bill said. "He's at home swimming in that new fucking pool of his." Neil recently got a bonus that made him the first owner of a full-sized pool in our neighborhood. "Aaron's the one who should have the pool. He was the swimming star in college."

"Neil's got Patrol tonight," I said.

"Hey, that's right," Curtis said. "Patrol."

I forgot," Bill said. "For once, I shouldn't be bitching about him, should I?"

Patrol is something we all take seriously in this newly restored "transitional neighborhood." The burglaries started eight months ago and they've gotten pretty bad. My house has been burgled once and vandalized twice. Bill and Curtis have had curb-sitting cars stolen. Neil's wife Becky was surprised in her own kitchen by a burglar.

The absolute worst incident, though, happened just four short bloody months ago, a man and wife who'd just moved into the neighborhood, savagely stabbed to death in their own bed. The police caught the guy a few days later trying to cash some traveller's checks he'd stolen after killing his prey. He was typical of the kind of man who infested the neighborhood after sundown: a twentyish junkie stoned to the point of psychosis on various street drugs, and not at all averse to murdering people he envied and despised. He also knew a whole hell of a lot about fooling burglar alarms.

After the murders, there was a neighborhood meeting and that's when we came up with the Patrol, something somebody'd read about being popular back East. People think that a nice middle-sized American city like ours doesn't have major problems. I invite them to walk many of these streets after dark.

They'll quickly be disabused of that notion.

Anyway, the Patrol worked this way: each night, two neighborhood people got in the family van and patrolled the ten-block area that had been restored. If they saw anything suspicious, they used their cell phones and called police. The Patrol had one strict rule: you were never to take direct action unless somebody's life was at stake.

Always, always use the cell phone and call police.

Neil had Patrol tonight. He'd be rolling in here any time now. Patrol was divided into shifts and Neil had the early one.

Bill said, "You hear what Don Evans suggested?"

"About guns?" I asked.

"Yeah."

"Makes me a little nervous," I said.

"Me, too." Curtis said.

For somebody who'd grown up in the inner city, Curtis was a very polished guy. Whenever he joked that he was the token black, Neil countered that he was the token Jew, just as Bill was the token Catholic, and I was the token WASP. Some might see us as friends of convenience, I suppose, but we all really did like each other, something that was demonstrated when Neil had a cancer scare a few years back The three of us were in his hospital room twice a day, all eight days running.

"Maybe it's time," Bill said. "The burglars and the muggers and the killers have guns, why shouldn't we?"

"That's why we have cops," I said. "They're the ones who carry the guns."

"People start bringing guns on Patrol," Curtis said, "somebody innocent is going to get shot."

"So some night one of us here is on Patrol and we see a bad guy and he sees us and before the cops get there the bad guy shoots us?" Bill said. "You don't think that's going to happen?"

"It *could* happen," Curtis said. "But I just don't think that justifies carrying guns."

The argument was about to continue when the bell rang downstairs.

"Neil's here," Bill said. "Now we can play some serious cards."

"You've already lost thirty dollars," Curtis reminded him. "I'd say that's pretty serious."

"SORRY I'M LATE," Neil Solomon said after he followed me up to the attic and came inside.

"We already drank all the beer," Bill said.

Neil smiled. "That gut you're putting on, Bill, I can believe it."

Bill always seemed to enjoy being put down by Neil, possibly because most people were a bit intimidated by Bill—that angry Irish edge of his—but Neil didn't seem the least bit afraid of him. And that seemed to amuse Bill all to hell.

"I may have a bigger gut," Bill said, "but I also have a bigger dick."

"His modesty is so becoming" Curtis said.

"That isn't what your wife told me," Neil said. "She said that *I* definitely had a bigger dick."

"Our usual elevated level of conversation," Curtis said, smiling at me.

Neil laughed. Neil is the opposite of beefy, blonde Bill. He's tall, slender, dark, nice looking. In college, he'd been a very good miler.

In the old days—up till two years ago—Neil had been the clown of the group. He had real wit, and wasn't afraid to be a little foolish in making you laugh.

In the old days.

But three years ago, at an office Christmas party his wife couldn't attend because she was feeling ill, Neil was unfaithful. The receptionist. The first and only time he'd ever strayed.

He got home late, very drunk, to find his wife sitting in the dark smoking a cigarette. She had never smoked in her life.

Her name was Becky and she was very slight and pretty in a warm, earnest way. She told him not to turn on the lights.

She hadn't, she said, wanted to spoil his office party, but she had some news, and it was bad news. She'd been having some troubles the last month and had gone to the doctor. He'd examined her and suggested a biopsy. Later that day he'd called her with the results. Uterine cancer. Needed to operate right away. Chemo and radiation to follow.

Five months later, Becky was dead. Neil was left with two things; a beautiful daughter named Rachel and more guilt than any human being could reasonably hope to shoulder.

These days, Neil drank a lot. And you could never guess what he was going to do next. One night I found him smashing his fist again and again into the wall of my garage. He knew he'd broken some knuckles. He was determined to break even more, until I stopped him.

Neil sat down.

I got him a beer from the tiny fridge I keep up here, cards were dealt, seven-card stud was played.

Sometimes I wonder how many hours I've spent playing poker in my life. Thousands, probably. And I can't even say I enjoy it, exactly. I guess it's the camaraderie. I grew up in a middle-class family of younger sisters, and so I suppose over the years my poker buddies became the brothers I never had.

I lost the first two hands. Even in stud, a pair of eights isn't all that worthy, especially when you're up against savvy players like Bill and Neil. They never lose their tempers or sulk, but it's obvious that they play with a lot of intensity.

Curtis said, "How'd Patrol go tonight, Neil?"

"No problems," he said, not taking his eyes off the cards I'd just dealt.

"I still say we should carry guns," Bill said.

"Fucking A we should," Neil said.

"Oh, great," Curtis said. "Another beer commercial cowboy."

"What's that supposed to mean?" Bill said.

"It just means that we should leave the guns to the cops," I said.

"You taking Curtis' side in this?" Neil said.

"Yeah, I guess I am."

"Curtis is full of shit," Bill said. Then he looked at Curtis and smiled. "Nothing personal."

"Right" Curtis said, obviously irritated with Bill's tone.

The battle over guns had been going on in the neighborhood for the past three months. The sides seemed pretty evenly divided. Because of all the TV coverage violence gets, people are more and more developing a siege mentality.

"Let's just play cards," I said, "and leave the debate bullshit till later."

WE PLAYED CARDS. In half an hour, I dropped fifteen dollars. It got hot in the attic. We have central air, of course, but in mid-summer like this, the attic can still get pretty warm.

The first pit stop came just after ten o'clock, and Neil took it. There was a john on the second floor between bedrooms, another john on the first floor.

Neil said, "The good Doctor Gettesfeld had to give me a finger wave this afternoon, gents, so this may take a while."

"You should trade that prostate of yours in for a new one," Bill said.

"Believe me, I'd like to. I mean, I'm getting tired of bending over and having him put his finger up my ass."

"Aaron and Curtis never get tired of it," Bill said slyly. "They love it when I put my finger up there."

"Another witticism," Curtis said. "How does he keep on doing it, folks?"

While Neil was gone the three of us started talking about the Patrol again. Should we go armed or not?

We made the same old arguments. The passion was gone. We were just waiting for Neil to come back and we knew it.

Finally, Bill said, "Let me see some of those magazines again."

"You got some identification?" I said.

"I'll show you some identification," Bill said. "It's about a yard long and it's nice and hard."

Curtis said, "Boy, your nose really *is* long, isn't it?"

We passed the magazines around.

"Man, I love lesbians," Bill said, as he flipped through the pages.

"I *am* a lesbian," Curtis said. "An honorary one, anyway."

I was just as exultant as they were. The older I got, the more real sex became, maybe because it was the only wild passion I had left in me. Walking down a sunny street, I fell in love a hundred times an hour. I always felt guilty about this, of course. I'd never been unfaithful and hoped I never would be. I'd destroyed a relationship in college by stepping out. She found out and never trusted me again. I just couldn't do that to Jan, not ever. There are some things you can never undo, and cheating on your loved one is one of them.

"You mind if I use the john on the first floor?" Curtis said.

"Yeah, it would really piss me off," I said.

That was the overpolite black man chained inside of Curtis. He never quite took the social liberties the rest of us did. Plantation politics were still a part of him, and it was sad to see. "Captain May I" would always be a sad reactive part of him.

I felt like a jerk for making a joke of it.

"Yes, use the first floor john, Curtis. Take a shower if you want."

"No," he said, "just pissing in your sink will be fine."

After Curtis left, Bill said, "I ride his ass sometimes, don't I?"

"You ride everybody's ass."

"I get to him. I can see it in his eyes."

"So go easier on him."

"Yeah, I suppose I should. There's just something I don't quite like about him. Never have." He looked down at the can of beer he had gripped in his fist. "Maybe I'm a racist."

"Well," I said, not quite knowing what to say. "Maybe you *are* a racist."

He sighed. "I'm going to work on being nicer to Curtis. I really am."

"Good idea," I said. "Curtis is a hell of a nice guy."

The first time I heard it, I thought it was some kind of animal noise from outside, a dog or a cat in some kind of discomfort maybe. Bill, who was still staring at his can of beer, didn't even look up.

But the second time I heard the sound, Bill and I both looked up. And then we heard the exploding sound of breaking glass.

"What the hell was that?" Bill said.

"Let's go find out," I said.

Something was bad wrong. I knew that in a clear, clean way that drained away all my beer fuzziness.

That sound, whatever it was, did not belong in this house.

I thought about the Patrol argument we'd been having. Right now a weapon would feel damned good in my hand.

Just as we reached the bottom of the stairs, we saw Neil coming out of the second floor john. "You hear that?" he said, keeping his voice low.

"We sure as hell did," I said.

"Yeah," Bill said, his face ugly with anger and suspicion. "And now we're going to find out what it is."

But in addition to wariness, there was an excitement in Bill's voice, too. He loved danger. It was like being a Big 10 lineman all over again.

He was an odd choice to be a medical man, a healer. There was a lot of hatred in him.

WE REACHED the staircase leading to the first floor. Everything was dark.

Bill reached for the light switch but I brushed his hand away.

My place. My turf. I'd do things my way. I put a sshing finger to my lips and then showed my old Louisville slugger. I led the way downstairs, keeping the bat ready at all times.

"You sonofabitch!"

The voice belonged to Curtis.

More smashing glass.

In the shadowy light from the street, Bill and Neil looked scared.

I hefted the bat some more and then started moving fast to the kitchen.

"Any fucker who lays a hand on Curtis," Bill whispered, "I'm personally going to fucking kill."

I almost smiled, remembering our conversation of a while ago. Maybe it took something like this to make him realize that he really did like Curtis.

Just as we passed through the dining room, I heard something heavy hit the kitchen floor. Something human and heavy.

A moan. A groan. Curtis.

"Cocksucker!" Bill screamed and went running hard into the kitchen, his face hard with rage, his fists tight and club-like.

He was at the back door. White. Tall. Blond shoulder-length hair. Filthy tan T-shirt. Greasy jeans. He had grabbed one of Jan's carving knives from the huge iron rack that sits atop a butcher block island.

The one curious thing about him was the eyes: there was a malevolent iridescence to the blue pupils, angry, almost alien, intelligence.

Curtis was sprawled face down on the tile floor. His arms were spread wide on either side of him. He didn't seem to be moving. Chunks and fragments of glass were strewn everywhere across the floor. My uninvited guest had smashed two or three of the colourful pitchers we'd bought in Mexico.

By now, Bill was crouching in front of the burglar.

Neil was ransacking the knife drawer, looking for the biggest blades he could find.

He gave Bill a carving knife, and kept the second one for himself.

Now Neil and Bill were both crouched in front of the guy, ready to spring.

"C'mon, motherfucker," Bill said, "make a move. I'd love to open your fucking throat."

Even though I was still near the kitchen door trying to revive Curtis, I could smell the burglar. Think of a city dump on a boiling July afternoon, that fetid sweet-sour odor. That's what he smelled like even clear across the room.

Curtis moaned, then, and I felt a ridiculous surge of joy. I guess I'd half-suspected he might be dead. I got him propped up against the wall.

His nose was smashed and it was pretty bloody. There was also a gash above his right eye. He kept touching the right rear side of his head.

I put my hand back there and felt through the damp curly hair a good-sized egg.

Our friend the burglar showed an unmistakable appetite for violence.

I looked back over my shoulder to see how Neil and Bill were doing.

They were still in a standoff situation. Every time they came in close, he raised his knife.

Bill swore every few moments. Neil feigned lunges just about as often. Then Neil's left leg would lash out, trying to catch the burglar in the crotch. But the burglar was quick and the burglar was savvy.

The burglar's face was fascinating in a repellent way. No sign of remorse. No sign even of fear. Just of trapped-animal rage.

He was pissed. He wanted to kill us because we'd had the audacity to catch him.

A noise. The back porch. Somebody tripping over something in the darkness.

The burglar's eyes snapped in the direction of the porch, and he then uttered his one and only word, "Run!"

The sonofabitch had brought a friend.

That was when I ran over to the knife drawer, quickly grabbing the longest blade I could find.

I was all reaction now. No thinking whatsoever. I felt the tremendous energy that Bill and Neil always showed whenever they were around violence. No time for fear.

I ran to the back door, ran into the narrow shadowy box that was the porch.

I could still smell last year's Winesap apples, a good, clean, sweet smell. Jan buys a bushel basket or two of them every autumn, then keeps them on the back porch until winter comes. During these months, we eat an awful lot of apple pie.

No one there.

I tried to see through the moonsilver shadows of the backyard. Clothesline. Two-story garage. Line of garbage cans. The kids' swing set.

And then he was there. Peeking around the far corner of the garage. The second burglar.

I burst through the back door, racing after him.

The night air was almost suffocating.

I crept along the length of the garage, keeping to the shadows, waving the knife in front of me. The blade gleamed in the moonlight. I imagined bright red blood along its edge, glistening.

Only now did I feel even a modicum of fear.

What if he had a gun, the second burglar? What if he looked just as crazy as his pal inside? What if he was waiting for me on the other side of the garage, ready to jump me and kill me?

Jan would say I was trying to be as macho as my brother Bob. He was now a detective in St. Louis. He still had ample opportunity to bust heads, and equally ample opportunity to regale us with his war stories at two or three family gatherings a year.

A noise.

I froze in my crouch. I noticed that the gleaming edge of the blade was now shaking slightly.

I could picture the bastard only a few feet away, just on the other side of the garage. Waiting for me.

I almost turned and went back. Almost.

But then I thought of the people who'd been killed and mugged in our little neighborhood over the past few years.

This bastard and his friends were making a safe, normal life impossible for us and our families.

I got good and pissed and forgot all about going back to the house.

A noise. Again.

The sound of a shoe on gravel.

Wherever he was, he wasn't far away.

I turned back just a moment to the line of four silver garbage cans.

In great vast pantomime, the kind of overplayed movements you see in silent movies, I lifted the lid off one of the cans then carried it back up to the edge of the garage.

I waited, listened.

Despite the seventy-eight degree temperature, I was shivering, sweat beading like ice cubes on my face and arms and back.

I heard bird, dog, train, car. But I did not hear him, even though I suspected he was only a few feet away.

I steadied myself, readied myself.

I would throw the lid into the alley, he would pounce on it and I would jump on him.

Once again I thought of how Jan would react if she knew what I was going to do. She would be scared, and even a little embarrassed, I imagined. My husband, the fourteen-year-old.

I threw the lid the way I would have tossed a Frisbee.

It landed in the middle of the alley, on a mound of tufted weeds and gravel.

Silence, a deep and unnerving silence.

Shadows, shifting shadows that seemed to move and merge and shift again.

I was six-years-old and in my bed and convinced that some monster was in the closet lurking, waiting.

When I finally went to sleep, the monster would come out and soon I would be nothing more than blood dripping from his long and razor-sharp teeth.

Silence.

My trick hadn't worked. He hadn't leapt out in plain sight.

Where was he? What was he waiting for?

I moved two steps closer to the front of the garage. Started to peek around.

And that was when I heard it.

The sound of shoe soles scuffling against the tiles on the garage roof.

By the time I turned around, by the time I looked up, it was too late.

He was already leaping off the roof and landing on me feet first.

I fell to the ground, stunned as my head slammed against the hard earth.

When he dove at me, I got my first glimpse of him—skinny, angular, muscular in a scrawny way. Black T-shirt and jeans. Short dusty blonde hair. Face hidden by dirt and sweat. Angry eyes peering out from a mask of filth.

He threw himself on me, tried to straddle me, meanwhile whipping out a switchblade and snicking it open.

I tried to roll away from him but he had me pinioned tight with iron legs. I saw him raise the knife, moonfire burning silver on its tip, and then somebody shouted, "Hey!"

When he saw Neil running toward us, he jumped to his feet and started toward the alley.

"You all right?" Neil said when he reached me.

"Yeah, but he got away."

"You get a look at him?"

"Not much of one."

I was on my feet. My head still hurt from slamming against the ground.

"Cocksuckers," Neil said.

He ran to the alley and looked left, then right.

"Bastard's gone," he said when he came back. "You all right?"

"Yeah. Anybody call the cops yet?"

We had just reached the porch.

"Nah, Bill and I thought we'd hold off for a while," he said.

"Hold off calling the cops?"

But he didn't have time to answer, because just then I heard glass smash to the floor inside, and break in a loud nasty explosion.

2

BILL STILL had the burglar backed up against the kitchen wall. Every time Bill would lunge for him, the burglar would grab a glass or cup from the sink and hurl it at Bill. Then he'd crouch and sway his long-bladed knife back and forth to keep Bill from coming any closer.

Bill was soaked with sweat. He didn't seem to hear me when I came in. He never took his eyes from the burglar.

I looked at Neil, who anticipated my objection. "Bill's fine. Don't worry about him."

"Where's Curtis?"

"In the john."

"I'll go check on him. Then I'm going to call the cops."

"Your house, Aaron. You can do whatever you like."

"C'mon, motherfucker," Bill said to the burglar. "Give me a reason to cut your fucking throat."

Knife to knife, rage to rage, they hunkered down, glaring at each other.

Curtis was at the sink in the downstairs bathroom. He'd wetted a washcloth and held it to the lump on the back of his head.

I opened the closet, found the flashlight. "Why don't you let me take a look at your eyes?"

"You think maybe I got a concussion?"

"Maybe."

I checked his eyes.

"How do they look?"

"I don't think you've got a concussion. You have a headache?"

"A pisser."

"There's aspirin in the medicine cabinet."

"I know. I already helped myself." Then, "Wouldn't it make more sense for Bill to come check on me, since he's a doctor and everything?"

"He's too busy playing gladiator."

He grinned. "You noticed that, huh?"

Then he extended his arm and said, "Look."

His entire arm trembled.

"Scared the shit out of me, man," Curtis said. "I thought I heard something in the kitchen and I went out and flipped on the light and he jumped me. He's got balls, I've got to give him that, breaking in when people are home."

"He probably didn't know anybody was here. We were all up in the attic and there aren't any windows up there. The rest of the house was dark."

He looked in the mirror and smiled at himself. "Thank God I'm still beautiful." Then, "The cops get here yet?"

"We haven't called them yet."

He watched my face in the mirror.

"You been talking to Bill?"

"About what?"

He daubed the washcloth over the sore spots on his face. "I tried to call the cops in the kitchen and Bill stopped me."

"He stopped you?"

"Yeah. Came over and took the receiver from me and said he'd call the cops when the time came."

"What the hell's that supposed to mean?"

"I don't know," Curtis said. "But whatever it is, Neil's going along with it. He was the one who sent me into the john. Said he and Bill would handle things."

"Well, I'm going to call the cops and right now."

"Glad you said that. I was getting worried. I mean, you're supposed to call the cops right away after something happens."

I walked to the door. "I'll fix you a drink when we get out there."

"Scotch would be nice."

"Scotch it is," I said. "And the best I've got."

"The week-old stuff?"

I laughed. "That's right. The week-old stuff."

I was expecting to find Bill still playing gladiator.

But the kitchen was empty.

"What the hell happened to them?" Curtis said.

The first thing I thought of was that the burglar had somehow overpowered them. Dragged them out into the darkness.

But Bill and Neil were big strong guys.

One man dragging them off was unlikely.

"Hey," Curtis said, "listen."

At first, I wasn't sure where the sound of the muffled voices was coming from. In old houses like this, sound sometimes bounces, and you can't quite be sure which room the noise is in.

Curtis walked across the kitchen to the basement door. He silently pointed out the fact that the door was ajar.

He opened it a few inches.

The harsh male voices came clear now.

Bill and Neil cursing at the burglar.

I walked over to the basement door and looked down the steps. They needed a coat of paint.

The basement was our wilderness. We hadn't had the time or money to fix it up yet. We were counting on this year's bonus to help us set the basement right. Curtis and I were still junior partners, but at our firm that still meant a good bonus.

We went down the steps.

The basement was one big, mostly unused room. There was a washer and dryer in the corner. And stacks of boxes lining three of the walls. Everything that didn't fit into the attic ended up in the basement. The long range plan was to turn it into a family room for the girls. These days, it was mostly inhabited by stray waterbugs.

When I reached the bottom step, I saw them. There were four metal posts in the basement, one near each corner.

They had him lashed to a pole in the east quadrant. His hands tied behind him with a piece of rope they'd found amidst the tools in the west quadrant.

They also had him gagged with what looked like a pillowcase.

His eyes were big and wide. He looked scared. I didn't blame him. I was scared, too.

"What the hell are you guys doing?" I said.

"Just calm down, Papa Bear," Bill said. That was his name for me whenever he wanted to convey to people that I'm this old-fashioned fuddy-duddy. It so happened that Bill was two years older than I, and this seemed to make him feel innately superior.

"Knock off the Papa Bear bullshit," I said. "Did you call the cops?"

"Not yet," Neil said. "Just calm down a little, will you?"

"You haven't called the cops," I said. "You've got some guy tied up and gagged in my basement. You haven't even asked how Curtis here is doing. And you want me to calm down, is that right?"

Bill came up to me, then. There was a pit bull craziness about him now, frantic, uncontrollable, alien.

"We're going to do what the cops *can't* do, man," he said. "We're going to sweat the sonofabitch. We're going to make him tell us who he was with tonight. And then we're going to make him give us the name of every single bad guy who works this neighborhood. And then we'll turn all the names over to the cops."

"It's just an extension of the Patrol," Neil said. "Just keeping our neighborhood safe, is all."

"You guys are nuts," I said, and turned back toward the steps. "I'm going up to call the cops."

That's when I realized how crazed Bill was.

He grabbed my sleeve so hard that it tore. He said, "We're going to sweat the bastard, Aaron. *Then* we're going to call the cops."

"You tore my fucking sleeve," I said.

We were only inches apart and it was clear that one of us would soon swing at the other.

"I'm sorry about your sleeve."

"This is my fucking house," I said, yelling right into his face. "Do you fucking understand that, Bill? This is my fucking house!"

I hadn't wanted to hit anybody in a long time. Right now I couldn't wait to hit Bill.

That was when Curtis got between us and said, "Let's go upstairs and have a drink on this."

He nodded to the man tied and gagged in the corner. "That asshole's not going any place."

"That's right," Neil said soothingly. "A nice, civilized drink and then some nice, civilized discussion. Okay, you two?"

They got us apart but we still glared at each other like two boxers with a real grudge.

BILL LED the charge getting the kitchen cleaned up. I think he was feeling guilty about our altercation in the basement.

After the kitchen was put back in order, and all the smashed glass swept up with a broom, I broke out four glasses and a bucket of ice, and we all sat in the breakfast nook where we had a clear view of the basement door.

"All right," I said. "Now that we've all calmed down, I want to walk over to that yellow kitchen wall phone and call the police. Any objections?"

"I think blue would look better in here than yellow," Neil said.

"Funny."

They looked more like themselves now, no feral madness on the faces of Bill or Neil. Curtis, who sat next to me, no longer looked frightened or agitated.

It was over.

I got up from the table.

And that was when Neil grabbed my arm

"I think Bill's right," Neil said. "I think we should spend a little time with our friend before we turn him over to the police."

I shook my head, politely removed his hand from my forearm, and started to stand up again.

"This isn't your decision alone," Bill said.

"Isn't it?" I said. "You want me to show you the mortgage? You want me to show you our homeowners' insurance policy? You want to see the light bill? That's my name on those things, Bill, not yours."

"Yeah, but this also happens to be my neighborhood, asshole. My wife and my kids live here and I say if we've got a chance to sweat this cocksucker, we should do it."

"When he breaks into your house," I said, "you can do anything you want to with him. In the meantime, I'm calling the cops."

He erupted without warning, coming across the table for me.

I was ready for him, cocking my fist back and starting to bring it down on top of his head.

Curtis grabbed me, and Neil grabbed Bill.

"Hey, for God's sake," Neil said. "We're friends here, all right, you two?"

The breakfast nook has a window where I sometimes sit in the mornings and watch all the backyard animals on sunny days. I saw a mother racoon and four baby racoons one day, marching single file across the grass. My grandparents were the last generation to live on the farm. My father came to town here and ultimately became vice president of a ball bearing company. When I look out this window, I often think of my father. He liked watching animals, too.

I looked back at the table and said, "We're not cops. We're just private citizens. And what we need to do is turn the guy in the basement over to the cops right now."

"You want to bet on how long it'll be before he's back on the street again?" Bill said.

"Hey," Curtis said. "You're the doctor. But we're attorneys. Officers of the court? You know what I'm saying? We've got to turn this guy over to the authorities and right now. Our asses are on the line, man."

"You shouldn't even have tied him up," I said to Bill and Neil.

"Yes, the poor thing," Bill said. "Aren't we just picking on him, though? Maybe you'd like to offer him something to eat."

"Just make sure you serve the right wine with it," Neil said. "I'm sure he's a gourmet."

"Or maybe we could get him a chick," Bill said.

"Yeah, with charlies out to here," Neil said.

I couldn't help it. I smiled. They were being ridiculous and that's just what we needed at the moment. A little bit of ridiculousness.

"I'm sorry I got so pissed," I said to Bill.

And held my hand out.

"Me, too," he said.

"You two want to go somewhere and make out?" Curtis said.

"He always has bad breath," Bill said.

"I just want to ask him one question, Aaron," Neil said. "That's not going to hurt anything is it? Just scare him a little. Ask him the name of the guy who was with him tonight."

I looked at Curtis.

He shrugged. "I guess we could give them a couple of minutes. But you promise you're just going to scare him?"

"Promise," Neil said.

"Absolutely," Bill said.

"Then we call the cops?" I said.

"Then we call the cops," Neil said.

"Okay?" I said to Curtis.

"I guess," he said, still sounding reluctant.

I LED the way down, sneezing as I walked.

There's always a lot of dust floating around in the basement to play hell with my sinuses.

The burglar was his same sullen self, glaring at us as we descended the stairs and then walked over to him.

He smelled of heat and sweat and clinging grime. The long bare arms sticking out of his filthy T-shirt told tattoo tales of writhing snakes and leaping panthers. The arms were joined in the back with the rope. His jaw was still flexed, trying to accommodate the intrusion of the gag.

"Maybe we should castrate him," Bill said.

He angled his face so the burglar couldn't see him wink at me.

Bill walked up to the guy and said, "You like that, scumbag? If we castrated you?"

If the burglar felt any fear, it wasn't evident in his eyes. All you could see there was the usual contempt.

"I'll bet this is the jerk who broke into the Donaldson's house a couple weeks ago," Neil said.

Now he walked up to the guy. But he was more ambitious than Bill had been. Neil spat in the guy's face.

"Hey," I said. "Cool it."

Neil turned and glared at me. "Yeah, I wouldn't want to hurt his fucking feelings, would I?"

I wish I'd paid more attention to Curtis' reluctance. This was a terrible mistake, bringing Neil and Bill back down here.

Then suddenly Neil raised his fist and started to swing on the guy.

All I could do was shove him. His punch landed but with less force than it might have had.

I was angrier than I should have been, I suppose, but I felt like a betrayed parent. Here my two spoiled brats had promised me to be on good behavior, and now they chose to break their word.

"You asshole," Neil said, turning back on me now.

But Curtis was there between us.

"You know what we're doing?" Curtis said. "We're making that jerk-off over there happy. He's gonna have some nice stories to tell his friends in the slammer."

He was right.

The burglar was the one who looked cool and composed right now. We looked like squabbling brats. As if to confirm this, a certain merriment shone in the burglar's blue eyes.

"Oh, hell, Aaron," Neil said, "Curtis is right."

He put his hand out to shake and then grabbed me and gave me a hug.

"This Patrol shit is making all of us crazy," Bill said. He jabbed a finger in the direction of the burglar. "And it's this motherfucker and his pals who're doing it to us."

"Now I'm going to call the cops," I said.

"Past time, man," Curtis said. "They can pick this asshole up and we'll be done with him."

I could see both Neil and Bill reluctantly going along with the plan now.

And that's when the burglar chose to make his move. As soon as I mentioned cops, he probably reasoned that this was going to be his last chance to do anything.

He waited until our attention was on ourselves and not on him. Then he took off running. We could see that he'd somehow managed to slip the rope.

He went straight for the stairs, angling out around us like a running back seeing daylight. He even stuck his long, tattooed arm out as if he was trying to repel a tackle.

He was at the stairs by the time we could gather ourselves enough to go after him. But when we moved, we moved fast, and in virtual unison.

Everybody was shouting and cursing.

By the time I got my hand on the cuff of his left leg he was close enough to the basement door to open it.

I yanked hard, and ducked out of the way of his kicking foot. By now I was as crazy as Bill and Neil had been earlier.

There was adrenaline, and great anger.

He wasn't just a burglar, he was all burglars, he was every sonofabitch who meant to do my wife and my kids great harm.

He hadn't had time to take the gag from his mouth.

I grabbed the tail of the gag and yanked on it so hard, he stumbled backwards down three steps.

At first, he kept trying to grab for the door. He even managed briefly to scramble back up two steps.

But I gave another yank on the back of his gag and he came back down right away.

I can't tell you exactly what happened the next half-minute or so.

He jerked around and took a wild swing at me. I grabbed his arm and started hauling him down the steps.

All I wanted to do was get him on the basement floor again, turn him over to the others to watch, while I went upstairs and called the cops.

But somewhere in those few seconds, when I was hauling him

back down, I heard the edge of the stair meeting the back of his skull.

The others heard it, too.

Their shouts and their curses died in their throats.

When I turned around, I saw the blood coming fast and red from his nose.

The blue eyes no longer held contempt. They were starting to roll up white in the back of his head.

"God," I said. "He's hurt."

"I think he's a lot more than hurt," Bill said.

Bill the doctor.

"Help me get him upstairs," Bill said.

We moved him as gently as possible. I was scared and sick. This was all so crazy. Just a little while ago, we'd been scanning sex magazines and playing poker.

By the time we laid him down on the kitchen floor, he started convulsing, his body jolting and twitching every thirty seconds or so, as if electricity were being pumped into him.

"Damn," Bill said.

You could smell that the guy had messed himself. The stench of feces hung sweet-sour on the air.

Then Bill was down on the floor next to him, checking eyes and mouth and pulse points in neck and wrist and ankle.

At first I didn't notice that the twitching had stopped. Then the guy stopped moving completely.

I watched his chest, eager to see the subtle rise and fall of his lungs.

There was no rise and fall, subtle or otherwise.

Bill looked up at me and said, "He's dead."

"No way," Curtis said. "No fucking way."

"Hey friend, you're the lawyer, remember?" Bill said. "I'm the doctor. And I say he's dead."

"Dead," Neil said. "Dead."

"I'm calling the cops," I said, and started for the phone.

That's when Neil grabbed my shoulder and spun me around.

"The hell you are," he said. "The hell you are."

3

I WAS at the hospital the morning my father died. My mother and sister were there, too.

Dad went into post-op and was then brought up and wheeled into his private room. He'd had open heart surgery.

A nurse came in and said we could go in and see him in another twenty minutes or so, after they were finished making him comfortable and everything.

Meanwhile, why didn't we just stay in the waiting room and read some magazines and relax? They'd come and get us when everything was ready.

This was ten years ago, but I still remember hearing the "Code Blue" announced.

I knew instantly that something had gone wrong with my father.

And so did my mother and sister.

My mother got up and started for the door but I stopped her, turned her over to my sister.

"I'll go find out," I said.

I ran down the hall to where I saw two teams of emergency personnel entering a room.

"Please," said a nurse when I tried to get in, "you'll have to stay out for now."

"He's my father," I said.

I think she still wanted to stop me, but I pushed past her.

I stood in the corner so I wouldn't get in the way of the hospital people. They worked fast and hard and you could feel their urgency. About all I could see of him was half of his face. He looked dead white.

A few minutes later, one of the doctors looked back at me and said, "I'm sorry."

I nodded.

When I got back to the waiting room, I opened my mouth to say something but my mother and sister didn't give me time. They just held on to me, as if they were drowning and only I could save them.

I let them cry till they were temporarily cried out and then we just sat there, the three of us, in this unfamiliar hospital, in this unfamiliar room, burdened with the unfamiliar knowledge of death and its finality.

No more father.

And we didn't speak, didn't say a word. It must have been fifteen, twenty minutes before one of us spoke.

AND IT was that way tonight, sitting in the breakfast nook, pushing the bottle of scotch back and forth. Saying absolutely fucking nothing.

None of us knew what to say, so we stared out the window or stared into our drinks.

The burglar was across the room. I'd thrown my old bathrobe across him. Blood soaked parts of it now.

After a long while, I said: "I think I'm ready."

"For what?" Curtis said.

"To call the cops."

"Yeah? What're you going to tell them?" Bill said.

"That we caught a burglar and wrestled with him and he accidentally hit his head and killed himself."

"You ever been interrogated?" Curtis said.

"Only that time I killed those three nuns," I said.

"What Curtis is trying to say," Neil said, "is that the cops are going to have a lot of questions."

"About what?" I said.

"About what happened," Curtis said. "You get a good look at his body?"

"What about it?" I said.

"One of you guys hit him pretty hard in the eye. Got the beginning of a shiner."

"So?" I said.

"So?" Bill said, "since the fatal wound is on the back of his head, how do we explain that he got a black eye?"

"Not to mention," Curtis said, "his broken finger."

"He's got a broken finger?" I said.

"Yeah," said Bill the doctor. "I noticed that. I must've busted it when I was tying his wrists together with the rope."

"And," Curtis said, "it's also going to be obvious to the coroner that our pal was dead a long time before we called the cops."

"You guys don't know jack shit about cops," I said. "And neither do I. I'm a tax attorney."

"We still know how the system works," Neil said.

"Enough to know that all of us could be in some deep shit here," Curtis said.

"What the hell're you talking about?" I said.

"What he's talking about," Neil said, "is that Bill here is licensed by the state medical board, and the three of us are licensed by the state legal board. And both of those boards frown on people who practice vigilante justice."

"Vigilante justice?" Bill said. "What the hell're you talking about?"

"Rope burns." Curtis said. "That's the first thing the coroner's going to notice about him. How he was tied up."

"We didn't want him to get away," I said.

"So we tied him to a post in the basement and then beat the shit out of him?" Curtis said.

"We didn't hit him that many times," I said.

"Yeah? How many bruises do you think the coroner's going to find on his body?" Curtis said.

I looked angrily at Bill and Neil. "You two assholes just had to play cowboy, didn't you?"

The phone rang.

We all sat and stared at it as if we weren't quite sure what it was.

Some newfangled contraption.

Sits on your wall and rings like a bell.

"I'll get it," I said.

"Maybe it's his mommy," Neil said, "telling him to come home."

"Funny," Curtis said.

By the time I picked up, the answering machine kicked in. Over my own voice saying wait for the beep and then leave your message, I yelled several times to let the caller know that a living breathing person was actually on the other end of the phone.

"Hi, honey," Jan said.

"Hi, sweetie."

"I'll bet I caught you right in the middle of a poker game, didn't I?

"Well, sort of."

"Remember our agreement."

"I know. No more than $25."

Because I'd once lost $100 one night and felt totally irresponsible and remorseful for a week after, we agreed that I'd never lose more than $25 in one sitting.

"Listen," I said, "I'm going to take this in the other room, Hon. I'll have Curtis hang up when I get in there."

"Great," she said.

I held the phone out to Curtis. He took it.

IN THE darkened living room, I picked up the receiver and said, "I sure miss you guys."

"We miss you, too," Jan said.

Curtis hung up.

"How are the girls?"

"Oh, just having a great time, Hon. Mom and Dad are spoiling them, as usual. Dad got a new Cadillac—he said that after all his years as District Attorney up here, he'd earned it—and they've got their outdoor pool now. So the girls have plenty to do. In fact, they were so tired, they went to bed voluntarily at seven-thirty."

While she was talking, I forced myself to take several deep breaths and to close my eyes while doing so. This helped settle my nerves a little.

"Wow, they must've been tired."

Pause. "You sound funny."

"I do?"

"Is everything all right there?"

"Is everything all right? What wouldn't be all right?"

"Your voice—you just sound—"

"A little drunk is what I probably sound." I said. "We've been doing our share tonight."

Pause. "Aaron?"

"Yeah?"

"You know our agreement."

"Sure, I know our agreement, honey."

"No matter what it is—we tell each other the truth."

"I *am* telling you the truth. Honest."

Two years before I met her, Jan got engaged to one of the campus football heroes. It was the kind of relationship that seemed ideal on the surface—strapping, handsome hero; winsome, bright fiancé. Everybody predicted great lives for them. He'd go on to the pros, she'd be his wife and the mother of his children. Even in our jaded age, a lot of people still like old-fashioned dreams like that.

There was one problem...the hero was a pathological liar. Rarely told the truth. The CEO father he boasted about was actually a bus driver in Columbus, Ohio. The manse he claimed to have been raised in turned out to be a shabby apartment house with slashed screens on the windows and dog crap all over the dirt front yard. And all the pro offers he was always talking about...a few half-hearted feelers from the Vikings, who were just doing a little bit of trawling and nothing more serious.

But that wasn't the worst. Oh, no. You might excuse all his fantasies as just protective coloration—he was poor and she was reasonably wealthy, right? He was ashamed of his background. Like a lot of people. So he told a few lies.

Then one day, Jan walked into his humid off-campus apartment and found him in bed with her own roomie. It didn't end there. Over the next week, she started asking *all* her close and trusted friends about her fiancé...and all but one of them confessed that they, too, had slept with him.

Devastated, she became a Big Ten version of a nun. She spent her junior year studying...and nothing else. Not a single date. And when she did start going out again, it was with guys she considered "friends" and not potential suitors.

It only takes once, having your faith in somebody destroyed that way. Jan had never recovered her trust. And even today, it was sometimes a problem. The slightest inconsistency in anything I said made her start wondering if I was lying. Or the slightest mood shift in my voice.

I was hiding something from her. That's what she always thought. I was hiding something.

That's all she'd ever asked of me, really, was to be honest. The night before our wedding, she said, "If you ever lie to me, Aaron, I'll leave you. And I mean it." I gave her my word and for the most part honored it. Over the years I'd told a few fibs, I suppose, mostly to keep her from worrying about our budget or my health, but I could honestly say that I'd been honest.

Until now.

"How're things at the office?"

"Oh, the usual. We go back to court next week for G & G. That's what I'm mostly spending my time on." G & G was one of our biggest clients, a shipping firm that was suing the Federal government for a tax shelter it believed was legal. The trouble with all such suits is that the Feds can pretty much decide on a whim—there's always some vague rule in the tax code that covers their ass—what is legal and what is not legal. But if it wasn't for the Federal government, half the lawyers in this country would be working at McDonald's.

When I was finished talking, I looked down at the magazine lying next to me on the couch. I had unconsciously ripped off the cover and balled it up.

"Oh, before I forget, the girls asked me to ask you if you'll take them to the new Disney film."

"Sure."

"Dad wanted to take them here. But they said they wanted to wait until you could take them."

I strained to laugh. "Let your Dad take them if he wants to. They always end up going three or four times to Disney films anyway."

"Well, now that you mention it, they do always see Disney films several times, don't they?" Then, softly. "I had a real nice time the night before we left."

"Me, too, sweetheart," I said.

Like too many married couples these days, Jan and I sometimes go two or three days at a time without spending any real time together. Even when we go to bed, it's mostly just to sleep.

But we decided to make the last night before they left very special. It was our tenth anniversary.

We put the girls down at seven o'clock, opened a bottle of champagne, put on some of the old disco records we used to dance to, and then proceeded to neck and giggle our way through the evening. We ended up making love twice that night, something we hadn't done in a long long time, and falling asleep in each other's arms. We'd needed that.

And like Jan, I too kept remembering the best moments of that night.

"I wish you were here right now," she said.

"Me, too."

Then, "You sure everything's all right?"

"Everything's fine. Honest."

"Dad asked if we might stay a few more days. And have you fly up on Friday night."

I liked my in-laws very much. They were good, decent people, and had always been exceptionally kind and open with me. We'd gone through a few family crises together—Jan losing our first baby seven months into her pregnancy, me going through a medical scare when I found a strange bump beneath my elbow—and had become good and true friends.

"The trouble is," I said, "There's just no way I can get away."

"That's what I told them," Jan said. "But it never hurts to ask."

"I sure love you and the girls."

"And we sure love you. Night, Hon."

After we hung up, I sat there in the darkness for several minutes.

I could hear the voices coming from the kitchen, but they were too far away to be articulate.

I felt safe in the darkness of my comfortable living room, the only illumination being the silver nimbus of streetlight against the pale drawn curtain.

It all seemed kind of funny, kind of harmless, actually. Guy breaks in and we play at being vigilantes and then the guy accidentally dies.

The cops would give us some hell, might even ask the district attorney if any charges should be pressed, but a doctor and three lawyers? No way the district attorney was going to press charges.

I felt much better about the whole thing.

All we had to do was be honest with the police, and they'd gnaw on our asses a little and then let us go.

I went back to the kitchen in an almost gleeful mood. We'd just let our fear and pessimism run away with us.

THE BODY was gone. That was the first thing I noticed. The second thing I noticed was that both Bill and Neil were holding handguns.

They were standing by the back door.

Curtis was on the floor, wiping up the moisture from the body.

"Where the hell'd the burglar go?" I said.

"Back porch," Neil said. "Bill had a tarpaulin in his trunk. He also had these guns."

He was a strange physician, our good Doctor Bill Doyle, far more interested in death than in life.

"What's the tarpaulin for?" I said. "The police'll just make you unwrap him."

Curtis stopped scrubbing and looked up at me. "We've kind've been talking things over, Aaron."

Any lingering euphoria I'd brought with me from the living room was now gone utterly.

"Talking what over?" I said.

Curtis looked at the other two, took a final swipe at the floor, then stood up. "Talking over what we should do with the body," he said. Then, "They're right, Aaron. There's no way we can call the cops now. They'll bring charges for sure. And you know what it's like at our offices. This kind of scandal hits the paper, they'll fire our asses for sure. I've got a huge mortgage, man. I can't afford to be fired."

"Curtis, are you out of your mind?" I said. "Of course we're going to the cops. And of course we're turning over the body. What the hell else would we do with it?"

"Throw it into the river by the little dam," Bill said. "You know, out on old Frazier Road. We've got it all figured out."

I almost smiled.

Four middle-class guys standing in a kitchen filled with all the latest appliances, gimmicks and gizmos—talking about throwing a dead body into a river.

There was something comic about it.

"What happens when it shows up down river?" I said.

"I checked your garage. You've got six concrete blocks out there," Neil said. "We tie some of them to the body before we throw it in."

They were together now, the three of them, standing in front of the back door.

Three good friends of mine. Men I thought I knew extremely well.

"I hate to spoil your fun, boys," I said, "but right now I'm walking over to that phone and calling the police. And I suggest that you take that body out of that tarpaulin."

I turned and started toward the wall phone.

Neil grabbed me. "Think about it, Aaron. Think about what the media'll do to a story like this. We'll be on the fucking TV news for two or three months. And then there'll be a trial. You realize how many laws we've broken now?"

I shook my head. "Laws you and Bill broke. Not me or Curtis. You two."

"Maybe I should remind you, asshole," Bill said. "You were the one who actually killed him."

"He was trying to escape," I said.

Neil said, "Think of what it'll be like for our kids at school, Aaron. You want to put your little girls through that kind of publicity?"

Neil looked at Bill and said, "And knock off that bullshit about how Aaron killed him. He died accidentally and we're all a part of it. Equally."

"I shouldn't have said that, Aaron," Bill said. "Neil's right and I apologize."

Curtis said, gently, "You know we're right, Aaron. You know we gotta handle it this way now."

"We could go to prison," I heard myself say in a dead voice.

"We could go to prison for what we've done already," Curtis said.

"But a jury—" I started to say.

"A jury?" Bill said. "A jury? God knows what a jury would do to us. You get a lot of poor people on that jury, and they'll just see us as a lot of middle-class bastards trying to get away with killing some poor burglar."

I started to argue but stopped. Bill had a point about juries. God only knew how they'd look at us and our predicament.

I looked longingly over at the phone. Then back at them.

"I'm going to call the police," I said. "And the only way you're going to stop me is to knock me out."

I looked at each one of them.

"You understand?"

They just watched me, silently.

I turned around and walked over to the yellow wall phone.

Funny, it felt as if I was walking a half mile instead of just a few feet.

I was already forming my story in my head.

Had to tie him up so he wouldn't escape. But he got free. And then we had this struggle. And then he accidentally hit his head. Sure. I'm a lawyer. Sure, I know we shouldn't have tied him up. Or struck him. But things just got so crazy—

I lifted the receiver. Dialed the central number for the police, which was on a small sticker right on the phone.

As the dial tone came on, I looked back at my friends.

Still in front of the door. Still silently watching me.

To my friends, I said, "I'm doing the right thing, you guys. I really am. I know a good criminal attorney," I said to the three of them. "He'll be able to handle this with no problem. Honest."

Still no answer.

"We throw that guy into the river, we'll never have another good night's sleep. We'll be too scared to sleep."

Then Bill was standing next to me. "Give me the phone, asshole."

Just then I heard a male voice on the receiver say, "Hello?"

Bill took the phone from me and said, "I dialed the wrong number. I'm sorry."

Bill hung up the phone.

I leaned forward, pressing my forehead to the wall phone.

There was no way we could innocently characterize what had happened tonight.

Every time we tried to explain ourselves, we'd just get into deeper trouble.

Even if we had a first rate criminal attorney helping us.

I slowly pushed myself away from the wall and turned around to face my friends.

"You want to help us carry him out to your van?" Bill said.

"Yeah," Neil said quietly. "We might as well get it over with."

4

I PULLED the van out of the garage and got the back doors opened so we could set the body inside. Curtis had offered to help me but I figured one man would be less conspicuous than two.

I went into the garage and hauled some cement blocks out, along with some rope. I loaded the van, pausing once to look at the deep rich summer night.

There were fireflies and moon shadows and the silhouettes of summer trees against the sky. I wanted to be a kid again, and not know one damned thing about being an adult. A kid just tucked into his bed for the night with a fresh stack of comics on his nightstand, and a Milky Way hidden in one of the drawers, Mom not wanting me to eat this close to sleep. I wanted to dream of freckled Becky Fisher and Spiderman prowling the city and owning the ten-speed I'd seen out at the mall.

I didn't want to know about prowlers and accidental death and taking bodies to the dam. When everything was set up, I went back inside.

All three of them were standing on the back porch, the body at their feet.

"Well, gentlemen," Bill said. "Let's get it over with. Curtis and Aaron, why don't you two grab the feet and we'll take the head. All right?"

The only light was from the kitchen. Everybody looked sweaty and tense.

"Ready?" Bill said.

I glanced at Curtis. He gave me a little grimace then bent down to the tarpaulin.

I bent down, too.

He was heavier than he looked. We spent a few minutes trying to get a good grip on him.

As we worked our way out the back door, Bill and Neil swung their end around for some reason.

They slammed the guy's head into the door frame.

"God, you guys," Curtis said. "Be careful."

"Yeah," Neil said. "We might give him a headache. I hear dead people get them all the time."

We got him down the three steps. He smelled pretty bad, even through the tarpaulin.

"Let's set him down a minute," Neil said. "I'm so fucking sweaty I can't think straight."

We all were. Fear and heat had soaked us. My eyes stung blindly with salty sweat.

I said, "Are you sure we want to do this, you guys?"

"What the hell're you talking about?" Bill said. "It's too late for that kind of bullshit."

"No, it isn't," I said "I could still go inside and call the police and tell them everything that happened."

"Maybe he's right," Curtis said.

"Man, are you two pussies or what?" Bill said.

"I can't believe this bullshit," Neil said.

They looked at each other and shook their parental heads. The tykes were acting up tonight and the parents were exasperated.

"In fact," Curtis said, "I should have thought of this earlier."

"Thought of what earlier?" Bill said.

"This cop, this detective, real nice guy," Curtis said. "He lives right down the street from us."

"And that proves what, exactly?" Neil said.

"That proves that I could at least call the guy and ask him to come over here and talk to us," Curtis said.

"That doesn't sound like a bad idea," I said.

I looked down at the tarpaulin on the ground. "Once we load him into the van—"

"This is bullshit," Neil said, leaning down and lifting his end of the body. "Now c'mon, you guys. Get your asses in gear."

"Damned right," Bill said.

Curtis sighed deeply, looked at me, then shrugged and bent down to pick up his share of the load.

When we had the burglar hefted again, and securely in our grasp, Bill said, "Now let's walk this sonofabitch right over to the van, shove him in the back and get this damned thing over with."

For the next minute or so, everything went just fine.

We walked across the grass to the drive. Walked across the drive to the van. Lifted the body slightly higher so we could push it inside.

And that was when a car pulled into the head of the driveway, insolently bright headlights fixing the four of us in their beam.

We froze.

The car continued to sit there, headlights glaring at us.

"Who the hell is it?" Bill said under his breath.

"I don't know," I said.

"He's just sitting there," Neil said.

"The sonofabitch," Curtis said.

"What the hell does he want?" Bill said.

Then we heard an electric window being lowered. Rock music throbbed inside the car. But all we could see of the car were its headlights, two pitiless eyes examining, probing us.

The music died suddenly.

"Excuse me," somebody unseen called from the car, "is this Manderly Street?"

The voice was young, female.

In the glow of the headlights, I looked at each of our faces. Pale masks, we were shiny with sweat and stark with fear.

"You're one block away," I said. "Go down to the corner and turn right."

"Thank you," she said.

The window went back up.

The throb of the electric bass could be heard again.

The car backed out of the drive, headlights swinging around wildly for a moment, then drove off down the street.

Darkness. Fireflies. Bird cry. Cold harsh sweat.

"Man," Curtis said, "what if they saw what we were doing?"

"Hey," Bill said, "we got enough trouble without borrowing any."

"He's right, Curtis," I said. "From the head of the drive, all they could've seen was four guys standing by the door of the van."

"The open door," Curtis said.

"Even so," I said, "they couldn't have seen anything. Bill and Neil's body blocked the tarpaulin."

"Shit, man," Curtis said, "we just shouldn't be doing this. You know what I mean? I mean maybe that was a sign from God or something—really—the car pulling into the drive like that."

Neil and Bill looked at each other.

Bill gently put out a hand and touched Curtis' arm. "It'll be all right, Curtis. It really will."

"God, I hope so," Curtis said. "This would just destroy my wife and kids. It really would."

A few minutes later, I was backing the van out of the drive.

WHEN YOUR CARGO is a dead body, you start to see the city in a different way. Every corner, every alleyway, is a potential threat. A cop car could be anywhere. We could not afford to draw the least bit of attention to ourselves.

I drove the speed limit. I kept the radio off. I slowed down at every intersection.

Neil and Bill were in the back of the van. A few days earlier, I'd taken out the back seats to haul lumber home. Our garage needed some work on the west wall. They sat back against the walls of the van, the body between them.

Curtis rode shotgun. Every half block or so, he'd wipe sweat off his face. I did the same thing.

Once in a while a carload of teenagers would pull up next to us at a stoplight. A few of them gunned their motors, wanting to drag. Most of them paid no attention to us at all. Couple boring middle-class guys sitting in the front seat of a boring middle-class van.

"Be great to be one of those guys," Curtis said.

"One of what guys?" Neil said.

"Teenagers."

"Oh."

"Driving around looking for girls."

"Yeah," Bill said. "The top down. The radio up. Six pack on the floor."

"Curtis is right," Neil said. "The best part of being a teenager was the nookie."

"Yeah, that's for sure," Bill said. "I got so much pussy in college, my dick almost fell off."

"Isn't it nice to know that doctors are just as sleazy as we are?" Curtis said.

"And modest, too," Neil laughed. "I mean, you'd never catch Bill bragging or anything."

"Not our Bill," Curtis said.

"You guys know what I mean," Bill said. "I mean, when was the last time you had some strange nookie?"

"We're married, Bill," Neil said. "In case you've forgotten, I mean."

"That's my point. In college you'd go to these parties and meet some chick and you'd be in bed with her twenty minutes later. And that's what these teenagers are doing tonight."

"Speak for yourself," I said. "The only way I could get laid in college was to get down on my knees and beg for it."

"Yeah," Curtis said, "not all of us were football stars, Bill."

Then Curtis said, "Oh, shit."

"What?" I said.

"Cop."

"Where?"

"That corner on the right."

Patrol car. Black and white. Parked back in the shadows, so speeders wouldn't see him until it was too late.

"Easy," Bill said.

"You're doing everything just right," Neil said.

"Damn," I said. "The light's going to turn. I'll have to stop."

I braked.

The other three points of the intersection were empty.

"Curtis and I are going to look straight ahead and not talk to you guys in the back," I said.

"Fine," Neil said.

The wait was endless.

"This must be the original seventeen-minute stoplight," Curtis said, keeping his eyes straight ahead.

"Hail Mary, Full of Grace," Neil said. He laughed. "I decided to give your religion a try, Bill."

"That isn't funny, Neil," Curtis said.

"We just need to cool out," Neil said. "Relax. That cop's not going to bother us."

"He's probably going to get laid somewhere," Neil said.

"Cops get a lot of nookie," Curtis said, "no doubt about that." He was trying to sound cool but his voice was trembling.

"Women love Nazis," Neil said.

"Hang on," I said. "And hope for the best."

"Now's the time for that Hail Mary, Neil," Bill said.

He sat there. Not moving.

The light changed.

If I went too slowly through the intersection, he'd certainly get suspicious.

Same as if I peeled out.

I gave the van a modest amount of gas and we started through the intersection.

"Just keep looking straight ahead, Curtis," I said.

"Oh, God," Curtis said.

"What?" I said.

"He's pulling away from the curb."

"You're supposed to be looking straight ahead."

"I'm seeing it peripherally."

"Just because he pulled away from the curb doesn't mean he's coming after us," Bill said.

"Yeah, it's probably donut time," Neil said.

"This is scaring the shit out of me," Curtis said.

I looked in my rear view.

The patrol car was turning the corner.

"Oh, shit," I said.

"What?" Neil said.

"He's following us," I said.

I heard a fist slam into the wall of the van.

"Sonofabitch," Bill said. In the rear view, I could see him kissing the knuckles he'd just damaged on the wall.

"We stay calm," I said.

"He still behind us?" Curtis said.

I looked in the rear view.

"Still behind us," I said.

"You've got another stop light coming up," Bill said.

"I see it."

The light was yellow by the time I reached the edge of the intersection. I touched the brakes. Gently. Then I sat there staring at the rear view.

"Hey," I said. "Keep looking straight ahead."

"What's he doing?" Bill said.

"Sitting there."

"That's all?"

"That's all."

"Can you see if he's running a check on the license plate?" Curtis said.

"Doesn't seem to be. He's just sitting behind the wheel."

"He's probably trying to fake us out," Bill said.

"Boy, that's not too paranoid," I said.

"The light's going to change," Curtis said.

"Just stay cool," I said.

The light changed. Again I gave it a modest amount of gas. We started into the intersection.

I went several feet looking straight ahead. Then I raised my eyes to look in the rear view.

"I don't believe it," I said.

"Oh, shit," Curtis said, "what'd he do? Turn on his siren?"

"No," I said, "he turned left."

"He turned left?" Bill said. "Are you sure?"

I glanced out my window. The patrol car was moving quickly away down the west-running street. He must have picked up some kind of urgent call. He was really rolling.

"Thank you, God," Bill said. "Thank you."

For the next six or seven blocks, we continued to congratulate ourselves on our good fortune. The cop wasn't going to stop us after all.

I suppose that gave us each a little more confidence. Maybe the cop was an omen. And maybe an omen that what we were about to do would work out, after all.

I actually felt relaxed for a time, just kind of cruising through the hot summer night the way a teenager would.

"Wow," Curtis said, "look."

He pointed to a McDonald's. The parking lot was filled with street rods, beautifully sculpted automobiles whose appeal was timeless.

"Think of the chicks you could get if you had one of those babies," Neil said.

"Look at the chicks over there now," Curtis said.

Like the others, I looked, too. And it was not long after that, maybe a half block past McDonald's, that I heard a siren.

This time a different patrol car filled my rear view.

This time the patrol car had his red lights going.

This time the cop in the car was waving at us to pull over.

"Oh, shit," Curtis said.

I pulled over. Reached in my back pocket for my wallet. Extracted my driver's license. Got it ready to hand to the officer.

"Stay cool, everybody," I said.

"Our ass is grass," Neil said.

It seemed like an hour had passed between the time the cop got out of his car and reached the driver's door of the van.

"Evening," he said.

"Evening."

"Back there by McDonald's?"

"Uh-huh."

"You were speeding."

"I was?"

"Clocked you at eleven miles over the speed limit."

"Oh, hell," I said. "I'm sorry."

He was a chunky, middle-aged man with a bland kind of face and deep sweat rings under the arms of his buff blue uniform shirt.

He raised a long, silver flashlight, looked at my license picture then trained the flashlight on my face.

"You been drinking?" he asked.

"Had a few beers earlier in the evening. Oh, and a drink of scotch."

He didn't give me a hint of what he was thinking, only leaned into the window and played his light around in the rear of the van.

"Evening," he said to Bill and Neil.

"Evening," they both said.

Then he played the light on Curtis.

"Evening," Curtis said.

The cop nodded hello.

I had the sense that he was satisfied with us, that we were good and reasonably sober citizens who were just wrapping things up for the night.

Then he shone his light in the back of the van.

"Where're the seats?" he said.

"Took them out so I could haul lumber."

"Where's the lumber now?"

"My garage. Need to fix up the wall."

To Neil and Bill he said, "Probably not real comfortable riding around back there, is it?"

"Only have a little ways to go," Bill said. "Be home soon, I mean."

"What's that on the floor?" the cop said.

"The floor?" Neil said. His voice had raised a full octave.

"Yeah. The floor. Between you guys. What is that?"

"The tarpaulin?" Bill said.

"Yeah, the tarpaulin. What's inside?"

"A rug I'm taking home to my wife," Bill said. "I was at an auction. I bought the rug and the tarpaulin, so I just put one inside the other."

The cop put the light in each of our faces.

"Where was the auction?" he said. He was asking Curtis.

"That auction house over on 28th Avenue," Curtis said.

"All four of you went?" the cop said.

"Yeah," Neil said, "figured we'd go with Bill here and hurry him along. That way we'd have more time for some fun."

The cop's light lingered on the tarpaulin.

To Curtis, he said, "You have some ID?"

"Is this 'cause I'm black?" Curtis snapped.

I rolled my eyes, fearing for the worst. A smart remark like that, he'd get us all out of the van, pat us down, and then go look at the tarpaulin in the back.

"I'm sorry, officer, I shouldn't have said that."

He handed his license over to me and I handed it to the cop.

Curtis and I glanced at each other. Fear had made me cold again.

"How about you other two?" the cop said, handing Curtis' license back. "You two have any ID?"

"Sure do," Neil said, his license in his hand already. He reached up and handed it to the cop.

Cop checked it with his flashlight and then handed it back.

Bill's ID was handed over last.

The cop had suddenly fallen silent. My stomach was starting to send missiles of acid up my chest.

"MD?" the cop said. "You're a doctor?"

"That's right," Bill said.

Cop held the light on the license a long moment, then angled it up for a closer look at Bill's face.

"Hey, Bill Doyle," he said. "You played football. For State."

"Right."

"I'll be damned," the cop said. "My boy and I were big fans of yours."

"Thank you."

"Never forget the day you kicked the hell out of Illinois."

"Got lucky I guess."

Cop handed Bill's license back.

"Don't mean to hard-ass you guys but you *were* speeding."

"My fault," I said. "I'll watch it."

"And I'd get that back seat put back in as soon as you can," the cop said. "Looks funny when you've got two guys crouched down in the back."

Then he smiled.

"Even when he's a football hero like Bill Doyle."

"Thanks, officer, we appreciate it," Bill said.

"You other guys doctors, too?" the cop said.

"No," I said, "lawyers."

The cop smiled.

"Well, I'll try not to hold that against you." He tapped the window ledge gently. "Watch that speed, Mr. Tyler."

"I will, officer. I sure will."

"Well, you gentlemen have a good night."

Everybody muttered a 'good night' of some kind.

I watched the rear view. Cop went back and slid into his seat. Put his car in gear and then made a U-turn.

Neil said, "'Anything I can do for you, Dr. Doyle? A blow job perhaps?'"

"'Would you like to bop my wife, Dr. Doyle?' Curtis said. "I'd consider it a privilege to watch.'"

"Very funny, you assholes," Bill said.

"Just be grateful we had a football hero along," I said. "Otherwise that cop might've gotten a lot more curious about what was inside the tarpaulin."

"I bet I sweated off ten pounds when that sonofabitch asked us about the tarpaulin," Curtis said.

"Yeah?" Neil said. "I bet I sweated off twenty."

THE DAM was roughly twelve miles north of the city. At one time, it was the primary dam for this entire area. But other dams were built more recently and much of the water was diverted from this old dam which, by comparison, was pretty tame in terms of water capacity.

My wristwatch read 11:47 when we pulled up near a heavy stand of jack pines.

We'd spent the last twenty minutes discussing how we were going to handle this.

Curtis and I would watch the road while Neil and Bill carried the tarpaulin, the cement blocks now tied to it, down to a spot just below the dam. With the body and all, it had become a heavy load. Even heavier, obviously, than when there'd been four of us. The blood hadn't soaked through. We'd wrapped his head in heavy towels before we'd closed the tarpaulin.

"The thing is to move fast," Neil said as we piled out of the van.

"The thing is to do it right," Bill said.

Curtis and I walked down next to the gravel access road and stood there while the other two went to work.

"Maybe this is gonna work out," Curtis said.

"Maybe."

The dam smelled of fish and heat and water. The roar of the water was thunderous.

"Man, what's taking them so long?" Curtis said after several minutes.

You had to shout to be heard over the roaring water.

I shook my head. "Don't know."

We both saw the car at the same time. It had just crested the hill above and was moving quickly down the gravel road.

We stepped back behind the evergreens.

The car seemed to slow slightly when it came abreast of us then picked up speed and vanished.

Nearly fifteen minutes had gone by.

Curtis leaned close to me and said, "Something's wrong, man."

I nodded. Leaned close to him. "You wait here. Watch for cars."

I walked back up the hill, staying close to the trees for cover.

When I reached the van, I checked out the back. The tarpaulin was gone.

What was keeping them?

I walked on over the hill.

The buttress dam was an older style with a curved wall, and the spillway and slide valves operated from a small cabin located near the dam. The cabin was rarely manned. Tonight it was dark beneath the starry sky.

At first I didn't see them. I walked down to the nearest side of the dam and then moved along the walkway overseeing the mighty splash and tumble of foamy water.

I found the rope lashed to a tree and then looked over the edge.

Bill and Neil were both clinging to the rope, trying to dislodge the tarpaulin. One of the ropes around the block had snagged on a stray rod jutting from the side wall.

They had one big problem. The rope they were using to hang on to didn't extend far enough to help them. And they were both obviously afraid of falling into the water and drowning.

The tarpaulin bobbed up and down violently on the surface of the water. It would probably bob like that for a day or two before the waves finally dislodged it.

I waved them up.

They were soaked when they reached the walkway.

"God," Neil said, wringing water out of his hair. "You see the problem."

We were all shouting to be heard.

"We've got to get that damned body free before somebody comes along," Bill said, sputtering water from his mouth. He made a face. "Probably not more than sixty, seventy kinds of deadly bacteria in that water."

"We need a longer rope," Neil said.

"No, we don't," I said. "We need somebody to dive into the water. That'd be a lot easier."

"That's damned rough water," Bill said.

"Hey," Neil said, "I forgot all about our friend here being a championship swimmer."

Bill shook his head. "No way. Even Aaron could drown in this stuff."

"We don't have a hell of a lot of choice," I said. For all its power, this was a small and relatively shallow dam. I could probably navigate it for a few minutes.

I went over to the walkway, took off shirt, shoes, socks, and grabbed on to the guide rope.

Bill grabbed me, shouted in my face. "You don't have to do this!"

"The hell I don't! The longer we're here, the better the chance we'll be seen!"

He looked at me a long moment and then nodded silently.

Neil patted me on the back, gave me a thumbs up.

I grabbed the rope and started the descent.

The wall was still hot from the baking day. Until I got close to the water line.

The water hadn't seemed this violent from up top. Down here it was a deafening frenzy.

I took a deep breath, let go of the guide rope and jumped into the water. Blindness. I lost all bearings momentarily. The water was warm and filthy.

A long moment of panic. Disoriented.

Then I fought my way to the surface, bobbing in time with the tarpaulin.

My eyes stung. My lungs burned.

I swam toward the tarpaulin.

When I reached it, I swam as close to the jutting rusted iron rod as I could.

Not going to be as easy as I'd hoped.

The dead guy's weight was only enhanced in the bobbing water. I had to lift him above the rod to set him free.

I spent the next five minutes trying to make it work, but it wouldn't.

It was like trying to bench press a refrigerator.

Forearms, arms, biceps, back all straining, I did manage to move him a few feet up the rod but there were still several inches to go.

And I didn't have the strength for it.

I had to stop, tread water, rest, reconnoitre.

The simplest thing to do would be to undo the rope holding the block to the body.

That would leave only two blocks. We needed to be sure that the body would sink, and stay sunk. We needed the third block. It might save time. But the body might also surface in just a few days.

In the moonlight above, I could see Neil and Bill watching me, urging me on.

As I tred water, I began to smell and feel the river. I felt filthy. There's nothing like a midnight swim in feces-infested toxic river water to make you feel good.

I started to float away from the tarpaulin. I reached out and grabbed the steel rod.

And felt it move.

And knew I had my answer.

Took ten intense minutes but I got it done.

I couldn't raise the body over the top of the steel rod. But I could twist and turn the rod until it was upside down and the rope simply slipped free.

Then I gave the body a shove, out into the worst of the slamming, slashing water.

By the time I'd swum back to the side wall and was working my way back to the walkway, the body was nowhere to be seen.

There was just the tumbling angry river water thrashing and smashing against the side walls.

When I got back up top, Neil and Bill kind of hugged me and we all did this little victory dance together.

And then we hauled ass back to the van and picked up Curtis.

THE ALCOHOL had no effect on me.

We got back to my house, my kitchen more specifically, and started working our way through a new bottle of scotch.

Four glasses. No ice. Just hitting the bottle.

We were all too tired to talk much. We were like jocks after a particularly wearing game.

Curtis raised his drink and said, "To the three best friends I've ever had."

"No shit," Neil said.

And we all clinked glasses.

"You think it's over?" Curtis said.

Bill nodded. "Sure. Even if they find the body, so what? How could they tie it to us?"

"God, I sure hope you're right," Curtis said. The phone rang. "Hello?"

This time of night, a phone call is always scary. First thing I thought about was maybe something was wrong with one of my kids. Or Jan.

"Is that husband of mine still over there?" Gwen, Curtis' wife said.

"As a matter of fact," I said, trying to sound light-hearted. "He is."

"Would you give him a message for me?"

"Sure."

"Tell him to get his butt home or he'll be sleeping in the garage tonight."

"I will convey that exact message, Madame."

"Our turn to have you folks over for dinner," Gwen said. "Have Jan call me when she gets back."

"Will do. And I'll pass the message on to Curtis."

"I heard, I heard," Curtis said from the breakfast nook.

"I need to get home, too," Bill said.

Neil and Bill used the john and tried to make themselves look as presentable as possible. They were pretty much dry but they still looked pretty funky.

At the curb, everybody started to get into their respective cars. Bill said, "I think we should all make it a point to stay away from each other for a few days. The way we normally would."

"Good idea," Neil said. "We should go on with our lives just like normal."

Then in the darkness, there are at last, Curtis said, "You guys really think it's over?"

I laughed. "It's over, Curtis. It's over."

BUT THEN, an hour later, lying awake in bed, thinking of Jan and the girls, trying hard not to think of what had happened tonight, I felt some of Curtis' anxiety.

Was it really over?

I don't know what time it was when the phone rang.

Some time in the latest and darkest and bleakest part of the night.

I rolled over and picked up the receiver, rubbing sleep from my face with my free hand.

"Hello," I said.

Somebody was there. Breathing. Not heavy breathing. Nothing dramatic like that. Just the steady normal rhythm of breathing.

"Hello," I said, again.

Then the phone clicked off on the other end.

I thought of the guy who'd jumped me from the garage roof earlier, the accomplice who'd been hiding on the back porch while we were taking care of his friend.

The accomplice was out there tonight.

Somewhere.

I tried to sleep but all I could do was listen to Curtis' voice in my mind, repeating, "You guys really think it's over? You guys really think it's over?"

5

IT REALLY is the sort of thing they put you in prison for.

The life of a tax attorney is rarely exciting. If you want excitement, you become a public defender or a trial lawyer.

But there are certain moments in a tax attorney's life when a rather ordinary situation has the potential to become a very dramatic one.

It's called the One Hundred Percent Negligence Rule, and the boys and girls at the Internal Revenue Service are very, very serious about it.

In it's simplest form, the Rule means this: you, as bookkeeper or comptroller, can be sentenced to prison for not paying withholding taxes—even if your boss orders you not to.

The way it usually happens is this—employer has cash flow problems. Decides that he'll pay some July creditors with his July withholding money. Three months later, he finds that he still has a lot of outstanding debts—and now he's behind in his withholding taxes as well.

In no time, he's five, six, seven, eight months behind and now he's got two problems. His cash flow is still killing him and now he's in deep trouble with the IRS.

This is where I usually get involved.

Now, only rarely does anyone go to prison over something like this, but it does happen. And people always look shocked when I say that incarceration is at least a dim possibility.

This was the kind of call I received five minutes after I stepped into the office the next morning.

I wore a new summer suit and tried to smile a lot. I was worried that I might still smell of toxic river water.

My secretary appeared in my doorway and said, "There's a woman on the phone, Aaron, and she really sounds upset. She really needs to talk to you."

I nodded and picked up, wishing I could savor the coffee I was now gulping down.

"Aaron Tyler."

"Hi, Mr. Tyler. This is Trudy. Remember?"

Remember? Who could forget? A pretty but very naive young woman four years off the farm, making her way in a mid-sized Midwestern city. Two or three bad affairs with sharks. And then forgetting to pay her taxes for two years. I'd believed her about forgetting them. She was so scared over the letter the IRS had sent her that she came up to my office and threw her arms around me, clinging tight. I guess I should mention that Trudy is a very erotic young woman—not especially pretty, not especially bright. But with her knowing blue eyes and curiously sexual overbite, not to mention her sleek and perfect body, she wears her eroticism the way other women wear perfume. I should also mention that Trudy got me into some trouble a year ago—not with the IRS but with Jan. Trudy sent a Thank You card reeking of sachet to my house. A few days later she sent me a pair of expensive leather gloves. For all the worldliness of her body, Trudy still had farm girl mentally. While she saw the card and the gloves as innocent, Jan saw them as proof that I was having an affair. She started thinking about her college boyfriend and how he'd betrayed her. It took me two weeks to convince her that Trudy was just a naive young woman and that there was nothing between us. So now she was asking me if I remembered? God, yes, I did.

"Sure, I do, Trudy."

"Can I ask you a question, I mean on the phone right here?"

"Sure."

"I don't have much money, Mr. Tyler. I need to be clear about that up front."

"One question and one answer free of charge. How's that?"

"I really appreciate this, Mr. Tyler."

"Aaron."

"Aaron, then."

"I'm a bookkeeper now. You know, I used to work as a clerk."

"Right."

"But I was good in math, so Ron decided to try me out as his bookkeeper."

"All right."

"For this manufacturing company."

"Uh-huh."

"And right now we're ten months behind in withholding payments to the IRS."

"That happens sometimes."

"What's really scaring me is that a lady in the office tells me I can be held responsible for that."

"I'm afraid she's right, Trudy."

"I could even go to prison?"

"It's unlikely but it does happen."

"But Ron—he's the president—he *makes* me pay all the other bills first."

Then she started crying. It was sudden, harsh.

"Trudy?"

"Yes." Crying.

"Almost nobody ever goes to prison over this thing. You know what I'd advise?"

"What?"

"That you start looking for another job. Then if the IRS ever questions you about this, you can say that you didn't want to go along with this Ron, and so you got another job. That would put you in a very strong position."

"I can't look for another job, Aaron." Still crying.

"Why not?"

"Because Ron and I are having an affair."

"I see."

"And he's married."

"Ah."

"And I'm in love with him."

"Well—"

"And I'm four months pregnant and I'm pretty sure the child is his."

What had started out as a rather routine call had just become the lyric for a country and western ballad.

"Pretty sure?"

"Well, I mean, I was at a party one night—Ron wasn't there, I mean—and I remember being so drunk that I fell on all these coats piled up on this bed and—well, I have some dim memory of something happening." She was snuffling up the last of her tears.

"Something happening?"

"You know. When I passed out. This really creepy date I was with. I mean, he might have done something to me."

"You couldn't tell?"

"Well, when I woke up the next morning my panties weren't torn or anything."

"I guess that's a good sign."

"And I wasn't sticky or anything. You know, down there."

"Another good sign."

"So it's probably Ron's child."

"Does Ron know about this?"

"He has a terrible temper."

"I see."

"A couple of years ago, he had an affair with one of the gals in the front office. And when he found out she was pregnant, he broke her nose."

"He broke her nose? Are you kidding?"

"Well, he was pretty drunk, and he apologized to her and everything. And then he gave her a raise. And paid for the abortion."

"Gee, that was nice of him."

"I'm probably making him sound just terrible."

"Oh, no. He sounds just peachy."

"He can really be a lot of fun sometimes."

I sighed. "Trudy."

"Yes?"

"Dump him and find another job."

"But I love him."

"Be that as it may."

"And I'm carrying his child. At least I'm ninety-five percent sure it's his child."

"Trudy."

"Yes?"

"You called to ask my advice, right?"

"Right."

"Dump him. And right now, right this morning, find yourself a newspaper and start looking through the want ads."

God has a role for each of us in this vale of tears. Trudy's role, inexplicably, was that of victim. With a capital V. He can really be a lot of fun sometimes. He broke her nose but he gave her a raise.

Trudy and all the other Trudies in this world break my heart. Women may not be perfect, but in general they're a hell of a lot more perfect than the general run of men.

This Ron was a predator—a selfish, dangerous, bullying predator.

No matter how much fun he was sometimes.

I hoped the IRS nailed his ass to the wall.

"Trudy."

"Yes?"

"I've got a lot of work ahead of me today, so I have to get busy here. But I really hope you'll think it over."

"About leaving?"

"Yes."

"And dumping him?"

"Yes."

"Maybe that's what I should do." Then, "Could I call you sometime?"

"Sure."

"I mean, when I tell him I'm, you know, preggers and everything, he might go ballistic."

"Call me if you need help."

"You're really sweet, Aaron."

"Thank you, Trudy. So are you."

PEOPLE DON'T believe me, but the IRS has actually gotten nicer over the past several years. For this, we can thank the singer Willie Nelson.

His tax troubles became a major story. So did the manner in which his particular IRS agents treated him.

Apparently wanting to prove that they would not be intimidated by a celebrity, the agents were rude, impatient, even hostile and threatening.

It's one thing to try and collect legitimate taxes; it's another to try and destroy a person's sense of safety and well-being.

When the press found out about this, the IRS saw a lot of downside public relations ahead, so it issued a new code for its agents.

For once, this was a federal code that actually worked.

All complaints about agents would be investigated. If the complaints were legitimate, the agent would be reprimanded or, in extreme cases, dismissed.

Tax lawyers and tax preparers laughed skeptically when we first heard about this code, but damned if the thing wasn't for real.

In the old days, I always accompanied my clients to the IRS offices. I was afraid they'd be bullied into admitting something terrible.

But these days, I rarely accompanied my clients. The IRS is no longer interested in intimidating citizens. It simply wants to collect owed revenues.

One other thing has changed: the IRS now works out reasonable repayment plans. They used to just attach everything you owned. But now they're much more like a bank, working out monthly or quarterly payments.

I mention all this by way of telling you that I'm not as busy a tax lawyer as I once was. My busiest time wearing that particular hat is, of course, the months nearest April 15.

The rest of the time I practice family law, probate law, and real estate law. With family and probate, my tax law experience comes in very handy. A good deal of family and probate deals with taxes.

I SPENT most of the morning in the small conference room talking to a woman who had inherited a five-hundred-acre farm and wanted to know how she could shelter some of her father's largesse from the inheritance tax.

I had to tell her that there wasn't a whole hell of a lot anybody could do. The inheritance tax allows for very few exceptions and loopholes. Very few.

I walked the woman to the front of our offices, stopped by the receptionist's desk to pick up my pink phone slips. There were three of them. One was business. The other two were from Neil.

When I opened my office door, I saw Curtis standing at my window, looking down at the river that divides the city neatly in half.

"Morning," I said, closing the door and walking inside.

"Morning," he said, not turning around to look at me.

"Something interesting out there?"

"The river," he said. "I wonder where the body is." Now he looked at me: "You think we put enough blocks on him?"

I went over and sat down behind my desk. I am a tidy man. The only thing you'll find on the surface of my desk is the matter I'm presently working on, the telephone, and one of those picture cubes for family shots.

My office, like the rest of Stearns, Lymon and Saunders, runs to mahogany wainscoting and somber carpeting, that drab but proper look lawyers always associate with success.

"You all right?" I said.

"You piss a lot when you're nervous?" he said, coming over and sitting down.

"Guess I haven't noticed."

"That's all I've done since I woke up this morning. Peed. You're lucky, by the way.

"Oh?"

"That Jan wasn't home. Gwen kept looking at me all during breakfast. My face doesn't look too bad, does it?"

Despite the beating he'd taken last night, he looked pretty damned good.

"You probably looked nervous."

"I guess I don't have much of a poker face, do I?"

I smiled. "No, I guess you don't." I leaned forward on my elbows. "Look me in the eye, Curtis."

"What?"

"Look me in the eye."

"For what?"

"Just do it."

He looked me in the eye. "All right?"

"Great. Now keep looking me in the eye and repeat after me."

He smirked. "You're a crazy sonofabitch sometimes, Aaron. People think you're so quiet and proper but they just don't know you very well."

"Now raise your right hand."

"You're shitting me."

"Raise your right hand. Humor me, Curtis."

He raised his right hand.

I said, "I, Curtis Reeves."

He sighed. "I, Curtis Reeves."

"Do solemnly swear."

"Do solemnly swear. You're fucking crazy, Aaron, you really are."

"That I will go on with my life as if nothing happened."

Another sigh. "That I will go on with my life as if nothing happened."

"And that I will relax and enjoy the many blessings."

"And that I will relax and enjoy the many blessings."

"That I richly deserve."

"That I richly deserve."

"There," I said.

"There?"

"There. It's called affirmation. You will something to happen hard enough, and it'll happen."

"I'm scared, Aaron. I can't help it."

"Affirmation, Curtis. Every time you get edgy, just close your eyes, take a deep breath and repeat that affirmation."

"Not word for word," he said, "I can't remember it all."

"Then just say 'Everything's going to be fine' to yourself."

He grinned. "That doesn't sound as impressive as the one you did. All that 'I, Curtis Reeves' bullshit."

"I'm glad you appreciated that." I laughed.

Without warning, he put his hands on his face.

I think he was trying to cry but not succeeding. Crying is not something most people of the male persuasion do with any facility. I always get self-conscious, even when I'm alone, as if the macho monitor is hiding some place, ready to jump out when I shed the first tear, and kick my ass for being such a pansy.

"Curtis."

He just stayed the way he was, face hidden.

"Curtis."

Slowly, he looked up. "I'm not sure I can handle this, Aaron."

"Sure you can handle it."

He put his hands down, watching them leave as if they were departing friends he would miss greatly.

"I'm the first person in my whole family to graduate from college. I ever tell you that?"

I nodded.

"Not to mention the first person to become a lawyer. And the first person to live out in Hamilton County. And the first person to belong to a country club, however modest that club may be. And the first person to drive a Beamer. You know what I'm saying? A black kid who came by it honestly." He looked out the window again. The rushing river was down there. The body was down there, too.

"And now maybe I'm going to lose it all. That's why I couldn't sleep last night. And that's why Gwen kept looking at me so funny. Because she sensed it—that last night I'd laid everything on the line." He paused, inhaled deeply. "You know what we did last night, man?"

"I know."

"A very, very serious felony. Hard-time felony." He looked down at his hands again. "I go to prison, man, I'm not any better than any of the guys I grew up with on Kensington Street. Hell, I'd be worse. Because I had the chance to make something of myself."

I wasn't quite sure what to say. Curtis had worked himself into a terrible state of anxiety. I've seen clients do that when faced with the IRS. They begin to believe the bleakest scenario their minds can concoct, and once they reach a certain point, there's no hope of bringing them back.

"We're going to be all right, Curtis. You've got to believe that."

The intercom buzzed. "Yes?"

"Call for you on line three, Aaron."

"Thank you."

Curtis was already up and walking over to the door. "I'll stop back later today."

"It's going to be fine, Curtis."

He smiled sadly. "Just don't make me repeat that pledge of yours, all right?"

"You're a good man, Curtis."

The sadness remained but not even a trace of the smile. "So're you, Aaron. So're you."

AT NOON I went for a walk.

On my way out the door, I saw Curtis talking to one of the other attorneys. I could've invited him along but I wanted to relax. I didn't need anymore of his anxiety right now. I'd convinced myself that everything was going to be fine and I wanted to go on thinking that.

Summer day in a mid-sized Midwestern city. The streets packed with walkers and joggers, a thousand pair of startling white Reeboks. On the benches surrounding the one square block city park women in summer dresses and men in short sleeves talk, munched apples, slurped Diet Pepsi's, read newspapers, paperbacks, or the occasional library hardback. A thousand smiles, a thousand white handkerchiefs daubing sweat off foreheads. At one time this used to be a sleepy little town. No more. There was real money here now, international money in manufacturing, research and investment, all reflected in the four new glass-and steel buildings that dominated the skyline.

A few blocks off the main streets was a large used bookstore where I spent a few lunch hours a week. *Read Books* began as a used best-seller store and became, over six or seven years, a huge two-story affair with every kind of book imaginable.

Curtis' anxiety had stayed with me. I needed to escape. So I passed up the non-fiction section, where I usually go, and headed right back to science fiction.

The golden books of my early teen years were the Edgar Rice Burroughs novels about John Carter of Mars. I was still in grade school when Burroughs came back into fashion. I had all sixteen of the Carters on a special shelf above my bed. They were the holy books.

One starry night, standing on a desert in Arizona, John Carter hears his name uttered across the vast reaches of space. He stands looking up at the sky, not understanding who is calling him or why.

And he is transported bodily, through a kind of matter transmission, to the planet Mars, where two factions war for dominance.

Whenever I was at my loneliest, or most frightened, I returned again and again to those books.

As I did today.

I stood there long enough to read the entire first chapter, Soft-Cover and Hardback, the two cats who lived in the store, taking turns rubbing against my legs.

And I was transported, no longer of earth, no longer burdened with my shameful little fears and drab little dreams.

And I walked a world filled with beautiful ladies. And lusty barbarians whom I would someday dispatch with my sword.

And in the long Martian night the women were so passionate, the wine and music so heady, the ecstasy threatened to lead to madness.

And you thought that tax lawyers were just nerdy little guys with thick glasses and three-piece Sears suits.

If only you could see inside our heads.

A MAN named Jennings felt that my last bill was excessive. He told me that while he would pay it, he would never do business with our firm again. A woman named Bascomb told me that she was sending me one of her bridge friends who was getting a divorce, and she hoped that I could help this friend, tax-wise, the way I had helped her, tax-wise.

One of the eight partners, Larry Reed, stopped in to tell me that he thought I'd done an exceptional job covering for him while he was in Europe. He'd had a little surgery—the problem had turned out not to be malignant—and then taken six weeks to recuperate and celebrate.

And Neil called. We'd been playing phone tag all day. Finally, around four o'clock, I returned his last call and we made a connection.

"You been listening to the radio?" he said.

"No," I said, feeling a panic I wanted to deny. "Is something up?"

"Nothing. That's my point. Nothing. Nada. Not squat, my friend. Home free."

I felt a ridiculous relief.

"How's our friend Curtis?"

"Fine," I said. Why worry Neil?

"I talked to Bill about two hours ago. He thinks we should all meet for drinks after work. I think he's right."

"I thought we were going to do everything just as we normally would."

"Hell, we all get together after work sometimes."

"Yeah, I guess."

"Hey, c'mon, we'll just have a couple of shooters and talk a bit."

"Yeah, actually that sounds nice."

"How about Nino's?"

I laughed. "Whirling breasts."

"Don't knock it, fella."

"Nothing but the high-class joints for us."

"I like the one who can make 'em look like propellers."

Nino's was a topless bar that allegedly catered to the carriage trade. The only evidence of that was that their drinks cost about three times more than they did in other topless places.

"See you right about five-thirty," he said. I called Curtis and told him the plans.

His first reaction was like mine. "I thought we were going to act like normal."

"Well, as Neil said, every once in a while, the four of us do get together."

"Not very often."

"It won't hurt anything."

"I suppose not," he said.

"Ah, I love that enthusiasm."

"God, I am a baby sometimes, aren't I?"

"No comment."

"Chuck you, Farley," he said, laughing. And hung up.

THE CALL came as I was walking around my desk to grab my suit coat from the coat stand.

"Yes?"

"A woman named Trudy on line two." Damn, I thought. "Thanks." I punched line two.

"I'm sorry to bother you, Aaron."

She was whispering.

"Listen, Trudy, is this something that could wait until tomorrow?"

"He knows."

"He knows?"

"He came up behind me and saw me circling things in the Help Wanted ads."

"Oh."

"And I'm afraid. Everybody's going home for the day. That means it'll be just the two of us—Ron and me."

"If you're afraid, just pick up your purse and walk out of there while there are still other people around."

"Oh, God, here he comes down the hall. I'd better go."

She hung up.

I suppose I should have given her at least a little bit of help but what could I say? If she was really worried about what he might do, I assumed she'd be intelligent enough to call the police.

A minute later, pushing my arms through the sleeves of my suit jacket, I headed for the reception area and the elevators.

6

IN MY college days, I logged a lot of hours in bars. I would go in with the sun shining and leave with the moon riding high. I liked the noise, smoke, loud music, and close proximity to girls. I also liked the camaraderie. My parents had spent most of their time doting on my older brother, and I suppose to them that made a kind of cruel sense. He was smarter, stronger, better looking, and infinitely more charming than I could ever hope to be. I suppose I found a kind of brotherhood in the frat bars. Alcohol has its own deluded truths, and I savored those truths. Hanging around bars filled with pretty young women, I felt not only adequate but downright popular. The fact that few of the pretty young women ever accompanied me back to my off-campus apartment did not chasten the delusion.

A few years after starting out in law practice, I was still hitting the bars. One slow and rainy Friday afternoon, a bartender looked at me and said, "You don't look like you belong here."

I wondered if she was kidding. "Why not?"

"The people who hang out in bars, they've all got problems. So they come here to forget them. A lot of them don't even know they've got problems. They just think that getting drunk every night is a normal life. If they didn't have problems, they'd be home with the missus."

"And I don't seem like one of them?"

"Huh-uh. You're nice looking, you're intelligent, and you stay pretty normal when you drink."

I smiled. "Does this mean you're throwing me out?"

But I thought about what she said, and slowly, over the next several months, I cut down on my bar time.

I started going to libraries, concerts, baseball games. And I surprised myself by meeting a lot more pretty young women than I'd ever met in bars. In fact, it was at intermission at a light opera that I met Jan. I didn't have a special interest in light opera—or heavy opera, for that matter—but I sure had a lot of interest in Jan. Two years later, we were married.

All these thoughts are in my mind whenever I go into a bar today. Because of what that bartender told me, I don't find the smoke, noise or music as evidence of the good life. I find it as a wall behind which the drinkers hide, hoping to convince themselves and each other that they're having a wonderful time.

Nino's had all the smoke, noise and music you could want. But what it mostly had were the dancers, thirtyish women with artificial balloon breasts, weary smiles, and g-strings made for stuffing with crisp green dollar bills. The problem I have with these dancers is that after a couple of drinks, I always wind up feeling sorry for them, and resenting the fact that they have to make their living pushing their crotches at a bunch of drunks.

Being one of those men who find understated women far sexier than the more blatant ones, I don't even find these women all that alluring. Not even the ones who can make their breasts seem to rotate like propellers, believe it or not.

Having been caught in traffic for the past half hour, I was running a little late when I walked up to the table where Curtis, Neil and Bill sat.

They'd taken a table in the back, one removed from all the activity on the runway. Presently, a black woman was rubbing the neck of a wine bottle between her legs.

Bill said, "The next time Aaron tries to tell us this isn't a high-class joint, I say we beat the crap out of him."

"All this place needs is country western music," I said.

Curtis laughed. "Yeah, man, then you'd *really* be in hell."

Neil said, "You want me to ask if any of those babes have any Reba McEntire records?"

"No, thanks."

And that's kind of how it went for the first couple of drinks.

We alternated small talk with looking at the women working out in the spotlight on the runway.

One of the women humped a pole, two of them did a kind of lesbian thing and one of them laid on her back and spread her legs for us.

Bill said, "This is like studying gynecology back in med school again."

Their admirers down front put on a better show than the ladies— blue collar and white collar mixed, most of them whooping and whistling and stomping their feet. They'd probably been in this place a hundred times, but somehow they had this great reservoir of enthusiasm for every predictable bump and every clichéd grind. I didn't know whether to disdain them or envy them. I guess I've always had the secret desire to be a man of simple tastes and pleasures.

"Boy, if med school had chicks like that in it," Curtis said, "I sure regret becoming a lawyer."

Easy patter. Couple trips to the john. Couple more rounds of drinks.

And not a single reference to last night.

We all hooted when the new woman who came out did her bit in time to a country western song.

I was back in a frat bar again. That kind of easy, empty kinship.

And then Neil said, "Anybody here going to be pissed if I bring up last night?"

Bill said, "That's why we're here."

Neil leaned forward, as did we all, in a kind of huddle.

"Anybody get a call late last night?" Neil said.

"What kind of call?" Curtis said.

"Somebody calling and not saying anything for a minute or two and then hanging up?"

"I got a call like that," I said.

Neil leaned back so he could see me better. "What time?"

"Late. Four o'clock maybe."

"And he didn't say anything?"

"Nothing."

"But you could hear him breathing?"

"Right."

"You guys get a call like that?"

Curtis and Bill shook their heads.

"Hey," Curtis said. "We're probably talking coincidence here. Right, Bill?"

But Bill didn't look so certain. "Maybe."

"There's one of those sonofabitches still out there, remember," Neil said.

"Right," I said. "The bastard who jumped me from the roof of the garage."

"If he wanted to nail us," Curtis said, "he could just go to the cops and tell them what happened."

I shook my head. "No, he couldn't. If he did, he'd have to tell them what he was doing. And I suspect that he's broken into so many houses, they might be able to put him away for a long time."

Neil snorted. "Yeah, at least a week or two, the way these fucking judges sentence people today."

"And there's one other thing, too," I said.

"What?"

"The Donaldson killing." This was the murder four months ago, right in the middle of our block, when the Donaldsons, an elderly couple, had been stabbed to death in their bed. A man had been arrested a few days later trying to pass some of their traveller's checks. The cops nailed one guy. But what if these two clowns from last night worked with the guy the cops arrested?

"Wow," Curtis said. "A burglary ring."

"Exactly," I said. "That's a real possibility. And it could be one more reason why this guy can't go to the cops."

"So he's going to start harassing us?" Bill said. "Phone calls, crap like that?"

"Possibly."

"I'd like to get my hands on the prick," Bill said.

"Then again," I said, "there *is* the possibility that the phone calls last night were coincidental."

"Unlikely," Curtis said.

Bill glanced at his watch. "Beth's folks are in town for a few days. I need to get home." Then he looked around the table at each of us. "I'm sure we each had a few bad moments today. That's only natural. But we're going to beat this thing. I know we are."

He probably sounded like this right after he'd given one of his patients a potentially fatal diagnosis.

"We just have to keep our usual low profile," he went on, "and keep our heads. That's the most critical thing of all. Not to panic. Ever. You guys understand that?"

We all nodded our heads dutifully.

"As long as we keep that in mind," Bill said, "everything's going to be fine. Everything is going to be fine," he said, again. Another glance at his watch. "I've got to go. Nice seeing you guys."

He stood up.

"I'll walk out with you," I said.

"Think I'll stick around a little while for the cultural part of the evening," Curtis said.

Neil grinned. "Yeah, I understand later that two of the strippers are going to debate the relative merits of a constitutional monarchy versus a republic."

"Talk to you guys soon," I said.

Bill and I stood talking a few minutes in the parking lot. Night was falling, the red sunset melancholy, the first stars vague in the sky.

"You think Curtis is going to be all right?" Bill said.

"I think so."

"Keep an eye on him."

"I will. We all need to keep an eye on each other."

"Not on me," he said. "I don't have any regrets about what we did last night, not about some fucking dirt bag like that. And I genuinely believe that if we stay cool, nobody'll ever find out about it. That's why

I'm worried about Curtis. He thinks this is the end of the world. But it's actually not much at all—if we just hang in there with it."

"I agree."

He looked at me closely. "Really?"

"Really."

He patted me on the elbow. "Great. Now I've got to haul ass."

He got in his bronze Jaguar XKE and drove off.

On the way home, I stopped at McDonald's and bought myself a fish sandwich and fries and a vanilla shake. No doubt about it. I was a regular party animal.

I sat eating in the parking lot, watching the last of the daylight die.

When they were very little, my girls sat on my knees and combed my hair. They loved combing my hair and I loved having them comb it.

I was overpowered by the memory as I sat there, so much so that I felt myself tear up.

God, I loved them and their mother so much, and I felt a terrible longing for them just now, a wild awful sense that I was never going to see them again.

AFTER GETTING home, I opened a beer and walked from room to room. I'd changed to chinos and a new T-shirt.

Jan had a passion for what is called the Victorian Renaissance Revival. During my early years of law practice, we had to settle for a little box of a house in a development. Not much she could do by way of decorating.

So eight years of pent-up decorating fervor had gone into this house, the Revival style running to a lot of ornamentation with details like inlay, marquetry, crests, and finials. There were also a lot of dark woods, claw feet, garlands, wreaths and cameos in the grand old rooms Jan had decorated herself.

At first, I'd felt it was all a little bit oppressive. Mine was an Ozzie and Harriet upbringing: you went to Ethan Allen, plunked down several thousand dollars, and two vast trucks showed up at your door in the morning and filled up your house with good, if impersonal, furnishings.

I wasn't used to the house I lived in having more of a personality than I did.

The house felt different tonight. I wondered if, in fact, it would ever feel the same again to me.

I kept seeing the burglar in the kitchen, his switchblade drawn, his eyes crazed as Neil and Bill tried to encircle him.

A man had died in this house. Not a man I cared much about, frankly, but a man nonetheless. He'd had a history of some kind, and somebody somewhere had loved him. And now he was dead.

I was about to walk down to the basement when the phone rang.

I picked it up in the kitchen, looking at the receiver as I lifted it.

With this very same receiver, I could have phoned the police last night. While there'd still been time.

But I hadn't.

"Hi, Sweetie."

"Hi, Honey," I said. "How're the girls?"

"Pooped out. Mom and Dad took us to the county fair today. I think the girls rode on every ride at least two times. Plus, they're beet red from the sun. How're things going there?"

"Oh, fine. Nothing much going on."

"No poker parties tonight?"

"Not tonight."

"You sound a lot better than you did last night."

"Yeah, I'm feeling better."

"You had me worried," Jan said. "When we hung up, I said to Mom that I thought there was something you weren't telling me."

"Oh, I'm sorry, Honey. I was just tired. Everything's fine."

"Well, now I believe that. Now you sound like your old self again."

"I think I'll watch the news and then go to bed. I didn't sleep well last night. You know how it is when you're gone."

"You probably miss me taking all the covers off you."

"And snoring," I said.

"And occasionally passing gas."

I laughed. "God, that really must've embarrassed you. You still bring it up and it was months ago."

"It was a very unladylike moment," she said. She tried to kid about it but I knew she was serious. There's a primness to Jan I've always liked. She's aware of this in herself and is able to kid herself about it.

"You know me," she said, "perfect in every way—except for that one moment of accidental fluffing."

"God, it's great to hear your voice."

"Yours, too," she said. "But I'd better get off. I've got to get the girls ready for bed. Mom says she's glad to do it but you know how it is with her arthritis."

"All right, Hon. I'll talk to you tomorrow night."

"I love you."

"I love you, too."

I spent the next hour with a can of beer and the TV remote, surfing between the forty-one channels we now receive. Nothing looked especially interesting. It seems we had better choices when we only had three channels to choose from.

Around ten, I went upstairs to the bathroom, washed my face, brushed my teeth, and then went into the bedroom to see what I had for reading matter. My reading taste runs to Ludlum and a handful of his imitators. I looked at the new Ludlum. I had enough for a final good read before finishing the book.

I was halfway down the stairs—I always make one final pass around the house, at bedtime, making sure the alarm is properly set and all the doors are locked—when I heard the knock on the front door.

My first thought was of last night, and the man who'd jumped off the garage roof and tried to stab me.

The knock sounded again, a timid knock, really.

The living room was dark. I snapped on a table lamp and went over to the front door.

As I raised my hand to touch the doorknob, I realized I was trembling.

"Mr. Tyler?"

The voice was female.

"Yes," I said through the door.

"I'm sorry to bother you, but I wonder if I could come in a minute."

"Who are you?"

"Oh, gosh, I'm sorry. Trudy."

A paranoid thought: Trudy was somehow associated with the second burglar, a Trojan horse as it were. He put her up to calling, and now he'd put her up to coming over here.

"It's pretty late. Why don't you call me at the office tomorrow?"

She started crying, then, and even though the door muffled the sound, her sobs sounded real.

"Oh, shit," I said, resenting anybody who'd put me in this position.

I'd open the door and find out that Trudy was one of those people who could cry on cue. And right next to her would be the second burglar. He'd have a gun in his hand and he'd blow me away.

Tax attorneys aren't supposed to lead lives like this.

I walked over and flipped off the alarm and then opened the door.

She was alone.

She had a black eye and there was what appeared to be blood all over her cheek.

"What the hell happened to you?" I said.

"Ron," she said. "He beat me up when I told him I was going to look for another job."

She daubed her eyes with a handkerchief.

"C'mon in."

"I'm sorry for bothering you. I don't know where else to go."

"Maybe you should've gone to the cops."

"That would just destroy him," she said. "All the publicity, I mean. I don't want to do that to him."

"He beats you up and you don't want to do that to him?"

But she was looking around the living room. "Wow. This place is so nice. All these Victorian things." She smiled. "Reminds me of my favorite movie. Mary Poppins."

She had one of those dear little faces and dear little bodies that make men feel protective. I don't suppose you could quite call her pretty but there was something so sweet and so earnest about her that you couldn't help but feel close to her somehow. She was sexy, too, in a waif-like way, the eyes a mercurial mixture of knowingness and innocence.

"Why don't you sit down? I'll get you a drink and then we'll have a look at your face."

"I'm really sorry."

"I know you are, Trudy."

"You were kind've mad when I knocked on your door, weren't you?"

I smiled. "Yeah, a little bit, I guess."

"I said a prayer while I was coming up your walk. That you wouldn't get real mad at me."

"Well, I guess it worked, didn't it?"

She smiled with her black eye and bloody lips. "Yeah, I guess it did."

I got her a scotch. Then I stopped in the downstairs bathroom and got a washcloth and some iodine and some bandages.

"I don't really drink very often," she said when I walked back into the living room.

She couldn't have weighed 90 pounds. She wore a yellow summer dress that came from one of the discount stores, and a collection of yellow costume jewelery that was endearingly tacky.

But it was her face that I fixed on, that suggestion of naiveté and grief that just broke your heart.

I spent five minutes washing her face and looking at her injuries. The blood came from her split lower lip. The black eye was in fact a purple eye. Her eyes were clear. She didn't appear to have suffered any kind of concussion.

"Gee," she said when I finished, "this is just like going to the emergency room." She had the laugh of a little girl. "Except they don't give you scotch."

She was on the couch. I sat across from her in an Edwardian chair.

"Turn him in," I said.

"I know I probably should."

"Guys shouldn't get away with hurting women like that."

"He said I betrayed him. That's the word he used. 'You betrayed me,' he said. He even started to cry. That's why I came here. I'd never seen him cry before. He said if I went to the police he'd be put out of business. He said the publicity would kill him."

"That isn't your problem, Trudy."

"Maybe this is my fault."

"How is it your fault?"

She shrugged her shoulders. "Oh, when my dad used to beat up my mom sometimes, she'd tell us kids that it was her fault that he got that way. You know, that she wasn't as good a wife as she should've been. You know, like only having meat loaf when he really wanted a steak or something. We lived on a farm and didn't have very much money." Then, "Maybe I made him be like this."

"You didn't make him be like this, Trudy. You've got to understand that."

"There were things—" She hesitated, looked down at her drink, "Well, it's kind of embarrassing to talk about." Then, "There were things he wanted me to do, you know, in bed and everything, and I wouldn't do them. They kind've scared me. I know they didn't scare other girls but they scared me and I couldn't help it."

She had sweet little feet and she kept them very properly together as she sat there, perfectly erect, and woefully heartbroken.

"How'd you find out where I lived?" I said.

"Phone book." She smiled sadly. "I really trust your judgement on things. That's why I stopped over. I thought it might be easier if we talked in person." Her eyes glistened with tears. She seemed to be a simple but troubled woman. Her loneliness was like a cage she moped in.

I smiled. "You'd make a good detective."

"No, I wouldn't. I'd let everybody go. My dad always told me that I was a sucker for a hard luck story. I suppose I am."

"You don't have to be."

"Maybe it's my nature."

"Dump him, Trudy. He's going to keep right on hitting you. And some night, he may hurt you a lot worse than he hurt you tonight. That's the pattern."

"But he was crying. I must've hurt him pretty bad for him to be crying."

"He was crying for himself, because he was scared. He wasn't crying because of you."

"Really?"

"Really."

She looked around again, those big sad eyes of hers dazzled by what she saw. "This is such a beautiful house," she said.

"Thank you."

"Your wife must be very proud of it."

"She is."

"That's a big reason I was afraid to come over here. Your wife, I mean. I didn't want her to think—"

"She doesn't think anything about it, Trudy. She isn't in town at the moment. She's with the girls visiting her parents."

"That's nice." Then, "I feel a lot better. I was really crazy after Ron hit me and everything. I ran out of the office and got in my car and I drove to this phone booth and I looked up your address and I drove right over here."

"I'm glad you did."

She smiled. "You're a nice man."

"And you're a nice woman."

"Not very smart, though. I barely got through high school. My sister Eve—she's two years older—she's the smart one in the family. She's a pharmacist's assistant at this pharmacy."

God, she was a sweet kid.

I stood up. "You go home and get some sleep. Lock your door and don't answer your phone. All right?"

"He'll probably try to call, won't he?" she said.

"Yeah, he probably will."

I walked her to the door. I took her by the shoulders and said, "Dump him, Trudy, all right?"

"I wish you were him."

I leaned over and gave her a fatherly kiss on the forehead. "The door bolted and the phone off the hook. All right?"

"All right," she said. "Thank you very much, Mr. Tyler."

"Aaron."

She giggled. "Aaron, I mean."

I watched her walk out to her car at the curb. It was an old junker of some kind.

When I heard the motor fire, I closed the door and went through the house, checking locks and bolts and lights.

Twenty minutes later, I was asleep.

THE KNOCKING was a part of my dream. Or I thought it was anyway.

But it persisted, louder and louder, a frantic edge to it now, and suddenly I was awake and rolling out of bed, responding instinctively to some kind of emergency.

Front door. Pounding. Voices. Male. I thumbed off the alarm and opened the door.

Todd Meyers and Jim Berryman stood in the door. They both lived on the block and I had a vague recollection that they'd drawn late shift tonight on Patrol.

"God, Aaron, sorry to bother you," Todd said. "But we wanted to ask you if you knew the woman in that car?"

I looked past them to the street.

Trudy's junker was still parked at the curb.

I'd heard her start the motor. I hadn't actually seen her drive away. I'd been asleep for an hour.

"Yes," I said, "she's a client of mine. Why?"

And that was when I heard the siren erupt just a few blocks away.

"What the hell's going on?" I said.

"Well, you know how Patrol people are always supposed to check out strange cars in the neighborhood," Jim Berryman said.

"Well, we checked hers out," Todd said.

"Somebody cut her throat, Aaron," Jim said. "Man, I've never seen anybody murdered before. She's a fucking mess. I almost blew lunch."

"Cut her throat," Todd said, shaking his head miserably. "I'm like Jim. I've never seen anything like this. Ear to fucking ear, man. Ear to fucking ear."

7

MOST OF them I'd never seen before, the people in the crowd. Oh, there were my neighbors, of course, people in robes and hastily snugged on walking shorts and jeans, their hair slightly mussed, their faces blurred with sleep, their mouths wide with yawns.

But most of them didn't belong to this area, the truck drivers and cab drivers and teenagers and old people who encircled the ambulance and the other official vehicles.

Some of them looked almost as scary as the corpse, these onlookers, with the red emergency lights washing their sweaty faces fiercely. The temperature was still in the low eighties. There was no breeze, and the air felt humid and dirty.

They seemed to take great pleasure from the scene, these people, their faces moving with bird-like quickness every time an official walked up to where Trudy's car was parked at the curb. Their eyes shone with lurid interest in every detail of the investigation, a dozen or so officials measuring, dusting and photographing the scene.

The body was still in the car.

That bothered me. I wanted to lift her gently and rest her on the grass in the backyard, protected from all sound but distant dogs, and all light except from the moon.

She was a sweet young woman and did not deserve to be put on display for the gawkers. A hundred years ago these prairie people would have shown up at dawn for the hanging that took place at noon, wanting to make sure they were close enough to hear the prisoner's neck snap.

Neil and Curtis came along soon after the police.

Neil wore his Yale T-shirt and running shorts. Curtis wore a yellow shortsleeved button down shirt and chinos.

"You know her?" Curtis said.

I explained quickly how it was that Trudy had ended up at my house that night.

"If I didn't know you better," Neil said, "I'd say you were getting yourself a little strange nookie."

I nodded. "I'm sure that's what the cops think, too."

"So you really think it was her boss who killed her?" Curtis said.

"Who else would've killed her?" Neil said.

"Are you kidding?" Curtis said. "Think about it."

But there wasn't time to think about it. A uniformed police woman came up and said, "Detective Patterson would like to talk to you."

"Sure," I said. To Neil, I said, "You guys want to go inside and have a beer. I'll see you in a while."

Curtis grinned. "You wouldn't happen to have any Domino's pizza in there, too, would you?"

DETECTIVE PATTERSON turned out to be Detective Michelle Patterson. I have to admit, my first reaction to her was disappointment. She couldn't have been older than thirty, or topped five-seven, or weighed more than one-fifteen. She had a cute, almost kittenish face, replete with freckles, and a sardonic and oddly erotic little mouth. Her copper-colored hair was cut short. Despite the heat, her white cotton blouse and tan skirt looked fresh and pressed. Even her light makeup, especially her vivid but subtle lipstick, looked fresh.

Maybe I was expecting a fat guy with a cigar.

She offered me a sweet tiny hand.

I wanted to go easy on her, not be one of those macho jerks who try to establish their natural superiority with a bone-crushing handshake.

But she startled me.

She had a grip so strong, it felt as if she was trying to grind the bones of my hand into a fine powder.

Behind her, on the sidewalk, I saw two plain clothes cops pointing down at something, and then getting down on their haunches for a closer look.

"This probably isn't much fun for you, Mr. Tyler," she said. "Going over your statement again. I'm sorry."

"You've got the hard job," I said. "You've got to figure out who did this."

"Officer Reisler tells me that you think you know who the killer is already."

"Well, I'd say her boss is a pretty good suspect."

"Yes," she said, "he'd sure seem to be, wouldn't he?"

I felt her eyes on me, her green, green eyes. She was a kid-sister kind of woman until you studied her eyes a moment. Then you knew that she could probably scare the hell out of any male detective you cared to name. We went over and leaned against the front fender of a patrol car. My clothes were soaked from the heat. I felt scratchy and dirty.

I went through the whole story, from Trudy's call this morning, to saying good-bye to her tonight.

Detective Patterson made no notes. She just listened. She showed no expression at all.

"That's about all I know," I said, finishing up.

"That's great. That's very helpful."

"But her boss—"

"I've already called him. He'll be down at the station when I get there in half an hour or so. Now, I'm going to ask you something, Mr. Tyler, and it's probably going to make you mad."

"I'm way ahead of you. And the answer is no."

"No?"

"No, as in no, I didn't sleep with her. Her coming over here was perfectly innocent."

I felt very proud of myself, being clairvoyant and all. Neil had been right. It probably was logical of her to suspect that there was something going on between Trudy and me.

"That isn't what I was going to ask you, Mr. Tyler."

"Oh."

"What I was wondering was if you had a lawyer."

"I am a lawyer."

"I mean a criminal lawyer."

"You're saying I'm a suspect?"

"No. What I'm saying is that I may ask you questions that you may not want to answer." The gaze never wavered. "I might also ask you to help us with some tests."

"Tests?"

"DNA, things like that."

"I can't believe this."

"I said I was afraid I'd make you mad. And I guess I have. I'm sorry, Mr. Tyler, but I'm only doing my job."

"You really think I killed her?"

"Actually, no. But I need to cover myself. Look at it from my point of view, Mr. Tyler. A woman comes out to visit you. Uninvited. She stays in your house for maybe—what? Half an hour, say?"

"More like twenty minutes."

"All right, twenty minutes. Then you walk her to the door, she goes out to her car, and before she can drive away, someone kills her. You're the last person I know for sure who saw her alive. So I've got to put you on my list. I'm trying to do a thorough job, Mr. Tyler. That's all."

Then she smiled and she looked cuter than hell. She also looked fourteen years old. "When you look like I do, Mr. Tyler, you have to do everything by the book. Nobody'll take you seriously otherwise." The kid sister face looked very serious. "Nice neighborhood like this, nice upper-middle class surroundings like this—I won't try and bullshit you, Mr. Tyler. I want to do everything right."

She didn't mention how good a case like this could be for a police career.

"All I understand is that I didn't kill her."

"I believe you."

"No, you don't."

She smiled her kid smile again.

"Let's say I believe you more than I *don't* believe you."

I looked around for Neil and Curtis. They were gone. They probably figured they couldn't help me much.

"I'm going inside."

"Fine by me, Mr. Tyler. All I need from you right now is a phone number where I can reach you during the day tomorrow."

I gave her the name of the law firm and the number.

"I can't believe this," I said. "The poor young woman is dead and you're wasting time on me instead of trying to find who really did it."

"You need to calm down, Mr. Tyler. You're making this thing into more than it is."

For some reason, I suddenly understood what she was saying.

It probably made sense to consider me a suspect. At least until she got a confession from Trudy's boss.

"I guess you're right."

She smiled at me. Cutely.

"Why don't you go back into that wonderful air conditioning of yours and have yourself a nice cold beer and then go to bed? This kind of thing is always stressful for everybody involved, and I really am sorry I have to be so by the book. But I do."

She caught me, then. I'd been sneaking the occasional glimpse of her merry little breasts as they rose and fell beneath her cotton blouse.

Our eyes met.

She put out her hand and ground my bones exceedingly fine once again.

"Things'll be better when your wife comes back," Detective Patterson said. "People always feel more vulnerable when they're alone like this."

I wasn't exactly sure what she was saying. But then this reflected my whole sense of her. You looked at her and wondered how anybody that delicate and appealing could possibly be dark and dangerous. And yet she was, she really was.

"'night," I said.

"'night, Mr. Tyler."

NEIL AND Curtis were in the breakfast nook. Neil was sipping a bottle of Bud, Curtis was sipping a bottle of Bud and eating what looked like a ham sandwich.

"I helped myself," he said.

"No problem," I said.

He had a ham on rye with lots of mustard leaking out over the side of the bread.

I sat down, and said, "Guess what?"

"Man, you look pissed," Neil said.

"I am pissed. Detective Patterson?"

"She's a cutie," Curtis said.

"Maybe to you. She thinks I may've had something to do with Trudy's death."

"You're kidding," Neil said.

"Not kidding."

"But it was her honey, that asshole boss of hers," Neil said. "He killed her."

"He would seem to be the logical suspect. At least to me."

Neil shook his head. "She's just being a cop, Aaron. You'll see. She talks to this dipshit who beat up Trudy, she'll see right away you didn't have anything to do with it."

I looked at Curtis. "You have mustard on your chin."

"You got any napkins?"

I got up and walked over to the sink and tore off a paper towel.

The house still felt strange to me, as if I was an interloper.

A man had died here last night. And even though I'd hated him, his death had forever altered this house for me. Then I remembered Trudy, two deaths here, in two nights.

"You're not drinking anything?" Neil said.

"You know what I really want?" I said.

"A martini?"

"A cigarette."

"Oh, man," Curtis said. "You're crazy. Think of how hard it was for you to quit."

"I know."

"And it's been how long?" he said.

"Here. Wipe your chin."

"Thanks, Dad," he said, taking the paper towel and wiping away the mustard.

"I had a cousin who quit," Neil said. "My cousin the rabbi, in fact. He quit for six years and his wife died and he went out and bought a pack and within a week he was back to buying cartons, again."

"Don't have a cigarette," Curtis said.

"Then maybe I'll have a beer."

"A beer," Neil said, "no cigarette."

So I had a beer, no cigarette. And when I was seated in the nook again, I said, "The second burglar killed Trudy."

"Oh, bullshit," Neil said. "Do you know how fucking paranoid that is?"

"He was watching the house," I said, "and he thought she was somebody I knew well, so he killed her."

"Why would he kill her?"

"He thought she meant something to me."

"That's exactly what I was thinking," Curtis said, chewing on the rest of his sandwich.

"Don't talk with your mouth full," Neil said. Then, "You guys are really crazy, you know that?

"We'll see," I said.

Neil looked at his watch. "I've got to get back and get some sleep."

"Me, too," Curtis said.

"So it's a coincidence?"

"Absolutely," Neil said. "Man, Aaron, you're supposed to be the level-headed one in our group. But now you're this wild-eyed paranoid. They'll go over and talk to her honey and then nail his ass to the wall. You wait and see."

Sitting there, I felt alone suddenly, and vulnerable in a way I used to feel when I was a boy. The world was such an overwhelming place, and it meant you harm. So many pitfalls to be wary of, so much random violence that could touch you virtually any time, anywhere. Faces were masks, words often lies.

"Thanks for the sandwich," Curtis said.

"Let's go out the back door," Neil said. "Avoid the circus out front."

After they were gone, I stood by the back door and looked out at the garage roof where the second burglar had crouched last night. I would replay last night over and over in my mind as long as I lived, the way the country watched the Zapruder films of JFK's murder so obsessively. Trying to learn something from it, I suppose; as if it held some wisdom for us if only we could understand it, like the mysterious words on the Sphinx.

Other images came back. The sickly feeling of my bowels when we had the corpse in the van and the cop was questioning us. The roaring dam. The tarpaulin caught on the steel rod. The filthy river water.

I felt eyes on me.

Neil was probably right. Last night's experience had probably turned me into an unlikely paranoid.

Good old sensible Aaron. Loyal, honest, dutiful.

But I still felt eyes on me as I stood in the back door looking out at the moonshadow, backyard and alley.

Maybe he was in the shadows, the burglar—watching it all, the cops and the ambulance and me.

Only now was the heat of the day starting to fade. A quick cool breeze came and turned up the silver underside of the leaves and dried the sweat on my face. Maybe I'd have a few hours of peaceful sleep tonight. I listened to the song of the soughing wind for a few long moments, a sweet reassuring music. I loved the sound of wind in summer trees. I went back inside.

In the living room, I stood in the darkness, parting the curtain for a peek at the street.

Most of the onlookers had drifted away. The excitement was long gone. A number of emergency vehicles had left, as well.

The white-jacketed attendants were only now putting Trudy into the ambulance. The body was in a bag and the bag on a stretcher.

Detective Patterson was walking around the car, giving it what appeared to be her final look for the evening.

There was a man with her. He was dressed in a short-sleeved white shirt, a yellow tie and dark slacks. He was bald and wore thick glasses that kept slipping down his long nose. He kept pushing the glasses back up his nose with his thumb.

Detective Patterson appeared to be asking him questions. She'd point to something and he would nod and say something to her.

This happened several times.

Finally, she walked around the car to the grass. She took out a penlight and angled it across the grass, all the way up to the sidewalk.

I thought of earlier, of seeing the two plain clothes cops pointing out something on the sidewalk. She was presumably looking at what they'd seen.

Detective Patterson and the man then followed the light. Moments later, they stood on the sidewalk looking at something.

Detective Patterson and the man got down on their haunches and examined the sidewalk closely and carefully.

She said something to him, and he nodded, apparently in agreement.

My bowels had that sickly feeling again.

The man took out a penlight of his own, got down on his knees, and almost touched his nose to the sidewalk itself.

What was he looking at? Or looking for?

The cold, slithering, sickly feeling in me came again.

I shuddered.

Detective Patterson raised her head abruptly and looked up at my house.

I had the impression that she'd suddenly sensed me at the window, peering out the slit between the heavy curtains.

I stepped back, letting the curtains fall together again.

Wouldn't looking out at her that way only make me look guilty?

I stood in the darkness, feeling trapped in my own house, my own fears.

So much had changed in the past twenty-four hours...

I sat in the dark breakfast nook with a drink of scotch for company, looking out at the moonlit world of the backyard. Nothing moved except the leaves and branches as the wind buffeted them.

Snapshots of the girls and Jan on sunny days; the sandbox I'd built for them; their first red swing set; Andy, the Lab we'd bought, who died beneath the wheels of a truck in the street out front; cook-outs with the new gas grill, and half the kids in the neighborhood filling our backyard in hopes of cadging some lemonade and cookies.

...and lying awake in bed a little later, snapshots of Jan came to me: her horrified face the snowy day she broke her ankle while we were skiing; her beatific beauty when I saw her holding our first child for the first time; her tender gaze after we finished making love, and lay silently in each other's arms; and the merry look of her blue eyes whenever she found something truly funny. I was more in love with her now than I'd ever been.

...I was just afraid that last night had destroyed our lives in ways I could not yet foresee...

I HAVE no idea what time the phone rang.

I was in the deepest and most troubled of sleeps.

I came up through the murky layers of consciousness just as I'd come up through the filthy water of the dam last night—

—and found the phone.

And put the receiver to my ear.

And muttered hello.

—scared to death that something had happened to Jan or one of the girls.

But there was only that faint steady breathing I'd heard last night, so late.

That faint steady breathing that had not become a reality in my life until a man had been killed in my basement, and the body carted off for secret burial.

Faint steady breathing.

"You sonofabitch," I said.

And then the click as he hung up.

I didn't sleep for a long, long time, and then it was a tangled and sweaty sleep, a fevered sleep.

8

EVERY EMPLOYER with fewer than a hundred workers has the thought of screwing the Feds by calling those workers independent contractors.

Most employers are smart enough to let this slide right on out their ear and evaporate in the ether.

Then there are the smart guys.

Smart guys can be male or female, black or white, Protestant, Jew, Catholic, straight or gay.

The thing they have in common, smart guys, is that they all think they've come up with an original way to swindle the IRS out of some substantial money.

You tell the Feds you hire mostly independent contractors, you have it made for a while. No withholding, and that's just for starters. No benefits, for another. No overtime. And on and on. You're pocketing lots of money.

It's a beautiful goddamned world.

At least for a while.

And then the Feds catch on. And then you're done.

The man sitting across from my desk the next morning—our meeting started promptly at eight o'clock so I didn't get much more than three hours of sleep—he was a smart guy.

His name was Brian Kemp. He owned a printing plant in a small town thirty miles east of the city. What he did, Brian Kemp, was a lot of sub-contract printing and stuffing and mailing for the largest printers in the state. They could mark up what he did for them thirty-five percent and make a nice profit. In some instances, they could mark it up fifty percent. And make an even nicer profit.

Brian made even more than that because of the sixty-two workers he listed, he called fifty-one of them independent contractors. Never mind that virtually all of them put in fifty, sixty hours a week—week in and week out—busting their asses at Kemp Printing. Never mind that most of them had been with him for more than five years. Never mind that they had to keep strict time-clock hours. Brian listed them all as independents. He'd been doing this for four years.

Three weeks ago, he got a registered letter from the IRS folks in Kansas City and shortly thereafter, he called our law offices.

This was my fourth meeting in two weeks with Brian, and every one of them went just the way it was going this morning.

"You're fucking telling me that I owe the government $211,000 in fucking back taxes?"

"That's what they tell me, Brian, and I don't think they're going to change their minds."

"So what the fuck am I paying you for, huh?"

"Brian, I deal with the laws. I don't make them. You can't prove that these people are independent contractors, because they're not."

"I can get ten of them to sit in a fucking witness stand and swear on a fucking stack of Bibles that they're fucking independent contractors."

Brian was a big user of the F word. I'm sort of partial to that word myself, but not as partial as Brian.

Brian, by the way, is this big blond hairy guy. He's got a busted nose and several busted knuckles and his three-piece suits always look too small for him and his two pinkie rings always look too big for him. He drives a new Lincoln Towncar, and scoots into Des Moines once a month for the Tough Man contests. We had beers one evening and he told me how disappointed he was that the guy who'd looked dead in the ring had ultimately survived.

"You'd really ask them to perjure themselves? They could go to prison, Brian."

"Yeah, well that's a lot fucking better than paying the fucking Federales $211,000, let me tell you."

That's another word Brian favors, a Sam Peckinpah word if you've happened to see *The Wild Bunch* as many times as I have. Federales.

"It can be worked out, Brian. Payment schedules, I mean."

"The fucking militia guys have it right. This government is so goddamned corrupt it makes me sick. Fucking Federale bastards anyway."

"We need to set up an appointment in the next week, Brian. We need to sit down and talk to these people."

He didn't miss a beat. "Anybody we can pay off?"

"I don't think so. And we can both go to the slam for even trying."

"I know a congressman. Harry Lyme, third district? Got drunk with him at Ducks Unlimited a few times. The guy's all right. He says in Washington, all you got is colored guys and fags and Jews on your fucking case all the time. He told this lesbo joke at this dinner some lobbyists had for him, and some fag busboy overheard it and told the fucking reporters about it."

"He sounds like my kind of guy, all right, Brian, but I'm not sure even somebody of his stature could help us much."

"What if I just refuse to pay?"

"Then they confiscate just about everything you own, fine you up to a quarter of a million dollars, and throw your ass in jail for five years."

"Cocksuckers."

"That word has been applied to them many, many times."

"Two hundred and eleven thousand fucking dollars."

"I'm sorry, Brian."

"If we have to pay the whole fine, do you give me some kind of discount on your fee?"

"I'm afraid the government disallowed our non-profit status several years back, Brian." He didn't get it. "Brian, of course we charge the same, win or lose. We have families to feed."

"I'm going to fucking call fucking Harry Lyme. I use your phone?"

"Be my fucking guest," I said.

HE CAME in with his cup of coffee, which meant he planned to stay a while. And he came in with that formal look of sympathy on his long New England face, which meant he'd heard about Trudy being killed at my place. His name was Wyman, Todd Wyman, and while he wasn't one of the founding partners. He essentially ran the law office on a daily basis. He was sort of like the world's most successful hall monitor. He wore, as usual, black suspenders, white shirt, red paisley tie, black suit pants, black socks and impeccably shined black loafers with prissy little tassels. He looked as if he'd understudied a world class funeral director, one who occasionally took a fashion risk with a paisley tie.

"You doing all right?"

"Doing fine," I said, not wanting to give him the satisfaction of knowing how chaotic I felt inside.

"You see the paper this morning?"

"Yeah," I said.

"Naturally, they had to list where you worked."

"Naturally."

"Not exactly the kind of publicity a firm like ours wants to have."

I started to say something but he held up a long narrow hand. "I'm not blaming you."

"Gee, thanks."

He sat himself down in one of my chairs, crossed his legs, blew a little on his coffee, and then looked at me with his damp brown eyes. "She was a client of ours, right?"

"Right...."

"And she came to your house last night?"

I nodded.

"And Jan's visiting her folks?"

"I didn't sleep with her."

"We don't want to get the kind of reputation divorce lawyers have, Aaron. You know, always hitting on their female clients when they're at their most vulnerable."

"Did you hear me? I didn't sleep with her."

"I really don't believe you did anything, Aaron, but face it, in a matter like this, perception is everything."

"She didn't even give me a hand job."

"That isn't funny, Aaron."

I sighed. "I don't suppose it is. But I don't know what the hell to tell you. I'm unhappy that I've embarrassed the firm but I didn't have anything to do with it."

"Didn't invite her to your house?"

"No."

"And didn't let anything happen when you were alone inside the house?"

"No."

"And don't know anything at all about her death?"

"Well, I know one thing about her death."

He looked ready to be very upset. "You do?"

I told him about her boss.

"You really think he did it?"

"He beat her up."

"That doesn't mean he killed her."

"No, but it means he's got to be one of the prime suspects."

"I assume the police have talked to him by now."

"I assume so," I said.

He said, "I'm not your enemy, Aaron."

"All right."

"I'm simply doing my job, which is to worry about the general welfare of this law firm."

I sighed again.

He was extending a hand.

Could I do any less? "I'm sorry, Todd. I haven't had much sleep and Trudy's death and everything—"

"You're going to weather this just fine. And I'm going to help you. And the first thing I'm going to do to help you is let you take the rest of the day off and go home and catch up on some sleep."

"I've got two appointments this afternoon."

"Already taken care of. I'll take one and Pete will take the other."

"That's damned nice of you," I said. And it was.

He stood up.

"I'm really not your enemy, Aaron. And someday you may actually come to believe that. Oh, when does Jan come back, by the way?"

"Tomorrow afternoon."

He made a kind of impish face. He didn't have a face for impish faces.

"That's what the old boy needs, wife and family by his side. That's all you need to get your life back to normal and put all this behind you." He smiled. "Enjoy your sleep. I envy you. I'm a little beat today myself."

As if to characterize this, he broke into a wide and very convincing yawn.

BY NOON, I was back in bed, reading a John Grisham paperback. I got through ten pages and fell into a deep and relentless sleep.

The sun had moved to the other side of the house by the time I woke up at four-thirty.

I took a shower, got into a T-shirt and Levis cut-offs, and went out to the kitchen to make myself some bacon and eggs.

I was just finishing up, wiping the last of the egg yoke off my plate with my toast, when I heard a knock, looked up and saw Neil at the back door.

"Hi," I said opening the door.

He didn't bother with pleasantries. "I think some sonofabitch is following me."

Neil is usually a neat dresser, favored single-breasted suits and pastel shirts with collar buttons. Today his shirt had pulled out of his pants, his dark hair was mussed and sweaty, and he smelled sweaty.

"Have a beer."

"I'd really appreciate it, Aaron."

We sat in the nook and drank a Bud Lite.

"Tell me about it."

"An old junker. Blue. Probably Pontiac. I remember fifteen years ago, General Motors was experimenting with all these different models for Pontiac and Buick. None of them ever caught on. This was one of them. Oh, I almost forgot. The car has a crumpled right fender. Some kind of accident. I tried seeing in the windows but he's got that dark stuff on them. Couldn't see a damned thing."

"When did you notice him?"

"On the way to work this morning. I just got real paranoid. Maybe you and Curtis are starting to rub off on me. But anyway, I started checking my rear view and here was this old junker of a blue car. When I think about it, I think he was following me all the way from my house."

"So he was parked near your house?"

"He'd have to be. How else would he know when I left for work?"

"He followed you all the way to work?"

"All the way," Neil said, waving his empty can at me. "Mind if I have another one?"

"Fine."

"You get his license number?" I asked as he walked to the refrigerator.

"He didn't have a front plate."

He got his beer and came back and sat in the nook.

Looking out the window, so I couldn't see his face, he said, "This shit's getting to me a lot more than I thought it would."

I heard tears in his voice. I said nothing. Just sat there. He'd talk when he wanted to.

When he looked back at me, he said, "Two years today."

Now his voice, as well as his eyes, were filled with tears.

"Oh, God, Neil, I'm sorry. I forgot."

"It's all right."

He turned away again so I wouldn't watch him cry.

"Rachel needs me at home—I mean, think of how fucking tough this day is for her—and what'm I doing? Spending time over here all caught up in my own problems."

We stayed silent a long time.

"I went out to the cemetery today," he said. "Put some flowers on her grave. I started bawling like a fucking baby."

"I'd do the same thing."

"Yeah, I suppose you would."

"She was a wonderful woman, Neil. And you're right to miss her."

He snuffled up tears. I thought of Trudy's tears last night. Happiness is so tenuous. It can be snatched away forever in a matter of moments.

"I should've made her go to the doctor sooner," he said.

"You didn't know, Neil. She didn't know herself until it was too late. You did what you could, Neil. And she did what she could. She didn't know anything was wrong."

Neil was now the single parent of a beautiful thirteen-year-old girl who still hadn't adjusted to her mother's death.

"I've got to find somebody," he said.

"You will."

"No, I mean somebody good and somebody fast."

Neil was proof positive that the singles scene was a real bitch for the fortyish male. He'd tried meeting women at dances, parties, bars, even his synagogue. Half the people on the block had taken turns lining him up. He did, in fact, meet a number of very eligible women. The problem was that they were eligible women who didn't happen to appeal to him. He judged everybody against Becky and found them wanting.

"I don't even care if she's Jewish anymore," he said. "I mean, if my parents don't like it, tough. I've got to find somebody for Rachel. That's the other thing."

"What is?"

"Rachel. I'm such a fuck-up as a parent. I mean, all this female stuff she's going through—you know, getting her period and wearing a bra and all that stuff—I probably say the wrong thing to her ninety percent of the time. She'll probably end up hating me."

Toward the end there, he'd been staring down into his beer. And then he abruptly looked up and said, "Oh, shit, I'm doing it, aren't I?"

"Uh-huh."

"Wallowing?"

"Wallowing."

"Maybe I need to wallow today."

"Maybe you do."

He checked his watch. "I'd better get home. Rachel's taking this cooking course. She's making this real special spaghetti tonight. I even bought her an apron for the occasion. With her initials on it." Then he grinned sadly. "I hate to say it but everything she cooks gives me gas."

He drained his beer and then walked over to the back door.

"I'll keep you posted about that blue car."

"I'll talk to Curtis and Bill, see if they noticed anything like that."

"That sonofabitch is out there somewhere, isn't he?"

"Yeah," I said. "He is." Then, "Neil?"

"Yeah?"

"You're a good man. You really are. And Rachel's going to be just fine."

"Thanks for saying that."

"It's true, Neil. It really is."

HALF AN hour later, I opened a fresh beer and carried it into the living room, turned on the TV.

The network news was just ending. I wanted to see what the local folks had to say about Trudy's murder.

Lead story. Team reports.

I saw my neighborhood, my house. In one brief shot, I even saw myself talking to Detective Patterson. The reporter said that Trudy had been visiting me in my house and that she had been found dead not long after. Then the reporter slyly added, "Tyler's wife and children were out of town at the time."

None of this was unexpected. The news people gave it maximum urgency and moment. Jack The Ripper hadn't received such dramatic coverage.

Toward the end of the report, Detective Patterson was interviewed on camera. She looked very pretty and very cold. She said almost nothing.

Then the reporter said, "Do you know anything about Aaron Tyler taking a leave of absence from his law firm?"

Detective Patterson remained her usual stony-faced self. "No, I don't."

The male reporter said, "I spoke with a Mr. Wyman at Aaron Tyler's office and he said that Tyler had called in this morning and taken an indefinite leave of absence. Do you draw any conclusions from that?"

"No, I don't," Detective Patterson said.

But I certainly drew a conclusion from that, as did everybody else watching the news. Good old Todd Wyman, who wanted me to know that he wasn't my enemy.

Good old Todd, just thinking of the firm.

Good old Todd.

I MANAGED to go an entire hour without picking up the phone. I had two more beers, tried some deep breathing exercises, and tried to convince myself that calling would only make things worse but—

"Is Todd there, please?"

"Yes, may I say who's calling, please?"

"It's Aaron Tyler, Matty."

A pause. "Oh, Aaron, sorry, I didn't recognize your voice. Just hang on. I'll get him."

Matty was actually a nice woman. She'd been very hospitable to Jan when I'd joined the firm, and she never forgot to send the girls Christmas cards with crisp five dollar bills in them. That she did this for all the lawyers didn't lessen the thoughtfulness of it at all. The only thing I couldn't figure out about Matty Wyman was why a decent, open, rather gregarious woman like her had married such a prim, stern, and duplicitous fellow like Todd.

Todd said, "Good evening, Tyler," as if nothing in the world was wrong, as if he was ever so happy to hear from his most favored of underlings.

"You sold me out, you bastard."

My anger didn't intimidate him in the least. "Actually, I was expecting this call. I'm just surprised you were able to restrain yourself this long."

"It wasn't easy."

"I just want to caution you, Aaron. I wouldn't say anything that might come back to haunt you in the future. I wouldn't burn any bridges, in other words."

"You sold me out."

"I did what was necessary. I tried to explain that to you this morning. My job is to protect the firm. If I fail to do that, then I'm out of a job myself."

"I didn't sleep with her."

"I believe you."

"And I certainly didn't kill her."

"I certainly believe that, too, Aaron. But that's not the point. We handle the business affairs of some of the most powerful people in this state. We have a square image, as you well know. We don't drive sports cars, we don't have mistresses, we don't endorse political candidates, and we don't become involved in scandals of any kind. Your involvement in this thing undermines everything the firm is supposed to stand for."

"But I'm innocent."

"Our clients don't know that. And neither does the public at large."

"The way you made it sound was that I took a leave of absence because I'm guilty."

"There, I don't agree with you, Aaron. Think about it carefully. You sounded guilty as soon as the press made three points—that Trudy visited your home, that your wife and children were on vacation, and that she was found dead in her car at your curb."

"And then you said I'd taken a leave of absence."

A pause. "I take orders, Aaron."

"Meaning what?"

"Meaning this wasn't my idea."

"Bullshit."

Another pause. "They had a meeting, Aaron. The senior partners. Soon as the story broke this morning. They discussed the matter for more than an hour. And then they took a vote. That was how they came up with the leave of absence idea. You can believe this or not, Aaron, but I didn't have anything to do with it." Then, "I would've voted against it, Aaron. I know you don't care for me much but I've always admired you. You're a valuable employee and you're good for the firm's morale. People feel they can confide in you."

I believed him. I didn't want to believe him. I wanted to hate him and blame him for all my problems. But I believed him. All his unctuousness and primness was gone. He sounded like a nice guy who genuinely cared about what was happening to me. The sonofabitch. I needed somebody to hate.

"I convinced them to make this leave with full pay," he said.

"Thank you."

"And full bennies."

"Very damned good of you, Todd."

"And I've taken the liberty of making a call for you."

"A call?"

"Bob Feldman."

"The trial lawyer?"

"Uh-huh. He's expecting to hear from you tonight. If you didn't call me, I was going to call you with his private home number."

"That's damned nice of you. I really appreciate it."

Whispers. Then the phone being passed to someone else.

"Aaron?"

"Hi, Matty."

"If you feel like a good meal tonight, I've fixed some pasta and a salad. We'd love for you to come over."

"That's very nice of you but I think I'll just hang around here."

"You could always stop over later for a nightcap."

"Thanks, Matty. I really do appreciate it, though. I really do."

"We're saying prayers that everything'll turn out all right, Aaron. And I'm sure it will."

"Thanks again, Matty."

"Here's Todd."

"Keep me posted, Aaron."

"I will."

"From the sound of things, I'd say the cops should have this wrapped up pretty soon. I called down to headquarters. They've had Trudy's boss in there twice today."

"He's the one who killed her. I'm sure of it."

"So am I," he said.

We said good night, I thanked him, and we hung up.

I sat in the living room with the curtains open looking out at the dusky street.

A group of kids rollerbladed up and down the middle of the street. Watching it scared the hell out of me. I kept having daymares—those little scenarios of dread that play like movies in your daytime mind—of a car slamming into them. But somehow, they seemed to know just when to pull over to the side of the street to let cars by.

For a time, I set my head against the back of the comfortable armchair and closed my eyes. The air conditioning was the only sound in the house. There was a restful regularity to the noise it made. I felt weary beyond my years. Weary, and scared. There were times in my life when I'd wanted an exciting life. The ass-bandit at the country club dance, the world-traveller who regaled rooms with his tales of far-off places, the entrepreneur who made making millions look so easy—at one time or another, I'd had fantasies of being all these guys. But now, suddenly, I saw how foolish and empty these fantasies really were. Little boy fantasies. But I was no longer a little boy; I was an adult. Most of the time I was, anyway, and thus the most precious gifts of all to me were the safety and well-being of my wife and two daughters. And now that had been threatened, because now I was threatened, both as a suspect in a murder case, and as a participant in the accidental death of a man who'd broken into my house.

I said a prayer. I wasn't even sure of the words, or even sure if anybody or anything was listening, but I said a prayer as devoutly as I could. Help me. Show me the right path. Give me wisdom. And courage. And please watch over Jan and the girls. Please.

The screeching brakes interrupted me, tire rubber against hot summer pavement.

Then a scream. A kid's scream.

I set my beer down and ran to the window. Something had happened a little ways down the block. I saw four or five kids standing in the center of the street, looking down at something on the pavement.

My daymare had come true—a rollerblader had been struck by a car.

I ran to the front door, threw it open, raced down the front steps.

By now, the people in nearby houses were also running into the street to see if they could help.

But people were mostly fixed on the poor kid lying in the middle of the street. I walked over to where he had been lying in the street. He wasn't there anymore.

Then I saw that his mother and father, the Parkhursts, already had him on his feet.

"I think he's all right," Ted Parkhurst said, brushing off his ten-year-old son. Phil was a gangly kid in a buff blue T-shirt and blue walking shorts. About the only damage I could see was a badly skinned knee. He was crying and both his parents kept patting him reassuringly.

"He's more scared than anything," Donna Parkhurst said.

When I reached the group, Ted said, "Did you see who hit you?"

Bobby Parkhurst shook his head, looking sort of embarrassed now. He was a gangly twelve-year-old in a red tank-top and Levi cut-offs.

"I just saw this blue car," he said. "It was kind've my fault. I couldn't stop in time and I skated into his fender."

The reference to the 'blue car' registered with me immediately.

"Was it an old car?" I said.

"I, I guess so, Mr. Tyler."

"Did you notice anything else about it? Was the fender smashed in or anything?"

Ted Parkhurst said, "Did you see the car, Aaron?"

Then I realized that I must sound pretty strange and crazy interrogating Bobby the way I was.

"I think I did," I said. "But it was driving away in the opposite direction."

"Did it slow down at all, son?" Ted said.

"Just a little bit," Bobby said. "Then he just drove away."

Will Templeton, a man who lived two houses east of ours, said, "What happened to our nice quiet neighborhood? First, last night finding that dead woman in her car, and now this."

As soon as Will mentioned last night, I could feel their eyes on me. I glanced at all of them standing there in a semi-circle.

"I'm sorry about what happened last night. For Trudy, most of all. She was a nice young woman. But also because it happened on our block. Not a real good thing for any of us or our kids."

I suppose they were all a little cynical about my words. To at least a few of them, I was undoubtedly guilty of killing her. To another few, I'd be innocent until I ran down the street naked and screaming a confession at the top of my lungs. Most of them, though, probably didn't know what to think. The circumstances—Trudy coming over when Jan was out of town—lent themselves to making me look guilty, but while most of them might think I was capable of cheating in the right circumstances, they'd have a hard time picturing me as a murderer.

At least I hoped they would.

"We'll get back to our nice, normal neighborhood very soon," I said, forcing myself to smile. "I promise."

I sounded as lame and empty as a politician begging for sympathy.

"That's all right," Dorothy, Will's wife, said. "Will just had to run his mouth a little." Will looked like a scolded child.

Several of them rallied silently to my defense.

A couple of them patted me on the shoulders and back. A couple more touched me gently on the arm and nodded good nights.

I walked back to the house, went inside, opened a fresh beer, drew the curtains, sat in the living room and snapped on the TV set with the channel surfer.

I tried convincing myself that it was a coincidence. Old blue car. There were a lot of old blue cars in the city. Didn't mean it was the same one that followed Neil. And how could we be sure that Neil was followed? Maybe that was coincidence, too.

Maybe Neil hadn't been followed at all.

Maybe maybe maybe.

9

I MADE the mistake of drinking too many beers before I went to bed. I wasn't drunk but I *was* waterlogged. I got up on four separate occasions during the night to empty my bladder. On the third trip, while swaying back and forth over the toilet bowl, I had a vision. At least that was how it struck me at the time. A moment of nothing less than genius.

The fourth time I stood swaying over the toilet bowl, with dawn a smudgy grey in the bathroom window, and a bunch of jays in the oak trees sounding so happy I wondered if they were on drugs, I was charmed again by the simple genius of my plan.

We were going to nail his ass, we were.

I couldn't get back to sleep. I lay in that half-life between sleep and waking. I got an erection and wondered vaguely about masturbating but I was too fuzzy and tired. What I needed was more sleep.

Finally, I slept. I think I did, anyway. I had dreams, murky and unpleasant dreams, though all the players died on the movie screen. None came back to consciousness with me.

When I got out of bed again, it was still only six-forty three. Too early to call the other three members of our little poker club.

I had to keep moving. Fatigue threatened to topple me every time I stopped moving.

I got out my Reeboks and my red gym trunks. Jan always jokes that they make me look exceptionally well hung. Who am I to discourage such an impression?

God hadn't turned the heat up yet.

The temperature stayed in the low seventies during my two-and-a-half mile jog.

Sunshine and cool breeze. Frenzied husbands hustling briefcases to BMW's, Saturns and Lynxes. Wives in housecoats bringing in the morning paper. People setting up their lawn sprinklers for the blistering day ahead. Yipping little dogs and yawning kittens. And one lone little girl who kept tapping a red balloon into the air with her blonde head. She made me think of my daughters and broke my heart.

Home, I showered, dressed, fixed myself Wheaties, a piece of toast with grape jam, coffee and some orange juice.

By the time I finished with breakfast, it was seven-thirty and time to call everybody.

Each agreed, if somewhat reluctantly, to stop by my place in the next ten minutes or so.

WE SAT in the breakfast nook. Mr. Coffee was certainly earning his keep today.

"I need to get going," Bill said. "I need to be at the hospital at nine o'clock."

"I'm in kind of a hurry, too," Neil said, glancing at his watch.

Everybody looked starched and pressed and fresh. The heat and the stress of the workday had yet to take their toll.

"This won't take long," I said.

I told them about last night, about the blue junker scraping the kid on the rollerblades.

"I told you," Neil said to me, "I told you that sonofabitch was following me around. Last night, he must've been checking you out."

"What the hell's he want, anyway?" Curtis said.

"That doesn't matter right now," I said. "What matters is that we find out who he is. Then we can worry about what he wants."

"How do we find out who he is?" Neil said.

"God, listen to you guys," Bill said. "Neil sees a blue car behind him, so he's convinced he's being followed. And last night some kid gets brushed by a blue car, so now Aaron's convinced it's the same car that may or may not have been following Neil. Did you guys ever hear of coincidence?"

"You think this is coincidence?" I said.

Bill laughed harshly. "Of course it's coincidence. What the hell else would it be?"

"Maybe he's stalking us," Curtis said.

Bill looked at us with great contempt. "You guys are fucking unbelievable, you know that? We did what we did, and it's over. Nobody's stalking us, nobody gives a shit."

"There was a second burglar," I said.

"Yeah, and by now the sonofabitch is in Chicago or someplace like that. He wants this to be over as much as we do. He doesn't want to go to prison, either." Bill shook his head and made a face.

"It's still funny that an old blue car was following me, and last night an old blue car was out in front of Aaron's place," Neil said.

"I think so, too," Curtis said.

"Well," I said, "there's one way to find out if somebody's following Neil."

"What do you mean?" Curtis said.

"We follow Neil," I said, voicing the little scenario I'd been working on since waking up. I was hoping they'd instantly see the genius of my plan and start telling me what a wizard I was.

Curtis said, "Follow him? What the hell're you talking about, Aaron?"

Neil was glancing impatiently at his watch again. "Hey, guys, sorry but I've really got to get rolling here."

"It's very simple," I said. So simple, I thought, that I have to do everything but a chalk talk so people can understand it. "Neil says he's being followed. So this afternoon, we—Curtis and Bill and myself— follow Neil home from work. We hang back a couple of blocks to see if anybody's following him. And if somebody is following him, then we start following the follower. And then he eventually leads us to where he lives. Then we nail the bastard, find out what he wants."

"I still think you guys are overreacting," Bill said.

"Right now, Bill," I said, "just go along with us, all right?"

Bill frowned but didn't say anything.

"He knows a lot about us, the second burglar, and we don't know anything about him. But if we find out where he lives—"

Curtis said, "Maybe it'll work."

"We've got to find out who this bastard is," Bill said. "I don't want any more phone calls. They scare the hell out of Beth."

"Then we agree?" I said. "Tonight after work, the three of us meet in the parking lot of the Grayson building, and then drive over to Neil's office. We park about half a block away. Neil comes out and gets in his car. We give him a half-block head start and then we start following him."

"He probably won't be driving the blue car anymore," Curtis said.

"We'll have to keep an eye out," I said. "We'll just watch for anybody who is behind Neil for more than a few blocks."

"What if he figures out that we're following him?" Bill said.

"Then he figures it out," I said. "No big deal."

"I'm out of here," Neil said, standing up from the edge of the nook seat. "I'll be in the parking lot after work."

The other two guys left with him.

I put the dishes we'd used in the washer and then started checking out the rest of the house. I wanted things to look good for Jan when she walked through the door.

I'VE NEVER been much of a flier. Jan insists that this is because I'm something of a control freak and to be a dutiful airline passenger, you need to surrender control entirely. You are entirely in the hands of captain and crew. I fly only when I have to.

I mention this because I had all my usual flying anxieties that afternoon when I went to pick up my wife and kids. I know that taking off and landing are the two most dangerous points in most air travel.

So, of course, whenever I'm waiting on Jan and the kids at the airport, I have all kinds of daymares about their plane crashing on a runway right in front of me. I see the flames. I hear the screams. I stand by helplessly. I want to take them and hold them, the three most precious people I've ever known, and hide them in some deep basement vault where nothing can ever harm us.

If only there really were such a place.

I had those daymares today when I stood among a large crowd of overweight people in lime green walking shorts and orange tank tops and Bart Simpson T-shirts and outsize sunglasses and white sunburn lotion on peeling noses and streaks of sunbleach in bottle-bleached hair.

They were all waiting for family and friends too, these people around me at the arrival gate, and as I watched them I wondered if they had the same fears I did, wondered if they saw life as precarious a business as I did. They didn't seem to. They were laughing too much, and talking too much, but maybe the laughing and the talking were just disguises. Maybe they had the same daymares but didn't want to admit it to others or even themselves.

Betsy and Annie were both wearing sunglasses shaped like little pink hearts. They looked like miniature movie starlets as they walked out of the arrival gate. They were dressed alike, too—white blouses, blue jeans, red Keds. I stepped out from the crowd and went running toward them.

Moments later, they were in my arms and I whirled them around, Betsy four and Annie eight, beings of blue eyes and cute little noses and flaxen blond hair and eager little smiles, pigtails for Betsy and a short bobbed do for Annie. They smelled of heat and shampoo and candy and sleep.

Then Jan was there, kissing me on tiptoes because she's only five-four, and sliding her familiar arm around my waist, her sweet clean face lovelier than ever in its thirty-ninth year. She looked crisp and efficient and erotic in a suburban sort of way, a way that I found endlessly welcome and endearing. In her pink skirt and white blouse, she was fresh and appealing, as the glances of several men attested.

Fifteen minutes later, we were in the car, rolling the windows down because the sunlight had turned the seats into searing surfaces that were a bit like sitting on a hot stove.

"Can I tell you about my dream, Daddy?" Betsy asked from the back seat, where she was seat-belted in next to her sister.

"Sure," I said.

She leaned forward as far as she could and giggled. "I was in bed."

"In the dream you were in bed?"

"Uh-huh. And Mommy came in and told me that there was a phone call for me. So I got out of bed and picked up the phone and guess who was calling me?"

"Who?"

"Tasha."

"Our cat Tasha?"

"Uh-huh. And she called me on the phone—you know, at Grandma's house where we were—and said she sure hoped we were coming home because she missed us a whole lot."

Jan, Janet Anne McNeil when we'd first met, was watching my face. She loved watching me smile at the things the girls did. She said it was one of the few times my smile didn't look sad.

"Cats can't call people on the phone," Annie said. She was the sensible one of the girls, an A student in all the subjects I barely got through, Math and Science in particular. She was like her mother. Betsy, however, was more like me, given to bits of fancy every once in a while. Like cats calling you on the phone.

"They can in dreams," Betsy said, reasonably enough. "Can't they, Daddy?"

"I guess in dreams cats can pretty much do anything they want."

"See," Betsy said to her sister.

"He's just saying that to humor you," Annie said. Then giggled. "Because he knows you're nuts."

Betsy giggled, too, "I'm not nuts, *you're* nuts!" and kind of gently pushed against Annie.

They spent half their time arguing and the other half giggling and playing. Arguments could magically become play sessions in a matter of seconds; and play sessions could become bitter arguments even faster.

"They've been like this all day," Jan said. I felt her studying me a moment. Because I was reaching the on-ramp to the cross-town expressway, I couldn't look over at her.

"You look tired, honey."

"I am," I said. "Didn't sleep too well last night."

"Diet Pepsi again?"

I'm a caffeine addict. Sometimes I push it. Watching a movie on the tube at night, I'll open a regular Diet Pepsi instead of a de-caf and then I pay the price. Tossing in bed.

Now I looked over at her. I put my hand out and took hers.

Maybe I should give her a little preview, I thought. Right now give her a little hint of the whole story about Trudy and how she was murdered in front of our place. I opened my mouth to speak but nothing came out.

Bad idea, this preview of coming attractions.

Better to tell her the whole thing when we were both able to talk at length. I'd have to edit out too much for the girls.

"Why don't we order a pizza in tonight?" I said.

"Really? All these days of baching it and you're not ready for some home cooking yet?"

"You've been flying all day. You really want to cook?"

"It doesn't have to be anything fancy," she said.

"Well, if you really want to cook."

"I'll make a pizza of our own."

"Great."

She closed her eyes and stretched. "It'll be so good to sleep in our bed again."

"Same old bed in the guest room?"

"Same old bed. And with the girls in with me, it's not real easy to sleep."

I smiled. "Especially with our cat Tasha calling you guys all night long."

She laughed and touched my arm. "I forgot how cute you are."

"IT'S SO great to be back home," Jan said, walking through the side door, the girls trotting on ahead of her.

Our three cats stood at attention in the middle of the kitchen floor, watching us with only a slight hint of indifference.

Took me three trips to get all the luggage in, took Jan nearly an hour to get everything unpacked.

I was sitting in the breakfast nook sipping a root beer and watching several big orange butterflies flit by when Jan came in and said, "Did you work today?"

"No."

"How come?" She seemed very curious.

"I took the day off. Wanted to be here all afternoon."

She came over and kissed me. Then, "You sure you're all right?"

"Fine. Really. Tired, is all."

"We'll turn in early tonight."

I took her hand. Even after two children, she was still my girlfriend. "I've really missed you."

"Me, too."

The phone rang and she went over and picked it up.

I watched her cradle the yellow receiver between jaw line and shoulder as she dug in the pockets of her blue walking shorts, looking for something.

"Oh, hi, Karen. Could you hold on just a minute? Thanks." To me, cupping the receiver in the palm of her hand, "She doesn't sound very good. I'd better talk to her. Would you hang up when I get in the den?"

"Sure."

She held the phone out for me. I kept it until I heard her say into the receiver, "Thanks, honey."

Karen Staley was one of her college friends who'd been diagnosed recently with clinical depression. Going through a divorce didn't exactly improve her condition. Jan was her lifeline. She'd even call Jan's parents' place to talk to her.

I'd planned on telling Jan about Trudy. It would likely be on the news tonight. I'd be mentioned and so would Trudy's boss. I wanted her to hear it from me. Unfortunately, I had to leave soon to meet Curtis and Bill near Neil's office parking lot. At least I didn't have to worry about Karen Staley telling her. Karen was calling from Chicago.

The girls were sitting on their respective canopy beds, which were covered with pink comforters and lined with a variety of dolls, teddy bears, pandas and elephants. The canopy beds came about when the girl down the block got one. It was the first time I'd seen the kids so relentless. We didn't have a chance. They had canopy beds within six shopping days of laying eyes on the one that belonged to their friend.

Annie had two cats on her bed, Betsy one.

"The cats really missed us, Daddy," Betsy said.

"They did, huh?"

"Yeah. You know how I could tell?"

"How?"

"When I came in and picked up Crystal and gave her a kiss, she didn't try'n pull away like she usually does."

"Yeah, that sounds like she missed you all right."

"And Tess let me kiss *her*," Annie said, in a more measured way. Eight year olds are usually a lot more dignified than four year olds. At least that's how Annie sees it.

I sat on the edge of Annie's bed and said, "You know what I wish you'd do?"

"What?" Betsy said.

"I wish you'd sit on this side of me and I wish Annie would sit on this side of me."

"Can the cats sit with us, Daddy?" Betsy said.

"Not for right now. For right now I'd like it to be the three of us. The cats can sit with us a little bit later."

Betsy looked down at Crystal the tuxedo cat and Tess the grey one. Tasha is an elegant tiger stripe. "You sit right here and don't move, okay?"

Crystal and Tess both watched her say it but neither of them said anything in return. They must reserve their comments for the phone.

When the girls were on either side of me, I eased the three of us back on the bed and then we lay there and I closed my eyes.

I had a kind of reverie, I suppose, just holding them in my arms tight against me, their little heads against my chest, blue and pink barrettes holding down the blonde waves, their giggles silver and sweet. They were growing up so quickly—everything moved at the speed of light these days—and I clung to them the way I would the sweetest memory in the world. A photo album of images played before my eyes— Annie's first front tooth; Betsy's chickenpox; Annie on her first bicycle; Betsy holding a tiny kitten in her two tiny hands; the soft simple sound of their breathing on the nights when we let them sleep with us, there being monsters in their closet, monsters who had shooed them right into our room. I wanted all time to freeze at this instant forever. No illness, no quirk of fate, no old age or infirmity for any of us.

But then other images flashed at me—the body in the tarpaulin hung up on the steel rod; the nosy cop sticking his face into the van window; the bloody slash across Trudy's throat.

The reverie was gone.

I opened my eyes. Checked my watch. I had to leave, meet Curtis and Bill.

"I'm sure glad you're home, you two," I said.

We sat up and I gave them some more hugs. But instead of peace I felt only frenzy. My life was so precarious now, threatened in so many different ways.

For the first time in my life, I found myself trying to imagine, in a realistic way, what prison would be like. I tried to tell myself that my anxiety was unrealistic. But was it? My mind wandered momentarily. When I focused again, Betsy was holding Crystal in front of me.

"Crystal said she'd like a kiss," she said.

I smiled, though it wasn't easy. "She did, huh?"

I gave her a kiss on her black and white forehead. Then the girls gave me one big sloppy cheek kiss each.

I stopped by the den and pointed to my watch.

Jan put down the phone. "Everything all right?"

"I told Curtis and Bill I'd meet them. I'll be back in time for supper."

"Be careful, sweetie."

"Don't worry, Miss Kitty. I will."

She laughed. We had this running joke how Miss Kitty on *Gunsmoke* always told Matt to be careful, even when he seemed about to embark on nothing more dangerous than walking down to the general store.

She puckered a kiss in my direction.

I was just about out the door, she was just turning back to the den, when I said, "There's something I'd better tell you."

When she turned back to me, she didn't say anything, simply watched me for a long moment.

Then, "I knew something was wrong."

I came back into the den and closed the door.

"You remember that woman who started calling me a lot when she was my client?"

"That Trudy, you mean?"

"Right, Trudy. Her."

"Oh, my God," she said. She looked pale already, before she even knew what happened.

"She came over the other night."

"Came over?"

"A visit. Unexpected. I mean, I didn't invite her or anything."

"She just showed up?"

"Well, she'd called me earlier in the day. She was having some problems with her boss. She was having an affair with him and he was being a jerk."

Now her cheeks reddened slightly. Anger. "So you slept with her."

"God, no."

"A very attractive woman like Trudy just shows up uninvited while your wife's away and—"

"And gets murdered."

Her expression changed instantly. She looked very young now, and genuinely shocked. "Murdered? Are you kidding?"

"Murdered. And right out in front of our house."

I kept looking at the clock. The boys were waiting for me.

"I can't tell you much more now, honey. I'm late already."

"You said in front of our house?"

"In her car. Not long after she left, apparently."

She looked upset. "What do the police say?"

I smiled, hoping I didn't look or sound bitter. "That would be Detective Patterson. A very relentless lady. I don't think she's quite ruled me out as a suspect yet."

"She thinks *you* had something to do with it?"

I shrugged, trying to look as if I wasn't worried. "She's got a lot of other suspects, honey." I looked at the clock again. "I've got to go. I'm sorry."

She walked over to me and touched my arm.

"Were you sleeping with her, Aaron?"

"Sleeping with her? Hell, no."

I tried to sound outraged but I'd been expecting her to ask that very question. Her football hero had left her unable to trust any man…and when an attractive woman like Trudy visits a married man…the question's bound to be asked.

But she wasn't buying into my outrage.

"No theatrics, Aaron. And no bullshit. Just a straight, honest answer. Were you sleeping with her?"

I took her hands and folded them into mine and looked at her. I didn't make a big deal of it. I just said it, a regular guy saying a regular thing, "I didn't sleep with her, Honey. Believe it or not, I've never been unfaithful to you, and I never will be."

"That's the only time you saw her since last year?"

"The only time."

"And you didn't invite her over?"

"Honey, I'm a happily married man. And happily married men don't invite women over to their houses when their wives are out of town."

She grinned. "Remember Tom Ewell in *The Seven Year Itch?*"

She was a big Marilyn Monroe fan, and *Itch* was her favorite Marilyn picture. It was one of my favorites, too, a rather pathetic middle-aged man having all sorts of fantasies about the gorgeous single woman living upstairs.

"We should rent that again sometime," I said. Then, "Now, I've got to go. We'll talk more when I get home."

But she wasn't finished with questions yet. "There's a lot you aren't telling me, isn't there?"

"Honey, I didn't sleep with her. Didn't lay a hand on her."

"The night before that, though, the night of your poker club. Remember I kept saying that you sounded funny. Something happened that night, didn't it?"

I kissed her gently on the mouth and said, "The next time Detective Patterson needs to hire a free-lance interrogator, I'll tell her about you."

Then I was out the door.

10

THEY WERE LATE.

I was parked a quarter of a block away from Neil's parking lot, with his silver Saab in clear view. I spent some time looking around to see if I could find anybody else sitting in his car watching Neil's car. From what I could see, the other vehicles parked along the street were empty.

I listened to the local news, which mentioned Trudy's murder but didn't mention me, and then I listened to some rock and roll. Usually, fast music picks me up, like a tonic. It didn't work today. It just sounded crude, loud and empty.

I checked out some of the buildings. This was the old part of the downtown area, the part built after the sprawling university but before the six tall buildings that comprised the new area.

Rush hour.

A kind of frantic edge to the people streaming out of the office buildings and hurrying to their cars. All they had to do was take their place in the long chain of cars headed for the expressways, and soon enough they'd reach their destination. The hot late afternoon air was already choked with the fumes of buses and trucks and cars. It would be positively silver-blue by the time the rush hour was over.

He came hurrying up the opposite side of the street, then crossed over when he saw my car.

Doctor Bill.

He looked like a soap opera doctor, muscular, intense, with an expensive hair cut and several hundred dollars worth of blue silk shirt and white ducks and canvas loafers on his body. Even from here, his anger crackled like summer lightning.

He was alone. Where the hell was Curtis? Was something wrong?

"Curtis get a hold of you?" he said when he got in the car.

"No."

"Got hung up at the office. The Gunderson deal. He said you'd know what he was talking about."

Gunderson owned a construction company that was being bought by a big firm in the east. Gunderson wanted us to find a way to shelter some of his profits. Given everything the feds were disallowing lately, it wasn't going to be easy.

After he closed the door, he said, "You see anybody yet?"

"Not yet."

"That's Neil's car, right, the silver Saab?"

"Right."

"I ask you something?"

"Sure."

"You smell pussy on me?"

"You serious?"

He nodded. "This new nurse at the office. I didn't want to hire her. She didn't have diddly experience in our kind of set up, the clinic thing I mean. But my partner insisted so I went along. I guess he figured that gave him squatter's rights." Bill grinned with great satisfaction. "He's going to be pissed when he finds out I got there first."

"The hallowed calling of medicine."

He chose to disregard my sarcasm. "But I don't want to smell like pussy when I get home tonight. I mean, the musk can stay on you a long time."

"You really don't think she knows?"

"Oh, I think she knows. But I never rub her face in it. That's the important thing. Cheat, but leave them their dignity."

"That's how it works, huh?"

This sarcasm he chose not to disregard. "You running for Pope, Aaron?"

"I just happen to like your wife." She was a sweet, compliant little woman who'd never quite gotten over the fact that a campus god had stepped down from on high and married her. She'd borne him four children, ran his house dutifully, and chose to ignore his endless indiscretions. Drinking one night, she'd come over to our place and spent two hours sobbing in the living room about how she suspected Bill of sleeping with a friend of hers. He'd shown up, angry and embarrassed, and dragged her angrily out to the car, and home.

"This is none of your business, Aaron."

"Then don't ask me if you smell like pussy."

He glared at me. "I guess that's fair enough."

"Yeah," I said. "I guess it is."

It should be obvious by now that Bill was my least favorite guy in The Poker Club. For him it would always be football Saturday, with him as the center of attention. As the hero of this never-ending crisp autumn afternoon, he expected to be forgiven all his sins, his rage, his arrogance, his peacock strutting.

The one thing nobody could ever explain was how he came to be such a fine doctor. He was patient, kind, tender, skilled, and genuinely concerned about the well-being of his patients. This went for young and old, black and white, rich and poor. He even contributed ten hours a week to the free clinic in the black section. The sonofabitch was the absolute best doctor I'd ever known.

"I guess I picked it up from the old man," he said into our stony silence.

"Picked up what?"

"You know. Being unfaithful."

"Your old man was like that?"

"He was worse. My mom had this incredible sister. I mean, talk about bodies. She was just fucking incredible. Anyway, one night the old man nailed her in his Buick right out in our driveway."

"Your mom ever speak to your aunt again?"

"Nah. She blamed her for seducing my old man. You know, like he was this little lost innocent lamb. Women really don't want to know the truth. They really don't."

"There's Neil," I said.

Neil was walking down the perimeter of the parking lot to his silver Saab. A tall, dark-haired man walked along side him. They were laughing about something.

Neil seemed especially careful about not looking around. He focused on his car, said good night to his friend, and climbed inside the Saab. Didn't want to tip off any observers that he was aware he was being watched.

A few minutes later, he pulled out into the street and turned right. I started my car. Sat there a long moment.

The street behind us was empty.

Then he was there. Coming down the street. The clunker befouling the air with grimy exhaust smoke.

Older Chevrolet, ten years, maybe. Blue. Rusted pretty badly. Grill smashed up a little. The whole car leaning leftward on bad shocks. And smoky windows so you couldn't see inside.

"Bingo," Bill said, seeing him, too.

"Bingo is right," I said.

He drove slowly so he wouldn't pull up right behind Neil at the first stoplight.

Then they were off, the blue Chevrolet staying about a half block behind.

"He kept on porking her."

"Who kept on porking her?"

"My old man kept on porking my aunt. I caught them one time outside this tavern where my old man and his cronies always went after work. My old man was a foreman at a ball bearing company."

"And your mom never forgave her?"

"She never saw her sister until about fifteen years later, when my aunt got sick. Cancer."

"So they made up?"

"They tried. But I don't think my mom ever forgave her. I think she wanted to, but she couldn't."

"Shit," I said.

"What?"

"I'll have to pull up right behind the blue Chevrolet."

"Maybe he won't notice you."

"Maybe," I said, sounding doubtful.

We sat at the light.

"Your old man still alive?"

"Prostate cancer." He smiled, and for perhaps the first time ever, I saw a kind of sorrow in his smile. "I loved the old fucker, I really did. Even with all the shit he laid on my mom." He shrugged and looked out the side window. "I'm more like him than I ever wanted to be. I can't keep my dick in my pants."

"You ever try?"

He laughed. "Yes, Monsignor, I actually did try there for a couple of years. Every time I got close to poking some nurse or something, I'd head for the can and jack off. I really did try. But finally I couldn't help myself. I just started fucking my brains out again. And now I can't stop." Another laugh, this one self-deprecating. "I got me a new jig saw for my workshop at home. Maybe it'll make me want to give up getting nookie on the side."

Doctor Bill Ryan had three passions: medicine, nookie, and making things in the workshop he'd built for himself in his garage. He was a very good carpenter and seemed to take almost as much pride in making things as he did in helping to heal people.

The light changed.

We started down the avenue again.

Traffic was slow, and tempers got shorter. Horns honked, middle fingers were jabbed angrily into the air, the occasional traffic cop looked sweat-soaked and ready to take out his night stick and open a few heads. And I wouldn't have blamed him. Most people were driving like spoiled children, determined to have their own way.

"You're pretty good at this shit," Bill said. "Following people, I mean."

"All those Robert B. Parker novels I read finally paid off."

"I always meant to read one of those. But I never got around to it. I guess I like historical fiction better."

"Damn," I said, tamping the brake just a tad.

I had to run a yellow light, hauling ass through a wide and dangerous intersection. If I didn't, I'd lose the blue Chevrolet with the smoked windows. Then we had a two block run with nothing to slow us down.

The next bottleneck was the street leading to the on-ramp for the cross-town expressway.

"Bastard's staying right on Neil's ass," Bill said.

"He sure is."

"I'd like to beat his fucking face in." This was the old familiar Bill. No more sorrow. No more melancholy. Rage.

"We should've gone to the police," I said.

"Hey, now there's a fucking positive attitude."

"We may get away with it, but it's always going to be on our minds."

"We didn't kill him on purpose."

"No, but we didn't report it the way we should have, either."

"You really want to go back through all this bullshit again?"

"No, I guess not."

Then we were on the freeway, four cars across, everybody doing seventy-five minimum. Killer drivers.

"Shit."

"What?"

"Lost them," I said.

We were heading into a steep bank. Neil and the blue car following him had disappeared completely.

"Just calm down."

He was right. I took several deep breaths. Calmed down.

The bank led into a valley and then I saw them below us, the blue car three cars back from Neil, Neil about six miles from his exit.

"Everything's cool," Bill said, seeing the cars at the same time I did.

The rest of the freeway run was relatively easy. I pegged seventy miles per hour and stayed there, gradually working my car over to the turn lane.

I had a moment of panic when a teenager zipped ahead of me out of the lane on my left. He'd almost overshot his exit. He didn't even seem to see me.

I jammed on the brakes, leaned the heel of my hand on the horn.

"Little cocksucker," Bill said.

The teenager put his middle finger up in the air above his front seat.

"Cocksucker," Bill said.

Another moment of panic.

We were shooting down the off-ramp right behind the rusted blue Chevrolet. But where was Neil?

Then I saw him. Front of the line. Already starting to turn left.

How was the blue car ever going to find him?

"That dumb ass."

"Who?" I said.

"Who? Neil. The sonofabitch should have slowed down so he wouldn't lose the Chevrolet."

"Yeah, I guess he should've. But he probably didn't have much choice. He had to turn."

"We're going to nail his ass anyway."

"Yeah," I said. "We can just follow the blue car."

So for the next twenty-five minutes, that's exactly what we did.

After trying and failing to catch up with Neil, the blue car slowed down and took a street that veered off to the right.

The car led us through a variety of crumbling neighborhoods. Poor whites lived adjacent to the university. Poor blacks started occupying houses about ten blocks east of campus. There was now a small Vietnamese neighborhood as well. When I'd started college here, the only foreign language you heard spoken was redneck. Now you heard a dozen languages in the air, an international bouquet of flowers.

In some sections of the city, the very oldest, you could still see the glistening century-old tracks of the town's first trolly system. In other parts, you could see two very beautiful immigrant Catholic churches, one built by the Irish, the other built by the Czechs. The exteriors of both were now defaced by graffiti.

"Watch out."

"I see it," I said.

Another intersection. Yellow light. It was going to be red by the time we reached the edge of the intersection.

I'd have to risk running it.

I punched the gas pedal and sailed through the intersection at sixty miles per hour.

A car came ass over appetite from my left.

"Shit!" Bill yelled.

The car was bearing down on us at at least fifty miles per hour.

He was going to broadside us. We'd be seriously injured, maybe even killed.

My stomach turned over.

I basically stood on the accelerator. There was a terrible lapse between the time I exerted the pressure and the time the engine got the message.

When the oncoming car was no more than five feet from my door, starting into a tire-screaming slide, my car suddenly jumped ahead, racing through the remainder of the intersection.

In my rear view, I watched the other car wrestle down to twenty miles per hour, all the other cars staying in place, not wanting to get anywhere near either me or the other car.

We lucked out twice.

We'd avoided the accident and the blue Chevrolet was sitting patiently at the next stoplight.

My whole body was shaking.

"Man," Bill said, "didn't you see him?"

"Guess not."

"Scared the hell out of me."

"Tell me about it."

We continued following the car for fifteen more minutes. When it reached a neighborhood known as Baylor Park, the streets were suddenly filled with black people.

Little kids played baseball. Young girls skipped rope. Teenagers strutted around with boom boxes on their shoulders and stood in insolent-eyed gangs, looking over the turf the drug dealers had long ago claimed as their private property. The older people were the ones that reflected the quiet hopelessness of life here. They sat on their crumbling front porches and watched the human parade, child into teenager into hopeless adults. Some of the kids, the ones with luck and pluck, but mostly luck, would make it out of Baylor Park someday. But for most of the people here, people of all ages and levels of intelligence, Baylor Park was as final as a prison sentence.

The blue car moved slowly up the street. People waved at it but because of the smoky windows, we couldn't see the burglar inside wave back.

We had found his home base.

He went up to the corner, stopped a moment, then turned right.

I stayed a quarter block behind him.

Tired of the air conditioning, I shut it off and rolled down the window. The air was filled with the rude noise of rap and a hundred smells, marijuana, wine, and the dying heat of the day.

I turned right just in time to see the blue car go up to an alley and turn right again.

There were so many kids in the street, I had to drive slowly and carefully.

At first, I didn't have time to check what it was that Bill had taken out of his sport coat pocket.

As we reached the alley, I finally saw it: a small .45.

"What's that for?" I said.

"What's that for? Are you kidding me, Aaron? What the fuck you think it's for? This asshole and I are going to have ourselves a little conversation."

He was stoned high and giddy and frantic on his own rage. In his football days, the rage won him a whole lot of fans. As he approached middle-age, his rage was just ugly and self-indulgent.

I turned into the alley.

The blue car was just pulling off the alley, to park in front of a sagging one-car garage.

"Bingo," Bill said.

And before I could say anything, Bill was jumping out the door and walking fast to the blue car.

He had a lot of nerve, Bill. Since he couldn't see inside, how did he know there weren't three guys in there with guns pointed at him, guns that would erupt at any moment?

But I'd seen his rage too many times before. It made him insensate.
I saw a coal black hand push open the car door.

I saw a coal black leg, just below the hem of a blue flowered
housedress, begin to push out of the car, a yellow K-Mart sandal covering
a rather large but definitely female foot.

I saw a meaty coal black hand find purchase on top of the car door
so it could help lever the rest of the body erect.

She was a grandmother of at least sixty years old, a sad and now
terrified neighborhood woman of probably two-hundred and fifty
pounds who was certainly wondering why the hell a well-scrubbed white
man was holding a gun on her.

I jammed my car into park and walked down to the blue Chevrolet.

"Where the hell is he?" Bill said. He looked and sounded crazed,
waving the gun in her face.

"Is who, mister? Mister, would you please put that gun away and
calm down? Guns scare me real bad."

"Move over," he said, shoving her as best he could.

Bill was obviously convinced that our burglar was sitting inside.

In his frenzy, he couldn't see that we'd simply been following the
wrong car. Nobody had followed Neil home but the junky condition of
the car and the smoky windows had convinced us otherwise.

Now we were scaring the hell out of a nice, harmless lady.

"I was just drivin' home, mister, that's all," she said, sounding as if
she was about to start crying.

"Ma'am," I said. "This is a terrible mistake. I really apologize."

All I could see of Bill was his backside.

He was bent into the car, searching for the burglar. Maybe the guy
was hiding under the seat. The world's smallest burglar.

I caught the way her eyes flicked left. I followed her gaze and saw
them.

There were at least twenty of them, men and boys of all ages, and
they were starting to encircle us.

"Who the fuck are you?" said a young man. He stepped up to me
and made sure I could see the switchblade that dangled unopened from
the fingers of his right hand. The covering looked to be genuine pearl.

"This is all a terrible mistake," I said, "And I was just apologizing to the woman."

"That's true, John," the woman said. "He was apologizing. It's the other one—"

Just then, Bill chose to extract himself from the car.

The twenty people standing in front of us cooled his temper.

"What you botherin' Thelma for?" John said. He was maybe twenty and wore a white tank top that showed off his considerable musculature.

"We made a mistake," I said. I looked at the woman. "I really am sorry."

"You think you can come into this fucking neighborhood and just do what you want, man?" John said to Bill.

Everything else happened so quickly it was unreal.

The blade on John's switch knife flicked open. John grabbed Bill and smashed him back against Thelma's car. John put the point of the knife to Bill's throat.

I had the wild sensation that John was going to actually kill Bill right then and there. The black face was a torment of rage.

I started to grab for John, knowing that his friends would now probably grab me.

But they didn't. They helped me grab John, pull him off Bill.

"Hey, friend," one of the older men said. "You don't want to do time for killin' some cocksucker like this one."

"Just let it slide, John, let it slide," said another older man.

Most of them wore cheap, shabby clothes and watched us with a mixture of contempt and curiosity. They smelled of aftershave and sweat and beer and wine and marijuana. It was a true cross section of blacks, some of the men with nose rings, others with dreadlocks, shaved heads, a few dyed blonde. But most looked like decent working-class people. In the waning sunlight of the wasted day, the purple hue of dusk gave the old garages of this alley a certain dignity and beauty. The hue gave the crowd a melancholy, too, as they watched us with their anger. But it was a weary and sad anger, one felt too many times before.

They held John as if he were an animal that could spring free at any moment.

Thelma said, "You'n your friend better get in your car and get out of here."

"I'm sorry," I said.

"We don't want to hear no more of your fucking words, asshole," said a white-haired old man. "Just git out of here. This is our place. Not yours."

I looked at him and then the others and felt ashamed. All their lives they'd been forced to live at the whim of white people. They hated us enough already. Now we'd given them even more reason to hate us. It was a strange feeling, feeling sorry for the people who in their heart of hearts wanted to kill us.

Bill looked shaken and numb.

I took his arm more roughly than was necessary, wrenched him around in the direction of the car, and then started walking.

When I got back behind the wheel, when Bill got himself seated, I put the car in reverse. No way I was going to drive past them.

"Fucking coons," Bill said, when I had at last reached the street again.

The crowd still stood in the middle of the graveled alley, watching us.

"Like to get some of my old teammates to come down here and kick some ass," he said.

"We fucked up," I said, "and scared the hell out of some nice old lady. I don't blame them for hating us."

"Yeah, well maybe you wouldn't feel so fucking understanding if some coon had put a knife to *your* throat." Then, "I'm not up for any of your bullshit, Aaron. So if I were you, I'd just keep my mouth shut, you understand?"

He didn't speak even when we were back where he'd parked. Just got out of the car, slammed the door hard as he could, and then went over and got into his own car.

11

THERE WAS A strange car in my driveway, a new dark blue Dodge with blackwalls and very little chrome.

The kind of car you usually associated with public officials who wanted to convince you that they really were trying to hold tight on spending your taxes.

I swung past the Dodge on the second lane of the driveway and stashed my car in the garage.

I walked back to the Dodge and looked inside.

There was a sawed-off shotgun in the back seat and a pair of handcuffs on the front seat.

I should have told her, made sure Jan heard it from me rather than from the police. I thought there would still be time when I got back. Now I knew better.

I went to the back door.

The girls were in the breakfast nook drinking what looked like fruit punch and munching on carrot sticks. Maybe the nutritional benefits of the latter would cancel out all the chemicals of the former.

"She has a gun, Daddy," Betsy said. "Right on her belt."

"Mommy said she's a detective," Annie said. "That's why she has a gun." I had to force myself to concentrate on the girls and the effort made me feel guilty. I owed my children my complete attention.

"She's nice, Daddy," Betsy said.

I leaned down and gave them forehead kisses.

In the living room, Detective Patterson was perched on the very edge of one of the armchairs. She did indeed have a small Magnum holstered at the side of her belt. She wore a dark blue skirt, blue hose, blue half-inch heels, and a brilliantly white blouse.

"Hi, Honey," I said to Jan. "Sorry I'm a little later than I thought I'd be."

"That's all right," Jan said. "I was just telling Detective Patterson here how you called me at my folks' about Trudy. It's such a terrible thing. I met her that one time about a year ago. Remember, honey?"

She was covering for me. I guess I wasn't surprised but I sure was appreciative. I just hoped Patterson never decided to check up on our long distance records.

"Oh, that time she stopped over and dropped off those papers?" I said.

"Right."

She was lying for me, too. She'd never met Trudy at all.

"I'm afraid I've been taking up too much of your wife's time," Detective Patterson said. "I know she'd rather be fixing dinner than talking to me." She glanced at me. "I didn't really come to talk about Trudy anyway. There's something else I need to talk to Mr. Tyler about."

My stomach got instantly queasy. As did my bowels. Patterson was a master of innuendo. If she didn't want to talk about Trudy's murder, what the hell *did* she want to talk about?

"Sorry to trouble you," Patterson said, turning her attention back to Jan.

"It's no trouble," Jan said. "I was glad to learn more about it." She looked at me. "Aaron didn't really tell me all that much." She gave me an icy smile. She was helping me with Detective Patterson but she wasn't happy about it.

Jan stood up. "But now I think I really should get supper for everybody. The girls are really hungry."

"Especially Betsy," I said. "She's so hard up for something to eat, she's dunking carrots in her fruit punch."

Nice, normal dad leading a nice, normal life. That's how I wanted to sound.

And what could be more normal than doting on the strange habits of your little girl?

Nice and normal.

But just what the hell did Patterson want to talk to me about, anyway?

"It was nice meeting you," Jan said to Patterson.

"Same here," Patterson said. Then to me, "You've got such a nice wife, Mr. Tyler."

Jan nodded good-bye and left the room.

Patterson got up and walked over to the front window, smoothing the front of her blue skirt with long white fingers. She had nice hips and legs. The gun attached to her belt gave her a kind of dangerous sexuality.

"Nice neighborhood," she said.

"Yes, it is."

"I've got two little boys. I wish I could afford to live in a neighborhood like this one."

I told her about the city's refurbishment program and how it had helped us afford this house.

She shrugged, still gazing out at the street. You could hear mothers calling their little ones in from the day's last games, pom pom pull-away and statue and hide-and-go-seek. There was a pleasant, sentimental sound to the voices, and to the sleepy half-moon that burnished the cloudy sky with soft silver beams.

"I still couldn't afford it, Mr. Tyler," she said, and turned back to me. "You may not realize it, but you're doing well for yourself. Very well."

"I know how lucky I am."

She came back and sat down across the room from me. "I heard you had some trouble last night."

"Trouble?"

"A car knocked a boy down."

"Oh. That. Nothing really serious."

"This is becoming quite a busy neighborhood."

"Yeah, I guess it is."

I wanted her to say it, whatever it was she'd come to say, but she wanted to prolong it. She knew how nervous I was.

"All your neighbors seem to like you very much."

Meaning she'd talked to my neighbors.

"That's nice to know."

"They said you're not only a nice guy but that you've got really good judgement, too. A Mr. Carter down the street said that he and his daughter were having a few problems and that you gave him some very good advice and that now he and his daughter are friends again."

"I just got lucky. Giving him the advice I did, I mean. It was just common sense, more than anything else."

"A couple of other people said the same thing. About how good your judgement is."

I smiled. "If I'm so good, why aren't I on the Supreme Court?"

She smiled right back. "That's what I was wondering." Then, "Do you know what adipocere means, Mr. Tyler?"

"I'm afraid I don't."

"When a body has been in water for a certain period of time, a drowning man for instance, the fatty tissues of the body begin to develop a kind of waxy substance. It's yellow. And that's adipocere."

I haven't done much trial lawyering in my career to be an expert at commanding a courtroom. But I have learned enough to keep my face blank.

I had to concentrate very hard not to react when Patterson used the phrase 'a body has been in the water.'

"This is like going back to law school," I said. "Learning a new term like this. How do you spell that?"

"A-d-i-p-o-c-e-r-e."

"I'll try to remember that."

"Have you ever seen a body that's been in the water a long time?"

"I guess not."

"Pretty spooky. I wanted to prove how tough a cop I was, so I did back-up on this drowning case when I was a young cop. I vomited right in front of my supervisor. I'd never seen anything like it. The whole face was so bloated it looked like a monster instead of a human being."

"I'm glad you're telling me all this before dinner."

Light patter. Nothing to hide.

"But fortunately, once in a while you get lucky."

"Oh?"

"Fortunately, a body that should have stayed in the water a long time gets found by somebody right away."

My entire body was covered with a cold, filthy sweat. I was trembling. I wondered if it showed.

"This is very interesting, Detective Patterson, but I'm not sure what it's got to do with me."

"You're afraid, aren't you?"

"Afraid?"

She stared right at me. She was enjoying this. Enjoying it a lot.

"You should see yourself."

"Oh?"

"Do you know that you've licked your lips three times in the last thirty or forty seconds?"

"No, I guess I wasn't aware of that. I must be thirsty."

Her gaze didn't leave mine. "You're afraid, Mr. Tyler. Afraid of what I'm going to say. It doesn't have anything to do with being thirsty."

"What the hell are you driving at?" I said.

The anger was clear in my voice. In this war of nerves, I'd just lost a major battle.

"I'm sorry I snapped at you."

"Quite all right, Mr. Tyler."

"But I really would like to spend some time with my family. As you know, they've been gone. And by the way, you haven't mentioned Ron."

"Trudy's boss?"

"Right."

"Well, I've interrogated him twice," she said.

"And?"

"And he's definitely in the running as far as suspects go. He doesn't have any alibi. He went out and got drunk and hit a lot of bars but nothing is very clear to him. He hired himself a very good criminal lawyer yesterday."

"Then I'm not a suspect anymore?"

"I didn't say the case was closed, Mr. Tyler. I just said that her boss was still definitely a suspect."

"I see."

"But that really isn't why I'm here tonight."

I smiled. "We're finally getting to the point."

"Yes, we are," she said. "Indeed we are, Mr. Tyler. I wanted to tell you that late this afternoon, a body wrapped in a tarpaulin was found down river from the dam. In the back pocket of the body, we found a tiny slip of paper."

"A slip of paper?"

"Yes, Mr. Tyler," she said. "And that's really why I'm here tonight. Because the slip of paper on the dead man had your name and address on it."

PART
TWO

1

A RE YOU all right, Mr. Tyler?"
"Of course. Why *wouldn't* I be all right?"

"You look upset."

I gave her my best lawyerly smile. "Did you ever have a body found outside your house?"

"I can't say I've had that privilege."

"Well, I have. And recently, in fact. And now you tell me that a man's body has been found in the river and my name was in his back pocket. This is all coming at me pretty fast. So if I *did* happen to look a little upset, I'd say it was pretty natural."

"You just said you weren't upset, Mr. Tyler."

Another lawyerly smile. "You're not taking courtroom classes at night are you? You're really good at badgering the witness."

"So you don't know why a dead man floating down river would have a slip of paper with your address on him?"

"No. But maybe he was a client. Or maybe somebody recommended my firm to him."

"You have any particular problems with clients lately?"

"Just the ones who ask me to cheat the federal government."

This time, she smiled. "And being a lawyer, you're far too ethical to do anything like that?"

"Do I detect a little displeasure with lawyers?"

"A little."

"I want to say something official here, Detective Patterson."

"Official?"

"Yes. I want to make a statement on the record."

"All right."

"I didn't have anything to do with Trudy's death, and I don't know a single damned thing about any man in the river."

"Period?"

"Period."

"We don't know who he is yet."

"I'm sure you'll find out."

"About six-foot, 180 pounds, dishwater blond hair, small scar on his right cheek."

"Like I said, I don't know a single damned thing about him."

Just then, Jan came into the room and said, "I just made some lemonade for the girls. Would you two like some?"

"Thanks anyway, Mrs. Tyler. But I have to be going."

I could see Jan watching both of us for some sense of what was going on in the room. I kept the smile on my face, trying to look as relaxed as possible. I'm sure Patterson had seen this kind of theater turn before, but I didn't know what else to do.

Nice, normal guy reacting in a nice, normal-guy way to news about some dead fellow floating down river.

"It was nice meeting you, Detective Patterson."

"Nice meeting you, Mrs. Tyler."

Jan smiled at us and disappeared back into the dining room.

"You've got a good one there, Mr. Tyler."

"And believe me, I know it. She's the best thing that ever happened to me. That and the girls, I mean,"

"They're just as cute as their mother."

I smiled. "Lucked out again."

She stood up. So did I. We met in the middle of the living room, just as the grandfather clock in the hall was chiming the half hour. The clock had belonged to my granddad, and whenever I heard it chime, I was transported back to my childhood hours at his place. He always had plenty of Double-Bubble gum (I could still smell it so fresh and sweet down the years), comic books (always DC, never Marvel for some reason), and whiffle balls. We used to play it by the hour. Even there at the last, when the cancer was becoming very painful, he'd managed to go out and pitch to me, always making a very big deal about how high and hard I could hit the ball.

She put out a hand. We shook. Her grip was still steel. "I know this is a pain in the ass, Mr. Tyler."

"You're just doing your job."

"Between us," she said, looking at me with formal directness, "between us, I don't think you had anything to do with Trudy's death, and I don't think you probably know anything about the body in the river. That's the first thing a cop has to learn. No matter how hard it is to accept sometimes, coincidences do happen. And I think that's what we're dealing with here—"

"Coincidences?"

"Exactly," she said. "And I'm sorry I have to be such a pest."

She was damned good at all this, she really was. I had no idea if she was being sincere, or if she was just trying to lull me into a false security, a security that might ultimately cause me to make some mistakes.

"Well, good night, Mr. Tyler."

"Good night, Detective Patterson."

I opened the front door for her and held it while she passed through.

The heat outside was still clammy and cloying.

"Boy, do I hate to leave this nice air conditioning," she said as she walked past me.

I stayed in the doorway until she got into her car and backed out of the driveway.

We both exchanged very earnest and civilized waves.

Just doing her job.

Nothing more than two coincidences.

Sorry about being such a pest.

I wondered.

I went inside. Jan was in the kitchen. "After the girls get settled in for the night, I want you to tell me everything that's going on here. Everything, Aaron."

She wasn't pleased with the surprise that had been waiting for her. I didn't blame her.

"I've changed my mind. I can't wait any longer. What did she want to talk to you about?"

I was looking in the refrigerator for a beer. "Who?"

"Oh, God, Aaron, I'm really not up for this bullshit. None of your coy answers, okay? I want you to tell me what Patterson wanted to talk to you about and I want you to tell me right now."

Jan is able to hide her feelings pretty well. While she was in the presence of Detective Patterson, she looked perfectly composed. But now I saw the strain and doubt Patterson's visit had put on her.

"I'm sorry," I said. "I was just making a little joke."

"Haul your beer over to the nook and we'll sit down, all right?"

But is wasn't to be.

In the next five minutes, the phone rang three times, twice for Jan, once for the girls.

There was no way we could talk in all this chaos.

I'd been given a little more time to figure out how much to tell her. I really wasn't ready to talk about the burglar. If things went well... maybe I'd never have to tell her about the burglar at all...

AFTER DINNER, while Jan was cleaning up the kitchen, I gave the girls their baths, tugged them into fresh jammies, ensconced them in their respective beds, and led them in their goodnight prayers.

At the end, I always said, "Now ask God for a special favor for somebody you know. We'll make this a silent prayer."

Betsy always told aloud what hers was and tonight was no exception. "You know Mrs. Durham down the street?"

"Uh-huh.

"She lost her kitty."

"Yes. I know."

"Do you think God would give her another kitty?"

"He might if you ask him."

"Do you think he'd give her a brown one like the one she had?"

"Maybe."

"And just as cute?"

"I'm done saying my silent prayers, Daddy," Annie said. "Is it all right if I lay down now?"

"Sure, Hon."

"I don't know why she has to tell you her silent prayer out loud anyway."

"I guess it just makes her feel better, sweetheart."

Betsy finished her prayer and scooted under her sheet. In the summertime, the girls rarely used blankets. We kept the temperature at seventy.

I leaned over and gave Betsy a forehead kiss and said, "I love you."

"I love you, too, Daddy."

I don't know why, but right then, hearing her little voice say that, I wanted to cry. I wasn't even sure I knew how to cry. But I wanted to sit down and bawl.

I kissed Annie goodnight and told her I loved her, and listened to her say she loved me, too. And then she said, "I called Heather tonight."

"How's Heather doing?"

"She said a woman got killed in front of our house,"

"She did, huh?"

"Yes. And she said that you knew the woman."

We weren't listening to Heather at this point, we were listening to Heather's mother, one of the congenitally unhappy housewives who spend their days polishing their neighborhood tales to a high fine luster.

"I didn't know her very well, sweetheart. And now's not the time for this discussion, anyway. Okay, Toots?"

She giggled. Even at age eight, she loved being called Toots.

At the door, I clipped out their lights.

"Will you leave the door open just a little bit?" Betsy said.

"She saw this movie at Grandma's that really scared her," Annie said.

"It did not," Betsy said.

"Then why do you want the door open?"

"So we can have a breeze."

Annie giggled again. "You're so dumb sometimes, Betsy. We have air conditioning."

"Well, you're dumb *all* the time," Betsy said on her own behalf.

"Let's zip 'em up," I said.

This time, it was Betsy who giggled. She loved the notion that her mouth had a zipper on it.

"Goodnight, girls. Mommy and Daddy love you very much."

IN THE den, I dropped into the recliner. On the stand next to me was the phone. I owed the poker club members a call. Tell them about the burglar's body being found.

But for the first time in our marriage, I felt intimidated by Jan. I was afraid she'd overhear something she wasn't supposed to.

A couple of times, I lifted the receiver, held it for a long moment, and then set it back down.

Both times, I cocked my head, listening for footsteps in the hall.

God, it was such a strange reaction. I was treating Jan like some sort of intruder or interloper.

I decided to wait until morning.

I was on the verge of changing my mind yet again—at least calling one of them and telling him what Patterson had said—but then Jan was coming through the door.

She wore a long white T-shirt she favors over pajamas in the summer. She had great legs, her new tan only enhancing their sexiness. She'd showered and smelled of wet hair and baby powder.

As she walked over to the couch, I couldn't resist looking at the bottoms of her buttocks as they moved so sensuously with each step.

But I decided against trying to lure her into the bedroom. She wanted her answers, not romance.

"You ready?"

I looked over at her and smiled. "You sound like Patterson."

"That's the point, Aaron. You talked to her, now I want you to talk to me."

"You know how cops are."

"No, as a matter of fact, I don't know how cops are. Believe it or not, being raised the way I was and all, I've never met many cops." She leaned forward on her elbows. She looked cuter than hell. But she didn't mean to. She wanted to look as cold as she sounded. "Does she think you were having an affair with Trudy?"

I shrugged. "I don't think she's ruled that out."

"Were you?"

"I thought we already went over that."

"I want you to tell me again."

"Just for the hell of it."

"Yeah, Aaron, just for the hell of it."

"I wasn't having an affair with her."

"Did you ever sleep with her?"

"This is starting to piss me off a little, Jan."

"Right now, I don't care, Aaron. Right now I need a whole lot of reassurance and you're not giving it to me."

"I never slept with her."

"Did you ever kiss her?"

"Jesus."

"Well, did you?"

"I gave her a paternal kiss when she was leaving the other night."

"A paternal little kiss."

"Yes, on the forehead if you want to be specific."

"I don't like the way I sound, either, Aaron, but the whole thing—she did have a sort of crush on you at one time … and then I'm away and she comes over … and then somebody kills her." She sat back and put her hands in her lap. "I really do need to be reassured, Aaron."

"I'd like to kill that sonofabitch."

"Who?"

"Your football hero. He did this to you."

"Aaron, you'd have doubts about me if I'd been caught in the same circumstances."

"The hell I would."

"Think about it. Really. Just give it thirty seconds or so."

I gave it thirty seconds or so. "Maybe a few. Doubts, I mean."

"See."

So I went through it again for her. Slowly. Trudy calling. Trudy coming over. The Patrol people finding her dead.

"And that was it? That was everything?" she said.

"That was everything."

"And Patterson thinks you had something to do with it."

"I suppose it's logical. Trudy was visiting here. Then she's found dead outside."

"My God," she said, "this is very serious."

I decided I might as well get the rest of it over with. "They've asked me to take a leave. At the office."

"Are you serious?"

"Yeah, unfortunately, I am."

"Those bastards. Do they think you did it?"

I shrugged, trying to minimize her anger. "It's just public relations. You don't want some guy who's involved in a murder investigation working on staff."

"I don't believe it. That place is your life, Aaron."

I sighed. "Not a hell of a lot I can do."

"How about Patterson? What do we do about her?"

I took due note of the 'we.' She was still my wife, still thinking of us together. I got kind of sappy right then. God, I loved her.

"I guess we'll just have to wait and see. That's all we can do."

She leaned forward and put her head in her hands.

After a time, I said, "You all right?"

She didn't say anything for a time. She took her face from her hands. "I just feel real tired now, Aaron. The trip and the girls and coming home to this. I'm just kind've worn out, I guess. I need some sleep. Just hold me," she said.

"My pleasure."

I forgot all about the news. I just let it drone on behind me.

I pulled her down to me.

I gave myself over entirely to the scents and feels and subtle movements of her body, and to my memories of her. Every once in a while the thoughtless male like myself gets overwhelmed by how much he loves his wife. It's a kind of epiphany, I suppose, a moment of truth that makes you realize how lucky and blessed you are to have such a life mate.

"I'm sorry," I said.

Her face was tender with warm tears when I kissed her. At first, it was all very platonic, me wanting to improve her mood.

But the kiss quickly became a passionate one, and then we were on the couch like high schoolers, and she was helping me undo my chinos, and then she was mounting me and I was up inside her, and we began to make love with a frenzy that became a kind of bonding. We spoke with our bodies, reassuring each other that our lives and love were just as good and nurturing and true as they'd always been.

Afterward, she jumped in the shower with me, and we made love again, her giggling when she got soap in her eyes, and me licking it off her eyelid like a dog, which made her giggle even more.

Then we went to bed, and right to sleep, both of us exhausted for a variety of reasons.

IN THE dream, the second burglar was creeping down the hall toward the girls room. He carried a butcher knife whose shining blade was deeply stained with blood.

In the dream, I woke up and ran to our bedroom door. But it was locked and no matter how many times I threw myself against it, no matter how many times I pleaded with God to help me, the door didn't open.

Then, the nightmare continuing, I heard the screams coming from down the hall as the second burglar crept into the girls' room, waking Annie in the process.

It was Annie who screamed. And cried, "Daddy! Daddy! Help us!"

But I couldn't help.

I couldn't get the door open.

And then Jan was next to me, trying to push and smash through the door, too.

Having no luck, she began to claw at the door, her nails tearing off, blood streaking the panel of the door in the moonlight.

The screams continued down the hall.

I saw the second burglar now, bending over Annie's bed, putting the butcher knife to her throat.

AND THEN the phone rang.

Total disorientation.

Was the ringing phone part of my nightmare?

I rolled over to my right.

Reached an uncertain hand for the receiver.

Lifted it up. Put it to my ear.

"Hello," I said.

What time was it, anyway?

I got my eyes open enough to see the digital clock. Three-forty-seven a.m.

"Hello," I said again.

And then I realized who it was, and when I realized it, I was jarred awake. Him.

The second burglar.

I listened to his presence, the quality of his silence.

The silence spoke of evil, modern evil, urban evil, of eyes that watched in the darkness, watched little children and good mothers, of eyes that coveted money and flesh and life itself—the rapist in New York who gave seven of his victims AIDS, the fiend in California who dragged poor little Polly Klass from her slumber party, and killed her in the woods half an hour later.

This was what I heard in the silence, in the darkness.

I slammed the phone down.

And lay back down, freezing in my own sweat.

Motherfucker.

Someday I would get my hands on him and someday I would—

Couldn't afford fantasies like that one.

Had to remain calm. Nice and normal. For Jan's sake. For the sake of the girls.

Nice and normal.

And then I heard Jan snoring and I couldn't help it. I smiled.

It's a wet, diminutive kind of snoring, hers, not the big bass drum kind that I get into.

And just then there was something so sweet about it that I reached over and put my hand on hers, gently so as not to wake her.

But I needed to touch her right then.

Reassure myself that I really did possess all the blessings God had given me.

After a time, I dozed off again, and had another nightmare.

This time I was back in the water at the bottom of the dam, trying to work the tarpaulin free of the metal rod.

But just as I was pushing the rod downward, a hand shot out of the tarpaulin, and seized my throat.

Inside the folds of the tarpaulin, I could see two eyes with a strange red glow watching me as the hand pushed harder and harder on my throat, as I began to sink beneath the filthy churning water...

I think I screamed.

I think I heard the echoes of that scream as I was waking from the nightmare.

I looked at the clock. Four-twenty-three a.m.

I looked at Jan. Still snoring peacefully.

I laid my fingers against her slender arm. My touchstone.

I lay like that for a long time. Freezing inside the membranous skin of my frozen sweat. Trembling.

Around five, knowing it was no use to even try to get back to sleep, I got up and went out to the kitchen and put Mr. Coffee to work.

2

THE FIRST CALL came just after seven a.m. Bill. He usually sounded in charge of every situation. Now, he sounded vaguely hysterical.

"I've been up all night," he said.

"What's wrong?"

"Somebody threw a rock through the French doors leading to the veranda last night. It set off the burglar alarm."

"It could've been kids."

"Will you listen to me, Aaron? It wasn't kids. It was that other burglar."

"It sounds more like kids."

"What the hell are you talking about?" He sounded exhausted, angry and completely at the mercy of his own bad nerves. "It wasn't some coincidence, and you know it, any more than that woman being killed in front of your house was a coincidence. It's the sonofabitch that got away."

"I still think her boss killed her."

"I don't. Not after last night. The burglar is stalking us. It's pretty clear."

"We need to meet after work today, the four of us."

"Why?"

I told him about the burglar's body being found in the water with my name in his pocket.

"We went through his pockets." He sounded like a frightened child.

"I know we did, Bill, but we missed it. We were pretty frantic when we searched him."

Instead of exploding, as I assumed he would, he lapsed into a long silence.

"Bill?"

"It's all falling down on us. All coming apart."

"Bill, listen. We have to think clearly. We have to reason this through."

"We should have listened to good old square Aaron. We should've called the police."

"I guess that's still an option."

"Yeah, sure it is. Look what the press is doing to you over Trudy. All those little innuendoes and sly hints. Imagine what they'd do to the four of us. Our lives would be over, Aaron. They really would be."

"Can you meet about five-thirty?"

"Where ?"

"Red Lion."

"Closer to six."

"All right. Closer to six. I'll call Curtis and Neil."

"I've got to pull myself together. Twenty minutes from now, I've got to tell a thirty-two year old woman that she has terminal cancer."

"It's going to work out all right," I said. "Everything is."

But even I could hear the anxiety in my voice. I didn't believe my own words, either.

JAN CAME into the kitchen around eight-thirty. Stretching. Yawning. Looking sleep-rumpled in her long T-shirt. Her bare feet made little kitten-cries as they moved across the waxed tiles of the floor.

"I had a great time last night," she said, sliding her arms around my waist.

"So did I."

"We ought to do that more often."

"That's what I was thinking, sweetheart."

Our sex life seemed to wax and wane with the various stresses put on us by outside forces. Sex may not be the most important thing in a marriage, but it's symbolic of certain intangibles that make a marriage endure. Sometimes we'd let ten, twelve days go by, and when we did, I always felt a bit distant from her. Sex was a bonding mechanism as much as anything. Not to mention a hell of a lot of fun.

She looked around me at the stove. Saw that I was heating up the griddle.

"Pancakes?" she said.

"Pancakes."

For some reason, the girls preferred my pancakes to Jan's.

"You go get the girls," I said. "I'll start the pancakes."

She leaned over so she could see my face.

"What time did you get up this morning?"

"Oh, early, I guess."

"There's a nice evasive answer."

I kissed her.

"My wife, the Grand Inquisitor. It was about five, I guess. I've been in the kitchen ever since." I lifted the pancake batter and poured some onto the griddle. Hiss and crackle of hot griddle; faint curling smoke rising from the surface.

The pancakes were on the way.

Just as I was using the spatula to pick up the first pancakes from the griddle, the girls came running into the kitchen in their pajamas.

"Mom said you were making pancakes!" Annie said.

"And Mom doesn't lie," I said.

"Oooo, pancakes!" Betsy said. She never had much to say in the early morning. Annie, on the other hand, could exhaust you with jabber.

Jan got them set up in the breakfast nook, poured them ice cold Minute Maid orange juice, gave them one Flintstone vitamin each, and saw to it they tucked paper napkins into the necks of their pajamas. Log Cabin syrup is really sticky stuff.

"Now it's your turn, Buster," Jan said, after I'd filled her plate with cakes. "Get over here and amuse us gals or I'll have to pistol-whip you."

Betsy giggled. She loved it when Jan talked like a gun moll.

"Yeah, Daddy," she said, "pistol whip." She laughed with a mouth packed full of pancake.

She had no idea what she was saying, of course, but to her the phrase pistol whip was about as funny as you could get. We ate.

By the time we were halfway through, Betsy had managed to make her little cheeks glisten with syrup. Even more impressive, she'd managed to get traces of glistening syrup in her hair. Presumably this happened when she raised a syrup covered hand to scratch her head.

"Say, 'pistol whip' again, Mommy," Betsy said when there was a lull in the conversation.

Jan smiled. "I wish I could amuse myself as easily as you can, Betsy." Then, "Pistol whip."

Betsy giggled some more.

Annie shot her a look of lofty disdain. Eight year olds apparently find nothing remotely amusing in the phrase 'pistol whip.'

The phone rang.

"I'll get it," Jan said, lifting up her plate. She was finished eating. She'd eaten two. I'd eaten six.

On her way to the sink, Jan scooped up the receiver and said hello.

"Hi, Neil, how are you?" Pause. "Oh, that's good. Did you want to talk to Aaron? He's right here."

Just before I reached out and took the receiver from her, my stomach shot a laser beam up my esophagus. No way Neil would be calling me with good news. It would be bad news for sure.

"Morning," I said, pretending that I was a nice, normal middle class guy giving a sunny greeting to his friend.

"You know what he fucking did?" Neil said.

I looked around the kitchen. Jan was at the sink, her back to me. The girls were slicing and dicing the last of their pancakes.

"So how's it going, Neil?" I said, sounding hearty as I could.

"He fucking smashed all the windows in my car. While it was sitting in my garage. I just went out there now."

I kept on sounding hearty. Dumb Daddy from a Dumb Sitcom.

"Well, it'll be great to see you tonight. That's the Red Lion at five-thirty, right? Bill just called to say that he could make it, too."

"We have to do something, Aaron. We really do."

If Neil was already this upset, I wondered how he would react to learning about the body in the river, and the slip of paper with my name on it.

"He's not going to give up," Neil said. "We have to deal with him."

"All right," I said, still sitcom hearty. "I'll see you tonight, then."

I walked back to the sink and slid my arms around Jan. "We're going to get together at dinnertime tonight."

"So I heard. Any special reason?"

"Well, Bill still wants to talk about that camping trip. My opinion is it'd be a disaster."

I started to kiss her neck but she slid out of my arms before I was quite aware of it. "Hey," I said. "I was going to give you a hicky."

"I'm not up for humor right now, Aaron. I want to know what the hell is going on."

"What's going on? What the hell are you talking about?"

Jan angrily wiped her hands on her apron. "You're a terrible liar, Aaron. You aren't talking about any camping trip. You're talking about something else. And I want to know what."

"God, Jan—"

"Does it have to do with Trudy?"

"Trudy? Why would we meet to talk about Trudy? They didn't even know her."

Her face was taut with anger. She was a little frightening when she got like this. I always think of her as gentle, sweet Jan. But that's my little sexist cliché. She's a damned strong, independent woman. And she can generally spot bullshit after about three words are spoken.

"You're lying to me, Aaron. And you know I won't stand for that."

I was about to lie to her some more when the girls appeared in the kitchen doorway. They'd gone outdoors after finishing their pancakes.

"You said you'd show us around the garden, Mom."

"Yes, I did, didn't I?" she said. She glared at me. "C'mon, girls, I'll show you how I'll plant the flowers."

The three of them went outside. I felt isolated, and scared.

Very scared.

SOMETIMES I just study my face. I'm not sure why. Not vanity, of course. I suppose I'm nice looking enough in a blunt, Midwestern way, but no movie star.

No, I think I study myself in the mirror to reassure myself that I actually exist.

The trouble is, the face I see in the mirror doesn't seem to have much to do with the thoughts trapped inside the skull.

The face would lead you to believe that here is a calm, rational man leading a calm, rational life.

But inside this mind itself, things are much different. Anxiety. Rage. An occasional sense of helplessness.

So we have the dichotomy between the mask and the internal reality.

This particular morning, I stared at myself in the mirror a good two, three minutes.

It was as if I was searching for clues on the surface of an alien planet.

When I thought of the dead burglar, I felt unreal. Good old Aaron Tyler would never get involved in anything like that. Not good old Aaron Tyler. Family man. Reliable citizen. Reasonably good father. Not good old Aaron.

Every few years, I get this scary notion that my life is all a dream, as if I'm watching *The Aaron Tyler Story* on the movie screen of my mind.

And someday I'll wake up and not be Aaron Tyler at all. The movie will be over. And I'll understand everything then, what cosmic force is behind the movie, and why that cosmic force wanted me to see the movie.

I looked out the bathroom window and saw the cardinal on the lowest bough of the oak tree in the backyard.

The cardinal was brilliant red. The grass was a brilliant green. The sky was a brilliant blue.

All these bountiful gifts, and I was a prisoner of my own fears, playing a poor man's version of Descartes: *I look at myself in the mirror, Therefore I exist.*

By the time I was finished with my shower and getting dressed, the girls were on the swing set.

Jan was in the small garden she tends at the back of our yard.

She wore gloves and was weeding a section of dirt.

"I'll be back in a couple of hours," I said,

She just kept working with her trowel.

"I'm sorry you're mad."

She looked up. She was even angrier than she'd been in the kitchen.

"You're still not telling me everything, are you, Aaron?"

"Now you sound like Patterson."

"She doesn't believe you any more than I do."

I didn't know what to say. I felt undone by her anger. Anything I'd say now would only make her angrier.

"Maybe I should leave," I said.

"Yes," she said, and then went back to her trowelling.

3

I'D NEARLY reached the shopping mall before I realized I was being followed.

Twice I looked in my rear view, the way I do sometimes, and there was a dark green Ford of considerable age behind me.

After the second time, and some twenty-five blocks after the first time I saw it, I got curious about it.

Kept an eye on him the rest of the way to the mall.

Just to test my paranoia quotient, I spent ten minutes in the large mall lot driving up and down the ranks of cars glistening in the hot Midwestern sunlight.

What seemed like dozens and dozens of sumptuous young maidens appeared and vanished in my windshield, tank tops and short shorts being the official uniform of the day. My first thought was that I wished I was back in high school again. The problem with that notion was that I hadn't exactly had great success with girls back then. The ones I had secret painful crushes on caused me to slip into silence whenever I was around them. And the ones I dated because nobody else would go out with them, I felt sorry for, as if I were deceiving them. They were nice girls and deserved somebody who wanted to be with them.

I parked on the west edge of the lot, in a section packed with cars.

I shut off the engine and waited, constantly glancing around the lot.

No sign of the forest green Ford.

More maidens, drifting between the lanes of cars.

Maybe my paranoia quotient was out of whack.

I'd seen him behind me three times.

The route I'd taken to the mall was a well-traveled one. Lots of people took it to get to the mall.

The Ford probably got to the mall, found a parking spot, and then the driver got out and went innocently about his business.

So much for being followed.

I was just opening the door, just about to get out, when I saw the green Ford at the far end of the line of cars I was in.

I closed the door quickly. Sat behind the wheel again.

He took a parking space far up the line.

The mall was east of my car. He was parked west. I'd have no logical reason to walk in his direction. Not without letting him know that I was aware of his presence.

I got out of the car and walked into the mall.

The day was so hot that I got sticky walking just three hundred yards or so to the east wing of the mall.

The air conditioning was fierce. It dried me off almost instantly.

I stood to the side of the double doors, watching the parking lot, seeing if he'd followed me.

I tried to picture him as he was the other night, when I saw him in the moonlight of my backyard.

The trouble was, I couldn't visualize him very well. I didn't really have any sense of his height—he hadn't struck me as short but then he hadn't seemed very tall, either—nor even the color of his hair except that it was light as opposed to dark.

Even if he walked right up to me, would I recognize him in the daylight?

For one thing, if he was following me, he'd probably taken the precaution of disguising himself in some way, so even if my memory of him were clearer, I wouldn't recognize him.

I stood there twenty minutes. I didn't see anybody approach who was even a likely candidate.

Middle-aged women, young mothers trying to keep their tribes in some sort of seemly order while they trekked through the mall, and the young maidens again, this time trailed by small groups of giggling boys who were afraid to approach them directly.

Nothing. Nobody.

I SPENT two hours in the mall.

I enjoyed myself. I stopped in the Barnes and Noble, going carefully through the History and Current Events sections. I bought Garry Wills' latest book. To me, he's one of the most astute thinkers in American politics, far brighter and more incisive than the show-offs who inhabit the Sunday morning political chat shows. Wills is too serious for a sound-bite format like that.

I spent another forty-five minutes at Suncoast Video, where I bought two Abbott and Costello videos, in one of which they meet the Wolfman. In the second, it was Boris Karloff they had to contend with. I'm way too young to remember their heyday back in the forties and fifties but one of the local stations ran their old movies when I was a kid, so I still have fond memories of them. I seemed to like the movies that the hard-core Abbott and Costello fans seemed to regard as the lesser ones.

I stopped at the imitation sidewalk bistro for a Coke.

The sociology of the mall had always fascinated me. In a Midwestern city like this one, the malls are where small town and big town come together. You have the sunburned farmer and country club lady shopping in the same jewelry store. You have the poor black kid sitting next to the rich white kid at the Orange Julius. And you have the frantic mother of four bumping into the beatific grandmother who is headed to her aerobics class. The concept of the melting pot is quickly vanishing, as most of us try to barricade ourselves away from urban violence. But sometimes it's pleasant to sit in a mall and see the diversity that still makes up our country.

I saw him.

My mind flashed on him jumping off the garage roof the other night.

The face-image of that moment matched the face-image of the man standing directly across from me, standing in the entrance to a sporting goods store.

When I first noticed him, he was just quickly looking away from me. As if he didn't want to be caught.

If I approached him, I was sure he'd leave.

I needed to trap him, somehow, turn on him so he would have to confront me.

He was perhaps five-ten, maybe one hundred sixty pounds, brown hair thinning on top, somewhere around age thirty. He wore a white short-sleeved shirt and dark trousers. No eyeglasses. No earrings. Not even a watch on his bare wrist.

The guy from the other night. The second burglar.

I finished my Coke, stood up and looked around momentarily, as if I couldn't quite decide where I wanted to go.

Just a nice, normal shopper making a nice, normal decision. That was the notion I wanted to project.

I saw the corridor that led to a section where two stores had closed recently. The traffic was light in this corridor.

A perfect spot.

I'd walk down there, as if I were going to use that particular EXIT door, and then when he got close to me, I'd turn on him and find out just what the hell he wanted.

I started to walk out into the main flow of traffic, chancing a glance in his direction.

He wasn't there.

I had this incredible paranoid sense that he'd snuck up behind me somehow.

I turned. Searched the crowd. Nothing. No sign of him whatsoever.

I turned back in the direction of the sporting good shop where he'd been standing.

He was in sight again. But he wasn't standing in the doorway of the shop. He was walking.

And he was smiling.

I'd smile, too, with a woman that gorgeous on my arm. She was a redhead and a beauty.

Husband and wife. Or lovers.

Whatever they were, they clearly had no interest in following around some attorney who was amusing himself by playing James Bond at a shopping mall.

"DADDY?"

"Uh-huh."

"How old do I hafta be before I don't hafta have training wheels?" Betsy asked.

"Oh, five. Or five-and-a-half."

"I'll be five in this many months."

She held up three sweet little fingers.

I took one more of her fingers and raised it next to the others.

"You'll be five in this many months," I said. "Four months."

"Then I don't hafta have training wheels?"

"We'll see, sweetheart."

"See what?"

"See how well you're riding your bike."

"Sean doesn't hafta have training wheels."

Sean was a boy in her preschool class.

"Did Sean tell you that?"

"Uh-huh."

"Sean kind of makes things up, I think."

"You mean like that flying saucer that time?"

"Yeah. Like that flying saucer."

"He said this green man came into his house and Sean gave him a Pepsi."

"Uh-huh. I don't think aliens would drink Pepsi."

"Then what would they drink, Daddy,?"

"Oh, probably chocolate malts."

She giggled. "You're being silly."

I leaned over and tickled her and she giggled all the more, putting up her arms and knees to stave me off—giggling all the while.

Then we settled down.

"Annie said that maybe you'd make me wait until I was seven."

"Was she mad at you when she said it?"

"I guess so."

"Well, she probably said it just to make you mad."

Just then Jan and Annie came through the sliding doors, Jan bearing a tray with four glasses of lemonade on it, Annie carrying a large yellow bowl of popcorn.

As Jan set down her tray, I saw that she had a white number ten envelope in one of her hands. I wondered what it was.

We all sat on the redwood back deck and watched the animals try to stay cool in the hot sun.

The envelope Jan had been carrying disappeared. I just assumed, then, that it belonged to her.

We all had so much sunscreen lotion on, we looked like actors getting ready for a stage performance.

We spent a good twenty minutes speculating on one of the small squirrels running up and down the hardwood tree near our property line.

The girls were fascinated as Jan and I told them how squirrels lived, and how they prepared for winter. Who said those college bio courses don't come in handy?

After the popcorn had been wiped out in a rutting frenzy by the Tyler family, Jan said, "Oh. I almost forgot."

She produced the white number ten envelope I'd seen earlier. She'd put it on her lap underneath the deck table.

I took it, looked at it. And knew instantly that it was trouble.

"Aren't you going to open it, honey?" she said.

"Sure. Probably just some kind of advertisement."

"There's no return address or anything. It came in the mail."

"Have you noticed that?" I said. "The junk mail houses, I mean? No return address? No pitches of any kind in front of the envelope, the way they used to have them? I guess they figure that if they're mysterious about it, you'll at least open the envelope to find out what's going on."

I was back to my nice, normal guy routine.

"So here, ladies and gentlemen, is another example of how direct mailing houses take advantage of our postal system."

I was speaking in an announcer's tone.

Betsy said, "Daddy's being silly, isn't he, Mommy?"

Jan laughed. "Very silly."

"A moment of silence, please," I said.

I tore the envelope down the side then blew on the opening to make it wider.

I pulled out the single sheet of white typing paper that had been folded into thirds.

"And here we have—"

This was the tricky part.

I had to read it quickly then crumple it up in disgust.

I glanced at the lone line of typing in the center of the page.

JUNE 23

"I was right!" I cried. I sounded like a game show contestant who'd just won a refrigerator. "A finance company wants to loan us $10,000!"

"Let me see, Daddy!" Betsy said, reaching for the piece of paper.

But I was already crunching it up.

When I looked over at Jan, I saw that she was watching me rather intently.

Maybe I hadn't been as clever as I'd thought.

Maybe my face had betrayed me when I'd unfolded the page and the date there.

"Want me to throw that away for you, Hon?" she said, holding her hand out, wanting me to drop the crumpled paper into her palm.

"That's all right," I smiled. "It's pretty heavy. I'd better keep it."

She smiled in return. Her mouth did, anyway. Not her eyes.

Not her eyes at all.

TWENTY MINUTES later, in the upstairs bathroom, I tore the note into many pieces and flushed them down the toilet. The envelope was no problem. Nothing to hide there. Just the postmark and my name written in ballpoint.

"YOU GOING to be here when I get back?" I said.

Jan was sitting in front of the TV. She glared up at me. "You got rid of whatever was in that envelope, didn't you? Before I could see it."

"Yeah, I guess I did."

Tears shone in her eyes. She said, "I want you to know how much this is scaring me, Aaron." She reached under a throw pillow and produced a most unlikely object—the .45 her older brother had carried in Vietnam. He'd been killed in a mine explosion. She had taken the gun from among his personal effects. Jeb, her brother, had been a marksman. He'd trained her to shoot. "You're scaring the hell out of me, Aaron. You really are." She laid the gun back under the pillow. "Just get the hell out of here, Aaron. Right now."

TEN MINUTES later, I was sitting at a stoplight five blocks from my home.

So was the green Ford that had followed me this morning.

Two cars back.

4

I WASN'T one of them anymore.

I got to the Red Lion about half an hour early. I thought it might be relaxing to sit in a booth near the back and just work on a drink and listen to the jukebox. The green Ford had driven on past me as I swung into the parking lot.

I had my choice of two things to look at, the steady flow of men and women to the restrooms in the back, and the parking lot outside the window.

It was watching the parking lot, all the sharp successful people getting out of their nice new cars and coming inside, that I realized how much my life had changed in the past few days.

They were all wound up after a day of various corporate treacheries, some of which they'd visited on others, some of which had been visited on them.

They'd talk about mission statements and goals and second quarter financial reports, and who was laying whom in the office, and who would be the prime candidate for the vice presidency opening up after so-and-so retired. That's how I'd spent the last eighteen years of my life.

But it all seemed remote from me now, and silly in the extreme.

My three friends and I were fighting to stay out of prison. Which lent everything a desperation I'd never known before.

It also lent my life a certain perverse exhilaration that I was only gradually starting to understand. I'd heard a lot of Vietnam veterans say that as much as they'd hated combat, it had focused them as nothing ever had before or since.

Fear, they said, had been their most constant emotion.

I was getting to know that feeling very well.

I watched the parking lot some more. I also kept thinking about the way Jan had been looking at me the past twenty-four hours. I felt sorry for her. I loved her.

I'd thought about sitting down and telling her everything. But then that would get her involved in it all.

And there were legal implications, as well.

While Jan certainly couldn't be considered an accomplice, keeping knowledge of a felony from the police just might interest the kind of publicity-hungry county attorney we had.

No, I couldn't tell her everything. I owed it to her and the girls to keep the worst of it to myself.

Curtis arrived first, bringing a bottle of Bud and a glass back with him. He sat down across from me, filled his glass, took off his gold tie bar, unloosened the knot of his tie, unbuttoned the top button of his shirt, and then brought the beer glass to his lips.

"Bill called me," he said.

"I thought he might."

"About finding the man's body. And your name in his pocket."

"Right."

"This is getting real, real spooky, Aaron."

"I know."

"Maybe we need to hire ourselves a good criminal lawyer."

"Maybe we do."

He took another long drink of beer. He watched me as he drank.

"You all right?"

"Yeah," I said.

"You've agreed with everything I said. But you're not adding anything of your own. You really think we should hire a lawyer and go to the cops?"

"Wait till Neil and Bill get here."

"We went through his pants."

"Yes, we did. Or I did. This is my fault. I was the one who searched him and I obviously did a lousy job."

"Oh, hell," he said, "none of us would've done a better job. I mean, we were all pretty crazy by then."

The waitress came. We ordered two more beers. This would make three for me in less than an hour. I'd pretty much reached my limit. My next order would be a Diet Pepsi.

"You know, in a weird way," Curtis said, "this is good for me."

"Yeah, right," I said.

"I'm serious. I mean, I've always thought that only black and brown people got into trouble like this. You know, where you don't really do anything but you wind up in jail for the rest of your life anyway. That's why I grew up hating white folks, I guess."

"You still hate us now?"

He smiled. "Not all of you."

"Speaking for the entire white race, let me say that I'm glad you find at least a few of us acceptable."

"I was only half kidding. About hating all white people."

"Yeah, I picked up on that."

"But my wife got me doing this meditation stuff I told you about, and it's really worked out good for me. I go home and meditate a half hour before dinner, and I've really calmed down."

He sipped some more beer.

"I used to be a real hater. I hate to admit that but it's true. I mean, fifty times a day I'd think of all the little things white people had done to me over the years. And I'd get all worked up. I'd see them smirking at me again, or making racist remarks, or firing my poor old man. He was a janitor and he worked for this guy for eight years and the only time my old man ever asked him for a raise, he fired him. I guess the guy figured there was a plentiful supply of niggers who'd work for next to nothing the way my old man always had. Or I'd see my little sister crying the day somebody spray painted 'NIGGER' on the side of our school. And I couldn't take it. I'd get all worked up, like one of those guys who goes back to where he works with an Uzi. You know what I'm saying? I'd spend half my day fighting these images that would come to mind, how people made fun of me and stuff like that, and it was driving me crazy. I couldn't stop even if I wanted to. But then I learned this meditation and it really helps. It really does."

"I'm sorry, Curtis."

"Aw, what the fuck," he said. But he had tears in his eyes. You can't deal with memories like his and not be affected. "All things considered, I'm a lucky guy to've been born in America, and had the opportunity to become a lawyer, and to have a nice family the way I do. A lot of people got it a lot worse than me, man. A lot worse. Random luck of the draw, and I didn't draw so bad. I really didn't." He smiled sadly. "I just don't want to lose it all now."

I'd often thought about that, how random it all was, genetics and geography playing the major role. A man and woman meet in Chicago and have a child. Same man, different woman meet in Los Angeles. Or different man and same woman meet in Orlando. Every variation being a completely different life history. And each variation affecting the world in a completely different way. A change of partners could produce Ted Bundy or Richard Speck; Mother Theresa or Prime Minister Rabin.

Most of us don't hope for fame or notoriety. Most of us are happy to have all our limbs, a well-functioning body, and an opportunity to prosper in modest ways in our society. But what if that man and woman produce a black child, or a crippled one, or a gay one, or a deformed one? Then that child is born, in our particular society, with a distinct disadvantage. And it's all random luck. There's nothing inherently superior about being white and straight, of course. It's just that you'll have an easier time of it in our society. And if you're not white and straight, then you have to adjust accordingly, and run up against our society's prejudices—just as Curtis had.

"Hey, friend," Curtis said. "I didn't mean to bring you down. I was just running my mouth."

I shrugged. "Nah. I think about this stuff, too. I wasn't a big Jack Kennedy fan but I happened to read part of that speech he gave about how unfair life is, and how we're afraid to really confront the unfairness.

I did a paper in eleventh grade on that speech and this teacher said that she totally disagreed with Kennedy because in the United States everybody has the right to make something of himself. And that's true. But it also misses the point of what Kennedy was saying."

He grinned.

"Hey, you don't have to convince me that teachers are stupid." Then, "There's Neil."

And there was Neil, pulling into a parking spot. And right behind him came Bill.

I didn't see any old green Fords anywhere.

Neil waited in the hot late afternoon sun for Bill to catch up with him. They came into the bar together.

"Bill's pretty strung out," Curtis said.

"I figured he would be."

"He's convinced it's all over, the police finding your name and address in that guy's pocket."

"We have to stay calm."

"Right. You ever try to keep Bill calm?"

They brought drinks with them. Neil sat on my side of the booth, Bill on Curtis'.

"The waitresses in this place have gone to shit," Bill said. "Remember the babes they used to have in here? Wore those cute little skirts and you could see the outlines of their butts in their panties?"

Neil said, "This must be medical terminology I'm not familiar with."

Bill laughed. "It's true. This place used to have great waitresses. Now they all look like middle-aged housewives."

"Let me speak up for middle-aged housewives," I said. "I've seen some damned sexy ones."

"Oh, I forgot," Bill said. "Aaron here thinks Hillary Clinton is a babe."

"I just said she was attractive. And she is."

"I'll make you a deal," Bill said. "I'll take Madonna and you take Hillary."

"Madonna's a pig," Neil said. "And her career's all over, anyway."

"You'd take Hillary over Madonna?" Bill said.

"Yeah. At least you wouldn't have to boil Hillary before you bopped her."

"I think the point is moot, anyway," Curtis said. "I don't think Hillary likes guys."

"You think she's a lesbo?" Bill said.

I laughed. "God. 'Lesbo.' You've been listening to Rush Limbaugh again, huh?"

"No," Curtis said, "I don't think she's a 'Lesbo.' I just don't think she likes sex. With anybody. 'Wham-bam-thank-you-ma'am' is probably what she prefers. You know, she just wants to get it over with. Ish. Ick. Acky-poo. Stuff like that."

At one point, I walked to the back and called Jan and told her I'd be late.

She didn't sound happy and I didn't blame her.

The waitress came by. Took our orders.

Bill studied her. Up and down.

When she left, he said, "I don't mean to pick on that poor girl but you have to admit she's pretty homely. And she doesn't have any tits."

"Nice legs, though," I said, feeling an irrational need to defend her. I felt sorry for her. None of us could stand up to the kind of assessment Bill had just put on her. Handsome and heroic as he might be, Bill still wasn't any Robert Redford.

"Let's knock off the shit and get to it," Neil said.

Silence.

"Agree?"

"I'd just as soon hear Bill run down that poor girl some more," Curtis said. "You notice how she had a scab on that one elbow?"

"She's probably a very nice young woman," Bill said, surprisingly defensive, given his usual arrogance. "All I said was that she wasn't exactly a beauty."

"What she is," I said, "if you'd noticed that she was wearing her inexpensive wedding ring on the right hand—what she probably is is a single working mother with one or two kiddies at home and a minimum wage job that depends on largesse from middle-class guys like us."

Everyone seemed aware of the anger in my voice. Sometimes Bill's arrogance got to me. You'd think a son of the working class would have compassion for working class people. He seemed to despise them, blame them for not having the luck he'd had. It all reminded me of the conversation Curtis and I had about the random factors that go into existence. Bill pissed me off and I wanted him to leave the waitress alone.

"Can we finally fucking get to it now, you guys?" Neil said. He was angry, too.

But not about the waitress.

He wanted to talk about dead men wrapped in tarpaulins bobbing in dam water.

I said, "Somebody's following me."

"You sure?" Curtis said.

"Positive. A green Ford. Bad shape. Maybe eight, nine, ten years old. I can't tell cars so well anymore."

"When'd you first notice him?" Neil said.

I told them about going to the mall, driving home, coming down here.

"That fucker," Neil said.

"Why's he doing this?" Curtis said.

"We're not going to find out until we nail his ass," Bill said.

"And just how do we do that?" Neil said.

"We follow him," I said.

"Yeah," Curtis said. "That worked out pretty well yesterday for you and Bill, scaring the shit out of some poor old black lady."

"There's a difference now," I said. "We know for sure it's him."

"That's a good point," Curtis said. "So if we follow him—"

"It's very simple," I said. "I've been thinking about it and I don't see how we can miss. You three guys get in Bill's car. We'll coordinate everything with cell phones. I leave the parking lot, the green Ford starts following me, then you start following him. I'll drive home, go inside as if I'm staying there. Then when the green Ford leaves, you follow it. I'll need to stay home for a little while. Jan's getting suspicious. I'll catch up to you when I can. But you can go ahead and follow the bastard. Anybody see any flaws in that?"

"Just one," Bill said. "What if he spots us?"

"He won't spot us if we're careful," I said.

"But if he does spot us, he might lead us into some kind of trap. You know, have a few buddies waiting in an alley he leads us into."

"How would he do that?" I said.

"Maybe he's got a cell phone, too," Bill said. "Maybe he figures out we're following him and then he calls ahead and gets his pals set up."

Neil said, "I vote to do what Aaron says. If he sets us up, he sets us up. We'll just have to take that chance."

"I go with Aaron, too," Curtis said.

The waitress was coming back.

"I guess her legs aren't that bad now that I see them again," Bill said.

What a magnanimous sonofabitch he was.

"But her tits still aren't for shit," he said.

And I marveled again that healing powers could be found in this angry and often ugly man.

God uses strange vessels sometimes.

"Let's go," Neil said.

"I'll go out first and get in my car. I'll be going up Windsor Avenue, in case you lose me."

"I sure hope this works," Curtis said. "It's time we lean on this sonofabitch."

"And lean hard," Bill said.

I went out into the dusk. Mosquitoes and steaming heat and the first fluttering glow of neon. Gasoline fumes and cigarette smoke and stray whiffs of perfume as women passed in and out of the Red Lion's entrance. Midwestern summer night was falling.

Five minutes later, I pulled out of the Red Lion parking lot. Half a block later, I saw the old green Ford.

It was two cars behind me.

5

NOTHING MUCH happened on the way home.

Once, I thought he might have fallen away. I didn't see him in the rear view mirror for two or three blocks.

Another time, I went through a yellow light, thinking he could make it, too.

He didn't.

I slowed down some to let him catch up with me. Neil and I were on the phone several times. Nothing to report, really.

Thursday night traffic is always frantic. Lots of bars, lots of parties to get to. People starting the weekend early. Everybody impatient and angry behind the steering wheels of their big metal killing machines.

Now that the sky was darkening, with the first stars imprinting themselves on the darkness, teenagers were also making their first appearance.

A couple of kids in a hot red Pontiac revved their engine and grinned at me. I declined the honor of peeling out from the stoplight.

There were a lot of backyard cookouts going on in my neighborhood. You could see the smoke rising from the outdoor grills. Visitors' cars lined the streets. I pulled into my driveway, the headlights illuminating the garage door. I thumbed the signaling device that automatically opened the door.

I tried to see it from the burglar's point of view.

What could be more convincing than a man opening his garage door and putting his car away for the night?

A nice, normal night.

The garage smelled of heat and car oil and mown grass. A kid had cut it yesterday for $25. He wasn't just saving to attend college; he was, apparently, saving to *buy* the college. I slipped in the back door.

Jan was at the stove. She wore a short blue summer skirt, a white blouse, and had a fetching red ribbon riding on the left side of her dark bobbed hair.

I took a beer from the refrigerator and slid into the breakfast nook.

She hadn't said hello. She hadn't even looked at me.

"I take it you're still mad," I said.

Said nothing. Just kept fixing the Spanish rice and green salad for dinner.

"This isn't any easier for me than it is for you," I said, knowing how whiny I sounded.

She carried the salad bowl and four plates into the dining room.

I felt dislocation again—as if I didn't belong there anymore. The burglar dying...in a way, he'd taken me along with him. I wasn't the same man I'd been before he broke in and fucked everything up.

When Jan came back, I stood up and walked over to her and took her by the wrist and turned her so she had to face me.

"You've never been like this before."

"That's because you've never lied to me before."

"I'm *not* lying to you. I'm really not."

"Bullshit. You know damned well you are."

She slipped out of my grasp and went over to check the Spanish rice on the stove.

"I feel pretty goddamned isolated right now," I said, sounding whiny again.

"Yeah? Well, what do you think I feel like, Aaron? I'm living with a man who won't tell me the truth."

I wanted to, of course, wanted to just tell her about the burglar and get it all over with.

But I wasn't sure what she'd do. I guess what I was afraid of was that she'd say to go to Patterson and tell her everything.

I wouldn't be a member of the bar again. Ever.

What the hell would I do for the rest of my life?

I said, "I have to go out after dinner."

She turned and looked at me. "Is that supposed to surprise me?"

"Neil wants me to help him with something."

"Right."

"Goddamn it!" I exploded. "It's the truth!"

She knew just how to handle me. She walked past me carrying the dish of Spanish rice and said, "Is it, Aaron? I don't think you've told me the truth since I got back from my parents' house."

I followed her into the dining room. "I won't be gone long."

"Fine."

"Fine? Is that all you can say?"

The table looked elegant as usual. She was one of those people with the Touch. However you get It, or where It comes from, I sure don't have It.

"I'll be home by nine or so. Then we can sit down and watch TV."

She glared at me. "When do you tell me the truth, Aaron?"

I sighed. "I'd still like to go on that picnic."

"I'd say you owe the girls that. You haven't spent much time with them since we got back." She nodded to the living room. "I'm trying not to let them know about our—troubles. But I think they can sense it." She sounded weary and sad. "Maybe you'd better go see them."

"I'll go see them right now," I said.

The girls were watching cartoons.

"How come Bugs Bunny looks different in this one, Daddy?" Annie said.

"This is an old one," I said. "They kept changing Bugs over the years."

"How come?" Betsy said.

"To make him look better."

"He was real skinny in the old ones," Annie said authoritatively.

"Yes, he was," I said. "By the way, you girls be sure and get rested up."

"Rested up for what, Daddy?" Betsy said.

"For the picnic."

"Picnic!" Betsy said. "Picnic!"

"Are we still going to the county fair, too?" Annie said.

"We sure are."

"Boy, that'll be great," she said.

"Now we'd better go eat."

I shooed them out to the kitchen and sat them down at the dining room table.

Once Jan joined us, Betsy led us in grace. She used to get grace and parts of the Star Spangled Banner mixed up. But she was four now and a lot more sophisticated than that.

Every time I glanced up from my meal, which I was eating very quickly, I found Jan watching me.

She looked alternately angry and afraid.

I wanted to put the girls into bed and tell Jan everything. But I couldn't.

The phone rang.

After I said hello, Detective Patterson said, "I hope I'm not interrupting dinner, Mr. Tyler."

"No problem."

"I was just wondering if you could stop down at the station tomorrow."

"If you want me to."

"Yes, I'd appreciate that. You can bring counsel if you'd like to."

"Why would I need counsel?"

"Well, I'm going to ask you some questions."

"I see."

"Some people like to have their lawyers present."

"I'll be fine by myself," I said. "Any news?"

"News, Mr. Tyler?"

"About either Trudy or the man in the river."

"If there's any news with Trudy, it's nothing I could discuss with you, Mr. Tyler. And as for the man in the river, we're still checking his prints. We put a drawing of him on all the local news shows. But so far nobody's come forth."

"What time tomorrow, Detective Patterson?"

"How's two?"

"Two's fine."

"I appreciate this, Mr. Tyler. See you then."

When I sat down again, Jan said, "Everything all right?"

"Just routine."

"She wants you to come down tomorrow?"

"More questions, she says. This is pretty routine."

But of course it wasn't routine. Not at all.

Jan obviously wanted to say more but she didn't want to distress the girls.

She finished her supper as quickly as I finished mine, then scooted the girls back to their cartoons.

I came out of the downstairs bathroom and walked to the back door.

"It's getting worse, isn't it?"

She didn't sound angry now—she sounded empty and scared. I wanted to hold her, comfort her but I knew it wasn't the time. I had the feeling that I was looking at a stranger again, as I'm sure she felt about me. There was nothing to say. Not now.

"See you in a while," I said, and left.

IN THE car, a block from my house, my cell phone rang.

"Bingo," Bill Doyle said.

"You found him?" I said,

"We're sitting in front of his place now."

"I need the address."

One of the worst sections of the city, as things turned out, down by the river, in one of those areas that had been fashionable when the city was relatively new about a hundred years ago. Steamboats and darkies endlessly unloading them for a few pennies an hour by the ancient waterway the white man had stolen from the prairie tribes.

"I'm on my way."

"Hurry up. I can't wait to get my hands on the bastard."

I couldn't resist.

"We got our hands on his friend, and look what happened."

He ignored me. "See you in a few minutes."

Everything seemed exceptionally vivid tonight, red stoplights, ice blue neon, mauve mercury vapor lights, even the silver moon and the ebony darkness itself.

A cacophony of teenagers' radios. A thunder of glass-pak mufflers. A cry of screaming tires. Shouts from girls on the street to boys in the cars. Thursday night.

Taco stands and supermarkets, strip malls and miniature golf, five-screen theaters and car dealers, futon stores and bagel bakeries. Drunks and druggies and cops and sleek imposing vans for boomers and their progeny. The city.

The darkness got even darker after a few miles.

The lights were fewer down here, and there were more open areas to consume the available light—the open areas where houses had been torn down. Every half block or so you'd see a vivid orange sign on a darkened house reading STAY OUT: CONDEMNED.

The night was filthy with the smells of garbage, dope, wine, sweat, and car exhaust.

I made sure my doors were locked.

I made sure that I didn't exceed twenty miles per hour.

A number of times, white motorists had been yanked from their cars and beaten, allegedly for endangering lives with their speed.

I hated to stop. There were always a dozen or more black teenagers on corners watching me as I waited for the light to change. I made sure to look straight ahead.

Finally, I reached the block.

I saw the car parked in the center of the block.

I pulled into the space behind it, parked, killed my lights, got out, locked the doors, and then went up and got into the back seat.

"He's in there," Bill said, indicating what had once been a very nice five-story apartment house back in the early part of the century.

Made of stucco, with a long, wide front porch, the apartment house rose with shabby majesty into the night. It had to be one of the tallest buildings in the entire area. Easy to imagine roadsters with rumble seats and flappers with feather boas filling those seats sixty years ago when the building was new. But those days were long gone.

Many of the windows had tape crisscrossing them. The yard glittered with broken beer bottles.

Stucco was missing in many places, a few pieces of it clinging to the walls.

Lights shone on only the first three floors. The windows on the fourth floor were mysteriously dark, as if the electricity hadn't been extended so high.

"You guys ready?" Bill said.

"Absolutely," Neil said.

"Me, too," Curtis said.

"One thing," I said.

"Here comes the sermon," Bill said.

"What were you going to say, Aaron?" Curtis said.

"We stay calm. And I'll do the talking."

"Why you?" Bill said.

"Because I won't hassle him. Is that okay with everybody?"

"Fine by me," Neil said.

"Yeah, me, too," Curtis said.

Then I said, "Where's his car?"

"Down the street," Curtis said.

"You get a look at him?" I said.

"Not really," Bill said. "He parked and walked back to the house here. It was dark. But don't worry. We'll be getting a real *good* look at the sonofabitch in just a few minutes here."

"Bill brought a gun," Curtis said.

"You asshole," Bill said. "I told you not to tell him."

"Why the hell'd you bring a gun?" I said.

"Because we don't know what the hell we're getting into and we may damned well need one. That's why."

"Give it to me."

"Suck my dick."

"I won't go if you bring a gun," I said. "We're in deep shit enough already without another body in the picture."

"You're in deep shit enough already," Bill said. "The cops think you killed that Trudy, and they found your name on the dead guy."

"I won't go, either, Bill, not with the gun," Curtis said.

"I agree with them," Neil said.

"God," Bill said. "Wall to wall pussies in this car. I don't believe it."

"Leave the gun here, Bill," I said.

"Pussies," Bill said again.

He took out the gun, held it up for us to see, and then made a big show of putting it in the glove compartment.

"You guys better get home early tonight," he said. "You'll need your rest for Girl Scout camp tomorrow morning."

Dog turds crunched beneath our feet as we moved toward the front door. We went inside.

The stench turned my stomach over. Food and marijuana and wine and puke and piss and still-stifling night air.

A baby crying somewhere upstairs. A woman screaming at a man somewhere closer by.

A line of mailboxes, the identifying letter of each apartment written in smudged pencil above the box itself. The mail slots were made of metal. Over the years, screwdrivers, knives and jimmies had been used to open them to steal welfare checks.

On one end of the mailboxes was a piece of white adhesive tape that read: MANAGER.

"Boy, there's a job I'd like to have," Bill said, looking around the vestibule. "Manager of this fucking dump."

In the high ceiling and the elegant painted-over woodwork, you could see the faded elegance of the place.

The baby crying again, aggrieved and lonely in the filthy night.

There were only two doors on this level, one on either side of the staircase that rose steeply in the center of the vestibule. There were dog turds on all the steps I could see.

We went up to the lime-painted door that said MANAGER in the same smudged-pencil letters above the mailboxes.

Curtis and Neil kept making faces each time they picked up some new scent.

Bill just looked furious. He wouldn't need a gun to kill anybody.

I knocked on the door, heard nothing, and then pressed my ear to it.

At first, I wasn't sure what I was hearing. Only slowly did I realize that I was hearing gasping. A woman gasping. But in such a way that I couldn't tell if it was pleasure or pain I was hearing. Or maybe pain that was pleasure.

Then the music started, her gasps were now joined by male cries, and then by grunts of girl and grunts of boy, and then it was unmistakably clear what I was hearing.

Two people screwing very dramatically in time to bongo music.

Somebody was listening to a porno tape inside.

I signaled for Curtis to come up to the door.

He did, and bent to listen.

At first, his face was blank. Apparently, he couldn't hear anything.

Then he grinned wide and white.

He took thumb and forefinger and made a circle and then started jamming the forefinger of his other hand in and out of the circle to simulate intercourse.

Neil and Bill stepped up next, pressed their ears to the door.

Neil started doing the bump and grind. Bill simulated masturbation. He made it seem as if he was a foot long.

The cries from the tape became even more insistent now. I no longer had to press my ear to the door to hear them.

And when the cries subsided, and the actors were spent, I raised my hand and knocked.

Silence from the other side of the door.

I knocked again.

Upstairs, a dog barked.

Bill said, "Knock harder. Pound the fuck out of it,"

"Yes, Massah," I said.

Curtis smiled.

The door opened. Just like that. And just like that, sensing it open, I turned and saw him.

I guess I didn't know what I expected the manager of a place like this to look like. He probably wasn't going to look like a candidate for a country club.

But there were poor people who took care of themselves, kept their threadbare clothes clean, their faces shaved and their manners intact. They seemed like damned nice people and you wish they'd get a lucky break now and then.

What I hadn't expected was a tiny man of no more than five feet three inches, weighing no more than one hundred and thirty pounds, wearing only a pair of filthy white briefs and a white body covered almost completely with tattoos. He was so covered, in fact, that he looked like the representative of another species. The filthy white briefs looked like diapers on an overgrown infant.

One more thing about him. His right arm was in a cast and both of his eyes had been recently blackened by violence.

"You guys want something?" he said in a wispy little voice. He sounded like a young girl.

"We're looking for somebody."

"Yeah?"

"Yeah." I described the man I'd seen the other night on the roof of my garage.

Just as I was winding up my description, the videotape started up again in the other room.

"You get yer bony ass in here," a voice shouted from the dark apartment behind the manager.

I couldn't tell if it was male or female.

"That's my wife," the man said. "She's got a real bad temper."

He nodded his head at his arm cast.

"Said I was lookin' at that gal up on the second floor," he said. "Gal went to LA and bought herself a new pair of tits." He grinned. "They're real nice."

"This guy I described, you know him?"

"Sure I know him. But I sure as hell ain't gonna tell you nothin' about him. Him and his friends come down here and try to kill me."

"So they live here?"

"I ain't gonna tell ya that, mister."

"Look, you little cocksucker," Bill said, and tried to shove me aside to get at the manager.

Fortunately, Neil grabbed Bill, and pushed him back.

"Let Aaron handle this," Neil said.

"Yeah, he's doing such a great job."

I watched their faces change. I wondered what they were seeing that could give them such pause, that could turn their faces into the sickening and terrified faces of little boys finally seeing the monster on a horror video.

I turned around to the door again.

The little man was gone.

In his stead was a vast black woman. She had to be six two and weigh three hundred and fifty pounds. She wore a huge and obscene aqua string bikini, the bra cups of which were stained with sweat and grime. Dreadlocks shot from her skull like wriggling greasy snakes.

She was inhaling deeply of a plastic tipped cigarillo.

When she opened her mouth to speak, her mouth literally shone, even in the dim light. All her teeth were gold.

"You askin' him about the vampires?" she said.

"The what?" I said.

She smiled with her gold teeth. "Little pussy. You even bring up the subject, he gets all scared 'n stuff."

"The vampires? That's who we were asking him about?"

She shrugged a massive shoulder. "That's what we call 'em 'cause we never see them except at night."

"I see."

"They're street people. You know, winos and homeless and riffraff like that. They know that sometimes some of these apartments ain't rented for a while, so they sneak up and spend the night there. Usually on the top floor. Don't nobody like payin' rent for them top floor rooms. Too much of a walk, you got groceries 'n shit like that."

"Aren't the apartments locked?" I said.

Her scowl made me feel like the tourist I was.

"Locked? You shittin' me? You think locks would stop these characters? They climb up the fire escape most of the time, and then they jimmy the windows so they can get inside. And as far as locks go, we don't even put no locks on them doors unless somebody's payin' us rent." She smirked. "Locks. Shit. Gimme a break."

And with that, she grabbed her giant breasts, which were rising slowly but certainly out of her grimy aqua cups, and stuffed them back down into the upper part of her bikini. Her sweaty ebony skin glistened.

"So what was you sayin'?" she said, leaning on an elbow against the door frame. She exhaled a long silver plume of cigarillo smoke.

"Actually," I said, "we had a particular person in mind. We wondered if he sounded familiar to you."

"Pale skin?"

"Uh, yes," I said, now that I thought about it.

"Kind of pale blond hair but dirty?"

"Right."

"Dirty clothes?"

"Uh-huh."

She gave me a golden smile. "You just described every single one of them bastards I ever seen. They don't look like they're...Americans or somethin', you know what I'm sayin'?"

I pictured the burglar lashed to the pole in my basement. I saw what she was talking about. He'd had an odd Slavic cast to his features.

"You see any of them around here tonight?" I said.

"Not tonight." She hesitated. "I been busy." Then she turned her head over her shoulder. "And I'm gonna be busy soon as I close this here door. So is that about it?"

"That's about it," I said.

A final golden smile. "He stole somethin' from you, huh?"

"Yeah," I said. "He stole something from us."

At which point, she gave her breasts another giant push upwards so that the tops of her bikini would cinch them tighter inside.

Then she slammed the door on us. Just like that.

WE WENT back out to the porch.

Despite the steamy heat, the air felt cleaner out here than it had inside.

"Anybody got any great ideas?" Curtis said.

"I say let's go search the fourth floor," Bill said. "Two of us, anyway. The other two can check out the back. He may hear us coming and shoot down the fire escape."

"That sounds pretty good," Neil said. "You want to take the backyard with me, Curtis?"

Curtis shrugged. "Sure."

"I wish I had my gun," Bill said.

"Don't start this again," Neil said.

Bill shrugged, angry. "I still say you guys are pussies."

"There goes Bill again," Curtis said, "trying to endear himself."

"C'mon," I said to Bill. "Let's go up there and look around."

THE HEAT and the smells got worse the higher we climbed. So did the noise.

This close, the screaming baby sounded as if it was in mortal danger. You could hear the click of dog nails as the angry dog on the third floor paced back and forth between barks. The woman sobbing sounded beyond consoling. The graffiti got rougher, too.

Now, instead of just dirty words, there were illustrations on the walls, vaginas and cocks dripping jism being the most popular subjects.

In front of one door, I saw a tiny red tricycle, and I felt sorry for the kid who owned it. Growing up in a place like this was unimaginable for a middle-class guy like myself.

A lone red light was the only illumination on the fourth floor. It was like standing in a photographic dark room. An angry wasp slammed at the red bulb again and again.

We stood silent, listening.

All the sounds of the lower three floors drifted up here now.

The heat bathed me in a dirty hot sweat. I wondered if I'd ever feel clean again.

I also wondered if maybe Bill hadn't been right, after all.

Maybe he should have brought his gun along.

Bill nodded to the door marked W with a crooked plastic letter. It was the door closest to us.

Bill stepped forward, pushed the door inward.

Apartment W opened itself to us.

I took out a small flashlight I'd brought along and led the way inside.

Moments later, we stood in the center of a large, empty room. Ironically, this room was cleaner than the hallway, though the graffiti was more striking. There was a large black drawing of a man taking a woman from behind scrawled across the ice blue east wall.

We started to search the apartment, me in the lead because of my light.

I heard something go *snick* behind me.

I glanced back to see that Bill had brought a formidable switchblade with him.

I was glad he had.

The once-white kitchen sink was urine-yellow with stains. The toilet bowl was filled with feces that hadn't been flushed down properly. The bedroom was littered with more used condoms and a small leather whip. Across the tip of it—up close—you could see blood and tiny pieces of dried flesh and hair.

We found nobody. Not a single stick of furniture had been left behind.

Once again, we stood in the hall.

Bill nodded to Apartment X.

This time, I tried the lock. Unlocked, just as the black woman downstairs had predicted.

We went inside.

Furniture had been left behind here, massive and lumpy armchairs and a couch that had been fashionable way back in the fifties.

I played my light over the pinkish slipcover of one of the armchairs. The slipcover appeared to be soaked in old blood.

In the kitchen, we found a freshly dead rat in the sink. Two other rats were eating what remained of its flesh. Blood glistened red on their whiskers. Their eyes gleamed with fear of us—and yet they couldn't stop dining on their former mate.

In the bedroom, Bill found a pink naked doll. Somebody had cut a vagina into its crotch. The vagina was distended and covered with some shiny substance. I tried not to think of the doll being put to human use, as it pretty obviously had been.

We were checking in the bedroom closet when we heard the noise.

Something slamming to the floor.

We stopped.

I tried to figure out where the noise had come from.

Something scraped across the floor.

On the other side of the west wall, I was sure of it now.

The next apartment: Y.

Somebody was in there.

We tiptoed out of X and went on to Y.

I touched the doorknob.

My breath was coming in gasps now, much like the gasps on the porno tapes downstairs.

But I wasn't having nearly as much fun working up my gasps as they had theirs.

The knob turned rightward.

I nudged the door.

We stepped inside Apartment Y.

The first thing I noticed was the filthy yellow air mattress on the floor.

A beer bottle with cigarette ash all over the neck had obviously been used as an ashtray.

I went over to check out a small cardboard box sitting near the air mattress.

There were several photographic proof sheets lying face down inside the box.

A large black spider rested on the white backsides of the proof sheets.

Even when I flicked it away, it moved only reluctantly, as if it was guarding a treasure of some kind.

I turned the proof sheets over and looked at them.

"Oh, my God," I said, a little more loudly than I'd intended to.

"What is it?" Bill stage-whispered back to me.

I held the proof sheets out to him.

He came over and took them from me.

"Shit," he said. "These cocksuckers should be killed."

He hurled the sheets back into the cardboard box. The photographs depicted young—very young, maybe as young as five—girls and boys committing sex acts with each other and with adult men.

Then we heard it again. Something being scraped across a floor.

Because the room was so large, and because it was empty, it was hard to know exactly which closet the sound had come from, the closet on the east wall, or the closet on the north wall.

Bill started communicating through hand gestures. He pointed to the north wall.

I stood up. Nodded.

We went back to tiptoes.

I walked over to the closet. Stopped. Put my hand on the doorknob.

Bill raised his knife, ready to plunge it downward like a dagger.

I tightened my grip on the knob.

I was going to open the door and throw it backwards.

The burglar might well be in there. Armed.

Sweat covered me once again. Bill gave a nod.

I turned the knob, flung the door open, ready to pitch myself to the left of the doorway when the burglar came charging out. Bill would waylay him in front; I'd jump on him from the back.

And that was when the other closet door, across the room, was also flung open.

And the burglar came boiling out of there like a rodeo rider on the meanest bull God ever created.

Bill ran across the wide empty room, grabbing the burglar just as he reached the window opening onto the fire escape.

I saw most of it in silhouette, two dark figures against the grubby electric light of the alley.

Bill raised his knife, the point long and sharp.

But as he was raising it, the burglar brought up a knee quickly, and smashed it so hard into Bill's groin that Bill simply folded in on himself, his knife skittering uselessly across the floor.

The burglar jumped up on the window ledge, forcing the frame upwards, and then tumbled cat-like through the open window.

I grabbed Bill's knife and went after him in the window.

He was still on the fire escape directly outside the window, so I didn't have much problem lunging for him.

I slashed the knife across his arm.

He didn't so much as whimper but I could see, directly beneath the sleeve of his T-shirt, that I'd cut him deeply.

Blood gushed from the wound.

Then he was running and I was shouting to Curtis and Neil, "Stop him!"

I saw them standing in the middle of the alley, looking up at the fire escape.

The burglar was clanging down the fire escape, sometimes taking two steps at a time. He continued to move with cat-like skill.

I wasn't far behind him.

By the time he reached the final eight steps of the metal escape, I was no more than ten feet away from him.

Neil and Curtis waited at the bottom of the steps, ready to leap on him, little more than vague figures in the grubby moonlight.

I started taking two steps at a time myself.

My mind futured ahead a few moments. I saw the burglar reach the ground. Curtis and Neil grab him. Hurl him to the dirt. Take him prisoner. It didn't work out that way.

When he had three or four steps left, the burglar lashed out with his right foot.

He caught Curtis in the throat. Curtis, strangling, crying out, gasping helplessly for air, crumpled to the ground much as Bill had.

Neil was treated to two quick kicks in the ribs and stomach.

He was soon on the ground himself.

Then the burglar was off and running.

I raced down the stairs, jumped over the prone forms of my friends, and started chasing the burglar down the alley.

He knew where he was going, wherever that was. All I could do was follow and hope that I could keep up.

We raced past dumpsters, garbage cans, ancient leaning garages, cats with eyes glowing green in the gloom.

The night was filled with sirens, laughter, cursing, tires squealing. The narrow black alley seemed to go on forever.

I started to stumble once but was lucky and kept my feet.

A hitch developed in my side.

I felt as if I'd been stabbed.

But I was closing on him. By the time we reached the head of the alley, I was close enough to hurl myself at him in a kind of tackle.

I got him around the waist, spun him around, smashed him up against the brick wall of a building. His whole arm was red from the cut I'd given him.

My breath came in dangerous spasms but I had strength enough to bring my fist up and smash him in the face.

I got one good punch in, a solid one to his mouth, but the next time I wasn't so lucky.

Just as I was arcing my fist to collide with his face, he sidestepped me and my hand went straight on into the wall.

Brick ripped flesh. Brick numbed knuckles.

He started to run away again. I was able to turn myself around and grab him by the shoulder.

I slid my arm around his throat and started choking him into compliance.

By this time, we were sweaty and bloody, the both of us, and willing to do anything to win this battle.

He brought up his left hand and hooked it backwards over his shoulder, catching me in the eye.

I screamed, blinded so much that my grip on him slipped. But before he could get away, I was able to grab his hair and slam his head against the brick.

This time, I could feel him wobble, his legs giving out beneath him.

I slammed him back against the wall and brought my knee up between his legs. The pain drove him forward. As he fell toward me I drove my fist into his face. I couldn't feel much. My hand was still numb from smashing into the brick.

They were shouting in the darkness down the alley, my three friends, and starting to pull themselves together.

Moments later, I heard their shoe leather slapping against the ancient bricks of the alley. They were silhouettes in the moonlight, moving ever faster toward us.

I made the mistake of turning my head slightly to watch them run toward me.

And then the burglar returned the favor, seizing my shoulder and jerking me against the brick wall.

He didn't use his knee, he used his fist, a quick and strong one. He pumped it deep into my groin.

I cried out just as he had cried out, and sank downwards, pain blinding me again.

He started running away.

And I started running after him. Where the strength came from, I don't know. Maybe rage can push you beyond your ordinary limits. Maybe rage feeds the soul, and thus the body, like nothing else.

He was running, I was running, and right behind him.

He beat me to the head of the alley by no more than twenty seconds.

If I hadn't stumbled, I would have caught him.

Then Curtis and Neil and Bill were helping me to my feet.

"Let's get him!" I shouted.

He was running again before I had time to gather myself from my fall.

We came around the corner of the alley just as the burglar had, and turned right.

Before us lay four square blocks of empty lots, blocks that had been filled with houses and stores until urban renewal had flattened them a few years back.

In the mauve glow of the mercury vapor lights, I looked out over this forsaken area of the city—it was a pretty damned big area—and wondered where he'd escaped to.

The building on the corner of the alley had a parking lot on the other side. He had gained thirty, forty seconds on us. At most.

But now he was gone.

"Where the hell did he go?" Bill said.

"There's no place for him to hide," Curtis said.

"Maybe a car picked him up or something," Neil said.

"We would've heard it," I said.

"So he just disappeared, is that what you're saying?" Bill said.

I didn't want to argue with Bill at the moment. I was in too much pain.

I stood looking over the empty lots stretching before us. One big sandbox for the neighborhood dogs and cats.

"We're going to nail that bastard," Bill said. "I swear it."

Curtis said, "How about settling for a beer instead?"

WE DIDN'T belong in this particular tavern and the working men who drank there took great pains to make that clear to us.

They'd sort of sneer when they'd walk by, or whisper things about us as they stood along the bar, and then grin with as much scorn as they could summon.

"Maybe we scared him," Neil said. "Maybe he won't bother us anymore."

"I hope so," I said.

Bill was having a glare-down with one of the men at the bar.

"He thinks I'm a pussy," Bill said. "I should go over and change his mind for him."

"Yeah, that's what we need," I said. "A little more violence tonight."

Bill swung around and smiled at me. "You call tonight violent? Listen, babe, you want to know about violence sometime, you ask me about the night my teammates and I kicked the shit out of the Michigan line at this kegger they were having. We crashed it and they weren't very happy to see us."

"He's staring at you again," Curtis laughed, goading Bill on.

"Maybe he just recognizes who you are and is too shy to introduce himself," Neil said.

"Yeah," I said. "Or else he thinks you're cute."

Bill was on his feet. For a moment, I was afraid he was going to start hassling the guy at the bar. Instead, he threw a twenty on the table for the two rounds of beer we'd had, and then walked out. He paused in the doorway for one last glower at his nemesis.

6

A LONE light shone in the kitchen window.
Jan generally left the light on when I was out at night, but now, playing against the crisp white curtains, I saw her shadow moving about.

She was waiting up for me.

One look at me, and she was going to have a lot of questions. And I knew that there'd be no way of putting her off tonight.

I ran the car into the garage and then stepped outside to linger a moment on the dewy grass.

Moon and stars looked crisp. I thought of the Edgar Rice Burroughs books I used to read, of the way John Carter was simply taken up to Mars.

Sometimes Mars sounded pretty good to me. Too bad there wasn't that booming civilization Burroughs had described.

I took a final look at myself.

I'd stopped at a gas station to clean myself up but it hadn't done a lot of good. The knuckles on my right hand were swollen and bruised. The knees of my chinos were torn and blackened with soot and reddened with blood. I had the start of a good-sized welt on the left side of my face.

I stayed a moment longer, taking in the sudden coolness of the evening, and the sweet safe darkness of the shadows. Maybe I could hide out in the shadows the rest of my life. No explanations required for my wife. No alibis required for the cops. No fights with the burglar.

Jan parted the curtains and looked out on the backyard. I could see her face looking at me but not seeing me. Her eyes hadn't adjusted to the darkness yet.

I stepped forward into the spill light from the kitchen and waved to her. I walked up the three steps to the kitchen and stood there in the good light, letting her look at me.

She just stood there looking at me. She came over to me and put out a slender hand and then didn't quite touch me, just left her white hand suspended in front of me.

"You sonofabitch," she said.

"Thanks for the kind words."

She started crying abruptly, tears filling her eyes and streaming down her cheeks. "You sonofabitch," she said again, and then she took me in her arms and said, fighting back more tears, "Now will you tell me the truth, Aaron? Please?"

I just held her for a long moment and then I said, "Yeah. I guess I owe you that, don't I?"

SHE SAID, "Did you have anything to do with that woman being killed?"

"God, are you serious?"

"Well, how would I know otherwise? You may not *be* guilty but you certainly *act* guilty."

I thought about Detective Patterson. Maybe she had the same impression of me. No real evidence of my guilt, but a hunch of it because of the secretive way I was acting.

"I didn't kill her."

"Or sleep with her?"

"Or sleep with her."

"Maybe you'd like to know who called me."

"What's that supposed to mean?" I said.

"Your friend, Detective Patterson," Jan said. "That's who."

"Why the hell is she calling you?"

"She apparently thinks that if she puts a little heat on me, I'll put a little heat on you. Then you'll tell her everything she wants to know."

"She doesn't have any right to do that," I said. "This is about me, not you."

"Well, apparently your friend, Detective Patterson, thinks otherwise."

I sighed and put my hand on her shoulder. She stared at me coldly. "I'm sorry for all this."

"The hell you are, Aaron. You're a lying sonofabitch and you know it!" She looked at me and said, "Do you know how much I hate being lied to? I'd like to tear your fucking face off right now!"

"Jesus," I said, looking at the stranger in front of me. "You're scary— you know that?" and she was, too.

"Tell me the fucking truth, Aaron. That's all I want. The truth."

She scared the hell out of me and I told her everything she wanted to know.

So she got it. All of it. Every single twist and turn, every single nuance of fear and dread, every single hope and prayer.

AN HOUR and a half later, we were in bed, after making sad slow love.

We lay side by side, watching the patterns the street lights made through the trees. The shadows danced on the ceiling.

"It's not too late," Jan said.

"For what?"

"Going to the police."

"Way too late. I'd be disbarred."

"Maybe not."

"For everything I've done? I wouldn't stand a chance."

"You can't live like this, Aaron."

"You mean *you* can't live like this."

My words had been harsher than I'd intended. I took her hand and held it to my chest. Her naked body felt nicely warm and silken next to mine.

"I'm sorry. I shouldn't have said that."

"No, you were right, Aaron. I can't live like this. And neither can the girls. Every time we see a stranger on our block—every time the phone rings—"

She didn't finish. She didn't need to.

"Maybe we scared him off for good tonight."

"Maybe. But even if you did—what about Trudy?"

"Her boss killed her."

"You're sure of that?"

"Sure. Positive."

"Detective Patterson doesn't seem convinced."

"She'll have a confession in the next few days. You watch."

"What if the burglar killed her?"

"Her boss killed her, honey." I rolled over and kissed her. "Things are going to be better. They really are."

"I still think you should talk to Detective Patterson and—"

"Let's just lie here."

"In other words, change the subject."

"Yeah? What's wrong with that? We need some sleep and talking about these things won't help us get any."

"I'd go with you."

"Go with me where?"

"To see Detective Patterson."

Now it was my turn to get angry. I threw back the covers and jerked from the bed. "Get off my ass, Jan. And right goddamn now!"

This time, my words were angry enough to start her crying. She rolled away, as far as she could get on her side of the bed without falling off. I stood there not knowing what to think, to feel. Everything was so different now. I was different now, too, in ways I was afraid to contemplate.

"Honey."

She still wept. "Our lives are never going to be the same again, Aaron. You should've gone to the police."

"I am going to see the police. Detective Patterson."

"You are? When?"

"Tomorrow afternoon. Remember? She called and wants me to stop in."

"What're you going to tell her?"

"Not the truth. It's way too late for the truth," I said.

A great sense of isolation came over me. I felt spurned, banished from my own wife. I'd never felt that before, not once since meeting Jan back at college.

Physically, she was only on the other side of the bed. Spiritually, she was a million miles away.

After a long, dark time I heard her small, wet snores.

And not long after, still feeling isolated, I finally went to sleep myself.

7

I'D NEVER realized it before, but the police station was a central meeting place for all kinds of people. This time of day, it was a busy place.

Housewives paying speeding tickets, lawyers counseling juvenile offenders in the hallway, the recently re-elected safety commissioner walking around glad-handing everybody, victims looking angry, perpetrators looking sullen, TV reporters checking stories...the station was crowded when I got there the next day for my meeting with Detective Patterson.

I waited fifteen minutes before being shown in. I sat in an uncomfortable straight-backed chair in a tiny cove with three chairs and a battered coffee table. The magazines were even older than the ones in my dentist's office.

Next to me was a fleshy middle-aged woman in a cheap orange blouse with a stain on the left arm and a badly soiled yellow skirt. She wore no hose. Her feet looked peasant-big and peasant-dirty in her cheap open-toed sandals. She was sobbing into a handkerchief and trying to talk so low I couldn't hear her.

But I heard every word, of course.

"They're gonna send you to reform school this time," she said to an insolent, muscular boy of maybe fifteen who sat next to her. He wore a tank top so we'd be sure to catch all his tattoos. And he wore his hostility so we'd be sure to know he was dangerous.

The way she was sobbing, I wanted to go over to her and slide my arm around her and comfort her. Her harsh red hands and ringless wedding finger bespoke a hard, grinding life. She was probably not a perfect parent—who is?—but she deserved better than this punk. He was breaking her heart and he didn't give a damn in the slightest. After I finished comforting her, I would extend the fantasy to slapping him around for about three or four hours.

A man in a blue suit came out of a door marked JUVENILE and said, "Mrs. Sullivan. The Captain would like to see you and your son now."

The kid made a protracted, self-conscious ballet out of getting up and following blue suit into the JUVENILE office. He stood up in sections and then lifted a comb from his back pocket and began to comb his hair. He had one of those irritating little rat-tails in back. Then he made sure to bump some chairs and make some noise.

Maybe I'd slap him around five or six hours. My own call came a few minutes later.

Detective Patterson herself came out to greet me.

"I appreciate you coming down," she said, offering me her hand. She wore a white Weskit blouse and a black knee-length skirt and black hose and black one-inch heels. She had very nice legs. She also wore a rather heady perfume. She looked at the welt on the side of my face, the welt the burglar's fist had left.

"Rough night?"

"I fell in the shower."

"That's a good one," she said, making her sarcasm as broad as she could. "I'll have to tell the other detectives about it."

"We're going to do a little fencing today, huh?"

She smiled. "I'm not being a very good host."

"No, you're not."

"Would you like some coffee?"

"That'd be great,"

We walked in through an unmarked door. Eight desks, four against each wall, lay before us. Three of them were occupied with men talking on phones. The desk surfaces looked pretty orderly for an urban homicide department.

In the far corner, a fax machine made monkey sounds as it jerked out its printed pages. In the opposite corner stood a TV set and a VCR set-up. The set had probably seen its share of gory murder videotape.

To the right of a door on the back wall was a Mr. Coffee. Patterson poured coffee into two cups that didn't necessarily look clean, handed me mine, and then opened the door with her free hand.

I followed her inside.

It was the sort of conference room you saw in a lot of small businesses that didn't care much about decor.

A long folding table ran down the center of the room. Six folding chairs flanked each side of the table. The far end of the table had a folding chair, too. The near end had no chair. The buff blue walls were bare. At midpoint on the long table was a large cassette tape recorder. Black. With a cord stretching to a wall plug. Next to the recorder was a pad and pencil.

"Let's sit down by the recorder," she said.

We sat down.

She said, "I'm sort of surprised you didn't bring an attorney,"

I smiled. "That's the nice thing about *being* an attorney. You don't need to bring one."

"You seem to be a cautious man. I guess I'm just surprised you didn't bring a criminal lawyer along."

"I'll be fine."

"This time I'm going to read you Miranda."

"Fine."

She read me Miranda.

Then, "How's the coffee?"

"Not bad at all."

She smiled. "In other words, pretty shitty?"

"Yeah, I guess that's about right."

"I'm going to identify this tape before we begin."

"Great."

She got the tape machine running and then identified herself and the date and then me into the little hand mike. There were two such mikes. One sat in a tiny black plastic holder and was aimed in my direction.

"The first thing I'd like to ask you today is about the dead woman, Trudy."

"All right."

"We've turned up a passing motorist who said he saw somebody running from Trudy's car at the curb. Our motorist says that the figure he saw ran in the direction of your house. In fact, it was his impression—he didn't stop to check it—that the figure ran *inside* your house."

"He's mistaken."

"So you didn't accompany Trudy out to her car when she left your house?"

"No, I didn't."

"You're certain of that?"

"Absolutely."

"Did you go out to her car at any time that night?"

"No."

"Did you go outside at all after she left?"

I thought about that. "No."

"You seem uncertain."

"I just wanted to make sure I was remembering everything correctly."

"And you didn't go outside at any time that night?"

"Not until the two neighbors on Patrol came to my door and said that they'd found a dead woman in the car at my curb."

"They both said that you seemed agitated that night. 'Disturbed' was the word one of them used."

"Of course I was disturbed. They'd told me that Trudy was dead."

"No. Before that. Just when you opened the door. They said that you seemed to be very nervous."

"Then they had the wrong impression."

"And the first time you approached the young woman's car was when you followed them out?"

"Yes."

"All right," she said. She jotted something down quickly on the pad next to the recorder. "Now I'd like to change the subject, Mr. Tyler."

"Fine."

She was watching carefully as she said this, looking for some kind of sign that she was beginning to unhinge me.

"The man in the river."

"Yes," I said. "My name on a slip of paper in his pocket. Front pocket or back pocket?"

"Back pocket."

"Oh. Right."

"We've made an identification from his fingerprints."

"I see."

"A Slavic immigrant. Name was Vaslos. Peter Vaslos. Ever hear of him before?"

"No."

"You sound very certain."

"I am. Peter Vaslos is not a name I'd be likely to forget."

"He had a criminal record. Minor. Arrested for two or three kinds of petty theft. But we think he graduated."

"Graduated to what?"

"We think he became part of a gang that specialized in breaking into homes."

"I see."

She paused before she spoke again. "I want you to answer this next question very carefully, Mr. Tyler."

"All right."

"What were you doing last Sunday night?"

"In other words, the night before Trudy was killed?"

"Yes."

"I was having a poker game in my attic."

"Can you give me the names of the people who were with you?"

"Of course." I gave her the names.

"These are close friends of yours?"

"My best friends."

"Do you play poker often?"

"Just about once a week."

"Always at your house?"

"We rotate."

"Did you hear anything in your house that night?"

"Hear anything?"

"Any noises. Somebody trying to get inside your house."

"No."

For the first time, I began to understand the direction of her questions, and for the first time, I began to realize that she was a lot more cunning than I was.

I felt myself start to sweat. A twitch started in my right hand. I kept the hand pressed against my leg.

"The piece of paper we found in his pocket?"

"Uh-huh."

"We think he'd been watching your place for a few nights and was going to burglarize it."

"I see."

"So you didn't see or hear anything strange Sunday night?"

"No, I didn't."

She parted the pages of the yellow writing pad in front of her.

About halfway down the sheets, she found something and extracted it from the pad.

She pushed it over to me. "This was shot in the morgue."

I stared down at the dead face of Peter Vaslos.

"He doesn't look familiar."

"Not at all?"

"No."

"Was your security system on when you were playing poker?"

"No."

"So maybe he *could've* gotten into your house without you knowing it."

"I don't think so."

"Maybe he got inside and heard you upstairs and then ran out."

"I don't think so."

"So if we were to dust your house for fingerprints, we wouldn't find any of his in your house?"

"Of course not."

"What would you do if you found a burglar in your house, Mr. Tyler?"

"Call the police as soon as I could. I'm afraid I'm not the hero type."

"We believe he was at your place the night of his death."

"But not inside."

"I'm taking your word for that, Mr. Tyler."

"I didn't hear or see anything."

My hand had stopped twitching. I wasn't sure why. Maybe I was getting used to lying.

"You said he was part of a gang," I said.

"We think so."

"Maybe he had a falling out with his gang. Maybe they killed him."

"Maybe, Mr. Tyler. Maybe."

Then she glanced at her watch. "You know what?"

"What?"

"I'm supposed to be in a meeting with the safety commissioner in three minutes."

"You mean we're done?"

She smiled. "You sound relieved, Mr. Tyler."

"Oh, no. I could go on like this forever. There's nothing I like more than being interrogated."

She clicked off the recorder. "You did a very good job." She stood up. "As long as you told me the truth here today, you don't have anything to worry about." She paused. She was wily. "You did tell me the truth here today, didn't you, Mr. Tyler?"

"Sure," I said. "Sure, I told you the truth. Why wouldn't I tell you the truth?"

Five minutes later, I sat in my car in the police parking lot and felt my right leg start to shake. It was going through some kind of hard spasms.

As long as you told me the truth here today, you don't have anything to worry about, Mr. Tyler. You don't have anything to worry about.

8

I DIDN'T notice him until I was about ten miles from home.
He was driving a yellow Buick of eight or nine year vintage. At one point, he got close enough for me to get a glimpse of his face. Or of his hat, anyway. He wore a Cubs cap. The long bill shadowed his face so much that I couldn't pick out any details.

I cell-phoned Jan and asked her if she needed anything at the supermarket.

I'd be driving right by there.

She wanted to know how it had gone with Detective Patterson and I told her just fine. I didn't tell her about Patterson's scenario. A burglar breaking into the house. And then something happening to him.

She wanted to know even more but I said, "You know what we should do?"

"What?"

"Have that picnic for the girls," I said. "There're picnic grounds out next to the fairgrounds. When we finish eating, we can take the girls over to the fair. They'd love it."

"But I don't have anything for sandwiches."

"I'll buy everything at the store. I'll get some ham slices and some wheat bread and some potato chips and some strawberry pop. They love strawberry."

"And don't forget some Hershey bars and some Good 'n' Plenty's and some red licorice."

"I'm kind've overdoing it, huh?"

She laughed.

"Just a little. How about getting some carrots? I'll slice them into sticks and we can put them in the picnic basket."

"I could always get a chocolate cake."

"Why don't you get chocolate and white cake? That way they could alternate slices."

"God, it's good to hear you laugh, honey," I said.

"And it's good to hear you all charged up about something."

I felt a ridiculous optimism about things. I almost felt stoned. "Everything's going to be fine," I said.

"Oh, Aaron, I wish I could believe that."

"You can, honey. You can. Detective Patterson's going to arrest Trudy's boss soon and—"

"Did she say that?"

"Well, not exactly." Another lie: "But she hinted at it."

"She did?"

Lying was a seductive habit: "She said she thought she'd have all this wrapped up in just a few days."

"But that doesn't mean—"

"Of course that's what it means. I didn't kill her, so I'm not going to get arrested. But her boss *did* kill her, and that's why he's going to prison."

"I'm really feeling a little hope now, Aaron. I really am. I just hope it lasts."

"We'll have our picnic, and you'll forget everything else. I promise you."

"I love you so much."

"Me, too, darling. But I've got to run. I'm pulling into the supermarket. See you in a little while."

I spent twenty minutes shopping. I don't usually enjoy pushing a clattering cart up and down supermarket aisles, but this afternoon shopping was a kind of confirmation that I was a free man. And a nice, normal one. What was more nice and normal than shopping?

I hefted too big bags out to the car, wrestled them into the trunk, and then climbed behind the wheel.

I looked in every direction possible but saw no sign of the yellow Buick.

Maybe he'd gotten bored and moved on.

I pulled out of the lot and started the rest of the way home.

A few blocks later, I glimpsed him again.

Following me.

We both sat at a light. This time he was right behind me.

He got cute, and I guess that's what did it. I was sitting at the light, thinking of how he and his friend had changed my life completely, and threatened the well-being of my family.

And then he rammed me.

He was clever enough to ram me gently, making it look accidental.

But it didn't matter. All my frustration and anger and fear overwhelmed me at that moment, and instead of the sensible middle-aged man I usually was, I became this macho teenager.

I became incomprehensibly angry. I was sick of him, sick of the situation, sick of the way my whole way of life had been ruined.

All this started because he and his friend had broken into my house. If only they'd passed on to some other house that night....

I hit the accelerator. No card-carrying teenager had ever laid more rubber than I did that instant.

I knew he'd speed up also. I wanted him to.

And then the game started.

I had no idea where I was going. I was just caught up in some mystical kind of macho contest.

I knew I could easily lose my license for what I was doing but I didn't give a damn. Not at that moment.

I turned to the river road, a twenty mile two-lane run that is extremely dangerous because of its curves.

He stayed right behind me.

Late afternoon, people reluctantly leaving the river to go home, the road was pretty much deserted. Out on the water I could see speedboats and a few sailing craft enjoying the ninety degree heat and the blue blue sky.

I hit eighty-five miles per hour and he stayed right with me.

I took the curves head on, sliding around a few of them, and he did the same.

A couple of times I saw him start to slide and I felt exhilarated.

I wanted him to pile up and die.

Cat-and-mouse we went out the river road, forcing a few slow-moving cars off to the shoulder, but mostly using the empty road to scare each other.

I decided to try a dangerous trick.

I slowed to seventy-five and then just before I hit an especially long curve, I hit my brakes hard and went into a slide.

I knew what I was doing, so I knew what to expect, and to handle the wheel accordingly.

He was totally surprised, so all he could do was jam on his brakes to avoid from smashing into me.

I floored my car and peeled away from him at more than one hundred miles per hour.

He went into a half-spin and then shot across the road.

He missed slamming into a tree by only a foot or so.

His car ran up the hill a good four or five yards before he was able to bring it under control.

I watched all this in my rear view. Smiling.

But he was an intrepid sonofabitch.

A few minutes later, I drove fifty out the river road and caught sight of several teenage girls sunbathing on the beach—a few minutes later he was in my rear view again.

Wily Coyote meets the Road Runner.

He was pissed.

He roared out from behind me and started to pass me just as we came into the curve. Then he turned his wheel hard to forc me off onto the shoulder, inches from plunging into the river.

Then he roared ahead, leaving me to try and keep my car from plunging into the river on my right. I spent a full minute fishtailing along the gravel shoulder before I was finally able to bring my car under control again.

I went around the long curve at a sedate forty-five miles per hour.

I saw him about a quarter mile up ahead. He'd pulled into a farm driveway on, the left.

When he spotted me, he whipped out of the driveway, leaving a storm of gravel dust behind him, and pointed his car in my direction.

I saw instantly what he was up to.

We were going to have ourselves a little game of chicken.

My first instinct was to swerve to the left. If he was going to drive me off the road, I wanted to take the land side. Running up a hill would be better than diving into the river on my right.

But when I started over into the other lane, he was smart enough to floor his car and start roaring straight at me.

The only thing I could do was swerve again, over by the river, to avoid him.

This time, wrestling the wheel of my car, I felt my rear tires start to slide toward the edge. The river was deep and the current fast.

I pulled out of the slide and then stormed back onto the road.

I was beyond rage.

I floored my own car now and charged him at more than one hundred miles per hour.

He must have guessed, properly, that I was in some kind of psychotic state, because he was smart enough to cut across the road himself, the yellow Buick skidding along the edge of the river as he fought to keep it from plunging into the water.

I watched in the rear view as the front end of his car started to dip along the edge of the road. I felt exhilarated again.

I could see people in the speedboats pointing to the Buick that was just about to tip into the water. Through my open window, I could even hear their screams.

He was going to go into the water for sure.

It was going to be wonderful.

Maybe he'd drown before anybody could get him. Then it would all be over.

Trudy's boss would get arrested and the members of the Poker Club would be free once again.

All these happy thoughts went through my head in less than a few seconds. I felt stoned again, positively high about being my old self once more, and having my old life back.

Then two things happened: he somehow managed to regain control of his car, and the motorcycle cop, siren wailing, appeared from nowhere and pulled up alongside the yellow Buick.

He didn't go into the water.

He managed to fight the Buick to a stop before it took its plunge.

The cop started shouting at the burglar as soon as he stepped from the Buick.

The cop didn't notice me. I was parked a tenth of a mile down the road, watching it all.

The cop was too damned mad to notice anything but the man in front of him.

But the burglar noticed me.

He squinted into the sun and looked down the road right at me.

Now he had one more reason to settle his score with me.

WHEN YOU grow up in large cities, you take amusement parks for granted. You have easy access to them in all the warm months.

But out here in the Midwest, you generally see Ferris wheels and tilt-a-whirls and The Demon only once a year, and that's at the time of the county fair.

The fairs are of two very distinct parts.

The first is the part that appeals to the rural folks. There are contests for the best milk cow, beef cow, horse and lamb. There are contests for best pie, best preserves, best beef and best pork recipes. There is new farm equipment, dominated by John Deere Greene, for everybody to see. 4-H has a booth and the Boy Scouts and the Girl Scouts have booths, too. The entertainment runs to rodeos and line dancing and local country and western bands, except for Friday night when a recording star generally performs in what is called the amphitheatre—really just several tall stands of bleachers arranged in a semi-circle.

This is the wholesome half of the country fair, the half that would make Walt Disney weep with joy.

The second part is very different. This is the midway.

Most of the men who run the midway look like street junkies— sallow, tattooed, their clothes grubby and grimy, their eyes steely and glinting, like the eyes of predatory birds. The women seem to come in two sizes, overweight and underweight. A few of the harder women look harder than any of the men. But most of the women just look worn out and long-suffering and even a little bit dazed, as if they can't quite comprehend what has happened to their lives. Because of plastic surgery and its achievements, a lot of the women have balloon breasts. And not just the strippers. You see a lot of tiny waisted, eighty-nine pound women running the cotton candy machines or the ring toss or the automatic rifle game and they've got these enormous science-wrought jugs. There's something sad about it, as if their only possible worth is in the size of their plastic tits.

This part of the county fair is noise, hustle, hype, stench, deceit, and not-so-grand larceny. And I love every moment of it.

As we sat on the far side of the fence, finishing up our picnic food, I listened to the calliope music, and to the clash and clatter of a dozen different games, and a dozen different loud-speaker voices, and a dozen different rides that made a dozen different noises...

...and I couldn't wait to walk the midway tonight.

"Daddy?" Betsy said.

"Yes, honey."

"You're not eating your Twinkie very fast."

"And you're worried that it's going to get all dried out, is that it?" She smiled.

"Put your hand out."

"How come?" she said.

"You know how come."

"Should I close my eyes, too?"

"If you want to."

"I like it when I have to close my eyes."

"All right. Close your eyes."

So she closed her eyes.

"Now put your hand out."

She put her hand out. I placed the Twinkie across her palm.

"Now can I open my eyes, Daddy?"

"Now you can open your eyes."

"Wow! Look, Mommy! Daddy gave me his Twinkie!"

Betsy loves drama. She obviously knew what she was going to find in the palm of her hand. But she had a hard time resisting such a dramatic moment.

"That's nice, Honey," Jan said.

"Thank you, Daddy."

"You're welcome, Hon."

"Can I go on the Demon, Daddy?" Annie said. I glanced at Jan.

"I'll have to take a close look at it," I said, looking back at Annie.

"Can I go, too, Daddy?" Betsy said.

"I'm sorry, Honey," Jan said. "I think you should wait until you're a little older."

"I'm almost five."

"Maybe when you're seven," I said.

I started picking up paper plates and cups. We'd pitch them in the trash bin, put our picnic things away in the car, and then walk over to the fair.

The picnic area was starting to empty now that dusk was setting in. There were a few dozen green wooden tables, as well as a half acre of freshly mowed grass atop of which colorful blankets sprawled.

The littlest kids were winding down for the day. Not even a four year old could keep up such constant frenzy all day long. They'd be cranky by nightfall, and probably in deep sleep by the time the family car pulled into the driveway.

I was just emptying the cardboard box into the trash bin when Betsy tottered over and said, "Please, couldn't I go on the Demon, Daddy?"

I put the box down and picked her up.

"Tell you what. Why don't we find something else you and Annie can go on together."

"Like what?"

"We'll look around when we get over to the midway. How about that?"

She smiled and gave me a wet kiss on the cheek. "Thanks, Daddy."

THE MIDWAY took me back to my boyhood.

I had a paper route from the time I was nine to fifteen. I always saved my winter money for summer fun, and the best summer fun was the midway at the fair.

I liked everything my parents, and all other responsible adults, hated about it.

I liked the noise, the stink, the small larcenies. It was great to stand out in front of the freak show and look at all the fantastic paintings of the creatures inside. I didn't actually go into the show until I was fourteen, and that one trip ended forever my interest in freaks.

But the rest of the sleazy circus was just fine. In our group of kids, we always tried to see who could go to the fair the most times in one week. My fifteenth year, I went seven days in a row.

These days, the magic wasn't quite as startling or bedazzling.

At night like this, the fair was mostly crowded with teenage couples. Every once in a while, I'd see a teenage boy with his hand on his girl's butt and I would try to imagine one of my daughters with such a kid. In order to take out my daughters, he would have to fill out this 35 page questionnaire I'd worked up. And I certainly wouldn't want him to walk around groping my daughter the way those boys groped those girls.

We bought cotton candy, strawberry pop, popcorn and caramel apples. No wonder dentists are so wealthy.

And then we came to the Demon.

You stood inside what appeared to be a circular coffin made out of plexiglass. You were whirled around inside that coffin at a very high rate of speed. People just getting off the ride had a hard time finding their legs. They wobbled and a few almost fell over.

"Are you sure you want to do this, Honey?" I said.

Annie nodded solemnly. "Chrissie did it and she's two months younger than I am."

I laughed. "Well, now there's a good reason to do something." I looked over at Jan. She seemed tense about the whole thing. "Tell you what," I said, "I'll let you go if I can go with you."

"Oh, Dad," Annie said. "That would look clunky."

Clunky was the word for the summer. It apparently covered everything that was bad.

"I'm afraid that's the only way you're going to get on that ride, Sweetheart." Jan was nodding. She looked relieved.

The Demon coffins were just starting to load up.

"Sweetheart," I said to Annie. "It's up to you."

She sighed deeply. "Oh, I guess so."

Joan of Arc couldn't have sounded more put upon.

"I could go with her, Daddy," Betsy offered nobly.

Jan pulled Betsy to her and said, "You're staying here with me, Kiddo."

We paid our money and we took our chances.

Annie was adamant about strapping on her own safety belt that cinched you into a standing position.

I hooked mine up and then reached across the two foot space separating us. I took her hand.

She gave me a little squeeze, then quickly withdrew her hand.

Wasn't this whole thing clunky enough without having to hold hands with your father, who was probably about the clunkiest guy in the whole universe anyway?

The first couple of minutes weren't so bad.

There was some shaking, left to right, up and down, but nothing to jar the bones or force a scream.

In fact, the ride was gentle enough that I had the ability to look down—we were about one story in the air—and watch Jan and Betsy watching us.

I noticed the man immediately. I'm not sure why.

The second burglar, like the first, was slender and fair and Slavic.

This man was bulky and had dark hair and a moustache and heavy, black horn-rimmed glasses. He wore a tan leisure suit that had last been fashionable when I was still in college.

I watched as he edged closer and closer to Jan and Betsy. They were totally oblivious to him. They were part of a larger group of people who were watching the Demon at work. And he was just one more unremarkable member of that group.

I kept trying to figure out why his presence alarmed me. But the alarm had been immediate and certain.

And then he went away. Just vanished. And I knew that I had experienced yet another paranoid run.

Then I didn't have time to think about anything other than not barfing up my picnic dinner.

The Demon proved worthy of its name,

Indeed, indeed.

I think I was screaming before Annie was.

The ride was like being trapped inside a giant cocktail shaker.

We were thrown violently leftward, then violently rightward, then turned upside down and shaken.

For a horrifying moment, I had the sense that the coffin was going to shake loose of its moorings, and we'd go flying out over the fair, to crash to our death somewhere in the darkness surrounding the grounds.

You read about such things two, three times a year.

Maybe this would be one of them.

The measure of the Demon's ability to frighten its riders was Annie's hand. It pushed itself inside mine, and clung there desperately.

"I'm scared, Daddy!" she shrieked.

"So am I!" I wanted to shriek. But as a card-carrying member of the Parents' Club I, of course, couldn't admit to anything so prosaic as fear.

"Honey, everything's fine!" I shouted back. "This is just part of the ride!"

She spent the rest of the ride screaming.

I didn't blame her.

And then it ended, abruptly, the way these rides often do.

One moment you're being hurtled to your death, the next moment you're unstrapping your safety belt and trying to regain your composure.

I was just as bow-legged, and just as wobbly, as everybody else who had exited the Demon. Jan and Betsy were pointing at us and laughing.

Annie was clinging to me, her arm around my waist, literally trying to hide behind me. I wondered why.

I looked for the man in the leisure suit and the dark glasses. He was nowhere around.

I relaxed and led the way to Jan and Betsy, dragging Annie behind me.

"Remind me to never eat a hot dog again before I go on a ride," I said. "It almost came back up."

Then Jan became aware of how Annie was hiding behind me.

"You all right, Hon?" Jan said.

I felt Annie's body tense against mine. And then heard her start stuttering out reluctant tears.

"Oh, Sweetheart, what's wrong?" Jan said, going to her instantly.

By now, Annie was crying full force.

I gently eased her away from me, so that her mother and I could get a good look at her.

I saw immediately what had happened.

There was a small dark stain near the crotch of her buff blue walking shorts. She'd wet herself on the Demon.

"Oh, baby," I said, my heart breaking. I wanted to pick her up and ride her off to some magic kingdom where nice little girls didn't have to suffer such embarrassments.

Then I realized that there was probably a simple solution to this.

"Pull out your shirt, Annie," I said.

Jan had bought the girl's summer clothes about a month ago. I remembered her saying that she was buying Annie's clothes a size larger than she needed because Annie was growing so quickly.

Annie just looked up at me.

"Here, Sweetie," I said, and leaned down and pulled the ends of her shirt out. This was a dark blue golf-style short-sleeved shirt.

As I'd hoped, the ends were long, reaching the bottom of the shorts. With her shirt out, nobody could tell she'd had an accident at all.

"Great," Jan said. Then, "I'm going to take her to the bathroom and clean her up. We'll be right back."

"I'm sure glad I don't wet my pants anymore," Betsy said.

While we waited, Betsy looked up and down the midway at rides she could possibly go on.

The trouble was, the rides for kids her age didn't interest her at all. She wanted the rough rides for older kids.

So then she turned in the opposite direction and started looking at the tent show. She was fascinated by the paintings on the exterior canvas of the freak shows.

Then, "That looks like Dracula, that picture of that man."

"Yeah, I guess it does."

"What kind've place is that, Daddy?"

"It's called the Tunnel of Horrors. You sit in one of those cars and they take you through the tunnel and then monsters jump out at you."

"Will Freddy Kreuger be in there, Daddy?"

I'm always amazed at the knowledge of popular culture my daughters have. This is something you pick up when you watch TV as much as they do. We try to steer them toward better fare on the tube, but they're tainted with their fathers' taste. I grew up loving horror movies and crime movies and westerns. They pretty much like the same things. Annie seems especially enamoured of *Have Gun, Will Travel*, which is certainly one of the most violent TV westerns ever run.

Jan was back with Annie in tow. A smiling Annie.

Jan said, "Why don't we find a ride for Betsy and then think about going home? I don't know about you, but these old bones of mine are ready to give out."

"Tunnel of Horrors, Mommy! Tunnel of Horrors!" Betsy said.

"What's the Tunnel of Horrors?" Jan said.

We walked in that direction.

"You sit in one of those little red cars," I said, "and a chain pulls you through the tunnel. And monsters jump out at you."

"She's four years old," Jan said, as if I'd lost my Parents' Club membership.

"I'm almost five, Mommy! Couldn't I go? Couldn't I?"

"I'll go with her," Annie said, protectively. "We'll sit in the same car together."

I looked at Jan.

"I can't see the harm if Annie goes with her."

"We'll sit right up close together," Betsy said. "Won't we, Annie?"

Annie nodded.

"Well," Jan said.

"It's perfectly safe," I said.

Jan looked down at Betsy. "You remember when we rented *Snow White* and you kept having nightmares about it?"

"I wasn't very old then, Mommy. Now I am."

"Boy, how can you argue against logic like that?" Jan said.

She frowned in my direction and said, "But if you have nightmares tonight, your daddy'll have to go get you, all right, Daddy?"

My membership in the Parents' Club had been restored.

I was still nervous about letting the girls go on the ride but I looked carefully around the midway. I didn't see any sign of the man I'd seen from the Demon.

"All right," Jan said, tearing two tickets from the bunch we'd bought at the front gate. "One for each of you."

Betsy looked especially cute accepting her ticket. She put forth the palms of both hands, as if her mother were going to set something very heavy on them.

"Just remember to stay together," Jan said.

I walked them up to the ticket taker and then walked back to stand with Jan. Just as they were handing over their tickets, Betsy glanced back at us, looking uncertain of what she was doing. One of the 'monsters' had just screamed over the PA system. To a four year old, the sound must have been bone-chilling.

"I hope this is a good idea," Jan said.

"It's like camp, honey."

She shot me with an elbow. "You always bring that up."

"It's true. Every time we send Annie off to camp, you worry if we've done the right thing. And she's always been fine, hasn't she?"

But she wasn't paying attention. She was bobbing up and down, left and right, looking for the girls.

"I don't see them," she said, anxiety in her voice.

"That's because those adults are behind them in line. Just watch the platform where the cars are. They'll be up there in a few seconds."

And so they were.

The cars resembled roller coaster cars, complete with bars to keep you from falling out.

The girls reached the platform and looked out at us, waving.
Jan waved back.

"They look so little."

"Honey, they'll be fine."

"Wave."

"I am waving."

"Oh." She glanced at me and smiled. "I just love them so much. I
want everything to be perfect for them."

"I know, honey." I gave her a squeeze.

And that was when the little kid, stumbling on ahead of his parents,
tripped into me and poured his cherry drink all over my tan chinos.

I now had myself another pair of chinos for doing household chores.
Whenever I stained chinos, they went into that part of the closet reserved
for work clothes.

The family was black and very nice and very apologetic.

"Let me take down your name and pay for the dry cleaning," the
wife said.

The boy, who was probably about Annie's age, looked frightened.
He stood very close to his father.

"There's no need for that," I said.

I wondered if I'd be this pleasant with a white family. Maybe their
color intimidated me. I didn't want to look like a racist.

But then the father said, "Greg, tell the man you're sorry."

And the kid promptly did it. Stepped right up to me. And said,
"Geez—I'm sorry, mister."

He was a slight kid, nicely dressed in a red golf shirt and black
walking shorts and a pair of white Reeboks.

"You didn't do it on purpose."

"Please let us pay you something," the wife said.

"No problem, really," Jan said.

"If you're sure," the husband said.

"We're sure."

We all nodded good-bye. The family went off and we turned back
to see how our daughters were doing.

"They seemed nice," Jan said.

"Very nice."

"Except you are going to need a new pair of pants."

I nodded.

The ticket seller was just saying, "No more tickets sold for this ride, folks! Sorry, but the cars are all filled up!"

At first, I couldn't find Annie and Betsy up on the platform. The cars had moved, some of them already into the mouth of the tunnel, which was shaped like the mouth of a monster opening wide in mid-scream.

Jan was having the same trouble I was.

"Do you see them anywhere?" she said, her voice edged with deep dark parental fears.

"They're probably in one of the cars that moved near the mouth," I said. "Let's walk over here. Maybe we can see them better from a different angle."

As we squeezed our way through the crowd—most of them parents who were watching their children the same as we were—the cars were jolted with electricity. They were ready to start moving.

"There," I said, after we'd shifted several yards to our left. "There they are."

Because of the angle, we couldn't see much of their faces. They were just two little girls sitting in the cars, all four hands on the safety bar, their grip indicating that they were a little apprehensive about the trip before them.

Shrieks and ghoulish laughter continued to pour from the mouth of the tunnel.

The cars started to move. And just as they did so, I recognized the man in the car behind them. The same man I'd seen near Jan when I was on the Demon with Annie. Dark hair. Moustache. Black horn-rimmed glasses. Tan leisure suit.

Now he was sitting directly behind my daughters.

He shouldn't have been there.

The cars began moving faster, disappearing into the black portal of the tunnel.

"Are you all right?" Jan said. She'd obviously been watching me.

"Fine," I said. I would have told Jan but I didn't want to frighten her.

"You sure? You look kind've funny."

"Just the heat, I think. I'm ready for air-conditioning and a nice, cold beer."

I was babbling, saying anything to distract her from the terror I was feeling.

As we stood there watching them, the heat and noise and shabby splendor of the midway started to repel me for the first time in my life. Jan took my hand. With the other, she waved at the girls, even though they couldn't see her.

Before she could say a word, I was squeezing through the crowd, pushing and shoving my way to the platform. Rusty hinges on old doors squeaked. Screams male and female. Incessant insane laughter.

You could hear, in between the mechanical screams, the real screams of the kids.

By now, bogeymen of all sorts would be popping out at them as the cars were tugged through the darkness.

Then I recognized Annie's scream and knew that this wasn't theatrical at all. She was really in some kind of danger.

I couldn't take it anymore. "Wait here!" I said to Jan.

The barker looked shocked to see me.

"Hey, pal, you'll just have to wait your turn. Ride's already started."

I saw people pointing at me, buzzing about the weirdo who was up there hassling the barker on the platform. Not even midways were fun anymore. Too many drunks and druggies wandering around.

"I want you to stop this ride!" I said.

"What the hell you talkin' about? We just started!"

Anticipating that he wasn't going to cooperate, I looked around the platform for the levers that stopped and started the machinery.

When I saw them, I started moving toward them. Fast.

He saw where I was going.

He was a slender guy in a grubby white short-sleeved shirt and dark dusty trousers. His thinning hair shone with grease. He smelled of heat and acrid sweat.

He ran ahead of me, put himself in front of the levers like a man defending his most prized possession.

I moved slightly to my right, hoping to fake him out. But he wasn't about to be faked cut. He moved to his right, too.

By now the crowd was shouting at me, booing me as if I was a villain in a professional wrestling match.

I took another lunge toward the lever, this time to my left.

But he was there, too.

I heard Annie's scream again.

It would take too long to wrest the lever from him. I had no choice but to go into the tunnel with the cars moving.

I turned around and ran across the platform to the mouth of the tunnel.

The barker was right behind me.

When he saw what I was going to do, he leaped on my back, trying to slow me down.

We wrestled for a long moment and then I finally put my fist deep into his stomach. It was enough to knock him off balance. He stumbled to one knee.

I ran into the tunnel.

Blackness. Screams.

The floor, which had been put together in sections, wobbled beneath me.

The air was rich with the scent of motor oil and the day's dying heat.

I followed the tracks of the cars, the angle of which I could see thanks to the light that seeped in through the cracks where the walls joined in back.

As I ran, I tripped the signals that launched the horrors of the tunnel.

Frankenstein's head popped out at me. After a few more yards, Dracula's visage appeared before me, his face bathed in an eerie green light.

The last monster I saw was a skeleton that dropped down from the ceiling and did a bony jig for me.

I pushed on past.

Thanks to the seams in the back walls, light was becoming a little more plentiful.

I saw the shape of the cars in front of me. All the kids were screaming now.

They were stopped to let a Freddy Kreuger look-alike threaten them with his knife-like fingers. He made an animal growling sound.

"Girls! I'm coming to get you!" I shouted but they didn't seem to hear me.

As Freddy's light, a blood red color, bathed the monster, I saw the man reach into the car ahead of him and grab Betsy. He must have been trying to nab her almost from the first moment of the ride. That's why Annie was screaming so hard.

The man got hold of Betsy, lifted her up, tucked her under his arm like a football, and then proceeded to work his way out of the car and toward the outline of a door behind him.

Annie kept hitting him and screaming. And Betsy started screaming, too.

All the other onlookers were frozen in place. Not one of the teenage boys lifted a hand to save my daughter.

A two-foot wide strip of wood separated the track of the cars from the black wall.

I heard somebody shout my name. Jan was there, shouting angrily at the man—he was now at the back door, Betsy still under his arm. "You bastard!" Jan screamed, "Let her go!"

Annie followed him, trying in her little-girl way to hurt him with her desperate punches.

I ran along the space between track and wall and when I got within three feet of him, I dove for him.

I was able, in that moment of surprise, to grab Betsy from him. I set her down. She ran to where Jan was standing with Annie a few feet behind me.

I got him around the waist, the way a tackle would, and slammed him into the wall.

I was able to put one good punch on his face. He groaned beneath the force of it.

He twisted away from the next punch so I started hitting him in the body. I wanted to kill him and that was obvious in the way I was grateful to damage him in any way I could. All the rage I'd accumulated over the past few days was freed in me now.

I grappled to my feet and slammed two hard kicks into his ribs.

I reached out and grabbed the man's hair. And it came off in my hand.

A wig.

Even in the gloom here, I could see the blond hair beneath the wig. The moustache would come off, too. As would the black prop eyeglasses.

And then I'd be looking at my old friend, the second burglar.

He scrambled to his feet and started for the outline of the back door.

He wasn't going to get away. I was going to stop him.

I felt my legs move up and down twice, and then Betsy was screaming, and I was falling. I'd stumbled over my youngest daughter who had, in fear, crawled in front of me somehow.

The trick now was not to fall on top of her.

I managed to get my hands out in front of me so that I'd absorb most of the fall.

I slammed into the back wall with such force that the entire tunnel shook. I had an image of the whole place crashing down on us in shaky sections.

The back door burst open.

Through the doorway, I saw a starry night sky and a long section of grass leading to cyclone fencing beyond.

I reached down and picked up the sobbing Betsy, and held her as I rushed to the door.

The man was gone. Right now, he'd be on the midway, working his way up front to the exit gate. Then he'd vanish.

"He tried to take Betsy!" Annie said. "And nobody would help us!"

I kept Betsy in my right arm, letting her lie her teary face on my shoulder, and with my free hand I held onto Annie.

It was time for the Tyler family to go home.

As we walked out of the tunnel, two beefy, sweaty security guards in dusty blue uniforms ran up. "What happened here? Are your little girls all right?"

"You're a little late," I said, angry that they hadn't been here sooner. We pushed on past them.

9

IN THE back seat, the girls went over and over their encounter with the man in the Tunnel of Horrors.

Annie put forth the notion that maybe the man wasn't a man at all, but a monster. They then discussed, in earnest detail, a monster movie they'd recently seen on HBO.

"And you know what they did to the monster, Daddy?" Annie said.

"No. What?"

"They burned him all up."

In the front seat, next to me, Jan stared out the window. She looked solemn and tired, as if she had been depleted of all energy.

An easy listening station played low on the radio.

I know that's hopelessly square, but there are times when rock and roll is too frenetic and classical music is simply too heavy. Then, it's very nice to listen to an airy little tune by Olivia Newton John or Natalie Cole.

"You all right?" I said.

"He tried to kidnap our daughter." Her small hands were white-knuckled fists in her lap.

"We need to call Detective Patterson and call her now."

"I've got a better idea."

"I'm sick of your better ideas."

I felt intimidated, the girls in the back seat. But at the moment, they were too engrossed in bad men to pay attention to their parents.

"I think you and the girls should go back to your parents."

"No, dammit!" she said.

This time, the girls did pay attention.

"Mommy's mad," Betsy said. "About the bad man. He really scared me."

We drove on, said nothing for many traffic lights.

I said, "I think that'd be best."

"I think telling Detective Patterson the truth would be best."

I looked over at her. "You're going to support the girls while I'm up the river?"

Betsy said, "How come Daddy's going up the river, Mommy?"

On a summer night like this one, the Dairy Queen was a popular place. There were at least fifteen people in each line, and there were two lines. Most of them were teenagers of the nerdier sort. The cooler variety wouldn't be found at DQ. They'd be out in their hot cars guzzling beers and copping cheap feels off their nubile girlfriends.

I pulled in and gave Annie three one dollar bills and told her to get what she and Betsy wanted. Annie piled out of the back seat immediately. But Betsy didn't move. "I'm scared, Daddy. Maybe the bad man's out there."

"You'll be fine, honey," Jan said. "We can watch you from here."

Annie put her hand out and Betsy took it and slid across the seat and out the door.

"Are you going to call Detective Patterson when we get home?" Jan said after the girls left.

"No," I said.

She stared out her window again.

"You're really not going to call her?"

"I can't afford to. You know that."

She swung her face back toward me. Her eyes were blazing.

"A man tries to kidnap your daughter and you can't even call the police?"

"Detective Patterson would have questions."

245 ♠ THE POKER CLUB

"Of course she'd have questions. It's her job."

"She'd want to know who the kidnapper was, and I'd have to tell her."

"This is our *daughter* we're talking about, Aaron."

"Do you want to see me go to prison?"

Her sigh was long and sad and in the middle of it I noticed the way her slender hand was twitching. Nerves.

I felt like hell. I loved this woman. And I'd managed to destroy her life.

"I'm worried for the sake of the kids," I said.

"Are you? Sometimes I'm not sure."

It was the wrong thing for her to say. I slammed my fist against the steering wheel. The horn accidentally sounded. Everybody lined up at the windows looked at us.

"Don't ever say that to me again, Jan. Ever." I talked as normally as I could but the people in line were watching us now. "I'm trying to hold this family together," I said. "If I got disbarred, our lives would be over. Everything we have planned for the girls—good colleges especially— would be shot in the ass."

But she wasn't impressed. She looked at me and said, "The fucker tried to kidnap our daughter, Aaron."

Before I could reply, the girls were back.

Betsy had already managed to drip DQ all over the front of her blue shirt.

"It's melting, Daddy," she said, as she crawled into the back seat, her cute little hands glistening with sticky goo.

"That's because it's so hot, Sweetheart," I said.

"It's all over my *fingers*," she said.

"Yeah, I noticed that."

As I spoke, I glanced at Jan.

Tears filled her eyes.

I put the car in gear, backed out, drove home.

THE PLANE left at eleven that night.

This gave us about ninety minutes to get everything packed.

Jan got the girls ready to go first and then went into our room and started filling her own bags.

"Anything I can do to help?" I said in my best toadying voice.

"I'd just as soon you wait downstairs," she said, not looking at me.

I TOOK the girls' bags down to the van and loaded them into the back.

The whole thing felt illicit somehow, packing up a van at this time of night.

Bed should be the destination of sweet little girls this time of night. Not the airport.

Back in our room, I said, "I got the girls all ready."

She finished folding a blouse and setting it almost reverently into her last suitcase. She still hadn't looked at me.

Then her head came up and she said, "I don't want to hear from you for a while, Aaron."

"All right." I didn't know what else to say. I felt crushed, and isolated again.

"I just need time to think."

"I know, honey."

"I just keep thinking about Betsy tonight. How close he came to—"

"But he didn't, honey. And that's the point. He didn't. This whole thing'll pass. It really will."

"It will? When? When he breaks in again and kills one of us?"

"He'll get tired of chasing us, honey. He'll go on to something else."

"How can you say that after tonight?"

She brought the lid of her suitcase down with great violence. She slammed the halves together and then locked it.

"I'll take those down for you," I said, nodding to her suitcases.

She was still furious. "I don't want you to be nice to me, Aaron. I want you to figure some way out of this whole situation for us. I'll be afraid to ever let the girls out of our sight."

So will I, I thought.

I went over to her and slid my arm around her waist and brought her to me.

She was playing her version of statue.

She didn't slide her arm around me. Nor did she respond when my lips touched hers. A cold, unmoving statue.

"I'm afraid I don't feel like kissing you right now, Aaron."

I hefted her bags and took them down to the car.

As I passed through the living room, I noticed the girls on the couch. They were both sleeping.

They'd never looked more precious or vulnerable.

ON THE way to the airport, I had a brief scare.

In the rear view, I thought I glimpsed the Buick the burglar had last driven. Uncontrollable anger seized me.

I worked my hands so hard on the steering wheel, I felt I had the power to snap it in two.

"Is everything all right?" Jan said.

"Fine."

"You don't look fine. You look angry."

"Just relax. Everything's fine."

But she kept on watching me.

She leaned over and whispered, "Is he following us?"

I had to tell her the truth. I whispered back, "I'm not sure."

She shook her head. Her hands made fists. "Oh, great. Just great, Aaron."

Though we were whispering, both girls were actually asleep in the back seat.

A few blocks later, at a stoplight, I was able to see that the car two blocks back wasn't the burglar's Buick. While it was the same year and model, and while the colors were quite similar, it was a different car.

"It's not him," I said,

"You're sure?"

"Positive. So now we can relax."

"Relax? Are you kidding, Aaron? Relax after what happened to Betsy?"

THE AIRPORT was closing down for the night.

The flight to Des Moines was one of the last planes out.

The girls zombie-walked their way through the airport, yawning every few yards. Usually, they enjoyed the airport, and insisted on seeing every inch of it.

I walked them up to the gate.

"Now you be good girls for Mommy," I said.

"Grandpa said he's going to take us miniature golfing the next time we come back," Annie said. "This'll be next time, won't it, Daddy?"

"It sure will, Pumpkin."

"He said we could roast wieners, too," Betsy added sleepily.

"You're going to have a good time," I said.

The loud speaker voice sounded lonely tonight as it announced last call.

"I'll call you tomorrow," I said to Jan.

"I'd rather you didn't."

I was going to try and kiss her but she seemed to sense this and started moving toward the metal detector. She walked all the way down there, a daughter on each hand, without looking back.

I STOOD outside watching the plane take off.

After a minute or so in flight, it banked westward and then disappeared into grey clouds the moonlight gave a silver glow.

I felt lonely standing there, the airport shut down for the night, the three people I loved most on the entire planet being forced away from their home.

I TOOK a quick shower and wandered downstairs for a drink of whisky.

I was sitting in the recliner, watching the end of a Jay Leno show, when the phone rang and woke me.

I cleared my head and then reached over and picked up.

"Hello."

Silence, the familiar silence, the soft steady breathing on the other end. The presence.

"The next time, motherfucker," I said, "I'm going to kill you. You understand me?"

I slammed the receiver down.

I was afraid I wasn't going to sleep. The call had upset me. Images of the Tunnel of Horrors came back. We'd come so close to losing Betsy.

Sleep was no problem.

Within five minutes of putting head to pillow, I fell into a dreamless, exhausted sleep.

I had no idea what time it was when the phone rang again. But I certainly knew who it would be.

Receiver in hand, I was just about to swear when Bill's voice said, "You have to get up, Aaron. And get over here."

I was still mostly asleep and couldn't quite decipher the exact meaning of the words. Bill seemed to be speaking in a different language.

"Get up? It's the middle of the night."

"They just found him about a half hour ago."

"Found who? What're you talking about, Bill?"

"Goddammit, Aaron. Wake up. They just found Neil."

"Neil?"

"Yes, Aaron, he's dead. Do you understand what I'm saying? He's dead, Aaron, and I know who fucking killed him, too."

"I know who killed him, too." I woke up enough to tell Bill what happened that evening at the fair.

Less than five minutes later, still buttoning my shirt, I was on the way down the stairs and out of the house.

PART THREE

1

THIS LATE at night, I was surprised by the size of the crowd. They were lined all the way up the incline to the top of Durham Hill itself. They would have reached the hill but all the emergency vehicles— and one extremely intimidating cop—kept them back. This was the Northeast end of the city's biggest park, the one with a zoo for the summer and a huge ice skating rink for winter.

There was a second surprise waiting for me as soon as I got out of the car: Detective Patterson stood over by an oak tree talking to Curtis and Bill.

Between the police cars and the TV lights, the grassy area leading to the edge of the hill was well lit. The grass looked brown and dead under the steady glare. Along the edge of the forest, which swept from east to west, you could see the glint of creature eyes watching it all. Apparently, even God's humblest creatures enjoy a good melodrama.

When Patterson saw me, she waved me over.

The cop with the hostile face had been on the verge of pushing me back until he'd seen Patterson's wave. But even then he didn't look all that happy about letting me part the yellow barrier of CRIME SCENE tape.

The night was hot, with no breeze for relief, and smelled of car oil and cigarette smoke.

Detective Patterson looked fetching tonight in her crisp white blouse and blue walking shorts and Reeboks.

When I reached them, I nodded and said, "What happened?"

Bill hadn't told me much on the phone. Just the location and that they'd found Neil. Dead.

"He was hiking," Bill said. "And in the dark, I guess he just didn't see the edge of the hill."

The drop was a sheer sixty, seventy feet to an asphalt road below. This area was part of the Nature Trail used by city slickers like ourselves. The Trail itself was twelve miles long, should you be so inclined to walk its entire length. In a fit of insanity. Walking out here was Neil's ultimate relaxation, especially now that his daughter was old enough to leave alone at night.

I walked through the dead grass to the edge of the hill. I was only a few yards away. Two crime lab people were down on their haunches searching the grass for anything that would help their investigation. A third man was spraying a small area of buffalo grass.

I stood on the edge and looked down.

There were several more emergency vehicles down there, and a white boxy ambulance.

In the center of the road, almost straight down, was a white sheet stained with blood.

A circle of human beings—who looked small and frenetic from up here—stood around the body.

And beneath the sheet was Neil.

I closed my eyes and thought about him for a moment. I suppose it was a kind of prayer. I thought of his guilt for cheating on his wife when she was already sick. I thought of how hard he'd tried to be a good father, and how he felt he'd failed at the attempt. He'd been a decent man, Neil had, and for a selfless moment there I mourned him purely— didn't think about the burglar, or how Neil had come to die, or what our next move would be. I just thought about Neil and his sweet wife and daughter, and how terrible this would be for her.

"I guess he had a lot of experience."

I'd been deep enough in thought that the words startled me.

"You sure get around," I said.

Detective Patterson shrugged. "I happened to stop down at the precinct when this came up. I recognized the name and thought I'd stop by out here."

She peered down over the edge.

"Your friends say he was a nice guy."

"The best."

"Funny he'd just step off a cliff that way."

"It happens."

She studied me.

"Yes, I suppose it does."

Then: "So you don't have any doubt it was an accident?"

I had to be careful.

"No, I don't, Detective Patterson. Do you?"

"Nothing I could prove."

"Are there any signs it wasn't an accident?"

"Not so far," she said.

She stared down at the road below.

"He's got a daughter."

"Right," I said.

"And he lost his wife to cancer a couple of years back."

"Yeah, he did."

"The poor guy."

I half-suspected she was being sincere. I supposed it was possible. Every once in a while, we all get overwhelmed by how some people just seem to have terrible luck. We have an insight into the dark forces of the cosmos that seem to pull our strings like malevolent puppeteers.

The reincarnation folks explain it as making up for being less than sterling in a previous life. But it was hard to imagine Neil—who really had been a sweet, sweet guy—being bad in any incarnation.

Mosquitoes started supping my blood. I slapped a few against my arms.

Patterson asked, "Have any of you talked to his daughter?"

"I stopped by to check on Rachel and gave her the news. I told her I'd stop back tonight," Curtis said.

"We were able to locate a Mrs. Rabinowitz," Detective Patterson said.

"His sister."

"Right. She has Rachel now."

"She's a very nice lady."

They left the sheet on him when they got him up on the gurney. I was glad. I didn't want to see his face.

"Anybody really hate him?" she said.

"No."

I didn't want to watch the grisly activity below but I couldn't seem to pull away.

"He ever mention anybody threatening him or anything like that?"

"No."

I let my gaze wander out over the river onto the other side of the road. Moonlight had blessed the water with a silver glow. The white birches on the far shore were dark and mysterious silhouettes.

She said, "He was there that night."

I turned and looked at her. I knew exactly what she was talking about but I needed to pretend I didn't.

"Was where what night, Detective Patterson?"

"Your house. The night of the poker game."

"Oh, that night. Yes. Yes, he was."

"Do you think he knew anything about the man in the river? Peter Vaslos?"

"Why would he know any more than I would?"

"Sometimes friends keep things from other friends."

"You're saying he had something to do with Peter Vaslos?"

"I'm just curious, is all. The body of a man shows up in the river with your name in his pocket. A woman is murdered in front of your house. And now a friend of yours dies."

"Accidentally."

"That's what it appears to be," she said. "For now, at least."

"You're saying what?"

"He could have been pushed."

"Could've been, yes," I said. "But it's unlikely."

"Is it?" She started studying my face again, obviously knowing how uncomfortable it made me.

A bulky man in a short-sleeved white shirt and blue trousers came up. He toted a badge on one side of his belt and a gun on the other. His white crew cut made his wide face even more imposing.

"Excuse me a minute," he said to Detective Patterson. He swatted a mosquito. "Damned things."

"This is Detective Craig," Detective Patterson said.

He offered me a hard slab of hand.

Then he took a penlight from his trousers pocket.

"Mind if I look at your shoes, Mr. Tyler."

I looked down at my feet.

"No problem."

"Would you raise the right one first?"

"Sure."

I raised the right one.

"Now the left."

I raised the left.

I felt like a horse that was being shoed.

"Thank you, Mr. Tyler."

"Sure."

He wasn't anybody I'd want in our poker club. His face revealed nothing of his thoughts.

"You need me for anything?" Detective Patterson said.

Craig shook his head.

"Everything seems to be under control," he said. Then to me: "We'll know a lot more when we get the time of death from the medical examiner."

"He couldn't have been down there too long," I said. "There's a lot of traffic on the road."

"That's true," Craig said. "But the road has been blocked off for the past week. An asphalt crew has been working up near the bend."

"Oh."

"So he could've been there a long time."

"I see."

"His daughter said he left to go hiking right after supper. That means, driving from his house, he would've gotten out here around seven-fifteen or seven-thirty. From where his car is parked, it would've taken him a good half hour to reach this point. So we're probably talking seven-forty-five, eight o'clock when he got here. Dusk. He go walking at dusk very often?"

"I'm not sure. I know he loved this trail."

"You ever go walking with him?"

"No."

"Your other two friends over there, they ever go with him?"

"Not that I know of. I think one of the things he liked about the walks was being alone."

"He have any enemies that you know of?"

Detective Patterson smiled. "I've asked him about that already, Fred. According to him, Mr. Solomon was universally beloved."

Her sarcasm irritated me.

"I didn't say that. I just said that he was a very nice guy and that he didn't have any enemies."

"That you know of," Craig amended.

"Right," I said. "That I know of."

A man in a green jumpsuit called Craig's name.

"Well, back to it," he said to Detective Patterson.

"Thanks, Jim," she said.

Some of the gawkers had started walking back to their cars. Whatever drama they'd sensed out here was definitely waning.

"They're like birds," Detective Patterson said. "They light when they know there's trouble and then vanish again. It's like they drive around and drive around until they find something really gory."

She walked me back to Curtis and Bill.

"You'll be happy to know that your friend here didn't enlighten me any more than you two did," Detective Patterson said.

She stood in front of us, looking first at Curtis, then at me, then at Bill. "You think you guys'll ever tell me the truth?" she said.

"You think you'll ever recognize the truth when you hear it?" Bill shot back.

"Peter Vaslos," she said. "Why'd he have Aaron Tyler's name on a slip of paper in his pocket?"

Curtis was the only one showing the effects of her pressure.

He licked his lips and his eyes darted nervously from me to Bill.

"We don't know who he was," he said. He spoke in little more than a whisper. "I don't know why you have to keep asking us the same questions."

Bill laughed.

"She wants to show us she's just as tough as any guy cop," he said. "She wants us to fill our pants 'cause she scares us so much."

"Anybody ever tell you you were kind've an asshole, Dr. Doyle?"

He smiled. "Yeah. Lots of people. I wear it like a badge of honor."

She looked at Curtis. "You've got some nice friends. A nice guy who won't be honest with me—and a bully who hides behind his medical diploma."

She took a step toward Curtis.

"Don't let them ruin your life for you, Curtis. You're gonna tell me the truth eventually. Just make it sooner than later, all right."

Curtis tilted his head down so that he wasn't looking into her face anymore.

"I'm trying to be your friend, Curtis. Think've how hard you've worked for what you've got. You don't want to throw it all away, do you?"

She looked at each of us individually again, and then started walking away.

After about seven or eight steps, she turned around and said, "Somebody wants to kill you guys. You'd better be damned careful."

CAR HEADLIGHTS washed the white door of my garage. We'd come into my driveway—my car first, then Curtis', then Bill's—fast, like stunt drivers.

I carried in the two six packs I'd stopped to buy on the way over.

Inside, Bill headed for the first floor john, and Curtis went to the phone.

I set out the beers and the glasses in the breakfast nook.

"Hi Honey, everything's fine," Curtis was saying to his wife as I sat down and poured my beer. "We're just having a few beers, Honey. That's all. Really. Everything's fine. Now you just go back to sleep and I'll be home in a little while." Pause. "I love you, too, Sweetheart."

He came over and sat down and said, "I need one of these."

Bill came back from the bathroom. Sat down.

"That bitch is on to us," he said.

"Patterson?" I said.

He nodded. Opened his beer. Poured it quickly and expertly into his glass.

"She doesn't have any particulars, though," I said.

"She doesn't need any particulars," Bill said. "She knows that somehow Peter Vaslos' body ties into our poker game, and that Neil's death has something to do with it, too."

"So you're sure he was murdered?" Curtis said.

"I can't believe you're even fucking asking me that," Bill said. "You really think it was just a coincidence that he fell off the cliff tonight?"

Curtis shook his head.

"Then she's right, isn't she?" he said. "The bastard really is going to kill us off one at a time."

We didn't say anything for a long time. Just sat and stared at our beers.

Curtis said, "There any chance you're wrong, Bill?"

"Wrong about what?"

"Neil. You know, it not being an accident or anything."

Bill shot him a disgusted look.

"I can't fucking believe you even said that."

Silence again.

Bill said, "I want to find that sonofabitch and nail him once and for all."

"Kill him?" Curtis said.

"Hell, yes, kill him."

"You really think you could do that?" I said. "You being a doctor and all."

He gave me the same disgusted look he'd given Curtis.

"You know something, Aaron? You sound like you're about eight years old."

"Thanks for the compliment," I said.

"If you mean the Hippocratic oath and all that bullshit, I think it's suspended when somebody's trying to kill you. I say we tear that cocksucker's heart out."

Silence again.

Curtis said, "I've been thinking about something."

I smiled.

"Unless it involves a whole lot of violence, I don't think Bill'll even want to hear about it."

Curtis picked up my humor.

"I was thinking we could go after the sonofabitch in a tank," he said, grinning.

"You know, flatten the entire apartment house where they sneak in."

"I guess I was thinking about using bombers," I said. "You know, three or four planes, and drop some bombs for a couple of hours, and our worries are over."

"Real funny," Bill said.

"On the other hand," Curtis said, "I was thinking of maybe burning him at the stake. You know, like a witch."

Curtis and I sat side-by-side, which made it easier for Bill to glower at us.

"You'll come around," he said.

"Come around to what?" I asked.

"To seeing it my way."

He watched us carefully.

"He isn't going to leave us any choice. He'll kill one more of us— and then we'll *have* to kill him. That's why I say get the bastard now— before one of you two guys get it."

"Of course," Curtis said, "there's absolutely no chance that you could be the next victim?"

"If he got close enough to kill me, I'd tear him apart right on the spot."

I believed him.

The silence again.

I'd left the six pack on the table. Bill opened his second beer. One had been enough for me.

Curtis said, "I think we should pay him off."

"Pay off the burglar?" Bill said. "You're out of your mind."

"Listen to me," Curtis said, leaning forward, excited, the way he got at the law office when he was pressing a point. "The guy's a punk. Probably a junkie. He steals to feed his habit. We offer him twenty thousand dollars or something like that, and he won't bother us anymore."

"Right," Bill said. "He won't bother us anymore until he goes through the twenty thousand dollars."

"I've got that covered," Curtis said, still excited. "If we give him the money, and he comes back on us, then we kill him. And you know how we do it?"

"How?"

"You give him an overdose of crack, or whatever he's using. The death looks accidental."

"You know something, Curtis," I said. "I've never realized before what a cold-blooded sonofabitch you are."

He looked as if I'd hurt his feelings.

I laughed.

"Hey, you didn't take that the right way," I said. "I'm proud of you." Curtis nodded.

"I don't think we want to murder anybody unless we've tried everything else first," Curtis said.

Much as I hated the second burglar for what he'd done to Betsy tonight, I had to agree with Curtis' reasoning.

I wasn't a killer, and neither was Curtis. Bill was, maybe. He gave the impression he could kill somebody without caring much. But I wondered what he'd be like when the time came.

I directed my words at Bill.

"Curtis has a good idea here," I said. "We give the bastard the money, he stays out of our lives at least long enough so that Patterson lays off us. She sees our lives returning to normal and starts thinking maybe she was wrong. And we can go back to living like decent human beings again."

"He killed Neil," Bill said.

"I know."

"And he probably would've killed your daughter."

"I know that, too, Bill. But what the hell else can we do? I don't know about you, but I'm sick of living this way."

"It's worth a chance," Curtis said.

Bill watched us for a time.

"Just where the hell do we get the money?" he said.

"Simple," Curtis said. "We kick in seven grand each."

"What if he wants more?" Bill said.

"We tell him to shove it," Curtis said.

"We don't even know how to find the sonofabitch," Bill said.

"We'll get another one of his late-night phone calls. You will or Aaron will or I will. And when he calls and just stays on the line, then we tell him what we want to do."

"How do we get him the money?" Bill said.

"Easy," I said. "Whoever talks to him says that we'll drop off the cash in the empty apartment on the fourth floor. Then we'll leave and he can go in and pick it up there."

"He'll think it's a trap," Bill said.

"Yeah, he will," Curtis said, "But eventually he'll start thinking about all that money just sitting there, and he'll go get it. Then he'll go on a spree and leave us alone for a while."

Bill sipped some beer. Sat back. Looked at us. Said nothing. Then, "This is a pretty chicken shit way to handle things."

"I want my life back," Curtis said.

"So do I," I said. "Jan can't handle much more of this and I don't blame her."

"My wife asks any questions," Bill said, "I tell her it's none of her business."

Then he smiled. "But I guess I'm not quite as pussy-whipped as you two. I just don't take any shit off of women."

"Fuck yourself," Curtis said.

"We could take one night," Bill said, "sit in the alley behind that apartment house, and we'd find him. And we'd kill him."

"Believe it or not, Bill," Curtis said, "I don't kill people."

"Not even a scuz-bag like this?" Bill said.

The phone rang.

The three of us looked at each other.

The burglar?

Who else would be calling this time of night?

I got up and walked over to the yellow wall phone and lifted the receiver.

"Hello."

"Hi, Aaron. This is Beth. Is Bill there?"

"Yeah." I wasn't sure what else to say. She sounded angry. "I'll get Bill. Just hold on."

He walked over and I handed him the phone.

I went over and sat down in the nook again.

Curtis and I didn't talk. Just sat there waiting for Bill to be done on the phone.

The funny thing was, Bill had turned away from us completely, and kind of slouched down, burying the phone between jaw line and shoulder. He obviously didn't want us to hear what he said.

"C'mon. I can't take that anymore." Pause. "Listen, please, I promise. No more late nights. Just don't—" Pause. "I hate the bed in the guest room. I always get that fucking crink in my back." Pause. "Of course I know that other husbands are home in bed by now." Pause. "You know how many nights you've made me sleep in the guest room this month?" Pause. "I'm sorry I used that tone of voice. I'm sorry, all right? I'm sorry."

All the time he was talking, Curtis and I kept looking at each other and smiling.

There's nothing more pathetic than a man who likes to pretend he's the absolute master of his home—and then has to grovel to his wife in front of his friends.

Anybody else, I might have felt a little sorry for him.

But Bill....

Then he slowly hung up the phone and turned around to face us. He came over and sat down. He looked embarrassed.

"I guess you really told her off, huh?" Curtis said.

"You asshole."

"Way you were wailin' on her, I thought we might have to call the police on a domestic violence rap."

Curtis looked at me and winked.

"You ever see a man push a woman around like that on the phone?"

"No, I never saw anything like that. It was pretty frightening," I said. "I had to cover my ears."

"Fuck you, you clowns," Bill said.

"I sure wish I wasn't pussy-whipped so I could push my wife around the way Bill does."

"Yeah," I said. "It's terrible being pussy-whipped. You think Bill could give us some lessons on getting un-pussy-whipped?"

Bill suddenly said, "I guess it's worth a try."

Curtis looked at me again but this time there was no frivolity on his face.

"You mean the twenty-one grand?" Curtis said.

"Yeah," Bill said. "I guess we may as well try it."

"Bingo," Curtis said.

"Seven apiece, right?" I said.

"Seven apiece," Curtis said. "Can you guys get yours by late this afternoon?"

"No problem for me," I said. "Bill?"

"No problem."

"Great," Curtis said. "Then the next time he calls, whichever one of us answers, we tell him, right?"

"Right."

"This'z going to work," Curtis said, sounding almost giddy. "And all this bullshit is finally going to be over."

"I sure hope you're right," I said, thinking of the uneasy truce Jan and I had struck earlier tonight.

We drank our beers.

"You know what I'm still trying to figure out?"

"What?" I said.

"That night you chased him from the apartment house and down the alley? Where the hell'd he go?"

"I still think about that, too."

"He just ran fast is all," Curtis said.

"This is what this jerk-off does for a living. He runs away. He's used to it. We're not."

I noted the 'we' he used.

"One thing I was thinking," Curtis said. "Maybe he climbed up one of the buildings somehow."

"Not enough time," I said. "And I would've seen him."

"Then where'd he go?" Curtis then made a science fiction movie sound.

"I'm starting to have doubts again," Bill said.

We both looked at him.

"About what?" I said.

"About this money bullshit."

"It'll get him off our backs."

"Will it? What if he has a week-long toot and then comes right back for more?"

"We've got to be a little optimistic here," Curtis said.

"Why?" Bill said. "All the shit that's happened, and we're supposed to be optimistic?"

I could see that Bill was in the process of talking himself out of the bribe. I grabbed three more beers from the refrigerator. Then I went back to one of the cupboards and got the Jack Daniels black label.

I just wanted it to all go away. And maybe with the money, it would. The bastard had probably never seen that kind of money before. How could he turn it down?

"You won't have any trouble getting the money will you?" Curtis said to me.

"No."

"How about you, Bill?"

Then I saw Bill's mouth draw tight and a faint flush of red coloring his cheeks.

267 ♠ THE POKER CLUB

Bill had long lived beyond his means. The house was too big, the cars too many, the vacations too plentiful. He made a good living, to be sure, but he was a general practitioner in an age of highly-paid specialists.

And Curtis had hit the real reason for Bill's reluctance.

"You need a loan?" Curtis said. "I can handle it."

Bill's anger was immediate. "I need a fucking loan, I don't need it from somebody like you, believe me."

I'm sure Curtis was wondering what 'somebody like you' meant, just the way I was. The way Bill was uneasy about black people, it had to be galling to have a black man offer him a loan.

"Let's have a drink to wrap things up for the night," I said.

I filled three shot glasses and dispersed them. I held up my glass in toast.

"First," I said, "to Neil Solomon. One of the most decent people who ever walked this planet."

"No argument there," Bill said.

"The poor guy," Curtis said, shaking his head.

We raised our glasses, and drank. I don't think the reality of Neil's death had really struck us yet. A grief counsellor once told me that sometimes the real impact of death doesn't set in for days, or even weeks.

"And to a nice, normal life," I said.

"To a nice, normal life," Curtis said.

Bill muttered something and reluctantly touched his shot glass to ours.

"So here's the deal," I said, after we'd downed our drinks, "We get the money and meet here right after dinner tomorrow night."

"Could we make it closer to eight?" Curtis said. "I've got some things I've got to do."

"All right," I said. "So we have the money in the apartment and then we just sit there and wait for him."

"What if he doesn't show up?"

"Oh, he'll show up all right," I said. "No way he can turn down this kind of cash."

"So after he gets the money, then what?"

"Then we surround him and scare the shit out of him."

"Oh, yeah?" Curtis grinned. "This is the good part, right?"

"Right," I said. "Bill, you bring your gun. We isolate the bastard and then we put the fear of God into him. We tell him that he can have the money with no strings, but if he ever tries to collect any more, we'll kill him on the spot."

"I'd like to kill him on the spot, anyway," Bill said.

"I know you would, and that's just what we need to convey tomorrow night. That this is our last chance with this asshole. That next time, he's dead."

"I've got an old switchblade," Curtis said.

"Bring it," I said.

Bill helped himself to more whiskey.

"I just keep thinking about Neil," he said.

"So do I," Curtis said.

"Maybe I won't be able to hold myself back tomorrow night," Bill said. "Maybe I'll kill the cocksucker right on the spot."

"You don't have to worry about holding yourself back," I said. "I'll be there to do it for you."

"So tomorrow night, here, eight o'clock, everybody brings his money. Right?"

"My wife won't like it," Curtis said, "me sneaking out of the house again. But I don't have much choice."

He smiled at Bill and said, "How about your wife, Bill? You think she'll like it?"

And that was apparently the wrong time to make that particular joke because Bill lunged across the table and grabbed Curtis by the front of his shirt and then slapped him across the face.

"I don't want anymore of your bullshit, you understand me, you black bastard? I don't want any of your money and I don't want any of your sarcasm? You understand me, jungle bunny?"

He was shouting.

I got up and grabbed his arms and eventually pulled him away from Curtis.

An awful silence followed my getting Bill to sit back down.

Curtis sat there staring out the window. I could see the tears in his eyes. He wasn't hurt physically. Those would have been the easiest wounds to heal. The verbal wounds were far worse.

'Jungle bunny' was an expression I hadn't heard since probably grade school.

"You owe Curtis an apology," I said, wanting to slap Bill as he'd slapped Curtis.

Bill swung his face up t me.o

"What're you supposed to be, Tyler, a fucking social worker?"

"You owe him an apology."

"Yeah? Well, he owes me an apology, too."

"For what?" I said.

"For riding my ass all night."

"He made a joke. Twice. That's hardly all night."

"He's always on my ass."

"That's bullshit," I said, "and you know it."

"Forget it, Aaron," Curtis said. "I don't even want an apology from him. He's just a bigot."

"I got pissed is all," Bill said, sounding defensive for the first time. He looked at me and then looked at Curtis.

Then, unbelievably, he actually looked embarrassed and sorry.

In a soft voice, he said, "Curtis?"

"Yeah?" Curtis' voice was angry.

"What I called you?"

"Yeah?"

"I shouldn't have. And I'm sorry."

He looked at me. I didn't cut him any slack. I glared at him.

Then Curtis was overwhelmed by the moment. Tears filled not only his eyes but also his voice.

He looked out the window, and fighting a sob, said "All my fucking life, man. All my fucking life." He looked at Bill then. "You think I wanted to be born black, man? Nobody in his right mind would want to be born black in this fucking country, believe me. There's too goddammed many white bastards like you running around. But most of us do the best we can. You may not believe that, white boy, but it's true. We do the fucking best we can. The same that most white folks do."

Then he slid out of the nook and stalked past me to the door.

"Real good, you sonofabitch," I said to Bill. "Real fucking good."

He just shook his head miserably. He looked dazed somehow, as if he suddenly couldn't cope with the reality of all this.

I followed Curtis out to his car.

He was already behind the wheel and turning it so he could drive around Bill's car.

I put my head in the open window.

"You all right?"

He grinned. "'Jungle bunny.' Jesus, man, That's almost pathetic. You know what I mean? I mean, he could've at least called me a 'coon' or something. 'Jungle bunny's' fourth grade." Then, "'Jungle bunny.' God."

His smile exhilarated me.

"He's an asshole," I said.

"You just finding that out?"

This time, I grinned.

"No, I think I've seen a few clues along the way."

He stared straight out his windshield, at the play of his headlights on the white garage door.

The temperature had dropped considerably. The night was pleasant and smelled of sweet flowers and that indefinable scent of summer night itself.

Fireflies were putting on hundreds of floor shows, diving, dipping, rolling over, soaring straight up.

"You believe the way that guy is pussy-whipped?" Curtis said.

"I have to admit, that one surprised me."

"It's the way he always talks about her. He had us convinced that he was the absolute lord and master of his place."

Then the melancholy was back in him. It was almost palpable.

"You going to be all right?" I said.

"Yeah."

"Just go home and get some sleep."

"It's my kids I worry about, Aaron. They'll have to grow up hearing all this bullshit, too. Some days, I'd just run home from school and hide in my room, the way I got treated by white kids sometimes. And now my kids—"

There were tears in his eyes again.

"We all need some sleep, Curtis," I said, gently.

He nodded.

The back door opened and banged shut.

Bill walked up.

"You guys're probably talking about what a jerk-off I am."

"God, and now he's clairvoyant," I said.

He leaned down so Curtis could see his face.

"Absolutely unpardonable behavior, Curtis. I'm sorry. I guess I was raised with this racist streak, and sometimes it comes out." He put a hand on Curtis' shoulder and said, "You're a good man and a good friend, and I'm really sorry for what I said."

I was shocked by the tears in Bill's eyes. And the choking sound in his voice. This was the healing side of Dr. Bill, the side you never saw unless you were a patient of his.

"I don't expect you to forgive me tonight," he said, the tears still in his voice. "But maybe someday you'll see that I didn't mean what I said. I really am sorry, Curtis."

Obviously, Curtis was moved by Bill's startling words and demeanor, too.

"I'll give it a try," he said, still staring at the play of his lights on the garage door. Then he looked at Bill and smiled, "'Jungle bunny.' Man, you need to update your vocabulary."

Then he put his car in gear and backed out of the drive.

When the driveway was dark again, Bill said, "I really hurt him, didn't I?"

"Yeah, you did."

"I can be such a sonofabitch sometimes."

"I sure wouldn't argue with that." Then, "Maybe we should use the money as a lure."

"A lure?"

"Sure. Get him alone, and then kill him."

"You really think you could kill somebody in cold blood?"

"Some scum-bag like this guy? Are you kidding?"

"We're going to give this an honest try."

"Should we wear our Boy Scout uniforms tomorrow night?"

The old harsh Bill was now back in control.

"You don't have the money, do you?" I said.

"Right now, I'm a little short."

"The XKE you bought last month?"

"I don't manage my money real great. I guess I have to admit that."

"How much can you raise?"

"Five Hundred."

"Wow."

"Don't tell Curtis, all right?"

"When do you think you can pay me back?"

"Three, four months."

"I'll need it."

"You'll get it."

He walked to his Mercedes sports convertible, clipped on the lights, and then leaned out and said. "Don't tell Curtis, all right?"

He was his old combative self again.

2

I SPENT the next morning playing house husband. After putting a load of laundry in the washer, I drove to the supermarket and spent sixty-one dollars on groceries which, I discovered, isn't difficult to do at all. After that, I stopped by a garden center and picked up two large bags of peat moss.

As I drove back home, I took note of the fact that this was a typical eighty-seven degree summer day, kids everywhere you looked, the occasional suburban lady lying in her yard in this year's new swimsuit, and the streets packed with the small trucks and vans that hauled merchandise to city stores. This could have been 1928 or 1969 or 1988. For all the scientific progress our society has made, very little of it shows itself to the casual observer.

Nobody had followed me, not so far as I could see, anyway.

I ran the car into the garage, dragged the sprinkling heads and hoses out, and started feeding water to the brown backyard.

As I was going inside the house to have a cup of coffee, the phone rang.

"Is this a bad time?"

Detective Patterson.

"Not at all."

"A yellow Buick mean anything to you, Mr. Tyler?"

"A yellow Buick?"

"An older one. Eight years maybe."

"I don't think so. Why?"

"We have a witness who saw an older model yellow Buick up near the site where your friend Mr. Solomon fell off the cliff."

"I'm sorry. But it really doesn't mean anything to me."

"All right, Mr. Tyler. Just thought I'd check. But if I were you, I'd keep an eye out for it."

"The yellow Buick?"

"Uh-huh."

"Why would I do that?"

"We're still not satisfied your friend's death was accidental, Mr. Tyler."

"I see."

"Well, you have yourself a nice day, Mr. Tyler."

She was good at what she did. No doubt about it. Her hunch told her that the yellow Buick tied to me just as Neil tied to me. She didn't know any of the details yet but she sensed that eventually all this would come coherently together for her. I was thankful for physical labor.

I was glad to take my shirt off and bake in the sun and have sweat streak down my face and neck and back and arms.

I wanted to be a simple man. Know simple pleasures. Have no complications in my life.

I worked for two hours in the baking sun. I should have worn gloves but somehow the calluses the rake and the trowel and the trimmer put on my hands felt good. Part of my simple man formula.

The phone rang. I ran in to get it but was too late. Curtis had left a simple message: "Sonofabitch called me about four-thirty this morning. I was up in the den because I couldn't sleep. He didn't say a word, of course. So I told him about the money. Said we'd put it in the apartment tonight. Sonofabitch still didn't say anything. Just hung up. I'll see you at your place tonight."

So much for my simple man idea.

Simple men didn't have dark figures following them around all the time. Simple men didn't have to raise a lot of money to pay off their stalkers.

I went back outside and tried my best to become one with the jays and cardinals and butterflies and chipmunks and racoons, especially the racoons. Ever since I was a little boy, I'd had this fantasy about being a racoon for a couple of days. Their lives looked like fun to me. They always appeared to be having a good time crawling up trees or exploring culverts or washing themselves in creeks.

But today I couldn't project myself into the animal kingdom. I was thinking about old yellow Buicks and nervous phone calls from friends who said they'd see me tonight with their share of the bribery money.

As I worked, a few neighbors called to me and waved, and I waved back.

There was no reason not to wave to me now. Nothing had been proven.

The Trudy stories had started to fade. The local news people had moved on to other tragedies.

If Trudy had been rich, of course, that would have made a difference. But in a small Midwestern city like this one, hundreds of farm girls arrive every year. It's just a matter of actuarial percentages that at least a few of them will meet bad ends.

Not real exciting journalism.

Not for the news appetites most of us had developed, anyway. We want the Roman circus, Christians and lions, in our living rooms each and every night.

Around noon, I decided to go in and have myself a bottle of strawberry pop and a sandwich of some kind.

I ate standing up at the kitchen counter. A few times, I glanced over to look at the place where the burglar had laid the night he died.

I started thinking about time machines, another fantasy I'd had since being a little boy.

Wouldn't it be cool if we could get in these little time machines and go back a few days and take back things we'd said or undo things we'd done?

This time, I'd insist we called the cops, and I'd take personal charge of the burglar myself.

Nobody would try to intimidate him in any regard.

I'd leave that totally to the cops.

If only. If only.

How much time most of us spend whispering those words to ourselves: *if only. If only.*

I decided to work another hour before taking a shower and going to the bank.

I waved to a few more neighbors, hauled out a few cob-webbed cases of empty Pepsi bottles and put them in my car trunk, and took some Windex to the garage windows. We had recently been under siege from neighborhood pigeons.

As I stood admiring the yard work I'd done—who said a simple man couldn't feel a simple pride in his labors?—the phone rang.

This time I was determined to get it before the answering machine kicked in.

"God, it's great to hear your voice," I said.

"How're things going?"

She didn't sound angry this time—just a little weary.

I paused before saying anything. "Neil's dead."

She said nothing.

"Jan?"

"It's never going to end, is it?"

"We're going to offer him money."

"You're what?"

Her tone of voice told me what she thought of our idea.

"It's worth a try."

I decided that now probably wouldn't be the ideal time to tell her that I was also putting in Dr. Bill's share of the bribe.

As she well knew, Dr. Bill earned about twice as much a year as I did.

She sighed. "It won't work, Aaron."

"It's worth a try."

"We're not exactly rich."

"We do all right."

"Not all right enough to pay blackmail money."

"At least it'll get him off our backs for a while so we can think straight."

"How much?"

"We're not sure yet."

"You're lying again."

"It won't be that much. I promise."

The anger was back in her voice. "I'd better let the girls talk now."

"God, Jan, please, listen—"

"Annie wants to say hello," Jan said.

"Hi, Daddy."

"Hi, Sweetheart."

"We're going to the movies."

"Great." I put as much enthusiasm as I could in my voice.

"And Granddad's going to sit between Betsy and me and share his popcorn with both of us."

"That sounds like an exciting afternoon."

"I better go, Daddy. Bye. I love you."

"I love you, too. Could I talk to your mom again, Honey?"

"She isn't in the den anymore, Daddy."

"Where'd she go, Honey?"

"I don't know but she isn't here."

"All right, Honey. Bye."

"Bye, Daddy."

I STAYED in the shower much longer than usual. The white noise of the water blasting my body and the steam clouding the shower door gave me the feeling of being in a cocoon.

Nobody could bother me.

Not even the most cunning burglar in the world.

After toweling off, I put on a fresh white shirt and tan chinos and my cordovan penny loafers. No socks. I was going sockless long before a certain TV show made that fashionable.

As I walked to the garage, I noted once again what a good job I'd done of cleaning up the backyard, doing all the things Jan would have done had she been here. Then I backed the car out of the drive and headed for the bank at the mall.

I was four blocks from my house before I realized I that I was being followed.

3

THE BANK was busy at lunchtime.

I went up to a teller and asked if she could give me a Bank Secrecy Act form. She slid one through the cute little cage she was standing behind.

I went over and sat down at a small table and got to work with a ballpoint.

Even when it's your money, the feds want to know when you're taking out anything more than $10,000 in cash. The same with deposits.

The form itself is nothing more than name, rank and serial number. No questions are asked about what you plan to do with the money.

But if the bank folks suspect anything wrong—kidnapping for withdrawals, say; or drug money for deposits—they can contact the appropriate law enforcement agency.

A few years ago, I'd needed large amounts of cash for rental properties I was buying. A real estate friend of mine said that certain kinds of people would agree to a lower price if you flashed the down payment at them in gorgeous green cash. "More rental properties, Mr. Tyler?" Darla Hobbins, who was one of the assistant managers, said.

She was the woman who helped me with most of my banking. Short, slender, unfailingly well-dressed, and all the personality of an ATM.

I nodded. "Yes. If he'll meet my price."

She gave me an abrupt and somewhat startling thumbs up. I wondered if she gave her husband a similar thumbs up when he'd given her an extreme amount of pleasure. I could easily imagine it happening.

Darla and her thumb decided to stroll around the bank, greeting customers. I finished with the form and took it back to my sweet-faced young teller.

"Thanks for doing this," she said, seeming slightly embarrassed about the whole thing.

"Just doing your job."

"But you're such a good customer and all. Anyway, I really appreciate it."

She slid fourteen natty one thousand bills into a heavy white envelope and slid the envelope over to me.

"Thanks, again," I said.

As I was pushing my way through the front glass doors, Darla Hobbins snuck up behind me and said, "Good luck with that rental property."

Her thumb must have been tired. He didn't put in an appearance.

I stood in the heat outside the bank, looking up and down the street as if I couldn't decide which shop to visit.

This was one of those shopping areas that had been refurbished at taxpayer expense. There'd been talk that the mayor's cousin actually owned a lot of these buildings and that the refurbishment had directly benefited him. But if that was true, neither the local papers nor the local TV stations had decided to do anything about it. Maybe they were forgiving souls, after all, and not the cynics we think. Or maybe one of their bosses owned property out here, too.

I saw two little girls walking along on either side of their mother, red balloons bobbing in the air above them. I had this kind of sentimental seizure. I could actually feel my daughters in my arms, smell their sweet, fine hair, hear their giggles.

I was deep in my reverie when I made the mistake of tilting my head slightly to the right.

The red Volvo was inching down the other side of the street. This is the vehicle that had followed me from my home.

What he was doing now, our friend the burglar, was making sure I was still inside the bank.

The funny thing was, he didn't seem to see me standing out on the sidewalk. I was momentarily hidden by a small crowd of late lunchers walking back to their office. The ancient red Volvo turned right, into the bank parking lot.

I glimpsed his face, still lost in shadow beneath the long-billed baseball cap.

He apparently couldn't find a parking place nearby. He'd likely been driving around the block all the time I was inside.

I waited until he exited through the back entrance of the lot. Then I rushed in.

I was going to follow him for a while.

He didn't catch on for a couple of blocks, even though I was right behind him all the way.

We came to a red light and he slowed and stopped.

After I applied my brakes, I hit the horn.

I could see his eyes in the rear view mirror. Now he'd figured it out.

He was apparently so shaken by seeing me behind him that he floored his car and fish-tailed through the intersection, barely missing a delivery van that was shooting down the street in front of him.

4

THE JEWISH religion has the right idea. Bury the dead person as quickly as possible, and get on with life. This extends to the type of burial, as well. Don't spend a lot of money on a fancy coffin and an impressive ceremony. Spend the money on the living.

There were probably fifty people at the funeral home when we arrived that night just before eight o'clock. The heat being what it was, you didn't see a lot of heavy suits. Men and women alike wore summery clothes.

I went over and said hello to Neil's daughter.

It's easy to sentimentalize somebody at the time of his death, to overlook flaws, to forget all about certain ugly habits or traits.

But with Neil, you didn't have to sentimentalize at all.

He'd really been a good and decent man.

Aside from Jan, Neil had been my best friend. I thought of his guilt over how he'd cheated on his wife the night she told him she had cancer, and how inept he felt as a father. He couldn't ever forgive himself—while he was surrounded by people who did far worse things. And were constantly forgiving themselves to go on and commit more atrocities.

I said a silent prayer into the ether, and then just sent him a thought across the dark border—a thought about how much I'd admired him and cared for him.

When I turned back, then, I saw the whole room as in a snapshot.

There were the old folks who would, soon enough, be lying in the front of the room in their own caskets.

There were the middle-aged people who looked somber and a little bit frightened. It's like reading the obituaries every day. There's something unnerving when you see that someone your age—41 or 42 or 43—has passed on. It really can happen to you.

And then there were the children. They seemed to be blissfully unaware of why they were here. They smiled at each other and a few even slipped through the knots of older people, and snuck off outside. A part of me went out the door with them, out into the noise and excitement and potential of the day itself. At their age, death is a blessed abstraction, and that is perhaps the greatest gift that youth possesses.

The furtive, almost embarrassed sobs, the faint but unmistakable odors that sneak up from the embalming room...these were the funeral home realities for the adults.

I saw his daughter, Rachel, standing alone momentarily, and I went over to her.

"I'm sure that you've heard this a lot tonight, Rachel, but if you need anything, please give me a call."

She was a slight and pretty girl with great dark luminous eyes and a mouth far too grim for a thirteen-year-old. She wore a dark blue dress and flats and a girlish blue barrette in her hair. She had great poise.

"He really liked you, Mr. Tyler," she said.

"I really liked him, too."

"He always said you were kind."

She started crying then, and so did I, at least a little, and I let her lean against me and put her face to my chest until she was done.

I felt her frail bones shake with the tears.

"I'm really going to miss him. He was really my friend, not just my dad."

"You know how he used to take you out on Saturday nights for pizza?"

She nodded. Tears stood huge and crystal in the corners of her dark eyes, and her fingers fretted with a tiny lace handkerchief.

"You can start going with my family," I said. "We usually go out on Saturday nights, too."

It was one of those things you say to push the sorrow away momentarily. But both Rachel and I knew that this would-be date would probably never happen. Or if it did happen, would take place only once or twice, and then never again.

She needed a father and a mother, not a stand-in family on Saturday nights.

I gave her a little squeeze on the shoulder and said another thing that you would expect to hear from an inarticulate adult.

"Everything'll work out in time, Honey. It really will."

She was sweet enough not to resent my babbling banalities.

"Thanks, Mr. Tyler."

"Sure, Sweetheart."

"I'd better get back now."

I nodded.

And then the rabbi was there, a very young man with a good, strong voice. He stood in front of the coffin and looked around for a long moment and said, "Neil's here with us tonight. That's what we need to remember. And I don't mean in the coffin behind me. But in memory. That's where he'll live on and on and on. In the life of memory."

And when he spoke of Neil, it was not, thank God, the slick empty words of a funeral routine of somebody who hadn't known Neil well...he spoke the hard, anguished words of a real friend.

We found a nice neighborhood bar and drowned some sorrows for a few hours.

"WOW, I'VE got to study up on the Jewish religion," Curtis said once we were back in the car and driving toward the other side of the city. "Those were really beautiful prayers."

Ordinarily, Bill would have made a joke about Curtis' remark. But now he was in the back seat restraining himself. I could almost feel the effort it took.

The rain started just as we reached the long bridge that spanned onto the north side of the city.

"Maybe it was really an accident," Curtis said. "Neil, I mean."

"I got this call from Patterson. She asked about a yellow Buick. She said an eyewitness had seen it up where Neil had died."

Curtis said, "What'd you say to her?"

"I said I didn't know anything about it."

I had a jazz station on, and they were playing a particularly forlorn Miles Davis piece from the early sixties, and given the night and the rain, a fierce melancholy seemed to grip everybody in the car.

"You see his daughter?" Curtis said.

"Yeah."

"I couldn't even watch her crying that way."

"Yeah," I said.

"Fits in with the day," Bill said.

"Yeah?" I said.

"Had to tell this twenty-seven year old guy that he had inoperable cancer of the pancreas."

"God," I said.

"I almost lost it," he said.

And here once again you had the enigma of Bill Doyle. When he was Dr. Bill you couldn't find a more caring or sensitive man. When he was just plain Bill, he was the kind of raw material the KKK was always on the lookout for.

"Change that station, Aaron. That jazz shit makes me suicidal," Bill said.

"Hey, that was Miles Davis," Curtis said.

"Yeah," Bill said, the old Bill now, "and you know about Miles Davis, don't you?"

"What about him?"

Was Bill going to make another racist remark?

"What about him is he's dead. And you know why he's dead? Because he listened to his own depressing music all the time."

I laughed. Couldn't help it.

"Bill Doyle, MD, and music critic," I said.

Curtis laughed, too.

"Is there anything you don't have an opinion on?" he said.

But Bill wasn't listening.

I found a station playing the Beach Boys' *Wouldn't It Be Nice.*

"Now there's music," Bill said.

"Got to admit," Curtis said, "that's pretty nice stuff."

We drove on in silence for a time.

The rain was coming harder now, the wind strong enough to whip the summer-heavy tree branches around pretty good.

In the slanting rain, you could see lovers running down the sidewalks, eager for shelter. But wet as they were, running as fast as they were, they still managed to hold hands, and for some reason—the funeral home still fresh in me—I was touched by this.

We crossed the second bridge.

And then we were in enemy territory.

Everything seemed darker and dingier here by sixty percent.

There was some dark and smoky monster hiding in a basement nearby. And the monster sucked up most of the light in this section of the city. And robbed the white people of all color, so that their flesh was zombie-pale. And beat down the shoulders and backs of black people, even little black children so that they walked with great weariness. And smashed windows. And rusted cars. And made men crazy enough to beat their wives. And urged children to run into the paths of cars. And take drugs when they were no older than eight.

The monster. In the nearby basement. Hiding.

"I sweetened the deal a little," Curtis said.

"Sweetened the deal?" I said.

"Put in a little extra dough," he said.

"What the hell are you talking about?" Bill said from the back seat.

"I put in my seven thousand, and then a little more."

"How much is a "little more?'" I said.

"Couple grand."

"Two grand?" Bill said.

"Yeah," Curtis said. "Two grand. What're you guys so uptight about, anyway?"

"You can't afford the seven and now you're giving him two more?" Bill said.

"How do you know I can't afford the seven?" Curtis said, his pride hurt. "You're the one who's always blowing his money."

"I just don't know why you'd do it, Curtis," I said.

"Because every little penny we give him, the less likely he'll come back on us."

He looked first at me and then at Bill and then back at me.

"I couldn't sleep last night," Curtis said. "I just kept thinking about Neil and his daughter. He was a great guy."

"He sure was," I said.

"And some bastard kills him," Curtis said. Then, "I can't live like this anymore."

"Neither can I," I said.

"This money is our last hope," Curtis said. "That's why I sweetened it. We may as well give it our best shot."

Silence again.

We were approaching the burglar's apartment house.

"Thanks for doing that, Curtis," I said.

"Yeah," Bill said, surprising me. "Thanks."

"Maybe this'll really work," Curtis said. "Then this whole thing'll be over."

We parked half a block away.

The rain was now a mist.

Curtis reached down and brought up a battered old blue gym bag.

"Here you are," he said, handing me the bag.

I angled myself around in the seat so that I could see both of them as I talked.

"I go upstairs and put this in the apartment on the fourth floor," I said. "Meanwhile, Curtis goes into the front lobby and hides in the dark part, in case somebody comes running down. And Bill watches the alley."

"What if he doesn't show up?" Bill said.

"Oh, he'll show up. All this money, are you kidding? Don't you want to talk to him? Scare the shit out of him a little?" Curtis said.

"You know I do," Bill said. "Let's go."

"All right," I said. "Let's go."

THE RAIN had cut the heat some but it didn't do much for the smells.

The mist now had an almost fog-like texture and as I walked through it. Carrying the gym bag in my right hand, I smelled that familiar mixture of scents that spoke to drugs, disease, despair and excrement.

A baby cried. A siren screamed. A vicious and angry dog barked.

I opened the front door of the apartment house and stepped inside. And caught my breath.

Somebody had vomited in the corner, near an ancient radiator.

Holding my breath, I walked past it up the right-hand staircase.

A symphony of sounds—sex, anger, harsh laughter, argument— and a collage of sights, words scrawled on the stairway walls, dog turds at my feet, a broken beer bottle, half a joint, and rat droppings that led to a small hole along the bottom of a third floor wall.

And almost no light.

Even though naked bulbs glowed along the corridor ceiling, they seemed to give out only a dirty, bleak light that cast shadows without giving much illumination.

I thought of the monster in the basement. Sucking up all the light.

On the fourth floor, I stopped, out of breath, and sticky with my own sweat.

I couldn't hold my breath much longer, not in this heat, and not climbing all these stairs. I'd pass out.

I inhaled deeply.

And damned near puked.

A junkyard on a filthy hot day. That was the only thing all these smells together could be likened to.

I saw the door I wanted and then started down the corridor.

There were no sounds up here.

I tried the apartment door I wanted. It swung inward with the merest touch.

Darkness.

I took the penlight from my pocket and clicked it on. Then I walked into the room. The same disgusting place. Air mattress. Scabrous furnishings. Smashed glass. And the oppressive smell of backed-up toilets.

I played the light around the entire room. I saw nobody. I went down the hall and checked out the other two rooms. Nobody. I tried the closets in the bedroom. Empty.

Maybe he really wasn't going to show up.

Maybe what he really wanted was us.

Maybe he wasn't interested in money at all.

When I reached the living room again, I stopped, thinking I'd heard something, some small but alarming noise that seemed to come from the closet directly across from me.

My heartbeat had increased considerably.

The sound again.

Some faint *scraping* sound, as if something was being dragged across coarse wood.

I played the light on the gym bag again.

This was supposed to have been a simple operation.

Now I had the sense again of being caught up in something unknown and dangerous.

Maybe the burglar was going to have it both ways.

Get the money—and leap out of the closet with a butcher knife.

I took a step toward the closet.

Stopped.

Took another step.

Stopped.

I could reach out and touch the doorknob. I could turn the knob and fling the door open.

And then what? What would I be facing? I glanced around the darkened room.

I was really getting paranoid.

I was now half-expecting him to jump out of the shadows behind me.

The bogeyman. That's what he was. He was the goddamned bogeyman, the modern one, the wraith composed of ghetto dirt and soot, the wraith who shambled and shuffled like the homeless people you see downtown, and whose sounds were the cries of babies born drug addicts and already dying of AIDS.

The bogeyman.

Waiting for me in the closet.

I had to get it over with.

I grabbed the sticky doorknob and yanked the door backwards.

Deep and total darkness.

I shone my penlight inside.

No bogeyman.

The closet was empty.

Then what had the *scraping* sound been?

I took a step into the closet. A dog had been in here at some point. His ancient turds filled a corner.

I checked the gym bag to make sure it was in a place where the burglar could see it.

And then I went over to the apartment door, opened it and took what I hoped was a final look at the place.

Maybe Curtis was right.

Maybe after tonight, it really would be all over.

BACK DOWNSTAIRS, in the vestibule, I found Curtis hiding in the shadows under the staircase.

"Somebody barfed," he said.

"Yeah, I kinda noticed that."

"I feel like knocking on the manager's door and telling him to clean it up."

"He's probably busy with those porno tapes."

"Yeah, and that big mama of his," Curtis smiled. Then, "Man, I don't know how long I can take this smell without upchucking myself."

"I'll trade places with you."

He smiled sadly. "I don't think I'd better be around Bill without having a referee handy."

"I thought you guys worked it out."

"Oh, he apologized and everything, but I know what he's really like."

"I actually think he likes you."

"You know, that's the funny thing. I know a lot of white guys like that."

"Oh?"

"Yeah. They don't have any trouble with blacks individually but they hate blacks as a concept. You know what I mean?"

"Yeah, actually I do."

"And Bill's like that. He'd jump in a river and save my life but I don't think he'd want a black family living on his street."

Just then, a male voice from the second floor shouted, "You fucking bitch!"

And then there was a thunderclap as the flesh of a fist met the flesh of another body. There's no mistaking that sound. Hard as professional wrestlers try to duplicate that noise, they never get it quite right. But you hear it all the time in boxing matches, particularly between heavyweights. It's a scary sound.

"I should go up there and punch that asshole out," Curtis said.

"Yeah, we probably both should."

Curtis shook his head and made a face.

We both knew we couldn't afford to interfere with what we were here to do.

"You all set?" I said.

"Ready as I'll ever be."

"This could be a long night."

"I'll be fine."

"I'm sorry about the smell."

He grinned. "Why are you sorry? You the guy who threw up there?"

I SLID behind the wheel and Bill said, "You sure took your time."

I told him about the rat.

"We used to shoot them," he said. "When we were kids. Go down by the river and the sewage plant."

"Sounds like a fun place to hang out."

"Actually, it was. If you were into killing shit, I mean. I saw rats the size of dogs. You pump three, four shots into them and, man, they exploded like grenades."

"Sorry I missed it."

The alley looked even narrower and dirtier than it had the other night.

Most of the one-stall garages literally dated back to the time of Model-T Fords.

I had to find one that was empty and wouldn't collapse when we drove inside.

There was an open dumpster that at least a dozen small rats were pouring out of. They must have been temporarily sated and no longer needed to plunder the garbage.

I found a small white-washed garage and pulled in there. This gave us a clear view of the back of the apartment house. Anybody coming or going in the back way, we'd be sure to see him.

The rain started again.

We sat in the car and listened to the rain, which had started in earnest again, drum against the garage roof. The roof was so leaky, the rain also drummed against the top of my car.

Bill whipped out a flask.

"You don't need that," I said.

"Were you ever a den mother?"

"If there's one fucking night we need to be straight, it's tonight."

"I'll have one little drink."

"One."

Then he lost it, waggling the silver pint flask in my face.

"No, I won't, asshole! I'll have all the fucking drinks I want! You aren't the boss! You're too much of a chicken shit to ever be boss of anything!"

He turned around in his seat. I could hear him breathing, great angry sobs of breath in his throat and chest.

Then the lonely sound of the rain again in the silence.

It all started to be dreamlike. I'd been feeling that sometimes lately.

I was a little boy in bed having this terrible, terrible nightmare.

Who were these people?

How had I ever come to be involved in all this?

Why couldn't I wake up from this dream?

"You want a hit?"

"No, thanks," I said.

"Sorry I yelled at you."

"That's all right."

"It really isn't any of your business how much I drink."

I looked over at him.

"Tonight it is, Bill."

He sighed, and put the flask on the floor.

More rain.

I could smell the old wood of the garage. The soaking from the rain gave it a kind of sweet decaying odor. Sometimes I liked to drive through old neighborhoods like this one and imagine what they'd been like when they were new. Ladies in summer dresses, men in striped summer sport coats and straw boaters.

"Wonder what he'll do with it?" Bill said.

"Do with what?"

"The burglar. With the money."

"Oh."

"You still pissed?"

"I never was pissed, Bill." Then, "I was just thinking about this neighborhood. Probably a real nice place a long time ago."

But Bill had never really been interested in sentimental moments.

"Drugs, that's for sure. What he'll do with the money, I mean."

"Probably."

"And pussy. Maybe get himself a hooker for a couple of nights. That's what I'd do, man."

"Aren't you afraid of catching something?"

"You're missing the point, Aaron. I'm not talking about me. I'm talking about *him*. What I would do if I was him."

"Oh."

"I'd get two. You ever had two broads in bed with you?"

"Just that one time with Mother Theresa and Dear Abby."

He laughed.

"Well, man, don't knock it till you've tried it."

"Meaning you've tried it?"

He stared out the windshield at the shining silver rain.

"Oh, yeah, back when I was a resident. There were these two cute little nurses. I always figured them for dykes. They were always hanging around each other and touching each other. You know how dykes are."

"Oh, yeah," I said, "if there's one thing I know, it's how dykes are."

"Anyway, one night at this Christmas party everybody got gooned up pretty good, including the chief surgeon, who got caught in the broom closet with this young black practical nurse. He was giving it to her up the ass. The chief surgeon. Giving it to her up the ass. I always think that anybody who ass-fucks women is a latent fag. I mean, that's just my opinion.

"Anyway, so it's late and I see these two cute little nurses getting their coats on, and I say, 'hey, shit, it's really snowing, I may have to stay at your apartment tonight.' And they say, 'sure, that sounds great.' Well, the truth is, I was kidding. But they weren't. They took me home. I called my wife and told her that there was too much snow to make it home and I'd be sleeping at the hospital. I called from my little office, I mean.

"Anyway, so I get to the apartment where these two gals live, and when they open the door, I see that the only light in the place is the Christmas tree. And these gals are naked."

"You sure you didn't read this in the *Penthouse* letter column?"

"I'm not shitting you, man. Honest to God. They're naked. And one of them drops down to her knees and starts blowing me. And when I come, they lead me into this dark room and really start working on me. Then I asked them to start working on each other. And they wouldn't do it. They said that they knew that a lot of people in the hospital thought they were dykes but they really weren't. And I guess I pushed them a little too hard. I mean, I really got fixated on them doing each other and letting me watch.

"Then they really got pissed—I was pretty drunk and probably a lot more belligerent than I realized—and then all of a sudden I blacked out. And you knew where I was when I woke up?"

"Where?"

"In my car."

"They threw you out, huh?"

"Yeah. But that wasn't the worst of it. Somehow they managed to get me down to my car naked."

"You woke up in your car naked?"

"Yeah. I must've really pissed 'em off, man."

"So what'd you do?"

"Well, my whole goddamned future was on the line. I mean, a doc gets arrested on Christmas Eve driving around bare-ass naked. I drove back to the hospital at about fifteen miles an hour and then I drove into the maintenance garage where I knew a couple of the guys kept their work uniforms. That's what I drove home in. This work uniform."

I smiled.

"I'd say that deserves a drink."

"Yeah," he laughed. "So would I."

And leaned down to pick up the flask.

And that was when I saw the burglar.

And that was when—with some kind of sixth sense—the burglar saw us.

He'd been walking briskly along—not seeming to notice the rain— when he suddenly turned and stared at us.

His head jerked. Startled.

That's how I knew he saw us sitting in the car in the garage,

He stood in the rain a long moment, as if making up his mind about what he wanted to do, and then he turned and started running back the way he came.

"You sonofabitch!" Bill shouted.

And flung open the car door, banging it hard against the too-near garage wall.

He couldn't control himself to walk between the car and the wall. He pitched himself up over the hood of the car, landed upright and started running after the burglar.

I didn't have any choice but to follow him.

I wasn't prepared for the rain. It was cold and hard, slashing across the head like tiny knives, slicing in the puddles at the feet so that even walking was difficult. Let alone running.

I was only a few yards behind Bill.

The rain blinded me. I had to keep blinking in order to see anything.

My shoes were already soaked.

I stumbled once, came down on the palms of my hands, raking them across broken glass. The alley was aged brick, many of the bricks jutting up at odd angles, perfect for tripping the unsuspecting traveler, especially the traveler who was foolish enough to run in the rain.

Pain traveled in a ragged burst up my arms and to my brain. I was up on my feet again, running.

No time to worry about the cuts in my hands.

The rain continued to slash and blind and pummel.

The burglar was so far ahead of us, I couldn't even see him now. I kept running, closing the distance between me and Bill.

And then he fell.

I wasn't prepared for it, of course, and in the obfuscation of the slanting rain, wasn't even sure, at first, what had happened.

One moment, Bill was ahead of me, his broad back and shoulders bobbing up and down, and then he was gone.

By the time I figured it out, I ran into his body on the ground, stumbling over him and then flying through the air for a few feet, sprawling ahead of him.

Bill had tripped, just as I had.

This time, I wasn't lucky enough to land on my hands. I landed on my head, the impact knocking me unconscious for a few long moments. A terrible pain streaked across my forehead.

I could hear myself cry out but the sound was lost in the susurrations of the silver rain.

Bill was already up and running again, shouting at the burglar, whom he could apparently still see.

But as he ran, I saw that he was limping on his right leg, which slowed him down considerably.

I caught up with him and shouted, "Are you all right?"

"Look!" he shouted through the rain.

The burglar was just now turning the corner. We were still several yards away.

"You run on ahead!" Bill said. "You can run faster!"

I nodded and took off running as hard as I could, though conscious of how my feet were slipping on the ancient brick floor of the alley.

I reached the corner. Turned. Looked for the burglar.

And he was gone.

There was an eerieness to the scene that lay before me. The flat blocks of vacant lots in the slicing rain. No way he could be hiding anywhere there.

I looked down the block to my left. The buildings, such as they were, had been built flush against each other. Slipping between them would be impossible.

The roofs were a possibility, I supposed, but to reach them he would have had to run to the end of the block and then climb a ladder or a rope.

He hadn't had time to do it. I was, at most, two minutes behind him. If that.

I started to walk out into the middle of the street, to see as far as I could.

No sign of a man running. No sign of anybody, actually.

A few cars were headed this way and I had to step up onto the curb. A dead patch of city like this, teenagers loved to come down here and race.

The cars went by doing at least fifty miles per hour, if not more, their headlights in the rain like the angry eyes of metal beasts.

Then Bill, out of breath, was standing next to me. "The sonofabitch got away?" he said raggedly. "He sure did."

"How the hell could he disappear like that?"

"That's what I'm trying to figure out."

I scanned the street again. Nothing remarkable about it at all, just another grimy city street with broken pop bottles, empty cigarette packs, sewer lids, smashed curbs, condom packages, and now gutters filled with rushing water.

"We know one thing at least," Bill said into my ear.

"What's that?"

"That he wants the money."

"I guess you're right."

"And I'll bet he's coming back for it in just a little while."

I looked at him and shook my head.

"You mean you want to go back to the car and wait him out?"

"Hell, yes, I do. It's worth a try anyway. Maybe he's greedy enough to come back. Anyway, he thinks he's a lot smarter than we are."

He stared at me and shook his head.

Standing there soaked, limping on his right leg, his trousers bloody just above the knee...he wasn't kidding.

"You want to sit around in these wet clothes?" I said.

"We'll dry out eventually."

After wringing our shirts as best we could, we sat in the front seat.

"The way you were bitching about my drinking," Bill said, "I shouldn't give you any of this at all."

"Serve me right, huh?"

He smiled.

"Damn right. You can be a regular hall monitor sometimes, Aaron. You know that?"

"And you can be a reckless drunk."

I took the flask from his hand and upended it.

"Cheers," I said.

"Hey," he said, "leave a little for me."

I handed the flask back to him.

"This is the life, isn't it?" I said. "Two grown men freezing their asses off like this?"

"Yeah. And it's in the eighties outside."

I studied the back of the apartment house. It was redolent of all those tenements you saw in the juvenile delinquent movies of the sixties that ran on TV when I was a kid. As a child of the middle-class, I had a hard time understanding what life was like growing up the way these people did. Just stand in the vestibule of this place and listen to the sounds of lust and rage and grief, and you saw a side of humanity that was almost numbing in its savagery. For all the hypocrisy and insularity of the middle-classes, I'll take that lifestyle any day.

"I'm still wondering how he did it," Bill said.

"Did what?"

"Disappeared."

Then he was silent a long moment.

"Man, I'm really soaked, how about you?"

"Yeah," I said.

"We ought to beat the crap out of him just for making us sit here like this."

Then: "I'm really going to scare the shit out of the bastard."

"The burglar?"

"Yeah. You watch me."

"That's *if* he comes back tonight."

"Oh, he'll be back," Bill said. "He'll be back."

ANOTHER HOUR and a half passed.

The rain stopped.

We rolled the windows down.

The humidity was oppressive.

We shared his flask a few more times. It was getting empty.

"I'd better go tell Curtis what's going on," I said.

"We told him it might take all night."

"I still think he'd appreciate seeing me."

"You'll blow our cover."

"No, I won't. I'll take backyards up to the front of the apartment house and then run across the head of the alley. Nobody'll see me."

"Man, just let him sit. He's doing fine."

"You'd appreciate somebody coming to see you. And so would I. I won't hurt anything. I'll be very careful."

I got out of the car and stretched. My shoes still squished and it took some adjusting to.

I leaned down and said, "I'll be back in ten minutes."

"I still think this is a bullshit idea."

"Yeah, I kinda got that impression."

I decided not to risk leaving the garage by the entrance. Instead, I climbed through a small rear window, tearing the stitching of my crotch as I did so.

I WALKED under a lot of clotheslines on my way to the head of the block.

There was moonlight now, a delicate silvering that made even this scabrous neighborhood look decent.

Dogs marked my passage by barking their asses off. I stepped in mud, dog shit, cat shit, rat shit, and a variety of viscous puddles whose origin I didn't particularly care to know.

I reached the head of the alley and stopped.

This was the only tricky part.

In case the burglar was lurking in the shadows down by our car, he would see me cross the alley up here.

I had to dash across so I'd be close to invisible.

I ran.

I didn't stumble, I didn't falter, I didn't in any way slow my pace.

I felt a ridiculous little-boy pride in how quickly I'd made it.

A nice lady was probably going to step forth and pin a blue ribbon on my swelling chest.

Little boys and little boy games.

THE SAME faint, sickly light shone in the vestibule. The only difference was the silence.

Even the most violent apartment dwellers, it seemed, were resting for the time being.

It's not easy beating up women. A guy gets arm-weary after a while.

I went up the steps of the porch and opened the door. The smells leapt at me.

I held my breath and went inside.

The vestibule was empty. The vomit was still in the corner. At least there were no rats.

The graffiti looked more lurid and vulgar than ever. I thought of the children who lived here, seeing all these words and genitalia crayoned on the walls. Every single day.

There was a new smell, a sour-sweet smell that I didn't recognize at first. And then I identified it. Feces. Human feces.

"Curtis."

I whispered. Perhaps too low for him to hear.

"Curtis."

I'd never heard this place so quiet. Tomb-quiet.

"Curtis."

Then I smiled. I had an image of him under the stairs asleep. As I would've been.

Sitting in the car with Bill Doyle exploding every five minutes tended to keep a person awake.

But sitting under the stairs by myself, I would have fallen asleep long ago.

"Curtis."

The silence was somehow troubling now. And then suddenly, I wanted to bolt.

I was going to find something here that would make things even more terrible.

I knew this for absolute fact.

I forced myself to walk forward to the staircase and then to walk around, so I could look in the area beneath the stairs where Curtis was hiding.

I took out my penlight.

I studied his face first.

The dark, handsome features were slackened now, the mouth filled with blood. Drops of it dripped from his lower lip to his chest. In death, his face was a fierce and aggrieved African mask.

The death wound, or so it appeared to me, came from the deep slash across the throat, though I counted six other wounds in his chest.

He had fouled himself. That's what I'd been smelling.

I reached out my hand and started to touch him—then stopped myself.

I couldn't afford to touch him.

And when I left, I'd wipe off the doorknob carefully.

And then I realized how callous I'd become. One of the best friends I'd ever had lay dead, and all I was concerned about was getting my prints off the door.

"I'm sorry, Curtis," I said. "I'm sorry."

And as I knelt on my haunches there looking at him, I heard the rain come again, even harder now than before.

"I'm sorry," I said again, thinking of the conversation we'd had a few nights earlier, about how hard it was not to hate people who despised and ridiculed you. And yet, as Curtis had said, you had to let go of them, because if you didn't, then they held you in hatred forever.

I just stared at him for a long moment, then. His quiet, intelligent and very shy wife was going to be devastated when she found out.

I'd told Jan about the burglar. But had Curtis told his wife?

There I was, being callous again, stooped here in front of my friend, but concerned only about myself.

But, realistically, wouldn't Curtis have been concerned about himself in the same circumstances?

Sometimes it's difficult to accept our own selfishness. Not that it stops us from being selfish. It's amazing how many things you can do despite a full load of guilt.

I had to get out of there.

Now.

Had to.

I stood up, knees crackling, back aching, hands still burning from where I'd scraped them on the alley bricks.

Curtis.

I'm sorry, Curtis.

I really am.

If I get a chance, I'm going to kill the sonofabitch myself. I really am.

And I was serious.

I knew it was a kind of madness, born of fear and exhaustion and anger, but I felt it nonetheless: the real desire to kill another human being. To feel his skull crushing beneath my hands. To hear him cry out for mercy. And finding no mercy in myself at all.

Suddenly, I knew what it must be like to be Bill Doyle.

I knew exactly what it must be like.

THE RAIN had started again by the time I got back to the car and the garage.

I was soaked when I slipped behind the wheel.

"You all right?" Bill said.

But I couldn't talk.

"Aaron? Did you hear what I said?"

The sound of rain, the smell of rain, the feel and texture of rain.

"Aaron?" Gently.

The smell of the garage, oil and wet wood and dust and age. Age immemorial. Death. Decay.

"Aaron, you're kind of spooking me, guy. You really are." Still gentle. But anxious now. Very anxious.

"He's dead."

"Who's dead?"

"Curtis."

"Oh, bullshit."

Turned on him then. Screamed in his face.

"You want to go back and look at his fucking throat?"

"Oh, shit. Oh, shit."

And brought his hands to his face.

He sat like that for a long time, his face covered up like that.

"That poor bastard," he said, after a time. "His wife and kids—"

"I'm gonna kill him. That burglar sonofabitch."

He looked over at me. I imagined he was shocked. Good old sensible Aaron talking like this.

The rain again. Silence.

"How old's his oldest boy?" Bill said.

"Nine, I think."

"He have any insurance?"

"I think he had a pretty good sized life policy."

"That's one thing, anyway."

"Yeah," I said. "That's one thing."

"God, I never should've said what I did the other night. I could see it in his eyes. How much I hurt him."

I suppose he wanted me to tell him a lie, tell him about how Curtis and I had had this conversation and Curtis said that the other night wasn't a big deal to him at all, and how Bill was actually a great guy.

The saving lie, Henrik Ibsen called it.

But I wasn't Ibsen.

And right now I didn't give a damn about saving Bill Doyle from anything, including his own guilt.

The fact was, one of the things I'd thought of, walking away from Curtis' corpse, was the argument he'd had with Bill the other night.

"Maybe he won't come back," Bill said.

"He'll come."

I just stared zombie-like out through the windshield at the empty alley. The rain continued.

"Maybe he got scared after killing Curtis, and took off."

"He'll be back."

Bill tried hard to laugh.

"It's funny."

"What is?" I said, still staring, unable, for some reason, to look at him without getting very, very angry.

"Couple hours ago, it was you who wanted to leave, and me who wanted to stay."

I didn't say anything.

"Maybe you're going into shock, Aaron."

"I'm not going into shock."

"Seems I'm the doctor here."

"Well, if you're the doctor, then you're a doctor who's full of shit, because I'm not going into shock."

Still staring straight out the window.

"You're pissed about the other night, what I said to Curtis, right?"

"I don't want to talk about it."

"You think I don't feel like shit?"

The rain. The smell of wet wood. The rain.

"Huh? You think I don't feel like shit about it, Aaron?"

"Just shut up, Bill. Just shut up."

It happened sometime in the next few silent minutes of us just sitting there.

It was like seeing a target pop up on a video game screen.

Only this target was the burglar.

And this target had a gun.

This target was the hunter. And we were the hunted.

One moment we were just sitting there and suddenly the burglar walks right in front of us, no more than five feet from the front of the garage, crouches down, and brings up a handgun and starts shooting at us.

The windshield started cracking.

Bill screamed.

The burglar pumped several more shots into the car.

I crouched down as flat as I could behind the wheel. Bill had managed to crawl down to the floor.

The shots kept coming, the windshield bursting apart under the repeated barrage.

Then the bullets stopped.

A ruse. That was my first reaction. He wanted us to think he was gone, and then when we sat up, he'd start firing again.

But I didn't care.

I just kept thinking of Neil and Curtis, and I didn't care. I just wanted the bastard dead.

I twisted the ignition on and floored the pedal before the spark had quite ignited.

"What're you doing?" Bill said from the floor. "He'll just start firing again!"

But I was lost to rage and driving, fishtailing out of the garage, wrenching the wheel hard to the right, and then finally getting the car straightened for a clear run down the alley.

At first, I couldn't see the burglar at all.

The hard, dirty rain obscured everything.

And then I clipped on my headlights, and there he was.

Running straight down the middle of the alley.

Bill was sitting up in the seat now and he said, "Run him down! Run him down!"

And that's exactly what I was going to do.

By now, I was doing seventy miles per hour.

I couldn't wait to feel the crunch of his body as the front of my car crushed him.

Then I was doing eighty miles an hour.

He tried to get tricky and dive off the alley. But it didn't work because as he turned, he stumbled.

He fell to one knee right in the middle of the alley, right in the middle of my headlights.

It was going to happen.

I was going to kill him.

It was going to feel wonderful.

And then I hit the brakes.

"What're you doing?" Bill shouted.

I just kept pumping the brakes.

We started fishtailing but I wasn't sure there was time to stop.

The burglar managed to make it to his feet again and then he just started running. Straight down the center of the alley again.

He was obviously trying to make it to the mouth of the alley where he could turn and cross the street as he usually did. And then disappear.

He seemed unaware that I was trying to stop the car.

He just kept running, running.

He reached the street and it happened instantly.

A car, speeding as cars usually did in this forsaken part of town, slammed into him just as he reached the street.

I sat behind the wheel, watching as the burglar was knocked high into the air and then came down and slammed against the pavement.

The car kept on going.

Silence again.

Rain. Hard rain.

"Drive up there," Bill said.

I put the car in gear and drove up there.

I pulled in at an angle to the body and then both of us got out of the car and went over and stood by him.

We were getting soaked again.

Bill reached into his jacket pocket and took out a rubber glove and snapped it on.

Then he leaned over and started feeling the burglar's pulse points.

Neck, throat, wrist, ankle.

"He's dead," Bill shouted above the rain.

And then he leaned over and spat in the man's face.

I could see that at least one of the burglar's arms and legs were broken. From the odd, awkward angle of the neck, that, too, seemed broken. The blood coming from his crushed skull was very dark when it started running down his back, but soon enough the rain washed it to a faded pink color.

Bill looked at me and then grabbed me and hugged me and said, "He's dead, man. He's dead and this whole goddamned thing is finally over for us, Aaron. It's finally over!" Then, "Now let's get the hell out of here before the cops come!"

We picked up Bill's car and he followed me to a storage garage Jan and I used. I ran the car in there. I'd have to tell her I had it in the shop for repairs and drive the Pontiac wagon we used as a second car.

5

I WOKE up just after dawn and went immediately to the shower. I stayed in there for over half an hour, running alternately hot water, then cold water. I was trying to sandblast all the dirt and grime from my pores. I was also trying to cleanse and heal all the various cuts, gouges, bruises and scratches I'd accumulated lately.

In the kitchen, I went directly to the Mr. Coffee. In sixty seconds I had a pretty good cup of coffee, and then I went into the living room where I used the remote to turn on the TV.

I sat in my robe watching the early news. I felt old and weary.

A domestic disturbance had turned into a homicide.

An east side bank had been robbed at closing time last night.

And a man was killed in a hit-and-run accident. The police were now holding three teenagers charged with his death.

So he was dead, and it really was over.

They went to a commercial break.

Curtis hadn't been mentioned.

When they came back, the news reader said, "Just as we were going on the air this morning, the police radio said that a man's body had been found in the vestibule of a west side apartment house. Police report that the victim is a black male. They are giving out no other information at this time."

I clipped off the TV and lay my head against the back of the recliner.

One of the cats jumped up in my lap, sniffed my coffee cup, decided she didn't want a caffeine habit, and then jumped down again.

Apparently, I hadn't made the coffee strong enough. I was falling asleep again. The phone scared me. I came up wide-eyed and trembling.

"Hello," I said.

"Tell me it wasn't a blonde."

"It wasn't a blonde."

"Or a brunette."

"Or a brunette."

Jan said, "I called until after one o'clock last night, and then I gave up."

I told her what had happened.

I let her cry. She took a while.

"Poor Curtis. Have you talked to Gwen yet?"

"Not yet."

"She's so damned nice."

"She sure is," I said. Then, "Maybe it's over."

Then I said, "How're the girls?"

I was afraid she might resent me changing the subject. But she wanted to change it, too.

"Sun-burned, but otherwise fine. Oh, and Betsy has a caterpillar."

"Oh, good."

"She's calling it Betsy, Jr."

I genuinely laughed. It felt great. "That sounds like her."

"And I think Annie has a crush on the boy two doors down from my folks."

"Let me guess. He's nine."

"Ten. And he can stand on his bicycle seat while his bike is going twenty miles an hour."

"No wonder he's stealing her from us."

Then, "I'd like to fly back today."

"That sounds great," I said.

"Really? No arguments about how we should stay here a little while longer?"

"No arguments."

"Oh, God, Aaron, that's so good to hear."

Just then, I heard a car in the driveway.

Car door opening. Car door slamming. Footsteps. Knock on the back door.

Bill Doyle's face.

"Bill's here," I said. "He probably wants to talk about last night. I'd better let him in. I love you, Honey."

"Love you, too, Sweetheart. We'll take the late afternoon flight."

"I'll see you at the airport tonight, then."

"Can't wait."

Bill didn't look so good. For one thing, he was still limping. And for another, the circles under his eyes were so pronounced they looked painted on.

He wore a crisp, fresh, white shirt and blue tie and blue slacks. He'd have his sport jacket in the car.

"Mind if I help myself to your coffee?" he said.

"Something's wrong, isn't it?" I said.

"Let me have some coffee first."

I stood there watching him, feeling my world start to sink back into the cold, murky waters of these past few weeks.

"What happened?"

He still wasn't answering direct questions.

He got his coffee and carried it over to the breakfast nook.

He spent a long moment watching a bunny frolic in the dew-silvered grass of early summer morning.

I sat across from him. I half-wanted to pour some bourbon into my coffee. I had a feeling I was going to need it.

"Tell me what's going on," I said.

He didn't say anything.

He just leaned forward a bit so he could get his hand into his back pocket.

And then he took a number ten white envelope that had been folded in half and tossed it to me.

It lay in front of me on the table.

I didn't want to touch it.

"What's that?" I said.

"Read the sonofabitch."

Reluctantly, I reached down and picked it up. Folded back the halves. Reached inside. Pulled out the piece of paper.

I APPRECIATED THE MONEY. I'LL BE WANTING $50,000 MORE IN THE SAME PLACE TONIGHT. OR A LETTER GOES TO THE POLICE.

"Where'd you find this?"

"My front seat," he said.

"When?"

"This morning."

"You're kidding me."

"Right, Aaron. I'm kidding you. I haven't had any fucking sleep for two weeks, my family life's going to shit, I'm limping around on a very painful knee, and I'm just in the right mood to play a little prank on my good ole buddy, Aaron. Of course, I'm not shitting you, asshole."

"But he's dead. I heard the news this morning."

"I heard the news, too."

"Then I don't understand how—"

I stopped myself.

"God," I said.

"Exactly."

"There's another one."

"That's right. There's another one. And he's coming after us, the same as his pals did."

I shook my head. "It's like they're some mutant breed, or something."

"Tell me about it," he said. He glanced at his watch. "I've got rounds at the hospital. I've got to get going. I'll call you tonight."

He carried his cup to the sink and ran water in it.

"Didn't mean to spoil your day," he said. "But since mine was spoiled, I thought I might as well pass the grief around a little."

He walked to the door.

"This one I'm killing, Aaron. And I'm going to kill him with my own two hands."

He held up his hands the way a surgeon does after scrubbing. "And I'm not shitting you, my friend. I'm not shitting you at all." He made his hands into enormous fists.

Then he was gone.

TWICE I went in to phone Jan and see if I could stop her from coming home now that the burglar's intentions were clear. But both times I stopped myself. She would just be angry and resentful. I would have to protect her and the girls without them knowing it.

I spent the rest of the morning outside pulling weeds in the garden, watering the grass, fixing the sprinkler head. Then I went back to the garden, pinching off the spent blossoms of the flowers and gathering up some vegetables. I wasn't exactly an award-winning gardener. I really didn't know what the hell I was doing, but I tried to ape what I'd seen Jan do over the years. I needed to keep myself occupied.

By noon the temperature was well into the nineties, so instead of walking outside, I went down to the family room and rode the stationary bicycle. A thousand years in the future, after an alien army has wiped out our planet, archaeologists are going to find five million family rooms with five million stationary bicycles, all in damned good shape because nobody ever used them. The archaeologist will probably mistake the bicycles for religious statuary. Here we had a whole civilization, they'll say, that got down on their knees every night and prayed to their bicycles.

I did it the easy way.

I slipped a Laurel and Hardy tape into the VCR and watched *Way Out West*, as I pedaled. Their song-and-dance routine in there is my favorite Laurel and Hardy moment. There's a male sweetness to it that few men have ever been able to capture on film. Not effeminate, not macho-treacly but genuinely sweet.

I pedaled my ass off for forty-five minutes and then I went upstairs and shaved and took a shower.

Gwen, Curtis' wife, called just as I was trying to gag down a bowl of Cheerios.

Food held no appeal.

She spoke between sobs.

She said, "He's dead, Aaron, he's dead."

I knew I had to pretend innocence. "What are you talking about, Gwen?"

"It's Curtis, it's Curtis. They found him murdered."

She went on to give me some of the gory details.

"My God," I said.

"It just doesn't seem real, Aaron. It just doesn't seem real. He wasn't honest with me."

"Curtis?" I said.

"Yes. He wouldn't tell me what's been going on the past couple days. Do you know what's been going on?"

"I don't know anything about this, Gwen, if that's what you mean." Then, "I'll do anything I can to help you and the kids. Do you need money or anything?"

She started sobbing again. "We don't need money—we just need Curtis. What was he doing in that apartment house?"

I felt terrible.

"I don't know."

"Did he use drugs?"

"Absolutely not."

"Did he use hookers?"

"Curtis? Are you kidding?"

I thought again of Ibsen's saving lie. But my lie of omission wasn't saving Gwen; it was saving me.

"Did he have a girlfriend?"

"He loved you, Gwen. He'd never been unfaithful."

"You're sure of that?"

"Positive."

"And he wasn't secretly gay or belonged to some kind of criminal organization or anything like that?"

"No."

"You know what I mean, Aaron. I'm grasping at straws here. I'm trying to make some sense of it."

Good, strong woman. If anybody could handle this situation, it would be Gwen.

"I had our whole lives planned out."

"I know you did, Gwen. I'm sorry."

"When he'd make full partner, and where we'd send the kids to college, and where we'd build our retirement home." She broke then, crying harder. "And now Curtis isn't here anymore. And he never will be again,"

I let her cry. There was nothing else to do.

A doorbell rang in the background.

"Oh, that'll be my sister to pick up the kids. They'll be staying with her while I go to the funeral home to make the arrangements."

"I'm here whenever you need me, Gwen."

"I appreciate that, Aaron."

Over the next hour, I cleaned up the den, went upstairs and put the master bedroom back into shape, and then picked up a paperback and went down to the den to read and relax.

I kept thinking about Jan and the girls getting home.

I kept thinking about the letter that Bill had found in his car this morning.

I tried to concentrate on the book. I couldn't.

But I did lean my head back against the recliner...and I did close my eyes...and suddenly....

I SLEPT for nearly two hours, feeling more rested than I had when I'd awakened this morning.

I was just slathering some cream cheese on a bagel when the front door rang.

Because it was the time when UPS usually dropped off packages, I didn't answer. The delivery man drops the packages off and leaves. The bell just signals us that he's been there.

I poured myself some coffee. The bell rang again.

Either it was UPS needing something signed, or it wasn't UPS at all.

I walked through the house to the front door.

"I hope this isn't a bad time," Detective Patterson said.

"Not at all. In fact, I just poured myself a cup of coffee. I'll be glad to do the same for you."

I felt her appraising the house as we walked through it. When we reached the kitchen, she said, "This is exactly the house I'd live in if I had the money."

"Oh, I forgot. All you saw last time was the living room."

She walked around, looking at the appliances, at the big butcher block island.

She touched things every once in a while, like a small girl half-afraid to touch something pretty in a shop.

In her tan outfit, Detective Patterson looked very pert and cute today.

"I forgot to ask you. You want cream in this?"

She said, "Black is fine."

I carried her coffee over to the nook.

"Beautiful view," she said when she sat down across from me.

"At night, there are baby racoons sometimes." I smiled. "It's better than TV."

She sipped her coffee.

"Thanks."

"You're welcome." Then, "You have kids? I have two little boys."

"You're kidding. You look so young."

"God's been kind."

"Your husband also a police officer?"

"My husband's dead, unfortunately."

"I'm sorry."

"Cancer," she said. Sad smile: "My son's convinced me to start dating again. Mike's been dead three years now. He says it's time. But I just keep comparing them to Mike and there's no comparison. He was a very good husband and a very good father."

Her lovely eyes glistened with tears.

She looked out the window for a moment. A stunning cardinal perched on the bird house, surveying our backyard with birdy dignity.

"I hate to see you lose all this, Mr. Tyler."

We were now back to business. "You sound like a bill collector."

"In a way, that's what I am," she said. "If you'll excuse a bad metaphor, I'm here to collect a debt you owe me."

317 ♠ THE POKER CLUB

"Oh?"

"The truth, Mr. Tyler."

"I see."

"One of your best friends was murdered last night."

"I'm well aware of that, believe me. His wife called me early this morning."

"And not long before that, another of your friends was murdered."

"I'm not arguing with you, Detective Patterson. Two of my best friends died. But it's completely coincidental."

"Like Trudy was coincidental?"

I didn't say anything.

"By the way, Mr. Grimes' alibi came through. A woman called us yesterday. She was the one drinking with him at that bar he told us about. She remembered him clearly. There's still the remote possibility that he would've had time to commit the murder and get to the bar but given the autopsy reports, it's unlikely."

"So he's free?"

"Yes," she said. "Free."

I think she appreciated the weight of that word on me. Free. I wondered if I would ever be free again.

"You and your friend Dr. Doyle are the only two left."

"Left?"

"Of your poker club."

"I guess you're right."

"Given what happened to your other two friends, you can't be feeling too safe right now." Then, "What was he doing down there? Your friend Curtis?"

"I don't know."

"Did he hang out down there?"

"No."

"Was he a drug addict?"

"Curtis? Of course not."

"Alcohol?"

"No."

"Hookers—female or male?"

I wanted to smile. I should've taped my conversation with Gwen and played it back for her.

"No. In fact, he was always saying that a man would have to be crazy to run around these days. You know, with AIDS and everything else out there."

She sat back in the nook and watched me for a while.

"You know, with Crimes' alibi coming through, this makes you our prime candidate again."

"I figured as much."

"You need me to help you, Mr. Tyler."

"I do?"

"Yes. And it's time to knock off the bullshit and ask me for my help. Otherwise—"

She glanced at the kitchen and then at the backyard.

"Otherwise, your accommodations may change in the near future. It'd be a shame to give all this up—not to mention giving up your family."

"I didn't kill her."

"Maybe."

"Positively, I didn't kill her."

"Maybe."

She leaned forward.

"Help me believe you, Mr. Tyler."

"I'm doing everything I can."

"No, you're not. You're lying to me."

I leaned back, as if trying to escape her.

"You may think there's no way back, Mr. Tyler, whatever you've gotten yourself involved in. But I can help. I really can. But you have to make your move now. You can't wait any longer. It has to be right now."

I wanted to, that was the thing. I suppose it's the principle of confession. Just giving voice to the burden of truth is a relief. She might even have some practical solution to my dilemma.

I leaned forward again.

I seriously thought about telling her.

I opened my mouth.

I half-expected to hear the words.

The truthful words.

But instead I said, "I'm enjoying this but I'm afraid I've got to get ready to go to the airport. My family's getting back this afternoon."

She watched me again. Closely.

"This is your chance, Mr. Tyler. Your last chance. And you're going to piss it away, aren't you?" Then, "By the way, in case you're interested, I know something about the men who live in that apartment house where your friend Curtis died. They're Rumanians. They came over here after the government fell a few years ago. They were street kids. Grew up in abandoned buildings and railroad yards. One of them got arrested shortly after they came over here. A police psychologist interviewed him at length. And you know what he found out? These boys not only ate cats and dogs to feed themselves, they also killed vagrants and hobos and ate them. They're cannibals, Mr. Tyler."

She was good, Detective Patterson. I felt like a little boy being dressed down by the most heinous high school principal known to mankind. Her last big punch was not direct intimidation but shock. You couldn't get much more shocking than cannibalism.

She watched me carefully to see how her words were affecting me.

I watched her right back.

"I really do need to get going."

And, in fact, I did. Jan and the girls would be touching down in ninety minutes.

She eased her way out of the nook and stood there waiting for me to escort her to the front door.

"Side door's fine, Mr. Tyler." She smiled. "I'm a servant of the law, after all."

I walked her outside to the drive. Bird-cry and the laughter of kids in a nearby backyard swimming pool.

We stood in the sunlight and she said, "You're going to regret this, Mr. Tyler."

"Maybe I am."

"You could lose all this."

I laughed. "You're good at this stuff."

"I practice."

"I believe it."

"The hell of it is, Mr. Tyler, I'm being serious. I mean, yes I'm trying to scare the hell out of you but I'm also trying to help you."

"I really believe you are."

"But you have to tell me the truth. What's all this about, these three people dying?"

That's when Bill swung into the driveway in his bronze XKE.

He got out of the car and walked up to us.

"Good afternoon, Dr. Doyle."

"Afternoon, Detective Patterson."

"He's all yours. I was just leaving."

Then to me, "If you change your mind, you have my card."

To Bill, "Good afternoon, Dr. Doyle."

And walked back to her car.

"What the hell's she doing here?" Bill said.

"C'mon inside, and we'll talk."

Then I just realized—what the hell was a doctor with a big practice doing here at this time in the afternoon?

I poured us coffee and carried the cups to the nook.

Bill had laid two things on the table: his .45 and his silver flask.

"See you're making yourself at home," I said.

He didn't respond.

He pulled his coffee cup to him, then upended his flask directly above the cup.

"You want some?"

"No, thanks. You seeing patients this afternoon?"

"If I was, I sure as hell wouldn't be drinking this."

I admired him for that. When he was playing doctor, he was true blue.

"You going to tell me about the gun?"

"You going to tell me about the cop?"

I shrugged.

"She wanted to tell me about Crimes."

"Trudy's boss?"

"Uh-huh."

"What about him?"

"His alibi came through."

"So now she's on our case?"

I took his flask and poured myself a wee one.

"She wants to help us."

"Right," he said. "Help us right into prison."

"It's pretty clear to her something's going on. I mean, after Curtis dying—"

"She may think she's got something, but she doesn't. If she really thought she had anything, she would've arrested us three or four days ago."

"I kind of like her."

He smiled.

"You always were a sucker for those little, pretty ones. I like a little more meat on them."

"Aside from her looks, I like her, too."

He shook his head.

"God, Aaron, I can't believe you sometimes. You're so fucking naive. That little gal would blow you if she had to—she'd blow you and then put you in the slammer."

"Maybe she likes me."

"Yeah, right."

I leaned back and stared at my coffee.

"I want it to be over now, Bill. I'm tired and I can't do this bullshit anymore."

"It's going to be over tonight."

He picked up the .45 and pointed it at a spot two inches left of my shoulder.

"POW, POW, POW."

I said, "Meaning what exactly?"

"I'm going to find him. And I'm gonna kill him once and for all."

"He wants $50,000."

"Yeah, well he's going to get a hot poker up his ass, that's what he's going to get."

I stared some more at my coffee cup.

"Forget it, Bill."

"Fuck yourself. I don't take orders from you."

"We've got to stay calm."

"What, and get some more phone calls and get some more notes left in my car, and keep wondering if this bastard is following me around the way he did Neil?"

"What if they kill Jan or one of your girls?"

There it was. The worst of all fears, and he'd given voice to it.

"You should see your face, Aaron."

"I don't want you to talk about Jan or the girls, you understand?"

"Don't be pissed at me, pal. Be pissed at them. They're the ones who ruined our lives."

"No, Bill, we're the ones who ruined our lives. If we'd have called the cops and turned the burglar over, none of this would've happened."

"And that's my fault, I suppose?"

"Mostly, yeah, it is your fault. But I didn't stop you, so it's my fault, too."

After a time, I said, "Maybe we should talk to her."

"That cop?"

"Yeah."

"Are you fucking crazy? The minute we talk to that bitch, our lives are over, Aaron. Do you understand what I'm saying? Our lives are fucking over."

"I don't want you to go find him tonight, Bill."

"Well, right now, pal, I don't give a shit what you want. I'm going to start running this show the way I want to. Understood?"

And with that he swept up his gun, and stuffed it into his pocket.

"I'll call you tonight," he said. "After I've talked with the sonofabitch."

"You don't even know how to find him."

"I'll find him. He'll be in that apartment house sometime tonight. I'll wait for him. No matter how long it takes."

"Then don't take the gun."

He glared at me.

"Don't give me anymore of your chicken shit, Aaron. We should've handled it this way a long time ago."

He slid out of the nook, stood up.

"Like I said, I'll let you know how it goes." Then, "Thanks for the coffee."

I let him walk out.

I didn't know what to say and I felt too weary for another confrontation. Bill's anger could wear you out. He had an inexhaustible supply.

At the back door, he stopped, turned around.

"Take care of yourself, Aaron."

He walked out the door.

I just sat there.

Listened to his footsteps. Listened to him opening the car door. Closing the car door. Starting the engine—

Then I ran out of the kitchen and out to his car.

I grabbed his door just as he was starting to back out.

"If you go over there tonight, Bill, I'm calling Detective Patterson and telling her everything."

"You sonofabitch!" he said.

And yanked on the emergency brake. And half-leapt out of the car.

"You call that bitch, Aaron, and I'll beat you to death with my own hands. And that's a promise."

"I'm not afraid of you, Bill."

We were no more than three feet apart, and I was terrified of him.

"Oh, yeah? Not afraid of this, huh?"

He slammed a punch into my stomach.

I doubled over, falling against his front fender for support.

"How about this, Aaron?"

Then he brought his hand up and put a punch right square on my mouth. I felt my teeth bite bloodily into the soft flesh of my lip.

This time, I sprawled backwards over the hood of his car.

He started coming toward me, and that's when my right foot raised up almost on its own, wedged itself between his legs, and then came up with rocketing force.

I hit him a great good one right on the testicular target.

He cried out, and doubled over, much as I'd just doubled over.

I was still winded, and blood was dripping down my jaw from where his punch had cut my mouth.

But I managed to pull myself upright, and then smash a fist into the side of his head.

He wobbled, and for a moment I had the ecstatic feeling that he was going to fall over backwards. I was living out a teenage dream of being a formidable foe in a fight. Maybe after this was over, I'd go look up a cheerleader and ask her to go out with me.

But my Technicolor fantasy was short-lived, because just as I closed in for another punch, Bill came upright suddenly and pounded a punch into my mid-section again.

My first reaction was that he'd cracked a couple of ribs.

Enormous pain lanced my right side.

And then I did it. Utterly lost it. Jumped on him and somehow got him in a headlock and then rammed his head into the hood of his car.

I got a good three foot run so his head hit the hood pretty hard.

He screamed the second time I was able to put his head to the metal.

And then I let him go.

I stood there, my shirt torn, sweat and blood sticking to my face, my breath coming in ragged gasps, my ribs hurting like fire, and I said, "I don't want you to go tonight, Bill. You understand me?"

And he stood there, his shirt torn, his face sweaty and bloody, his breath coming in gasps, and he said, "I always thought you were a chicken shit."

"Well, you were wrong."

But I was as surprised as he was about how I'd acted.

"I don't want you to go tonight."

"Yessuh, I got the message."

"So what's your answer?"

He glared at me.

"You sonofabitch."

"That isn't an answer," I said.

Inside, the phone started ringing.

"What's your answer, Bill?"

"Your phone's ringing."

"Yes. I'm well aware of that. But I need your answer first."

I took a menacing step toward him, so that I was almost shouting in his face.

"What's your answer?"

The phone continued to ring.

"Alright, all right," he said. "I won't go."

"Good. Now I want the gun."

"What the fuck are you talking about?"

The phone continuing to ring.

"The gun. Now."

I held out my hand.

"You asshole," he said.

He made a face and muttered something.

And then he dug in his trouser pocket and pulled out the gun and put it in the palm of my hand.

"I appreciate it," I said.

And then I hurried inside to get the phone.

I SPENT twenty minutes on the phone with my boss, telling him how well things were going, and that the police would likely be dropping me as a suspect very soon. He kept apologizing for the way things had been handled, but said that he had no choice. I kept saying I understood. He was bullshitting me and I was bullshitting him, but hey, that's what most relationships are all about anyway, right? He'd called me, I could tell, out of guilt. Sort of like going to confession. Now he could go have his four after-work martinis and forget all about me.

I spent another twenty minutes in the bathroom cleaning up. I had a lot of tender spots on my face and arms and chest. The past few days had taken their toll physically.

The traffic on the expressway was heavy, particularly as I got near the airport. By the time I found a parking space, I didn't have long to wait for Jan and the girls.

I swept up both girls and gave them big sloppy kisses. They gave me big sloppy kisses right back.

Jan, on the other hand, gave me a very precise and very dry kiss right on the lips. Then she slid her arm around my waist and hugged me.

I carried the girls to the car. We drove back to PICKUP and the red cap loaded the trunk and then we were off.

"Oh, God," Jan said, "It's so great to be going home."

"Home for good," I said, knowing she wanted me to say something optimistic.

"So everything's going all right?"

I smiled, reached over and took her hand.

"Everything's fine."

"Really?"

"Really."

She knew I didn't want to say any more in front of the girls, so she allowed herself the luxury of believing that things were, indeed, all right.

The brow wasn't furrowed. The slender hand didn't give the involuntary twitch. The eyes didn't gaze off with great pain and worry.

She was herself again, friend and girlfriend and wife and mother. I gave her hand a squeeze.

WE DECIDED that I would make some hamburgers on the grill while Jan and the girls unpacked and took showers.

It was as if they wanted to wash the road dust away, making themselves pristine for being home again.

I am not your average backyard chef. In the course of making six hamburgers, I generally lose two or three. I drop them or burn them. Some damned thing, anyway. I always take the casualties over to the fence where Ronnie, the neighborhood beagle, is more than happy to get them. That's one reason Ronnie and I have such a good relationship. Any time I want to get my hand all wet and sticky, I just dangle it over the fence and Ronnie works on it for a while.

As Jan came out the back door, carrying a tray filled with buns and condiments, I saw her again as a college girl. The blue shorts and crisp, white, sleeveless blouse gave her a fresh and sexy appearance and I found myself sentimental suddenly for our dating days. I still couldn't believe my luck in persuading her to marry me. She could have done one hell of a lot better and we both knew it.

"How many did you lose?" she said, as she set the tray down on the small picnic table.

"None."

"Truth, now."

"One."

She looked up at me and smiled.

"Truth?"

"Two."

She grinned.

"Did Ronnie lick your hand?"

I held them up. "Want to feel how sticky they are?"

"No, thanks," she said, shaking her head at me as if I was a bad little boy.

I went over behind her and slid my arms around her, my groin touching her backside.

"Umm," I said. "Feels good."

She turned around slowly inside my embrace and said, "Are things really better, Aaron? I'm afraid to really be happy."

She wanted to hear yes and I wanted to tell her yes.

"Don't be afraid. It's all going to work out."

The girls burst out of the back door a minute or so later.

"Shot from cannons," I said, as I usually did when they made their entrance that way.

"Shot from cannons, Daddy!" Betsy said, and tottered over to me for another kiss.

The girls wore yellow playsuits with yellow barrettes in their hair. These were their only fancy play clothes and I knew that Jan was sort of celebrating. She was going to will our lives to be better.

We had burgers, potato chips, dill pickles, strawberry soda (Betsy liked it when we all drank the same thing), and butterbrickle ice cream. Hard to beat a meal like that.

After dinner, Betsy had a stomach ache and had to sit out the furious badminton game between Annie and myself. Usually, both girls play me. Today, Annie had the pleasure of beating me all by herself.

By this time, Betsy was feeling better so I dangled her over the fence so Ronnie could lick her face. Ronnie had to stand on his hind legs to do it, but apparently it was worth the effort. He made a lot of slurping noises as he lapped her with his tongue. And Betsy giggled a lot.

Then, remarkably, it was dusk and Jan was in the back door telling the girls that it was time to come in and get ready for bed.

"This was their third shower for the day," I noted, as they flashed by us pink and naked, running down the hallway.

"Three?" Jan said.

"Sure. They probably took one at your folks' this morning."

"That's right. It *is* three."

"The two cleanest girls in the northern hemisphere," I said.

The girls and I gave each other somewhere around four hundred goodnight kisses, and then they shuffled off reluctantly to bed, Annie doing her usual dramatic presentation of how awful it is to be an eight year old who's sent to bed every night at eight-thirty. There's a theater scholarship in that sweet little girl's future.

Jan and I made out on the couch.

"I'm too tired to make love," she said. "Is that all right?"

"Fine."

"So we can just neck?"

"We can just neck."

So we necked and had a great time.

Sometimes that's better, anyway. Necking. Rather than doing it, I mean.

You start appreciating her a little more in detail. You can concentrate on what a good kisser she is. Or the way her ears get warm when she's excited. Or the tenderness of her gentle hand on the back of the head as she holds you. All this can get lost in the passion and frenzy of Doing It. It's nice, every once in a while, to get back to basics.

Afterwards, we watched the last twenty minutes of a Fred Astaire-Ginger Rogers movie and I said what I always say when I see them

329 ♠ THE POKER CLUB

together, that not until I was grown up did I appreciate Ginger Rogers' good looks. For some reason—probably because she was in 'old' movies—she'd never much appealed to me before. But now I saw that she had indeed been a wonderful golden sarcastic babe who was every bit as elegant, in her slightly vulnerable way, as Fred Astaire himself.

When I glanced over at her, I saw the reflection of the TV screen glistening in her damp eyes. "What's the matter, honey?" I said.

"I'm just afraid to be happy, that's all."

I took her in my arms and held her.

By the time the movie ended, she was sleeping soundly, head on my shoulder.

The anxiety of the recent past had taken its toll. She was rarely tired this time of night.

I felt an overwhelming tenderness.

I picked her up as gently as I could and carried her into the bedroom. She didn't ever stir as I slid off her blouse and walking shorts.

Clad in bra and panties, she rolled over onto her stomach, the sleeping position she usually favored, and kept right on softly snoring.

I kissed the back of her head, luxuriating in the clean smell of her hair, and then went out to the kitchen for a shot of 7-Up.

I was going to turn in early myself.

The tensions of the recent past hadn't exactly left me in great shape, either.

I was just finishing up my 7-Up when the phone rang.

Fortunately, I was standing in the kitchen, right next to the wall phone, when it rang.

I got it on the first ring.

"Aaron?"

Bill. I could tell instantly that he was calling me from his cell phone.

"I thought I'd give you some warning."

"What the hell are you talking about?"

"I've decided to do it."

"Do what?"

"I've decided not to take anymore shit from this asshole. You know what I gave you this afternoon?"

His gun.

"Yes."

"Well, I've got another one."

By now, it was apparent that he was very, very drunk. He slurred most of his words. But he was one of those Irishman who could stay functional right up to the moment that he fell flat on his drunken face.

"Bill, listen—"

He hung up.

I leaned my body weight against the wall. I forgot all about the phone until it began ringing busy. I set it back on the hook.

The silence.

I'd come to hate the silence of this house. The silence of the burglar lying dead on the kitchen floor. The silence following Jan and the girls going to her parents. The silence after being told that Neil was dead.... I was thankful for the sudden hum and throb of the refrigerator motor kicking on.

It was all going to come undone tonight, I knew. Bill was drunk and Bill was angry and Bill was going to blow this whole thing up in our faces.

I didn't have much choice.

I had to try and stop him.

6

ALL THE way across town, I kept punching up Bill's cell phone number. And getting no response.

He'd probably waited until he was just a few blocks from the apartment house before calling me.

There was no cooling rain tonight. Even going on eleven o'clock, the temperature was in the mid-eighties. The Midwestern humidity was merciless.

The teenagers were out in great, noisy numbers, hanging out in front of pizza places, bars that made their money catering to the underage, and movie theaters where the last show was just about to get underway.

There were even more of them in cars. Every stoplight I hit, I felt their gazes on me—curious gazes, wondering what some old fart like me was doing out so late on a weeknight.

Neon and mercury light and lighted storefronts gave the downtown area the brightness of false day. Everything was fine as long as I was basking in that artificial glow.

But then I crossed the river into almost utter darkness.

I tried Bill's cell phone again. No response.

There were two black kids sitting on the front porch of the apartment when I arrived. Summer lightning flashed behind grey rain clouds as I approached the porch.

Cats yowled, fighting in the shadows. Baby-cry and muffler-rumble and rap music joined the cat noise. They were maybe sixteen, seventeen, and they seemed highly amused by my presence.

"Hey, man," the one in the yellow T-shirt said. "That's a fine car you got."

"Thanks."

The one in the red T-shirt said, "You lost or somethin' man?"

I smiled.

"Probably looks that way, doesn't it?"

"Bet he's here to see Taffy," Yellow said.

"You here for Taffy?"

"I don't even know who Taffy is," I said.

I wanted to go up the steps and into the building, but I figured I needed all the allies I could muster in a neighborhood like this one.

I said, "You see a white guy pull up here in an XKE?"

"XKE?"

"Fancy car." I smiled. "Looks a little like the Batmobile?"

They both grinned. They were a little rough but they seemed like nice kids.

"Oh, yeah, that one," Red said.

"Around back," Yellow said.

"The alley," Red said. "Seen him drive it back there. Figured he was meetin' his man or somethin'."

"His man?"

"Yeah, you know," Yellow said. "Man with the drugs."

Then they smiled at each other.

They'd known they were dealing with a rube, but not until this very moment could they appreciate how much of a rube I was.

"How long ago he get here?"

Red shrugged. "Twenty minutes, maybe."

Yellow said, "You ain't the law, are you?"

"Nope. I'm just trying to find my buddy, before he does something stupid."

"Well," Red said, "if he want to do somethin' stupid, man, he come to the right place."

"Guess I'll check around back."

Just by turning the corner, you walked into the invisible wall of odors emanating from all the overflowing dumpsters.

Chittering rats ran in and out of the dumpsters. The big metal containers were apparently like shopping malls for rodents.

The long, brick alley was empty.

There were only three small, dirty pools of light from the narrow light poles. Everything else was darkness.

I checked the backyard. No XKE there, either.

I walked down the alley, looking in garages.

I kept wiping my hand over my face. I was sweating and the sweat was stinging my eyes. My clothes were soaked from sweat and felt clammy and unclean against me.

I wanted to be home in the air conditioning, next to my wife in bed.

I found the XKE a quarter of the way down the alley.

He'd done a good job, my friend Bill, pulled it all the way in, then swung the overhead door down. You wouldn't know it was there.

A perfect spot for watching the alley.

Apparently, the burglar had put in an appearance and Bill had followed him.

The heat was worse in the garage. The sweet decayed smell of hundred year old wood filled my nostrils. A noisy rat ate something in the corner shadows of the garage. It ripped and tore its repast relentlessly.

I walked out into the alley, turned around, and looked back at the top floor of the apartment house. Utter darkness.

I listened. No telling or unusual signs.

Time to go.

I just wished I didn't have the feeling that somebody was watching me.

I looked left, right, up, down. I could feel someone hiding, peering out.

The burglar. I was sure of it.

But what choice did I have?

I could get in my car and go home. But that would leave Bill to work things out on his terms. And if he did that, we were sure to be in jail by morning....

I pulled down the last section of fire escape and began the ascent.

On the way up, I passed a couple making fierce love and a woman singing something to an infant in Jamaican and an old man crying out in nightmare.

I walked on tiptoe, rust from the fire escape coming off on my hands.

Then I was higher than the light pole and the shadows grew even deeper, and the smells even more sour and gagging.

When I got to the top floor, I stopped and listened for any sign of life up here. None.

I kept thinking of Curtis, and how I'd found him.

I crept up to the window of the center apartment. It was open a crack at the bottom. I eased it up and put my head inside.

Darkness. The smells once again of filth and decay. Silence.

I climbed through.

The floor was sticky. I tried not to think about what might have made it sticky.

Gradually, the room began to take on shape and dimension. I saw all the familiar sights in the living room, the air mattress, the closet, the hallway leading to the bedroom.

I didn't see Bill. Or the burglar.

I took a step in deeper and immediately stepped on a piece of glass that broke with a loud cracking noise.

So much for my quiet entrance.

I was halfway across the room, moving on tiptoes once again, when I heard the rats.

I spanned the light of my flashlight across the living room. Trash. Junk. But no rats.

And then I saw the partially opened closet door. And the two rats sneaking out of there.

Again, a terrible image of Curtis filled my mind.

Propped up against the wall beneath the stair. His throat gaping open. Blood crusting his neck and shirt.

A noise.

I spun around, half-expecting somebody to jump me.

I saw a battered end table wobble on a half-broken leg. And then I saw the rat that had just leapt on the table, causing it to wobble.

I became aware of the heat again. Greasy, filthy sweat covered me.

All I looked at now was the closet door.

Would I find Bill behind it? One way to find out.

I took five quiet steps, put my hand on the edge of the door, pulled the door open all the way, and looked inside.

He'd probably been a handsome animal at one time, brown and white mutt who'd probably been prowling through the apartment up here when the rats simply outnumbered him. He was handsome no more. At least twenty rats feasted on him now, his dead glassy eyes reflecting none of his pain or indignity.

The rats were so busy, not one of them turned to look at me. The noises they made were obscene.

Sickened, I closed the door and continued looking for Bill.

The hallway leading to the bedroom and kitchen was empty, scabrous and grimy in the beam of my light.

I tried the bedroom on the right first, playing my light over the pornographic drawings scribbled on the walls.

I was half-afraid to open the closet door. Not only was I leery of finding Bill, I was afraid of finding more rats feasting on another poor animal.

But the closet was empty, dusty too, causing me to sneeze.

I turned around to head back to the hallway and that's when I heard it—the pressure of body weight on wooden flooring.

Somebody was just outside the bedroom door.

I flattened myself against the wall on the left side of the door.

Another creak of wooden flooring.

He was sneaking into the bedroom.

I clipped off my flashlight, holding it now like a club.

I had to be fast and I had to be accurate. The moment he came within range, I had to split open his skull. Otherwise, he'd use whatever weapon he had, and kill me for sure.

Another creak.

I felt smothered suddenly, as if I couldn't quite catch my breath. Hyperventilation. Pure terror is what I was experiencing.

And then he was there.

Sneaking through the doorway.

And I pounced on him, bringing my flashlight up and starting to smash it down against the back of his head and then he turned and pushed the gun in my face and—

"You stupid sonofabitch!" Bill whispered. "It's me!"

The strength in my right arm faltered and the flashlight I'd been using as a club stopped in mid-arc.

"You scared the shit out of me!" I whispered back.

In the grimy light through the bedroom window, his face was glazed with sweat. And his .38 glistened.

"You see those rats eating that dog?" he said.

I nodded.

He shook his head miserably.

Then he leaned forward and said, "I already checked out the other bedroom. We've got to check the kitchen."

I looked at his .38. "You're not going to shoot him."

"Guess we'll see."

We were still whispering. "C'mon," he said.

He nodded and I followed him out of the bedroom and back into the hallway.

The kitchen was small and L-shaped, the refrigerator and stove on the right, the sink and cupboards on the left. There was a closet, too. The door was closed.

Rat turds were everywhere. They crunched beneath our feet.

I played my light across the room. Even the kitchen had filthy drawings on the wall.

I opened the refrigerator door and was literally knocked backwards. There was no light. The refrigerator hadn't had any electricity for a long time.

Six or seven rats had crawled in there and somebody had been nice enough to close the door on them.

Their bloated corpses lined two shelves. I was afraid I was going to vomit.

And then he came running out of the closet behind us.

I heard him and turned and trained my light on him, his dead-white skin and glistening eyes startled by the beam of my flash. He wore a dirty white T-shirt and jeans and his arms were covered with the heads of various kinds of snakes, the tattoos as gross and alarming as the drawings on the walls.

He brought a huge, gleaming butcher knife down toward Bill's right shoulder.

"Watch out, Bill!" I shouted.

Bill, startled, still watching me, hadn't had time to get into position yet. Even if he'd wanted to fire, he couldn't.

The knife plunged downward.

All I had time to do was club the burglar a glancing blow on the side of the head.

He made an animal grunt of pain then reached up, seized the flashlight, and hurled it against the wall, where it fell like a meteor until it hit the floor.

By now, Bill had time to squeeze off a shot, and he did so, but it was too late.

The booming shot echoed and re-echoed in the small kitchen.

But neither the shot nor its report slowed the burglar down at all.

He slammed into us like a broken field runner pushing past two stodgy linemen. I managed to grab a handful of hair and I think Bill managed to put a fist deep into the burglar's side but the man escaped. For half a minute, anyway.

Then Bill tackled him from behind, and shoved him hard into the wall.

I got his hair again, and grabbed the flashlight from the floor. Then I got my arm around his neck. With the headlock, I was able to drive the top of his head into the wall.

I didn't hear the *snick* of the switchblade until it was too late.

The burglar managed to open his blade and slice it across the top of my ribs, inflicting pain instantly.

Blood started soaking my shirt within moments.

I heard myself yell out and then, in rage, I reached down to grab the burglar's arm. I was going to take the knife away from him and cut him up a little. See how he liked it. The blood was making me crazy. I didn't care about anything, in my panic and fear, except hurting him real bad.

But he was too fast for me.

This time, he sliced me across the right arm. I had to give up my hold on him.

He managed to swing around and arc his right foot into Bill's stomach. Bill, *woofing* air, dropped to his knees, his gun clattering to the floor.

Moments later, the burglar was running down the hallway, toward the front room.

"Get him!" Bill shouted.

I was bleeding pretty steadily now, from both my arms and my chest, but the panic was gone now. All that remained was the anger.

"You sonofabitch!" I screamed. And went after him.

He was already scrambling through the window to the fire escape. I got there in time to put a fist hard into the side of his head. It stunned him enough to slow him down and make him drop the knife.

I grabbed his hair again, shoved his head three or four times against the window frame, and then I reached down, without letting go of him, and picked up his knife.

I slashed him deep and hard across the shoulder and was ready to do some more damage when he leaned outside the window and smashed his fist through the pane of glass.

Glass fragments and shards exploded into the air, cutting me in a dozen places.

I fell back for a moment, brushing the glass from my face, giving him time to escape.

"Get him!" Bill said, pushing past me, going after him.

I was functional again after thirty seconds or so.

By now, Bill and the burglar were clanging down the fire escape.

Bill shouted to him every few seconds.

The burglar didn't even look up. Just kept racing down the stairs.

Bill stumbled once, started to pitch down the steps, but then corrected himself and began running down the stairs as fast as his injured leg would take him.

I was right behind him.

We hit the ground at about the same time.

The burglar was already running down the dark, brick alley.

We went after him.

Bill had his gun out.

I didn't give a damn anymore. I wanted to see the sonofabitch hurt and if that meant that Bill killed him, then that's the way it would have to be.

Bill fired once, the report of the gun almost as loud as it had been in the bedroom.

The burglar kept on running, in and out of pockets of shadow, disappearing for long seconds at a time.

Bill fired another round.

Only occasionally was I aware of the pain and the blood now. All I wanted to do was get my hands on the bastard.

"He's going to vanish again!" Bill said as we saw the burglar approach the corner.

And maybe he would.

Turn the corner.

And we, only a minute or so behind, would be unable to find him.

It had happened twice before.

"Not this time," I said.

And I started running faster than I had since my track days in college.

Running. Leaving Bill behind. Getting closer and closer to the burglar.

Every McDonald's double-cheeseburger, every Sara Lee cake, every Mars bar, every Lay's potato chip I'd ever eaten made itself known to my cardiovascular system.

But I didn't care.

I kept right on pumping the legs, pumping the heart, pumping the rage.

He turned the corner.

He was a quarter block ahead of me.

He'd lost us before by at least a full minute.

Now I'd cut the time in half.

Maybe I was going to find out where he'd vanished to.

I got to the corner.

And he was gone.

No rain to impede my vision tonight.

I saw the whole run-down area. Empty streets. Empty lots. Empty buildings.

He'd pulled it off again.

And then Bill was beside me, reeking of sweat, gasping for breath in the steaming night.

"He vanished again?"

"Looks like it," I said.

"No way."

And then I saw it.

My gaze was just reaching when it moved almost imperceptibly. If my eyes hadn't been trained on that particular spot, I never would even have noticed it.

"Damn," I said, "that's where he goes."

"What the hell are you talking about?"

I could see him frantically scanning the area in front of us.

"The sewer lid," I said.

"The sewer lid?"

And then he looked at me and half-smiled.

"Hell, yes. The sewer. That's where the sonofabitch goes."

THE SEWER didn't smell as bad as the burglar's apartment. That was the first thing I noticed.

The second thing was that it was maybe ten degrees cooler down here.

The third thing was the darkness. Perfect, utter darkness.

When I reached the bottom of the ladder, I found myself standing in two inches of dirty water.

I played my light on the tunnel ahead of me. Filthy brick walls.

There was maybe four feet between walls for walking. The tunnel ran long and straight, then turned abruptly. There was no sign of the burglar. He'd obviously been able to make it around the corner.

Bill leaned over and whispered, "I've got the gun. I'll go first."

He went first.

I kept playing the light off the walls as we walked. Every ten feet or so I'd see large holes in the wall where time and decay had done their job. The holes were large enough for a man to hide in.

Bill stopped abruptly.

At first, I couldn't hear anything except cars overhead. Their rumble and thrum on the ceiling of the sewer.

Then the sound came to me, faintly.

Somebody was walking through the water just around the turn ahead of us. I could hear the splashing sound.

"Kill the light," he whispered.

We walked very slowly for the next twenty yards or so. This was the stuff of boyhood nightmares. There were very sharp stones on the floor of the sewer.

Total darkness. Filthy water that could be filled with small but unimaginable monsters. And a man who desperately wanted to kill us.

Bill stopped again.

I ran into his back.

"Listen."

The sound of water churning again. Closer this time. He was moving again, the burglar....

The first shot dug pieces of brick from the wall. I felt shards of the brick bite into my face.

Bill had hurled himself against the wall, crouched down. My eyes had adjusted enough to the blackness that I could see him doing this.

I crouched down, too.

Silence. Pain from the knife wounds traveled up my chest every once in a while, and made me blink back a kind of grogginess.

I had the sense that the burglar was peering around the corner, waiting to take his next shot.

We didn't have to wait long.

The burglar put two more bullets very near our heads. In the yellow explosion at the tip of the barrel, I caught a glimpse of the burglar's face. Dead-white skin, gleaming eyes. I thought of what Detective Patterson had told me. Rumanian street urchins. Cannibals.

"You sonofabitch!" Bill cried.

And then, insanely, he was up and running, charging the burglar.

Bill fired two, three times.

Echoes of gunfire played up and down the sewer.

And then silence.

Then—the burglar running back down the tunnel, retreating, then splashing sounds he made now joining the echoes of the gunfire.

All this played out in darkness.

Bill's breath coming in gasps.

Then—silence.

"We need to get around that turn," Bill whispered. Then, "Shit!"

"What's wrong?" I whispered back.

"Put your light on my leg."

I put the light on his leg.

I wasn't sure if it was a water moccasin—which it probably wasn't—but it was definitely a shiny black snake of approximately three feet in length and it was coiling its way up Bill's leg.

I can't tell much else about it because I wasn't particularly keen on looking at the damned thing. I've never figured out why we hate and fear snakes so much. One part of our brain is reptilian—the same brain our very first ancestors had, humans being reptiles even before they were apes. But hate and fear them, we do.

Almost without thinking, I reached down and grabbed the snake and ripped it free of Bill.

I tossed it as far back of me as I could, the sleek black tubular thing writhing and snapping as it vanished into the gloom.

"Thanks."

I nodded.

I clipped off the light.

He whispered, "You don't have to go with me, Aaron. You can stay here."

"No way."

Now I wanted to catch the bastard as badly as Bill did.

We forged on in the darkness. A couple of times, I winced. The sharp little rocks were like hungry teeth, biting into the soles of my shoes.

When we reached the turn, the texture of the air felt slightly different.

It took me a few moments but I finally realized what was responsible for this: somewhere far down the dark sewer there was an opening, a culvert most likely, that led to the outdoors. It was a mixture of outdoor air and sewer air that I was feeling now.

Bill stopped and said, "I need the light."

"For what?"

"I'm going around the corner. I'm going to surprise him. Hit him with the light and then get a couple of shots off."

"Man, that's really risky."

"I can handle it."

"You sure?"

Now he was angry. "Just give me the fucking light, all right?"

I gave him the flashlight.

We stood within inches of the turn.

What Bill was going to do was go around the turn, crouch down, clip on the light and then fire at his suddenly illuminated target.

Maybe he was right.

Maybe this was the best way to pick off the burglar.

"Now!" Bill whispered.

And then he was gone.

I peered around the corner to see the flashlight suddenly go on.

The burglar was trapped in it.

He was holding his gun in firing position and the moment the flashlight beam reached him, he started squeezing off shots.

Bill hadn't counted on this.

Bill had thought the element of surprise would momentarily immobilize the burglar.

Bill screamed.

I knew he was hit.

I crouched and duck-walked around the corner, wanting to catch him before he fell backwards into the water.

I needed to save him and kill the light.

The burglar kept on firing.

Bill was falling fast. I wondered if he was still alive.

I got him in my arms and started dragging him backwards.

The burglar kept right on firing.

I was just pulling Bill around the corner when I saw the hole in his forehead.

I no longer wondered if he was still alive.

I got him around the corner and propped him up against the wall.

His head lolled on his right shoulder. His angry blue eyes stared straight at the wall across from him.

They'd killed off every one of us but me, the burglars had. The best friends I'd ever had.

I reached down and took the flashlight and the gun from his hands.

By rights, I should've been the one who was dead. Bill had been a hell of a lot more ferocious than I'd ever been.

Or maybe not.

Maybe now I hated him so much that I was ferocious in my way, too.

No doubt what the burglar would do now.

Run.

Run as fast as he could for the far end of the sewer. He'd find the opening and escape.

But I wasn't going to let him.

I got my finger set on the trigger and I gripped extra hard on the flashlight and I crouched down and I went back into my duck-walk and I eased around the corner.

If I made any noise, he apparently didn't hear it because there were no gunshots.

But maybe he was already making his way down the sewer to his escape.

But he couldn't do that silently. I'd be hearing him now.

No, he was still somewhere nearby, waiting for another good shot.

His brothers were dead. He probably hated me as much as I hated him. He was probably even more eager to kill me than I was to kill him.

Just then, he spotted me and fired.

Two more momentary bursts of yellow flame from the barrel of his gun.

Echoes of gunfire.

He'd missed me by two or three feet. His eyes weren't as good as I'd feared.

Silence.

Now what?

And just then, another sharp rock jabbed its point deep into the sole of my shoe.

I started to duck-walk a little further down the tunnel and that was when he fired again.

This time, he came very close.

Two shots. Quick succession.

I twisted myself into a ball and slammed against the wall. I was wide open. There was no protection.

But he gave up after two shots. Temporarily gave up, anyway.

The bottom of my foot still hurt from the rock. I eased my foot out of the water to extract it. It seemed to be jammed deep into the leather sole.

The point was knife sharp and the rock bigger than I thought it would be.

And that's when I got the idea.

We both fired at sound.

Sound was all we had to guide us.

I kept rolling the rock around and around in my hand, planning my shot.

He'd only be taken in by this ploy once.

I had to take full advantage of it.

I came up from my crouch. Needed to be standing up straight. Ready. Far, far in back of me, around the corner and way up near the sewer entrance we'd come in, I thought I heard something. But that could easily be noise from the outside.

There was no time to worry about it, anyway.

I had to trick the burglar. I got myself ready.

In order to throw the rock well, I needed a free hand. I tucked the flashlight under my left arm. The gun was in my left hand.

The rock was in my right. I threw it.

It didn't make as much of a sound as I'd wanted it to, slamming into the wall, but it was enough to get the burglar to be distracted and open fire.

That's when I quickly put the gun in my right hand and clipped on the flashlight.

He was frozen in time and space for just a moment, realizing he'd been tricked and immobilized, at least momentarily, by this knowledge.

"Stay right where you are and throw your gun down," I said.

He didn't, of course. He swung around so that he was facing me and opened fire.

He got me in the shoulder. The pain was instant and traveled throughout my body.

I got off my own shot and got him in the shoulder, too. There was one difference.

I'd held onto my gun. His had dropped into the water at our feet.

I edged toward him, studying his face in the beam of my flashlight, which I'd lodged in a small hole in the wall.

I wanted to feel sorry for him. I wanted to see his humanity and know that whatever else he was, he was a member of the same species I belonged to.

But as I drew closer, studying the oddly glowing grey eyes, I saw that he was no kin to me. Not in any sense.

He simply observed me without any feeling of any kind. Bill's death had meant nothing to him. Simply another night's work. No pleasure, no pain. Just doing what he had to do.

I thought of Neil and Curtis and Bill, and of the hell this man and his brothers had made of my life—and all I'd done was have a stupid poker game one night.

My life would never be the same again. Ever.

"Are you afraid to die?" I said.

He just watched me. No emotion.

"Did you hear me, motherfucker? You and your brothers killed all my friends. So now I want to know if you're afraid to die. Huh?"

I pushed the gun closer to him.

Still no emotion on his face. The pale white skin. The glowing eyes.

I kicked him, then, very hard and right between the legs.

I'd succeeded in putting pain on his face. His features were lurid with pain.

I kicked him again.

This time he screamed, the sound echoing down the sewer the way the gunshots had.

He crouched even lower, favoring his groin.

But his pain had made me careless, made me think that I was in control of the situation.

He sprung at me, coming in right under the gun, seizing my wrist so that I couldn't get a shot off, and then slamming me up against the wall.

He was trying to get the gun out of my hand. I held on to it desperately.

He returned the favor, pounding his fist into my groin, and then driving his fist into the wound above my rib.

The pain blinded me. I heard myself cry out.

He hit me once more in the groin, doubling my pain, and then he grabbed my hair and began banging my head against the wall.

The gun was still in my hand.

This time he went at me directly, grappling my wrist with both of his hands, trying to pry the gun from my fingers.

But he left himself open.

My knee shot upwards and found his groin again. I felt his hands loosen on my wrist.

But he had lost none of his cunning.

He let one hand go from my wrist and seized my throat so hard that I was losing air immediately.

He smashed my head against the wall and kept on choking me. The strength of his one hand was enormous.

I had a sense of my own impending death. There was a madness about him now that hadn't been there even thirty seconds ago.

He was determined to kill me now. Nothing less would satisfy him.

He reached up and ripped the gun from my hand without too much difficulty.

And all the while, he kept on choking me.

But once he had the gun in his hand, he let go of my throat.

I fell away from the wall, gasping, trying to get my breath and my bearings.

He was bringing up the gun.

Pointing it directly at my right temple.

He was taking very careful aim.

He was getting ready to fire.

He was going to execute me.

I glanced at the flashlight and the odd angle from which it protruded from the wall.

If I could even brush against it, I could knock it down into the water.

In the darkness, I could—

I moved.

A smile came across his filthy face as he got ready to kill me.

And then a voice said, "Don't move!" Jan's voice.

"Put the gun down," she said. "Or I'll blow your fucking face off." He turned and glared at her, still holding the gun to my head.

That was when she fired, the bullet tearing into his elbow. But even with a bullet in him, he didn't let go of the gun he was holding.

Then he started slamming the gun against my head as I jerked his bloody arm right and left, trying to free the gun. I held on until I felt the weapon loosen in his grip and then I grabbed it—

I held the gun on him now.

And reached down and picked up the flashlight.

Its beam was still strong. I trained it on him.

I put the gun back where it belonged, right next to his face.

"Like I was saying, asshole. You killed my best friends. And now I'm going to kill you."

And I really was going to kill him, too. Or at least that was the feeling I had.

All the fear, all the frustration of the days since the poker game— Pulling the trigger would be easy.

And feel very, very good.

But that was when the voice said: "Don't kill him, Aaron. Please. For my sake."

I turned and saw Jan there, her brother's .45 in her hand.

"Please don't kill him, Aaron. Please. Think of the girls. That's why I followed you. So you wouldn't do anything crazy."

I broke. I pitched the gun into the water and I let the flashlight fall back into the water and I just started hitting him.

I must have hit him six or seven times in the face.

Then, a big black uniformed cop came over and gently but firmly pulled me off the burglar.

Detective Patterson and her men had their own flashlights. They came over and broke it up and they put the burglar into handcuffs.

She said, "You don't look so good, Mr. Tyler. I did what your wife did—I followed you."

I stood there, dirty, sweaty and wanting only to see Jan.

"We still need to have that talk, Mr. Tyler."

"I know. Could we make it tomorrow?"

"Nine a.m. My office. You may get out of this wit just probation, but you won't be practicing law anymore."

She played her flashlight around the sewer. She nodded to the burglar. "I imagine he'll be able to clear you of killing Trudy Wyatt—"

"I hope so."

She looked at me a long moment. "You should have gone to the police in the first place." Then she turned and led the way out.

As we rounded the turn, I could see other flashlight beams playing in the darkness near the sewer entrance. The burglar was being led away.

We held hands as we walked to our car. There were three police cars parked at the curb, their emergency lights flashing. The burglar was in the back seat of one of them. He glared at me as we passed him.

"How'd you catch up with me?" I said.

"I broke a lot of speed limits."

After we'd walked a little more, she said, "It'll work out, Honey."

"I probably won't be able to practice law."

She laughed.

"A lot of people would take that as real good news. One less lawyer."

I stopped her right there, right in the red haze of emergency lights, and took her in my arms and said, "I'm sorry I made such a mess of things."

"Yeah I'm sorry, too. But I'll get over it."

And then we got in the car, wet and reeking of the sewer. It took the hospital nearly three hours to get me cleaned up and fixed up. Then we drove home.